Acclaim for Edna O'Brien and *Time and Tide*

"Brilliantly expressed . . . O'Brien is one of the great writers
in the English-speaking world."
—*New York Times Book Review*

"O'Brien's melodious, fluent prose is one of the sweetest
pleasures of contemporary fiction . . . *Time and Tide*
displays her gift eloquently."
—*Los Angeles Times*

"Mesmerizing . . . echoes the fierce brilliance of her earliest
works. A dazzler, a hypnotic saga of love and loss that
sweeps you up in wave upon wave of emotive eloquence."
—*Seattle Times*

"O'Brien's prose is so rich and original, her characters so
urgently present, that a strange kind of elation is induced,
reading about events that arouse our deepest fears."
—*Mirabella*

"Vibrantly alive . . . almost painful to read. A testament to
her consummate writing skill."
—*San Diego Union-Tribune*

"Another virtuoso performance."
—*People*

Edna O'Brien is the author of eighteen books, including *Down by
the River, House of Splendid Isolation, Lantern Slides* (winner of the
1990 *Los Angeles Times* prize for fiction), *A Fanatic Heart, The
Country Girls Trilogy, The High Road,* and *Mother Ireland* (all available in Plume). Born and raised in Ireland, she lives in London.

TIME

~ AND ~

TIDE

Edna O'Brien

A PLUME BOOK

PLUME
Published by the Penguin Group
Penguin Putnam Inc., 375 Hudson Street, New York, New York 10014, U.S.A.
Penguin Books Ltd, 27 Wrights Lane, London W8 5TZ, England
Penguin Books Australia Ltd, Ringwood, Victoria, Australia
Penguin Books Canada Ltd, 10 Alcorn Avenue, Toronto, Ontario, Canada M4V 3B2
Penguin Books (N.Z.) Ltd, 182–190 Wairau Road, Auckland 10, New Zealand

Penguin Books Ltd, Registered Offices: Harmondsworth, Middlesex, England

Published by Plume, a member of Penguin Putnam Inc. This is an authorized reprint of a
hardcover edition published by Farrar, Straus & Giroux. For information address Farrar,
Straus & Giroux, 19 Union Square West, New York, NY 10003.

First Plume Printing, July, 1999
10 9 8 7 6 5 4 3 2 1

Ⓟ REGISTERED TRADEMARK—MARCA REGISTRADA

The Library of Congress has catalogued the hardcover edition as follows:
O'Brien, Edna.
Time and tide / Edna O'Brien.
—T.p. verso. I.Title.
ISBN 0-374-27776-1
     0-452-28051-6 (pbk.)
PR6065.B7T56   1992   823'.914—dc20
92-3962   CIP

Printed in the United States of America

PUBLISHER'S NOTE
This is a work of fiction. Names, characters, places, and incidents either are the products of
the author's imagination or are used fictitiously, and any resemblance to actual persons, living or dead, events, or locales is entirely coincidental.

To John and Suzanne Mados,
my staunch friends

Pour your eternal dreams, samples of blood
From one glass to another.
                    —Osip Mandelstam (translated by
                                   James Greene)

The spider spins her web
on dark days.
                    —Proverb

Prologue

"Do you believe her?" she said. Once said, it cannot be unsaid. That is the thing with words. You cannot wash them and wipe them the way you wipe dishes, which was what she was doing, merely to cancel out the brutality of what she had just said. Four words. Four treacheries. He said nothing, his anger taking a great inner lurch, and then he walked out of the kitchen, leaving the tap running. At least from now on when she came to turn it on or off, the handle would yield to her grasp. How many times over the years had she marvelled at his strength and his brother's strength, children, her children possessed of a power and a determination that she had never mastered. Now the breach. Not long ago by chance she had read something that was a premonition of this, read it in a doctor's waiting room and copied it out slowly, methodically, so that it spoke itself back to her in her long kitchen, which looked like the deck of a liner, the floor a bleached blue with pale blue walls to match. Now they were both gone. Paddy to his watery rest and Tristan about to set out for Penny's top-floor flat, with its cushions and its empty bird cage suspended on a long plaited golden cord. She had gone there once and was coldly received, so coldly that she took in every feature of the room, even the missing bars of the cage in which Penny kept her toiletries, brush and comb, and bottles of deepest blue-reliquaries of what? She could imagine Tristan arriving with his luggage, maybe even carrying a can of beer, making light of his sudden but irreversible appearance, and Penny's secret whoops of victory that she had won out over that all-important, hovering creature, the Mother. Between mothers and would-be mothers this great chasm.

"In the morning of life the son tears himself loose from the Mother, from the domestic hearth, to rise through battles to his destined heights. Always he imagines his worst enemy in front of him, yet he carries the enemy within himself, a deadly longing for the abyss, a longing to drown in his own source, to be sucked down into the realm of the Mothers . . ."

It spoke itself in the long blue kitchen with the sun marching in, in elongated slants, their fat shadows beside them and the creeper coming through both window and window frame, so that the effect was of an indoor garden. Yes, the grave words fell on each little thing, the drawers half open, where she or maybe even Tristan had taken out a knife, a wooden spoon, or a clean tea cloth. She never did close drawers fully. Her husband had castigated her about that, said it was manifest of the same dithering as when she walked down the street and showed a deficient character by her cowardly back.

What could she do now to retrieve things. She thought of rushing down the stairs to his bedroom with as normal a manner as artifice can manage and asking, "Would you like a cup of tea?" or, "Let's talk," but she could not do it, and maybe there was another reason, an unthinkable reason, which is that she wanted him to go, simply because it was something she had always dreaded. One little skein of thought at odds with all else said it had to be, this separation, and that one day he would feel the selfsame sorrow over a child of his, a son or a daughter, and in that instant know the cruel indissoluble overlapping of memory which binds us to our past. He would take the dog, too, take Charlie. Charlie was Paddy's dog, but had grown fond of her, gave her the paw, licked her knuckles, and watched, slavering, as she cut up his sausage for a treat, forgetting that she had commited him that lunatic week to the dogs' home. Tristan had gone there and retrieved him. Found

Charlie among all the other woebegone rejects, brought him home, washed him, pampered him, and cared for him as he was about to care for Penny. Why?

"Do you believe her?" she had said when he told her that Penny, that black scowl of a girl, was pregnant and that probably it was Paddy's but she couldn't be one hundred percent sure, nor could Paddy at the bottom of the Thames, perhaps by now not even there but gobbled up by the sea creatures and the sea monsters. She clung to the little story he used to tell her about the souls of drowned bodies becoming seagulls, and in her river walks she looked for them, expecting one that might seize her with a look that was not birdlike.

Although her lips said these hard, rancorous things, inside, her heart, or wherever it is that feelings dwell, was spilling, so that she wanted to contradict what she had just said, wanted to say, "I'm saying these things because you have all gone from me, you have cut yourself off from me. Come back to me; even let Penny be civil to me and I will not say these hard things, because they are not what I truly feel." How should she still be here, wiping dishes, wiping anything that was on the stainless-steel ledge, spoons, knives, forks, now washing the dog's bowl, the fawn bowl that said DOG and had the remains of yellow corn in it, the meat all eaten up because Charlie liked the meat, even though it oozed a brown, gravy stuff, when she should be mending the rift? She would wash this bowl, and while she washed it something would happen. A redemption, one of those miraculous swings which meant that he would come up the stairs, whistling to denote a truce, and say that he was not leaving, at least not for a few days, and then when he did leave, it would not be in high dudgeon but in a state of grace. Grace. She had had so much of it once. Do these traits die or just get drained out of one, or do they remain, waiting for a resurgence? It must of course seem to Tristan as if all her pity had gone out of her, or solidified, and yet that was not true; no, that was not true.

She could hear him packing or, rather, moving furniture in the room just underneath. Why did he have to drag furniture in order to pack? She couldn't tell. It was probably putting books and clobber into boxes, and along with all those things he would take as well the miniature rocking horse with its milky white paint, which in places was scratched, and the Chinese leather hatbox that she had given him and the sword that someone, an earlier girlfriend, had given him towards the end of their romance, and the several suits and jackets which he never wore but wouldn't part with. She bet her life that the metal hangers, a medley of them from the dry cleaner's, would be on the floor in a heap, a bequest on which she could skewer herself, take a lordly lunge.

Once, in New York, on stage, she saw a woman, a black woman, reenact aborting herself with one of those hangers, and so befuddled were her thoughts now that she believed that the child she was aborting in her was a memory child. She yearned to forget everything, even them. But nothing is forgotten. It follows you from the city to the country, stoops with you as you bend to tie your shoelace, trots into the shed where you get the hose, even pursues you down into the bowels of a ship if you happen to be a seafaring man. Yes, their voices clear as bells, lightish in tone, oh so long ago, like a refrain filtering back from beyond the cold immensities.

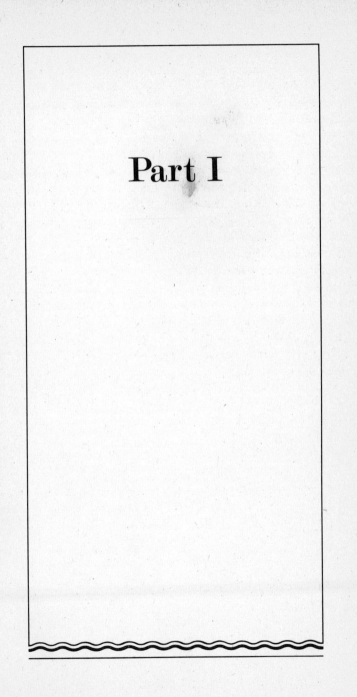

Part I

1

My Uncle Billy had a ten-foot willy,
Showed it to the girls next door.
They thought it was a snake
And hit it with a rake
And now it's only four foot four.

Prodigal they were, with song riddle and recitation. They even climbed the apple tree although forbidden to and shook the apples in a welter . . . "A dozen for thruppence . . . a dozen for thruppence," they said, careless now of being reprimanded. Their father was asleep. Now and then they tore into the kitchen, openly said her name, said, "Is she here yet, Nellie?"

The arrival of the new girl had in some way infected them as if they knew she was going to bring excitement into their lives. They loved excitement. They trotted out the word "bored" as an adult might, thought Saturdays quite boring, Sundays very boring, what with the constitutionals on the common and having to behave like good boys all the time, while inside, two reckless little hearts were beating and conspiring.

"My Uncle Billy," she was hearing, sometimes to different tunes; sung in unison, or a duet, sung in opposition, sung until they were hoarse and had to pause for a moment and ask for drinks, soft drinks. They loved the sound of the word "soft."

"You'll have sore throats by evening," she said, pointing to their Fair Isle sweaters, many-threaded, lying on a bit of muddy garden. What would her mother say? Her mother had knit these sweaters and sent them by registered post. Her mother loved them, lived for their annual summer holiday, wrote months ahead to tell what she would be cooking, indeed offered them a choice, asked if for their first meal they would like boiled chicken or roast; the advantage of boiled was the broth which, of course, she would season. They seemed to like seasoning. Yes, her mother loved them. Princes, she called them. Two little princes. Barbarians. She also asked in her letter, her mother did, if they would bring bags for the jams and jellies that she had made for them. She listed the flavours: black currant, bramble, and of course crab apple. While they were there she spooned these jellies onto scones for them, and they ate until, as they said, they had "little corporations." Her mother had told them that word and other grown-up words, such as disgusting. Porridge was disgusting. She sat them alternately on her knee and sang:

> Dan Dan the Dirty Man
> Washed his face in the frying pan,
> Caught his hair in the leg of the chair,
> Dan Dan the Dirty man . . .

When they were there they went to bed very late, long after dark, making much about seeing stars and moonlight and so on, since they could not be pleasantly seen in a city. Far too precocious. Her mother brought them lemonade and biscuits to bed, brought the tin so they could choose. They argued over this, both of course wanting the same ones, and called each other the ugliest names, which often escalated into pillow fights. One prevented the other from having his favourite biscuit by bruising it to pieces when it was the last one; then after the inevitable bawling there had to be a peace, and like nice little chaps they had to make up. That was her mother's doing. When they shook hands they laughed, even marvelled at the show of temper and the fluency of bad words that they had at their disposal. When her mother wasn't looking, one of them crept out and brought the dog, Dixie, up. Dixie was not supposed to be up there, not supposed to be in the house at all, even Dixie herself knew it. She cowered and tried to bolt halfway down the stairs, but they dragged her by her big amber mane, brought her into the room, fed her biscuit crumbs, gave her a sup of lemonade, poured it onto the bone lid of a jewelry box, in fact did heinous things. Dixie was warned not to bark or yelp and not to do number one or number two.

"No, no. One," one said.

"Oy oy. No, no. Two," another said, and saying it and repeating it, they laughed until they feared they would burst. When her mother came to kiss them good night, Dixie was under the bed, with the green chenille bedspread low down, and as her mother tried to tuck it in they told the most elaborate lies, such as they had fever or had claustrophobia or some other high-flown thing. Hearing of a fever urged the grandmother to make them a hot drink, and this they did not refuse, because they hated going to sleep; they hated dreams and all that and already claimed to be the victims of nightmares.

What would become of them? Nell thought that morning, admitting that this hilarity they were showing was a little too much. They knew something. They guessed. That's why they laughed and spluttered and shook the remaining apples onto the grass, then dived down and scooped bits out of them and left the scooped-out apples on the lawn, rendering them useless for stewing or jam. Anyhow, the wasps were on them at once.

It was autumn; wherever she looked there were wasps— converging on the butter dish, buzzing on the onion-shaped lid, around the ledge where she had geraniums and cacti to brighten things up, on the draining board, in the garden itself, in the scooped-out apples, and once in the sole of her foot as she ran to fetch some clothes in before a shower. It was like a nail through the foot, quite piercing. Yes, they knew, or they sensed; that was why they put on this perennial show, to leaven things.

"Is she here yet, Nell . . . Nello?" Paddy said. Paddy was the elder, and having said it in such a peremptory way, he waited a second to see if perhaps she was going to chastise him. She wasn't.

Tristan then repeated it. When they said her Christian name like that, it meant they were indifferent to any correction, they were in a kind of intoxication.

"Not yet," Nell said, adding that probably the new girl had missed the bus and was now at a bus stop awaiting another. The buses came to the lane every twenty minutes. They lived on the outskirts of London, and transport to and fro was not easy, another reason why she disliked the place. "The Styx," she called it, but of course only to herself. Her husband, Walter, had chosen it, said it was healthy, there being a park opposite, and that the trees produced the necessary oxygen for the children's lungs. Nothing wrong with their lungs, she thought. They were now pelting each other with butts and the sleeves of their sweaters.

What would her mother say if she knew, but of course she did know. Her mother had never liked her husband, Walter; none of her family had, tried to stop her, but she bested them, ran from an upstairs room where they had locked her, got out a window and down the stone, holding on to each ridge as if by the skin of her feet, bolted down the back avenue so as not to be seen, and then very casually, as it were, thumbed a lift, telling the lorry driver that she had to go to see a doctor in the city. In the city she took a bus to the capital and then another bus to his abode, told her sorry tale, was gently treated by him, given coffee from a brown earthenware pot, coffee and stone-ground biscuits. She would never forget it. He was glad to take her in; he was lonely, too, had been without female company for a few years. Later that day he even drove her to a big town not far from them and sent her with money to the drapery shop to buy clothes, because she had come hands down except for the clothes on her back. She bought underwear and stockings and a nightie, and a pink dress with little swellings all over it like blisters. He did not like it very much. He liked her. She was afraid of him. She was obedient.

Her family wrestled to get her back—first force, then pleading, then her mother's heart attack, then her mother's second heart attack, then her mother on three kinds of pills, and so on. In the end they were almost happy to see her married, or "fixed up," as they called it. Better than seeing her as a concubine. Marry in haste, repent at leisure. Oh yes, her mother guessed that it was not roses. She could see it clearly on the last holiday, when her husband and she never addressed a word to each other and when even on the nights when they played cards around the kitchen table Walter made sarcastic remarks about her brainlessness. Her mother guessed and felt inwardly vindicated, but outwardly said nothing. The row did not come about that, about her husband's alienation from her; the row of course came about the children and their upbringing. She was in the scullery washing up; she washed up a lot to appear good in her mother's eyes and also to pass the time, because there was nothing else to do; she washed cutlery and dishes and tin cans in which milk had been, in which there was a lingering sour smell. She washed them and rinsed them. She was washing shelves, the shelves that were covered with linoleum with a pattern of robins on it. Her mother was gutting two chickens in the kitchen on the table on layers of newspaper. Cockerels for next day's lunch. She called Nellie in quite sternly.

"Nellie," she said, "come in here for a moment."

From the tone Nell feared the worst and quaked. She held a cup and a tea cloth in her hand to give herself authority, to give herself something to do.

"Where are those children going to be educated, in what kind of school?"

"We don't know yet, we haven't decided," Nell said, using the royal we. She and Walter and the children were leaving Ireland and going to England, and Paddy, the elder, was ready for school, since he was five.

"Are they going to a Catholic school?" her mother asked.

"I told you, I don't know yet," Nell said, and watched her mother draw the innards out with gusto, then drop them anywhere, often missing the newspaper that was supposed to take this refuse. Brown, khaki, and red innards were all jumbled together, the little beating livers frail and helpless in contrast to the roped neck and the plump grey gizzards.

"You must give me your word," her mother said.

"I won't . . . They're our children," Nell said, whereupon her mother flared up, poked savagely in the cavern of the bird, and broke the sac, letting acrid stuff spill over the pimply flesh. One word led to another. Words flying about like implements. Walter came from the next room, her father from another room where he had been reading the morning paper, and now four people were arguing, accusing, saying festering things, until suddenly her husband grasped her arm, a thing he had not done for many a moon, led her away, and said, "We don't have to put up with this barbaric behaviour."

They packed quickly, carelessly; her husband went out into the fields to call the children, and she dreaded being alone in the bedroom in case her mother came up for a second harangue. She flung things into bags, even flung ornaments by mistake, which she had to take out again. The children came up to the room crying because they had to leave their weapons and all their toys in the fields, their hallowed haunts where they had seen foxes in daylight and pig badgers at dusk.

"Forget your toys and your guns," their father said, and told them to wash their hands. Finding that both taps in the bathroom were without water, he cursed aloud and said, "If they would care as much about body hygiene as soul hygiene, it would be better for all of us." The children spat on their clayey hands and wiped them grudgingly with a towel.

They were disconsolate at having to go downstairs and say goodbye to their grandparents, formally, like little gentlemen. One could see, by the way they walked, with their shoulders hunched up, that they knew that there had been a debacle. Their father escorted them, looking serene, almost jaunty. She carried the bags out to the car and slumped into the front seat, sinking down, hoping to become invisible. Self-immolation was everything. She saw her father approach, his tweed cap far back on his head and his eyes crazed with fury. She thought for an instant that he was going to open the car door, haul her out, and kick her, as he so easily might.

"Your mother in there crying her heart out and you don't go and put your arms around her," he shouted through the open window.

"Tell her I'll write," she said in what was patently a terrified voice. To make peace now would be everything, but it was quite impossible. The unspent rows of many years were crammed into this one. Yes, if they could say everything, haul every single griev-ance out of their innards the way her mother had hauled out the chicken entrails, roughly and ferociously, then it might be all right, they might start afresh, poison or no poison. Yet she could not do it, because she could not foresee where it would all lead. It might go too far. Rows can. Her own side of the diatribe she could predict, but not her mother's. Her mother might just say some-thing to her that she could never obliterate from her mind, some remark that would tear at her being day in and day out, some blame or some disgrace that she could not live with or, rather, that she could live with only in a state of mortification.

"Little shite," her father said, staring into her face so closely that she could see his bristle, see each hair and smell the coffee he had recently drunk. He had changed from tea to coffee and liked one from a jar that was flavoured with chicory.

"Tell her," she said a little more vehemently.

"Little shite . . . and you always were . . . always . . . from the minute you were born." A death blow there and then.

The children came and got into the back of the car, snivelling. Her father and her husband exchanged a few sharp unpleasant words, and then, as they drove off, the dog darted from beneath the hedge, caught up with them, and ran in front of the car, trying to impede it.

"Even their dog is a lunatic," her husband said, while the chil-dren, seeing the animal, wept afresh and put their hands out to give it reassurance. That made things worse. The dog now leapt to the window as they said endearing things to it, while Walter pressed on the horn and made a sound that could be heard in the village a mile away. The children were crying unashamedly. Their father leant back, lifted each one by the lapel of his jacket, and set him down again smartly, mercilessly. Unable to protect them, unable to account for herself, she suddenly screamed in a manner that was alarming even to herself.

"Get me out of here . . . get me out of here," she called, and stunned the children into silence. Her husband asked her to please cut out the hysterics and to be so kind as to get out, drag the unwieldy animal down to the gate, and open the gate so that they could finally make the much desired departure.

Walking along with the yelping dog as her companion, she thought that she would probably not see the place again, except perhaps for a funeral. Even the cows resting under the trees seemed to glare at her, seemed to be full of sullen ill will. Some dog hairs were coming off in her wet palm. The car hooter still sounded incessantly and imperiously. Her mother and father would hear it and add it to the litany of resentment that was now being voiced. Yes, it was a bitter ending.

She passed the horsechestnut tree where they used to tell her that she had been born and which she preferred to the Blue Room with its damp walls, its slop bucket, and the array of holy pictures that were both supplicant and chastising. How beautiful the tree looked, the leaves with their first coat of russet, but a rich thriving russet that had nothing to do with withering. That would come later. Yes, she was seeing everything despite her frenzy, or maybe because of it. The elderberries were so bright and shiny they seemed to be saying something. Saying "We are elderberries, take note of us." The gate needed painting. Shavings of dried paint ran along the wrought iron, and each time it was opened or shut, another little consignment fell onto the ground. The car caught up with her, coming at a stately progress. The last thing her eye caught was a bed of nettles so dense and luxuriant that it seemed to rasp with green fire.

Yes, her mother had guessed then about her crumbling marriage but had said nothing. Not then. They made it up, of course, insofar as anything so visceral can be salved. The children went to a non-Catholic school, and when her mother wrote to them she merely voiced the hope that they would not forget the country of their birth. She wrote to them separately and reminded them of walks, treats, orchards; said that their treehouse was safe until the next summer and their pet dog as mischievous as ever. Next summer. Nell dreaded the word, the obligation in it; matters on which the future hinged gave her the jitters.

2

"Oh . . ." she screamed, and jumped. The new girl was in the kitchen without her realising it. She had left the hall door ajar, and now here was a tall, shy, dark, stringy creature, surprising her, catching her with tears in her eyes and a soggy dishcloth in her hand. A crippling start.

"The door was open," the girl said, in a quite brazen way and without a trace of apology. The children arrived in a flash, pleased to see a young girl in a very short summer dress and sandals. She brought youth and lightheartedness in with her.

"This is Rita," Nell said to them, though they had already asked her name and tried to put it in a rhyme. Rita warmed to them at once. She put her arms out to include them, and as if they knew her well, they sidled into the crook of each arm and allowed her to rock them back and forth as if they were on a slow-moving swing.

"Dotes," she said as she smiled at them. She smiled at Tristan more. Tristan was the younger by a year. Paddy always said that it was not fair that Tristan got the most petting and that he, "Dogsbody," had to carry things, coal for the fire and the like. Tristan pleaded babyhood.

"Brown eyes is habbing a rest," he would say, emphasising the little lisp that he had, and Paddy would raise a fist and vow revenge. They were smiling at the new girl, sensing that she would play with them when their mother was tired. They did not like when their mother was tired or when she went out. To stall her, they often hid her high-heeled shoes, and once put a dab of perfume behind each ear as they had seen her do and said, "Shall we go . . . the carriage awaits us, madam." Now Rita was here and there were two mothers to minister. There was something about her that made Nell uneasy. It was the way she spoke to the children and not to Nell, who after all was employing her. There was a hostility somewhere but well concealed with half-smiles and the clutching of a handkerchief. Nell also thought to herself that she could be imagining this and that perhaps the girl was just shy. Her face was stark white and there was a spikiness to her. They were from the same village, but Rita was younger. In fact, she remembered Rita with a gaggle of other young girls playing or chasing geese across a field, always up to some mischief or other. She remembered her having an accident on a hay cart, and there indeed was the scar on her cheek to show it. Rita was taking toffees from her pocket, which she must have brought on purpose to give them. Their father would not approve, as he forbade them sweets.

"Their father would not like this," Nell said, trying in some feeble way to exercise her own authority.

"Is he a bishop?" Rita said, and laughed, and once again Nell felt the dark, subterranean powers of this young girl. Quite quickly they decided terms—Rita's wages, her half-day, and the weekends that she would be free. Then she was shown the small room that was to be her bedroom. She just stared down at the cork-lined floor of her bedroom, with the yellow Afghan rug over it, and said that if it was all right she would move in on Monday.

She arrived in the afternoon with her belongings, which were pitiful. All she had was a small plastic bag with a nightdress and a few things in it, and in her hand a little tin box which contained her hairbrush, a bracelet, and a picture of herself and some other girls at confirmation. Nevertheless, she was soon laughing with the children, doing bannister slides and piggybacks; so much so that their father, who was an irksome man, put his head through the door of his study and said, "Could we have a little quiet, please." All Rita did was put her hand to her mouth in a sudden gesture of apology and then laugh uncontrollably, once he had closed the door again. She pushed the children out into the garden, and Nell could hear them out there, yodelling. It was autumn, London autumn, and a mist hung over everything; it wandered about like some spirit; it even seemed to encase the bunches of green grapes in the conservatory, make a halo around them, grapes that were hanging in clusters, but that he refused to cut.

Yes, Nell thought, things will be better from now on. Things had been dire. Her husband and she lived in mortal enmity, and whereas once upon a time she had gone into his study in the evening for little friendly chats, she now saw him only when she delivered his tray with his meals. The children were allowed in for an hour before bedtime. He played music, classical music, most of the day, and in the afternoons, from three to five faithfully, he took a walk. Nell could not say exactly when things went wrong, so wrong that they were no longer retrievable. Formerly, he had had his periods of huff; he would not talk, except to issue an edict or make a stinging remark, but after a few days he would relent, put his arms around her, taking her unawares, and say what a grump he was. Those moments reminded her of what it must have been like for Jane Eyre when she sensed a certain thaw in Mr. Rochester's granite demeanour. To Nell, Jane Eyre and Mr. Rochester were very near, far nearer than her neighbours.

Neighbours suddenly made her realise that the new girl was making too much of a racket and that the woman next door was bound to complain. The woman next door and she had been friends of a sort, which is to say that they had conversations over the garden wall, the woman telling her of her childhood outside Edinburgh—the very fine mountain ranges, then her marriage, coming south of the border and settling in London, where her husband was a caretaker in a hospital. He had died a few years before and since then she had hardly left the house. Nell often gave her a hunk of cake or a jar of apple jelly, and their little evening rituals began to be as regular as the shuffle of the birds disappearing into the trees to roost. One day, in a fit of goodwill, the woman had confided that her hair had been the very same colour as Nell's, copper-coloured, but that she had had to have it cut for her wedding; nevertheless, she'd saved it and had it made into a wig. She ran into the house, brought it out, in its round leather box, lifted the lid with a flourish, and said, "You didn't believe me, did you?" But Nell had believed her and felt sorry for her in some way and it was that show of emotion that made the woman give her the wig and beg her to wear it when she went out in the evenings, to parties. Nell rarely went out except to see a man, in secret, and that, too, was beginning to be hazardous.

"I couldn't take it," she said to the woman.

"Please, please," the woman said, and assured her how it would make her happy, how it would make her feel young again. She had been, she said, a bit crusty of late, never having a good word for anyone, screaming at the children who had come in fancy clothes at Halloween, refusing to talk to the people on the other side of her house because of the dreadful smell of boiled cabbage that issued from their kitchen, but now, by giving the wig, her spleen was dissolved, her faith restored. A week later she asked for it back, giving no excuse, simply calling out in a bossy tone, "I would be grateful if you would give me back my valuable."

Nell thought it a joke and said, "Oh, go on, Mrs. Johnstone!"

"I'm waiting," Mrs. Johnstone said, so Nell brought the wig out in its box and returned it to her shamefacedly. After that, there was a sort of tribal feud, Mrs. Johnstone complaining if the children screeched or if a branch of the forsythia sagged over into her garden. Nell could never understand what had happened and believed it to be some awful bitterness in the old woman which, one day, having miraculously subsided, had resurfaced again. Mrs. Johnstone was often to be heard hitting the divided wall of their house because the classical music was overwhelming, or she would put tart notes under the front door, saying she objected to the washing on the clothesline or the children's language. Nell's husband wrote her a stiff letter, telling her that she could call the police and see where she'd get!

Nell thought of these things now as she heard Walter moving around in his study, the music as usual pouring forth. She felt powerless; she was afraid of him, just as she was afraid of her neighbour, afraid of everyone. She was too frightened to tackle him, to ask what had gone wrong, even to ask him to put the music a bit lower. Her children were her only friends; she clung to them, indulged them, let them get away with murder—they had biscuits at all hours and were allowed to keep torches under their beds and to make treehouses out in the common, which was forbidden. To say she loved them was inadequate; she needed them, they were her sustenance. Now she could hear them, laughing and malarkeying, and she thought the new girl will be good for them and maybe the marriage would be retrieved somehow.

As she thought this, she saw a picture in her mind of Lazarus coming back from the dead; she saw Jesus touching him, and she saw the pallor leave his cheeks and then the blood flow back into them like cochineal. It was as bad as that. Her husband took to the bed when she vacated it at seven in the morning; once, when she tried to kiss him, he froze, and as she drew back with tears in her eyes, he said that it was very salutary to observe people who could cry at the drop of a hat and wear their hearts on their sleeves. The bedroom smelled of camphor balls, because he insisted on putting them between his sweaters. She always dressed out on the landing, the children peeping at her through the jamb of the door, pretending to be someone else, in fact doing a Scottish accent copied from Mrs. Johnstone and giving each other false names. One was called Orlando and the other was Jeremiah, and one would say, "Orlando, look at her bosoms," while the other would retort, "No, Jeremiah, it's her knicks," and then they would duck down and slam the door, believing they were going to be meted out punishment. Soon after, the door would be opened a crack again, but by then she would be downstairs, making their breakfast. He insisted that they have porridge, which they hated, and to make it seem that they had eaten it, they picked it up on their spoons, licked it, and then returned it to their plate to form mounds. "Me eat more than thee," one would say to the other. They carried on all this affected talk either to amuse themselves or to cajole her, or to elude their father. Sometimes they called her Nell instead of Mama, and occasionally they asked her why Dad was so cross, but then they would forget about it and go back to talking about the treehouse that they were making in the common, or the homework that they had forgotten to do.

Hearing them with the new girl, Nell had a sudden pang. She thought, Suppose they get too fond of her? Then in some mad manifestation of ownership she ran out into the garden and kissed them suddenly, telling each one that he was her angel. Rita ignored this and dared them to chase her to the end of the garden and back.

There's something subversive about her, Nell thought, not quite realising what she meant, and then she went back towards the house, looking at the last of the roses, which though blooming were milky, had a chill on them, an intimation of death.

The father decided to have supper with them that first evening, and was amused by Rita telling them of her exploits in the country, claiming to have cut turf, to have saved hay and milked cows and goats. Also, she said, somewhat slyly, she had sucked the milk from the goats when she was parched with thirst. Walter seemed to like her, at least enough to say that if she ever wanted to play a Come-all-ye record of her native soil, she could enter his study and ask him. The offer was prompted by his overhearing her singing. She sang to the children as she was laying the table; it was a lament; October winds around the Castle of Drumore. After dinner, when he asked her to sing again, she went scarlet, her very white face went red, and she sucked in her cheeks, so that her hollows were pronounced, swearing that she couldn't sing, not a note. Nell could see that he liked her shyness and her country ways.

3

It was decidedly better. The children felt happier. He ate with them sometimes now, and Rita never complained about having to iron or to hoover. She called Nell Missis and she would say, "Missis, tell me what to do today?" Then she would clean her room, or put a lick of paint on a windowsill, or do anything. Moreover, Nell could get out—she went to the shops in the daytime, walked around these big shops, mesmerised, tried things on, and now and again she bought something, something small, like a scarf or a hairslide and, once, a black satin bolero which was reduced in price and which she believed gave her a certain piquance. Then, of course, every couple of weeks or so, she saw this man in a café or a teahouse and they held hands and elaborated on what they would do if they only had the chance. He was also bound by guilt and duty, and said that he had been so depressed that he had made a will, leaving everything to his children. They sometimes had a drink when the pubs opened, and sitting down together with the fire on and buoyed a bit by drink, they got closer and became rasher. She was always home before dinner, and on the days that she saw this man she was much more buoyant, a fact which her husband must have noticed, because he followed her, tracked her down, witnessed a rendezvous, and listened in to a telephone conversation of hers.

She did not know any of this yet—all she knew was that a rank poison floated through the house as thoroughly as the autumn mist had. At Christmas he gave the children and Rita presents, and to her he wrote a plain postcard which said, "Happy Nothing." She'd got the children drums and he objected so to the din that within an hour these garish, silver-crusted implements were seized and put in the loft upstairs. That night, they had both been invited to neighbours', but he refused to go. She went alone. The daughter of the house flirted with everyone, including her own father. Her father had been in the war and limped but the daughter insisted that he do a tango with her, showing to all present his dotage of her. "Daddy, Daddy," she kept saying. The wife ate a lot of the mince pies and told Nell how that day her mother-in-law had looked into the lavatory bowl and in the clear water had seen, for the first time, her epiglottis and had screamed with fright. The drinks were quite liberal—it was a wine cup—and for one who didn't drink much, Nell soon got tipsy and went home and paraded into his study and said she had the answer, she had the solution to their problem, that if they went to the Lake District all would be well, their marriage would be restored again. She had just heard about Lake Windermere and all those lovely inns from the neighbours. They could also visit the Brontë Museum, see the little shoes that these sisters had worn, see their gravestones. "Please," she said in a coaxing voice.

"Please," he said, lifting her eager arm off his shoulder as if it, too, were an old glove. He said to breathe her alcoholic fumes on some more willing fool, as for instance the idiot she consorted with, whose three front teeth he had vowed to knock out. It was then, Christmas night, that he showed her a copy of the letter he had written to that idiot's wife, and she knew now with a horrifying clarity why her friend had not shown up Christmas week and not even sent her a card or called to explain. She had rung the newspaper office where he worked, only to be told by his secretary that he was unavailable and to please not ring again. The letter appalled her; it was addressed to his wife by her Christian name—it told of the maudlin rendezvous of the two deceivers and then expressed satisfaction in ridding him of his few front crooked teeth.

"You didn't," Nell said, holding the letter.

"I can imagine *their* jolly Christmas," he said, and continued to cut up envelopes with a paper knife, a thing he did out of economy, and perhaps to amuse himself.

4

The months bore on inexorably, and although she knew that the marriage was doomed, she could not do anything other than weep. She could not leave him, that was certain; she could not stay with him, that, too, was certain. In some vague, unvoiced way she was willing her own death; her teeth began to pain and she was almost relieved when two of them had to be removed. This confirmed the mortality that she was counting on. She was not yet thirty. The children, sensing her despair, grew more and more towards Rita, and at bedtime it was Rita they wanted to bathe them and make bubbles, Rita to toss them in the big bath towels, fling them onto the bed, singing, "What shall we do with the drunken sailor—toss him up in a blanket, oh." Her husband's communications were by letter, terse bulletins such as "The sheets need changing" or "No more burnt parsnips, if you please." Once he wrote on a large sheet of paper—"Now and then he did not think that all women could possibly be bitches, but reality was always at hand to reassure him." She tried to tackle him about this; it was in the hallway when he was dressing to go for his walk, putting on scarf and gloves, the damp pouring in from outside, so that the hall itself was as cold as the garden. He was frugal about the oil heaters and allowed them lit only after six in the evening. She held up the offending page and he smiled, pleased that it had had its nettling effect.

What does he think, what's going on in his mind? she thought as she watched him go down the street, tall, aristocratic, aloof. A few crocuses were coming up in their garden, and in her dismal state, they looked like little yellow blades that had cut their way through the dark mournful clay. She prayed for a world catastrophe, her mind ran to such lengths as war, or earthquake, whence he and she would be flung together by this larger doom. She could not believe that they had once been close; in fact, she would take out the box with the photographs in it and peruse them while he was walking. She did not recognise herself, that young girl, many years younger than he, that young girl of only a few years before standing on the steps of the house where they had lived, wearing a jacket of his and feeling a little shy, but proud, knowing that he loved her. It was before the children were born; she was almost a child herself, running from room to room, singing or reciting verses and looking at the souvenirs in his china cabinet. His first wife had lived there with him and these souvenirs were from that time; there were two pink porcelain menus on which were written the fare for some party that they had had; there was turkey, she seemed to remember, and chestnut stuffing and pumpkin pie; the writing was in the wife's hand. At that time she used to be very jealous of such things and once had even tried to wipe out the writing, but now nothing racked her, only the thought of this hideous marriage, her body withering away, his dislike of her rampantly voiced, as if he had always wanted to dislike her, as if in fact that's why he had chosen her.

Then there was Rita, Rita dancing attendance on him, having his slippers warmed when he got in from his walk or asking him a crossword clue, and yes, definitely yes, flirting with him in a concealed way, wearing bows in her hair at dinnertime and asking him questions that seemed serious, like the population or agriculture in China or India.

Soon, Rita was refusing to take a half-day, first on the grounds that she no longer wished to see her sister—they were now enemies—and then on the grounds that the children had asked her, begged her to stay at home. The children and she were full of secrets; at table they whispered to each other and spoke this strange secret language, so much so that Nell began to feel that perhaps she should leave, perhaps she should look for a job somewhere, maybe even out of London. But that was unthinkable; they were her children, there was a tie between them that no one could cut, despite secret language and "What shall we do with the drunken sailor" antics. Her children knew it, too; they had only to look at her and between them passed such a flow, such love, a tender kind of love so that their eyes would cloud over, because of course they knew that there were things amiss, sensed how wretched she was. On Sundays, when Rita went to a ceilidh, Nell sat with them in their bedroom and they talked and talked; they talked about other children at school, friends, enemies, what they would like for their next birthdays, and thinking about presents and birthdays, they always raised their eyes to the ceiling, towards the loft, where the drums that she had given them still were, shedding, as she thought, their silver dust.

"There's rats up there," one of them said.

"There's not!" Nell said, and then they all laughed, not knowing why they laughed. She would have little squares of chocolate for them on those evenings, and then, because they had already brushed their teeth, she would run a bit of toothpaste around their mouth, on the tip of her finger, pretending it was icing. Oh yes, between them and her there were bonds that no father or no Rita could breach.

"Dad says you wanted us to go to a different school, across the main road where we'd get run over by a lorry and killed," Paddy said.

"That's crazy," she said, and repeated it. "That's crazy."

"He took us down there one day; he said main road thus: school on other side, Mother wants children to cross main road in order to be run over."

"Is that true?" she asked of Tristan, and he nodded. This was intolerable. This was lunacy. To them she said somewhat feebly, "But I got you into your school, I went and saw the headmaster, I begged him to take you," and then she stopped herself, knowing that telling them her woes would not solve anything. When she kissed them she said they were not to think any sad thoughts, they were to think only of summer, when they would all go home to Ireland, the three of them, that is, and walk in the fields.

"And I'll see a blind bat, a fox, and a fairy again," Tristan said, and boasted as always that he had seen these marvels while his brother had not.

Downstairs she could hear her husband on the other side of the door, moving about.

"It's prison," she said, "we're prisoners." She kept saying it over and over again. Not a thing altered in her mind or in the room except that now and then a piece of glowing coal settled down into the bed of the fire and was replaced by a new lump that she put on automatically. She heard Rita come in, put her head through his door, and ask if she could get him a snack or leave something for him on a tray. He declined, asked her if the dancing had been enjoyable, and reminded her that she was to cut his hair during the week; yes, she was his barber as well.

"I could do it now," Rita said, agog.

"Tomorrow," he said, and added that he was doing letters, he was attending to a lot of urgent business matters. What business matters? Nell wondered, and her heart began to pound. At times he had threatened that he would take the children away to New Zealand, where he had a relative, and she thought that maybe one day she would come back from her weekly appointment at the hairdresser's and find the house stripped and them gone.

She called Rita into her room; she called her curtly, as if to say, "I am mistress here, it is me to whom you should be offering snacks or supper on a tray."

"Have the children ever talked to you about being sent to a school across the main road?"

"They did say something," Rita said, blushing a little.

"Said what?"

"I don't remember."

"He's poisoning their minds, he's turning them against me," she said.

"You're not all there, missis," Rita said with a shameless bravura.

"What makes you say a thing like that?" Nell asked, rising.

"You're imagining things," Rita said, and by the gleam in her eyes, Nell saw that for some reason the girl was visibly excited at the thought of her mistress's despair.

"What have you got against me?" she asked quickly, foolishly.

"I don't know what you mean," Rita said, and refused to be drawn out on the matter. They had come from the same neighbourhood, Rita from a poorer family, could that be it; she, Nell, had shone at school, and Rita had been a dunce, could that be it? Nell felt that it really was not those things, that it was not the past at all but that it was this very instant and that Rita really wished her not to be there, casting a gloom over their lives, quizzing the children in an unnatural way, no wife to her husband, a sourpuss. No knowing how their meeting might have ended if it wasn't for the fact that Paddy let out a cry, said his throat hurt.

"Have you the thorns, love?" Rita said, and rushed up the stairs to tend to him. He was getting one of his bouts of bronchitis, which would tie him to his bed for days, coughing, being sick, and asking his brother to bring him back old comics from school. The two women stood by his bed, one on either side, taking turns feeling his forehead. His mother gave him an aspirin, and eventually, as if he was duty-bound to console both of them, he said, "I'm sorry to be a nuisance, to be a crock," and Rita kissed him and went out, and then his mother kissed him and stood there in the dark confirming her love of him, or was it her need?

5

In bed, Nell scanned in her mind the list of her friends and wondered which one she could go to, to seek advice. They hadn't been
living very long in England and didn't have many friends, except
for those neighbours where she had got drunk at Christmastime;
but since then they had had their own drama: their beautiful
daughter had got pregnant by some man who belonged to a religious sect and had gone off with him. She felt as she lay there that
some dreadful plot was afoot, either from her husband downstairs
or from Rita. She felt all the cards were stacked against her, and
she was now so unclear about herself and the state of her mind, she
was not sure whether perhaps Rita was correct in telling her that
she imagined things and maybe Rita bore her no ill at all, and
maybe her husband was sitting downstairs waiting for her to come
in with open arms and say, "Darling, darling"; but these thoughts
she knew also to be ridiculous. She made little resolutions, such as
that she would buy a tonic, that she would buy a thermometer,
because it was not enough just to feel her son's temperature by
putting her hand on his forehead. Yes, he would be sick next day,
and she would sit in his room, and he would ask her those grave
little questions that he always asked when he was sick, about God
and dying. Once, he told her that he had had a bad dream and it
was of little coffins and he and his brother were in them, each in
his own coffin, doomed.

"Nonsense," she said, "nonsense," and she had put her arms around him; but she could feel that in some way the sadness that was going on had imparted itself to him, and one day when he was a grownup he would remember this and tell someone about his bouts of sickness, and the strange girl they had from Ireland who preferred his brother to him, and his mother always a bit forlorn. She jumped out of bed and rushed into his room; he was sound asleep, but she knew from the muttering that he was developing a fever.

The break came on one of their birthdays. The garden was full of children, children laughing and going "Bang, bang, bang!" and some of them sneaking up to the table where the eats were and touching them with their fingers. She had put a trestle table up and covered it first with red crepe paper and then with a lace cloth, her best lace cloth; it looked sumptuous. The first little setback was when Tristan, whose birthday it was, broke a glass. He was drinking his orangeade and determined to show off; to prove a point, he slammed the glass so that it split onto the cloth and onto the red crepe, and soon the cloth itself had this wandering red pigment to it. He looked around to see who had noticed, and seeing that his mother was not cross, he laughed loudly and said, "Aren't I the brave boy not to cry?" She smiled at him and went over and began to clear up the glass, so that none of the children would cut their fingers. There was wrapping paper everywhere, and she picked it up, too, thinking how happy they were, how lighthearted. Their father had not yet appeared; the children were playing war games while Rita was going around, kissing them, tying their laces, and in every way being essential. There were jugs of orangeade, iced buns; there was an assortment of sandwiches, and later the cake. The boys much more overexcited than the girls, brandishing sticks as guns and letting out cries while the girls whimpered and went to Rita to ask for a handkerchief or to be let into the house because the boys were too rough. Once brought into the house, they immediately asked to be brought out again. Nell glanced over the wall from time to time to see if her neighbour was looming, but for three days she had not appeared at all and Nell reckoned that probably she was ill. She thought that perhaps she should knock on her door and ask if she needed any help, but she was afraid to.

It was while the party was in full swing and they were just about to light the candles, the seven candles on the pink angel cake, that her husband sauntered out, very quietly, wearing his best hound's-tooth jacket and with a peculiar look on his face. He watched while Rita lit the candles and Tristan blew them out, and then waited as everyone sang, "Happy birthday, happy birthday to you," but he did not join in. She knew he was going to call her. He did not call her by speaking, he just curled his finger and she followed. Inside the house he closed the door that led to the garden and she thought, This is going to be rough, maybe fatal.

"That cheque that came this morning, you haven't signed it on the back."

"No, and I'm not going to," she said. The cheque was for work she had done; it was quite a substantial amount; in fact, it turned out to be a larger cheque than even she had imagined. In the past when she had worked and received money, she always gave the money over to him, but this time she decided that it was her own money and she wanted her own account.

"I've never heard anything so audacious in all my life," he said.

"But it's my money," she said, and she knew that her voice was quaky and that there were tears welling up in her eyes, the way they welled up in her eyes as a child when she tried to explain something to her mother, tried to explain that she had not done wrong, that she had not deliberately broken a cup or spilled salt, but that it had just happened. Also, she thought, Why did I leave this cheque here for him to see; why didn't I try to cash it somewhere and at least show my independence? One word followed another; he took a fountain pen from his pocket, dipped it in the black ink—they were in his study—and said, "Sign it, sign it!" She was adamant. Then he gripped her arm and brought her upstairs, and as they went upstairs she had this premonition that she was not going to come down in one piece. In the bedroom he closed, then locked, the door; pushed her down on the bed; his hand like a vise on her throat, as he said in a very calm voice, overcalm, "If you don't sign it, your life will not be worth living!"

"How! How!" she said, realising that it was madness to ask him to be reasonable.

"I've just told you," he said. "Your life won't be worth living," and then he added that he would take the children away and she could howl to the streetlights.

"You can't! They're both of ours!" she said, and he laughed as his fingers ground into her throat. Ridiculously, she thought of Dracula. She also felt the breath being squeezed out of her.

She got away somehow, went towards the door, and by the fact that she took the pen, she was saying that, yes, she would capitulate, she would sign it. She went down to the hall and signed her full name, even her middle name, on the cheque, went into the kitchen, looked at the children in the garden shouting and scampering about, and thought, I cannot spend another minute under this roof. She walked back into the hall, opened the creosoted cupboard where the coats were, put on her grey coat, and went out of the house, for what she knew would be forever.

6

She walked and walked. She walked first to their school and half
thought of going in search of the headmaster, who lived nearby, to
tell him her plight, but then decided that that was a mistake.
Instead, she walked to the surgery, where the doctor had seen her
twice, had prescribed a tonic for her and had given her a bit of a
lecture on not giving in to her nerves. She walked away from there
to one street, then another, and looked at signs in windows, while
in the back of her mind was the worry, not yet fully acknowledged,
that she had nowhere to spend the night. There was a woman she
had met through her work who lived a few miles away and she
took a bus to her house. The woman was surprised to see her, but
rallied and said, "Come in, pet, come in," and she went in and sat
down on a sofa that looked out on the Thames and onto a sloping
bridge. It was a footbridge where people could come and go to the
underground. At first Nell rambled, said there was nothing wrong,
that she had just been in the neighbourhood, but gradually she told
it: how she had just left her husband and children and that she was
desperately unhappy and that she did not know what to do. The
woman made her tea and toast and kept saying, "No one can help
you, pet, only yourself!" but that of course she would do anything
she could to help. At dusk, Nell thanked her and apologised for
having barged in, and although she wanted to say, "Do you think

I could sleep on your floor tonight?" she did not say it; she could not bring herself to.

She left, promising the woman faithfully that she would be in touch with her; she even said that maybe they would have dinner together, and in her mind wondered at her absurdity. All the money she had was the ten-pound note in her pocket, the housekeeping money that he gave her each Friday morning, as she bitterly recalled, money that was really her own. Out in the street it was dark, and automatically she took a bus back towards home. She went to the police station at the end of the lane and a young officer kept asking her the same questions—why she had come and whether she had been molested by her husband. She explained that she had not been molested, but that she had almost been, and that she had nowhere to go. The young policeman said he was sorry that he could not help her and suggested that she go home and talk it over.

Her next stop was at the local hospital, where she sat in the Outpatients' Department along with a lot of people who seemed to be in greater need than herself. People came in bleeding, others came in wrapped in blankets; one couple, who were decidedly peculiar, came in laughing, both of them sporting black eyes. The very bad casualties were brought in on stretchers and were not left in the waiting room but carried through to the rooms, where obviously nurses or doctors saw them. When it came to her turn, a very officious nurse interviewed her and said, "What is it, dear?" but by the way she said "dear" she implied, "There isn't that much wrong with you, you have no wounds, no injuries, so why are you wasting my time?"

Once again, Nell repeated what had happened, how she had been in the garden, how there was a birthday party, how she had had this showdown with her husband and had left her house without saying goodbye.

"That's not very intelligent, dear," the nurse said.

"Is there anything you can do to help me?" Nell asked.

The nurse took one key from the big bunch on her belt, opened the wall cupboard, and took out a bottle from which she removed two sleeping capsules. They were bright turquoise.

"I suggest you go home, dear, take these, and sleep it off," she said.

Nell took the two pills, and holding them in the palm of her hand, she thought that she would swallow them when she went out into the street and then wait to see what happened. In the end she didn't. She took two more buses and went to a railway station where she knew tramps slept. She knew this because she had read about it in the newspapers; she also knew that they were unlikely to attack her, because they were all fairly forlorn people, like herself. She sat all night on a bench, while on the other end of the bench there was a woman so bundled up with coats that she did not seem like a human at all. Various people came and went, some just to reconnoitre, then shuffle off again; some to find a favourite corner, bundling themselves up in blankets or coats, one opening a big black tattered umbrella and putting it between himself and the rest of the world. Even the pigeons were quiet, and because there were no trains through the night, not a sound came from any of the tracks. Many of the people coughed. A couple of porters went by from time to time, but did not bother them, did not even seem to see them. Her mind was made up. She had friends in the country; she would go to the children's school at lunchtime the following day and fetch them. They would take a train to the country and then she would decide what to do.

The children ran to her and said, "Mama, Mama!" They did not ask why she had not come home and they did not even mention if their father or Rita had been alarmed. She whispered her plan to them. They were to go back into the cloakroom and get their coats but not say a word to any of their friends, and then come out quickly, because they were going on a journey, on a train.

"Safari . . . safari . . ." they said, and ran off like two little conspirators. They were back in no time, not only with their coats, but with their satchels as well, remarking on their own ingenuity. She brought them to Woolworth's to buy some toys; she bought them a plastic weapon each, she reckoned that if they were going to be in a strange house in a distraught state they needed toys. She had already telephoned her friend in the country and asked if they could come. Her friend was newly married, and was madly happy, and said, "Of course, darling, you come here and we'll jolly you up."

The children were incredulous because when they arrived the husband told them he had a very pleasant task for them, which was to demolish the greenhouse. It was old and a hazard, and the best way to demolish it was with stones. He broke a few panes, just to demonstrate. From inside the house, where Nell sat with Sally, she could hear the shattering glass and the shouts of glee which followed each crash. She was drinking wine and getting a little fuzzy as she told the same story: the months, the years of desperation, the showdown over the cheque, the night she had spent at Waterloo Station, and the dash to the school to abduct them. Sally kept filling her glass and saying, "Awful, too awful for words." From time to time Sally's husband came in and said, "Still nattering?" then kissed Sally and went out again. Sally said that she could not believe her luck; she had held a torch for this man, this genius, for several years, but he was married to that other cow, she never even knew that he fancied her and never would have known but for a ball when they sneaked away and went into the woods and were so happy that they actually ate the daffodils. "To die, darling!" she said, hinting about their intimate life, and Nell felt that her presence there was really an inconvenience, bringing gloom into this enclave of bliss. As a precaution, she said that of course she and the children would not stay long, and Sally said, "You get a good night's rest and then you can think."

Thinking was beyond Nell. She bored them at dinner, talked too much; bits of her life fell out of her mouth, like bits of bread. The children ate a lot and even drank wine, and then sallied off to bed without a murmur, tired from having demolished the greenhouse and then playing cops and robbers in the woods. Nell knew she was boring her host, because from time to time he got up and called Sally out; once it was to see the full moon and another time it was to see a badger. In bed she could hear them laughing and talking, and she thought what a relief it must be for them to be alone at last, without her litanies. She took a sleeping capsule that Sally had given her and fell into a drowsy, dream-clotted sleep, so that when Sally stood over her the next day she could not remember where she was or how long she had slept. It was noon, Sally said. Nell had slept all that time; then, as she jumped up, Sally said the children had been playing outside since breakfast time, and a new garden shed had been delivered, which R was erecting. She called Robert R, even to his face. She had brought coffee up, but of course, there were fried eggs and risotto on the Aga, waiting. Nell tried to remember things, to get her bearings, as she felt the tiny buttons of the strange nightgown that she was wearing, and saw the long wardrobe with a tassel attached to the key. She was coming back to reality.

"Darling!" Sally said, as if it was some accidental little thing that had cropped up in her mind. "Darling, you're in luck; we have to go into London today, R has an assignment, they want him to write some beautiful theme music for a film, so you have the house all to yourself." Nell thanked her, but really felt that they were going out of boredom, they were going to be free of her. In fact, they left before lunch, because R decided that he wanted to take Sally for a treat and was lucky enough to get the last bloody table at the Connaught. Nell sat in their kitchen, and with a start of bewilderment it came to her that there were actually people in this world who were happy, who had warm stoves and nice crockery and who lolled over meals and joked with each other. For some reason then, she made a tour of the house. She saw all Sally's clothes, summer clothes in one wardrobe and winter clothes in another. Their bed was a four-poster with russet fringing and their room full of baskets of flowers and books flung on a chaise longue, new books that didn't seem to have been opened. She sat on their bed, sat on the russet counterpane and stared at the phone. Beside it was a little bureau and she opened a drawer to search for a telephone directory. She was on the point of doing something, something definite. In the drawer was a note that she could not avoid reading; it was from R to Sally. It was about spanking her and doing naughty things to her; it was written in a schoolmasterly manner and was telling its pupil what to wear. She was to wear a short leather skirt and not to forget her bristle hairbrush. Smack. Smack, it said as a signature. Nell closed the drawer and dialed the operator for the London code. Her husband and she had one mutual friend, a man. She rang him and received a very heated tirade. Her husband had already been on the phone to him twice, was demented, did not know where his children were, was at his wits' end—he who had had this happen to him once before, a wife who had skeddaddled with a child; how could she do it? How could she do it?

"I was desperate," she said, going wan with fear.

"So is he!" he said.

"I thought you were my friend," she said, to coax him.

"I *am* your friend," he said.

It was agreed that she and the children would take the train that afternoon, that she would deposit the children with another woman she knew in North London and then meet her husband in this man's flat and thrash things out.

"I can't go back to him!"

"I think he realises that," her friend said and laughed, and by the laugh she knew that he would be on her side.

She got there early. She was pale, and, as the friend said, "deep into mourning." On the way she had gone to the dry cleaner's to get a suit out, but as she hadn't the docket they wouldn't give it to her.

"I'll just have to get that docket," she said, as if it was all-important.

"Not just now," the friend said, and then the doorbell rang, and before she let him answer it, she clutched him and begged him to be nearby at all times, not to go out, in case of any unpleasantness, or in case her husband tried to throttle her again. He assured her he would be in the next room. Her husband was indeed changed; she could tell how the shock had affected him and he appeared to have cried a lot. He was dressed in his best suit, best shirt and tie, and he kissed her fondly on the cheek, a thing he had not done for years. He enquired about the children; he asked if they were all right and enquired if by any chance they had done their home-work, then said to their friend that a cup of tea wouldn't go amiss but was really asking to be alone with her. She heard herself say, "Sorry," and then regretted it, but in fact it had a desirable effect.

He said he understood; after all, she was young and it stood to reason that she needed to sow her wild oats.

"Not really," she said, thinking of the letter that he had sent to the man's wife and how the man had never got in touch with her again and probably hated her now.

"We're decent people, we're grownups," she heard him say, and he went on to explain that, as he saw it, they both loved their children very much, loved them enough to share them.

"Why don't you let them come back?" he said. "And when you have a place of your own, you can have them two or three nights a week and I'll have them the other nights, or vice versa."

It was almost too good to be true, him yielding like this, bending, saying that they could share the children when only forty-eight hours before he had said that he was taking them away, far away. She had no idea where she could get a flat or what she could use as money, but he was telling her that it could be amicable, and that was all that mattered.

"Will Rita be staying on?" she asked a little tentatively.

"For a while," he said casually. "Then I think she should move off and go to college." The three of them then had tea and joked about things, about how one night they'd all gone to the theatre, a play written by another friend which proved to be so dull that they had to pretend in the interval that she had a sudden dizzy spell and they had to carry her out. They talked for about an hour, and then seeing that indeed he had melted, Nell rose and said she would go to North London, collect the children, and bring them home so that they could sleep in their beds that night. She herself had found a place to stay for a bit, because the woman whom she had called on the day she left him was going out of town for a few weeks and had offered her the flat, free.

"So things are working out," she said, as if it was not separation and divorce that she was embarking on but some kind of joyride. In the streets she saw the bits of purple lilac trod into the ground. There were boys in the trees shaking the branches, shaking them violently; she looked up and smiled at them; another time she might have been cross. Her children would be glad, they would be in their own room that night and she would see them every day.

Not a day of her life would pass without seeing them, and she would work hard and find a place for them to live; the nightmare was over.

The woman in North London was quite relieved, glad for Nell's sake, as she said, and equally glad not to have to put sleeping bags down in the sitting room. The children took it in their stride, seemed rather pleased at being dispatched at a moment's notice from one place to another, eating at all odd hours, and being kissed by strangers who called them "love." She had borrowed money from this woman, promising to pay it back soon. First they took a taxi, then a train, then from the station took another taxi. As they went up the hill towards what had been her house, she felt her heart go "thump thump" again, and she remembered the manner in which she had left, she remembered how going down the road she was certain that he would come after her and drag her back. As they passed the artificial lake, which was now just a sheet of black, it occurred to her that she would never walk there again and see the oldish men with mesmeric patience and bamboo rods fishing from the bank.

7

The lights were on and the house had a glow of welcome to it, a welcome that she never sensed when she lived there. She asked the taxi to wait, opened the door, and the children ran out, ran through the open gateway to the hall door, where they knocked impudently. Their father, who was wearing his old tattered pullover, stared at her with a peculiar kind of smile. He kissed them, said that they were just in time to see a favourite television programme of theirs. Inside, they called, "Rita, Rita." Then he looked at Nell and the smile became a little more frigid as he told her formally how much he wanted to thank her.

"For what?" she said, for he was no longer the amenable person who had drunk tea in her friend's house, he was a man livid with rage.

"You realise," he said, "that you have just lost them legally; as their mother you have just deserted them," and he laughed. Then, without any to-do, he pushed the door forwards, so that what she saw was the white hall door and the glass-beaded paneling which was opaque.

She hit on it and said: "Wait! You can't do this!"

And through the letter box, which he lifted slightly, his voice said, "Like hell, I can't!"

She said a few more things, such as she would get the law on him, such as she would get her children back, such as he was a bastard; but he had shut the letter box, so that she couldn't be heard through the flap. After five minutes, maybe more or maybe less, she knew there was nothing she could do but walk away. She paid the taxi. The driver saw by her face that things had gone wrong. He said, "Don't let it get you . . . luv." Walking down the street, she felt murderous and conceived every kind of revenge, saw herself shooting him, striking him, hiring bodyguards to kill him . . . anything, anything to get her children back. They would not miss her that first night, of course; they would not realise what was going on, but in a few days when they knew that they were not coming to her, then what—weeping and agitation and maybe refusing to speak to her again.

She wrote to her mother, wrote with all the urgency and muddle of a child, knowing that it would be welcome news, in spite of the shock. Each day she awaited the reply.

Holding her mother's envelope, which was thick and sturdy, she felt a moment of strength, of forgiveness, and of a burgeoning hope that life was going to be all right, that the worst had been. Out on the street, she halted by a lamppost to read it leisurely, and also because there were tremors in her heart. That was natural. A fat letter, a wad of words. Warm, comforting words. Instead, a diatribe. Her mother said that it was no surprise, that it had been crystal-clear for all to see, that even the most casual caller could tell how bitter and loveless the marriage was; then she dilated on each and every failing of his, reminding Nell of the trouble she had taken with meals for him, because of his faddiness, only to be put in the halfpenny places, to be treated like a skivvy. Next came the forbearance of her father, who had taken scarcely veiled insults from a man who was not fit to clean his boots. But that was the past and what mattered now was the future. Her mother was asking her to make some vows concerning that future. She was to kneel down as she read the words, kneel wherever she happened to be, and swear on her oath that she would never touch an alcoholic drink as long as she lived and, more importantly, that she would never have to do with any man in body or soul. She stood there in the street and thought, I'm going to do something terrible; I'm going to disgrace myself right here. It was a fairly smart street, with antique shops—a tiny oak staircase, replica of a larger one, the single item in one window, and in another a beautiful china cabinet with carved rosettes and, above, the lamppost with its hanging basket of fresh, leaking flowers, so gay and jaunty, and she thinking, This woman, my mother, is not my mother, because she has no pity; this is a mother who is made of stone.

On compassionate grounds, as he said, he decided to let her have the children a couple of evenings a week. The evenings were never certain, it depended on him, on Rita, and on whether the children had behaved themselves well enough to be allowed out, so that it was always a question of waiting for their phone call and of going to the station to wait. Often she waited for an hour or more. She began to know the station better than her own room. She knew the tracks and the clumps of cinders between the tracks and the gloriously inappropriate advertisements for holidays and suntan. Grass banks sloped steeply down from the little back gardens where clothes were hanging. Many, like herself, looked bedraggled, but some were full of vitality: young girls going on a date, dressed to the nines. The children always came running to her, as if they feared that somehow she might not be there. Sometimes they grumbled—their father had made them do this or do that, he had made them hoover their own room, and there on the platform, with a great flourish, they reenacted working this laborious machine and having to stop to pick up bits of fluff and Rita's used matches. Another time it was milk bottles; Tristan had picked up the milk and suddenly felt the load was too much and said, "They're slipping, they're slipping!" but his father took no notice of the warning, until "Crash! Crash!" they slipped, and he said feebly, "They've slipped." Paddy tried to help him sweep up the broken glass, but he was not permitted to.

"Let him do it, he dropped them," their father said.

"It will all soon be resolved," she said, not knowing if indeed it ever would. She had after all deserted them, and she felt too frightened to go to a lawyer, frightened about this crime of hers, and then of course there was money. Money was her second biggest bogey; she had gone to a bank manager recommended by a friend, and he took pity on her, agreed to let her have an overdraft. He was a fatherly man, said he knew what it was like, he had lost a son; he didn't say how.

She got a job as an editor with a publisher, part-time, and then to supplement her income she read manuscripts at home; many stories not too different from her own, except the women in them had a little more pluck.

"Why don't I do something?" she would say when alone in her little flat or when waiting in the station, but fear had paralysed her. Fear that she had done some great and incalculable wrong.

The flat that she got was small, but she loved it—a studio with a skylight, where she could see endless roofs and television aerials, nearby a steeple, its pale verdigrised dome like a gigantic fireman's hat. The city seemed unfamiliar; it was as if she were in a strange place and not in London at all; Paris, she thought, although she did not know Paris. The children loved it, too; they pranced about marking their territory, and each time left some of their possessions. She had bought a huge bed and they slept in it with her, their feet and arms in the night lolloping over her. Love affairs were out. Now and then she went to the odd party, and once she met a singer she liked; he was very smooth, had a kind of bandleader quality, with his suede shoes and his very soft leather jacket and black polo-neck sweater, and yes, she did imagine being in his arms, and for some reason she wanted to be wearing black velvet to match his outfit, as if the two outfits rather than the two bodies would merge and ravish one another. In truth, she was afraid of being with anyone, afraid of being caught and therefore losing her children, but even more than that, afraid of being inadequate to the situation, the room somehow too shabby and she herself too emotional. He seemed interested enough in her, passed her some compliment about her ivory skin, her crop of hair, but was appalled to find that she didn't have a telephone in her own flat, that it was a landing telephone which sometimes other people answered.

"I've applied for one," she said.

"Good for you," he said, and winked and trotted over to the table where there was a buffet—lasagna swamped in an overwhite sauce, bowls of lettuce, and French bread that was not cut but broken into clumps. She assumed that was probably the sophisticated thing to do.

Sometimes she told herself that it was all bearable. She saw the children, they loved her, she spoilt them with comics and sweets, and in ten years they would be grown up enough to make their own decisions. Ten years! she thought. Then again, as she waited at the station and they did not come, she fumed and made fantastic threats. He used to keep her waiting and say to them blithely, "Let's see how flapped she gets." He never got out of the car, just opened the door and let them out, like puppies coming through the hatch. The car was grey; he had bought it after she left, possibly to lift his spirits. It was a vintage car and very recognisable from a distance. So imagine her surprise when one day, going on the bus to fetch them, she saw it going in the opposite direction, the hood down, a young girl next to him in the passenger seat. At first she thought it was Rita, but no, it was another girl, long hair adrift in the wind in come-hitherish spill. She couldn't believe it. She jumped from her seat, which was near the door, and mindless of the consequences, she leapt from the moving bus and soon was running down the road after the grey car, which was already out of sight. Her rage was matched only by her disbelief. Who was this girl? Where were they going? Had the children met her?

At the school gate the children were grumpy from having been kept waiting. One said that his shoelace was undone, and as she bent down to tie it, he said, "I thought you'd gone, disappeared." To make amends, she bought them chocolate ices, and soon they were sallying along, surprised to learn that they were going to their dad's house first to pick up some belongings of hers. She still had the latchkey. She had of course taken her clothes, but her excuse now was that she would take a few jugs, things that had belonged to her mother, and a paperweight that someone had given her, a paperweight with a dandelion seed inside it. Going up the street towards the house, she made them walk near the wall and the gateways, believing that they were less likely to be spotted that way—she had a story prepared in case he had returned. She would say that one of the children had left a textbook that he needed for his homework, a book on sea urchins.

"Fibber!" Paddy said, glad that she was now in some sort of confraternity with him, because he had told it at school that his mother had tuberculosis and had gone to a sanatorium and would be away indefinitely. The headmaster had not communicated this to her but to Walter, who wrote her a note and said that it would be estimable if from now on she would try to put an end to fantasising, as she was polluting her children's minds with her lies.

She let herself into the house very quietly, and was quick to notice a couple of changes that had been made since she left. There was a new, coarse rush mat to wipe one's feet on and he had put varnish on the hall cupboard. Rita seemed to be out. It was, in fact, her half-day, which was why Nell had collected them directly from the school instead of meeting them at the station. Nevertheless, she let out a little holler and the meekness and the ineffectuality of it annoyed her. She sent them into the kitchen, saying that she wanted to go into their father's study to be alone.

"To look in his locked box?" Paddy asked.

"Nosy," she said, and gave him a little biff.

The study was full of clutter, but on his desk was the incriminating material that she had come in search of. She read an advertisement from a woman who was looking for accommodation in London, a woman with a child. She was certain that the woman in the car was this same woman; quickly she copied out the box number and determined that she would answer the advertisement under an assumed name and find this woman's name and address. She believed, momentarily, that her struggle was over; the existence of this woman would be grounds for adultery, and hence, she would be able to get her children. She was almost triumphant, when Rita burst into the room, curlers in her hair and an eggshell mask on her face making her look like a ghoul; she was obviously preparing for a date.

"What are you doing here?" she said.

"What are *you* doing here!" Nell said in reply. She thanked her stars that Rita had not seen her rummaging at the desk.

"This is my house still," she said as she went to the bookcase and took out three books, all of which had his name printed on them.

"Their father will be very cross about this," Rita said.

"Fancy that," she said, and made a big show of calling the children in from the kitchen and saying that they would have to hurry as they had an appointment at a hotel for tea. Even as she said it, she thought that she was going a little mad. Rita kissed them as they went out of the house and said to Tristan: "Who do you love most?" forcing him of course to say that he loved her.

Going down the street, she was still terrified of being seen by any of the neighbours, or worse, by her husband on his way back with the girl. Paddy complained that Rita didn't love him but made a favourite of his brother and often he was sent out of the room while she told his brother secrets and once he was made to scrub the bath with a pumice stone.

"She'll have to go," Nell said, and that night she wrote a letter to Walter to say that she found Rita unsuitable for the children, but as she had no sensible grounds for this, she decided that posting the letter would only lead to more trouble, and instead she put it in a jug, one of the jugs she had taken from the house.

He began to let her see the children far oftener, so much so that she bought bunk beds and put them in the sitting room. He was hardly ever home. Nell believed he was with the girl, who lived in the country, and one day it came to her that for two months now she had had the solution to her plight. All she had to do was to find the young girl and himself together and she would have her evidence. The woman who had once lent her her flat suggested that they drive to this hamlet in the country where the girl lived and catch him there. She had got the address from the advertisement, which she answered under the assumed name. They set out after the children's tea, and Nell was so possessed of victory that she told the children that very soon they would be with her all the time.

"Goody, goody," they said to her and the babysitter. He was an old man with war wounds whom she had met in a playground and who had professed to love children. Little did she know that he wanted to interfere with them; he often asked them if he could unknot their pyjamas. Being a pair, they defied him, but they were a little wary of him all the same. They never told her, of course; instead, they told Rita.

The drive was far longer than she had anticipated. They drove first along the motorway, passing those neon-lit garages with metal signs that flapped because of the wind, overtaking a lorry or two, being overtaken; the woman telling her about her own life: her husband, their two best friends with whom they did everything, went on holiday, played bridge, and so forth, and one day coming home unexpectedly to find her husband and the woman in bed, her bed. They stopped to get coffee, and sitting in the cold car drinking it, Nell asked herself, "What is the logic of this escapade?" Two lorry drivers stood by their lorries, eating sausages and drinking tea, and one of them tapped on their window to see if they wanted to be chatted up.

"I'll have the darkie," the woman said, but when the men refused to go away, she put her finger up in a gesture of "piss off."

Nell could hardly believe it when they entered the sleepy little town by the sea. It was very late by now, and almost all the lights in the houses were quenched. The sea lay at the end of the street like a gigantic grey mat; the wind had died down and everything was deathly still. There it was, parked at the end house, the stately grey motorcar—the evidence. She let out a shout of joy and grasped her friend's arm and said, "That's it! That's it!"

They stopped and pulled into the driveway of a house that was undergoing renovation. She did not know what to do. They debated whether they should go and knock on the door and assume that either the girl would come down or he would come down. "Then . . . then what?" she asked aloud. She decided that it was best not to, she would hire a detective and have him do it; after all, it needed an outsider, someone impartial, to give evidence in the court, because go to court she now would. To satisfy herself, or to give vent to some streak of spite, she decided that she would ring the telephone number—she had it from the advertisement. The girl had answered her letter on letterhead paper and said that, yes, she did need accommodation, but she was very particular about the accommodation she would get, that she had a small boy.

Her friend waited, holding the door of the telephone kiosk open, and as Nell put the money in, she regretted doing it, found her heart leaping, even though she knew very well that she had no intention of speaking.

A sleepy voice, the girl's, said "Hello" once, then twice, waited, and then said, "Why don't you fuck off, whoever you are." This was a very matter-of-fact girl, not like her.

She imagined them close together, with a window that looked out onto the sea, and for some reason she imagined a big jug of country flowers in an ewer and the furniture being all pine.

8

The next day, though quite unslept, she went to a lawyer, told her story, which, as she said, was a bit of a rigmarole, and sought his advice. He was a very busy man and, from what she could see, very influential. While she was there, he took three telephone calls; two of them entailed what to do with the effects of a famous pop singer who had committed suicide—she had read about this suicide in the paper. The lawyer was quite crisp as he discussed gold watch, gold cuff links, and various other personal effects. When she rose to leave he made a little flirtatious remark about taking her for supper, *à deux,* once they had her mess sorted out. He knew a very good detective, he said, just the man, had caught an earl with his trousers down. It all seemed so unreal, so hard, that to keep a grip on herself she thought of her children, their eager faces, the smell of their bodies in the evening after their bath, the way they gobbled sweets, and she wondered for the first time in her whole life if when they were grown up they would accuse her of all this—"this mess," as the lawyer called it. His office was full of tasteless furniture, onyx boxes, clumpy ashtrays, gaudy prints such as one might see in any department store.

The detective that the lawyer chose was so busy himself that he sent a junior, thought for some reason that it was a walkover. The junior got to the hamlet in the middle of the night, just as she had done and just as had been planned, rang the doorbell, and, when the woman came down, asked her if she was having a relationship with Mr. So-and-so. The girl asked him who he was and he was fool enough to tell her that he was an enquiry agent from a detective agency. She asked him if he thought she was a "Doris," daft enough to tell him anything, and said that as a mere addendum she kept lodgers, since she had an extra bedroom. She did not allow him in.

The upshot of all this was that Nell's chances, which up to now had been slender, petered away. Her husband realised what she was up to and wrote a letter to say that he could not be responsible for his actions, and that if she was to take the children by some foul means, he would be working night and day to get them back, no sleeping or waking moment of her life would be secure, he would see to it that her life was hell.

It was a question now of not cracking, of somehow holding the sediment of her thoughts together until she gathered the ammunition to start again. Her sons had taken up hobbies; for one it was trains and for the other it was stamps. Tristan made a small profit one day simply by buying a stamp in a shop on the Strand and selling it in another shop a few doors away. This created discord. In a mad moment of appeasement she took them to the Savoy for lunch. Once inside the glittering lobby, their delight was so great that they ran around, thumped sofas, then snatched stationery from a little occasional desk and wondered aloud whom they should write to.

"Sorry, madam . . . but the young gentlemen must have ties," the headwaiter said as they stood on the threshold of the Grill Room.

"Mr. Meanie . . ." she said, realising that it was an absurd thing to say to an agitated headwaiter, who was already perspiring, even though the clientele had not foregathered. He prevaricated, disappeared, and returned with two very garish ties, which, when donned, made them look like children impersonating clowns. They ate like wolves. They ate steak and kidney pie preceded by a cold soup, which they returned on the grounds of it being cold. Afterwards they had steamed pudding. The red jam threaded into the very yellow cake mix made them enquire saucily if she could spare the time to make one at home. They always referred to her house as home. The waiter, who by now had befriended them, whispered the secret recipe of the steamed pudding in a conspiratorial voice, then launched into a scenario of when they would be young men, coming to his restaurant after the theatre, with ladies on their arms. They giggled over this, and she saw as through a peephole into a future when she would not be essential to them.

The courtyard outside the hotel covered with some red, trampled-upon carpet added to their wellbeing, as did the sight and sound of doormen feverishly hailing cabs. They had a notion that at last they were removed from real life, the life of buses and school and homework. They tried to imitate the whistles of the doormen all the way home and argued as to who could whistle louder.

Not long after, she went to their midterm open day and there among the cutouts, the pictures, and the painted lanterns she read her Paddy's prize-winning composition, featuring the day out. He claimed to have tasted a dry martini and eaten a whole baby chicken. This, too, will have repercussions, she thought as they breezed past her with friends and asked if she had come by taxi. Everything would have repercussions.

It took the best part of a year before she summoned the courage to go to another lawyer, and this time it was to someone much more staid. She would sit for her weekly appointments, recalling detail after detail: the latter part of the marriage, the split, an affair she had had, how kind the man had been, an American who, though he returned to his wife and family, promised that he would always be there as a friend. Her mother sent dire warnings about the disgrace of divorce and repeated her constant anxiety about the children growing up in a pagan land.

The romantic attachment that their father had been having seemed to have ended, and he was leading a quiet life now, except for occasionally going out to the theatre and once, it seems, taking Rita to an exhibition. The children told her this, among other things, and sometimes late at night, when she went to their bedroom to cuddle them, one or the other of them would say he believed that their father would kidnap them.

Tristan was so pale he looked as though he was anemic. Walter wrote to her about this, saying her unhappiness had induced it. There was nothing for it but to fight. Her solicitor agreed with her, but was a "teetchy bit bothered," as he said, about the affair that she had had and, moreover, about the circumstances in which she had left home.

"He had an affair!" she said, fraught, and the solicitor, an elderly man, closed his tired lizard eyes for a moment, hearing once again the raised voice that sought retribution.

It was then that things began to get really rank, like a poison, destroying her every thought. She heard through her lawyer her husband's case against her, a case reinforced by Rita's sworn testimony and by the doctor and the headmaster. She was worse than a deserter, she was a harlot. Rita was to say that she saw her go out of the house on Christmas night, defecting on the children, who begged her to play with them, and return after midnight drunk and maudlin. She was to describe a woman of modest means who could leave in the morning and return home with several hundred pounds' worth of clothes on her back, which had obviously been procured in some seedy way. Her husband was to reaffirm his agony in trying to conceal from the children the bitter fact that their mother was mentally unstable. The local doctor described her as being a bit "airy-fairy," while the headmaster told how on Sports Day she had brought a very elaborate picnic basket and was doling out largesse. Hourly the cards were being stacked against her. She had hired a child molester as a babysitter, she had made her children anemic; her only kisses and fondnesses were when she was being seen, her love a charade.

"Lies . . . lies . . . lies," she told her lawyer, her voice loud enough to extend beyond the thin walls where the secretary sat with a hot-water bottle on her lap, typing more of these diatribes. Her solicitor joked and said that one day they would make light of it.

Her own evidence paled by comparison. She had little to say

except the obvious, which was that they were not compatible and perhaps never had been. She also had to go to four men she knew, one of whom she worked for, and tell them that her husband claimed that she had frequent sex with them. They laughed it off, but even their laughter made her uneasy, as if no one quite grasped her ordeal.

Eventually, they decided on a strategy. She would seek her divorce, not on grounds of adultery, but on cruelty, which as he said, was rampant. Many things were written down in his long, sloping hand, with his old-fashioned fountain pen. She heard herself tell him about being in a shop with her husband when she had just come to England and ordering a pound of smoked salmon, but not having enough money to pay for it, because the price on the plastic holder that was wedged into the skin of the fish was per quarter pound. She saw her husband smile at her discomfort as she told the irked shop assistant that where she had lived things were always sold by the pound.

"Yes, but I've sliced it, haven't I?" the assistant kept saying. This, and a million other things—not allowing her to keep her own money, not speaking for weeks on end, then notes laden with bile.

The day she served the papers on him, the children were in her house, she made certain of that. She had her own telephone by now; it lay off the hook like a dark cobra waiting to pounce. The children and she sat and watched television, and had beans on toast on their laps. She had told them that she had served the papers but didn't know if they had heeded it or not, because their favourite programme was on.

Later, before they went to bed, Tristan said, "When I go to school tomorrow and my friend Marvell says, 'My mummy has a fur coat,' I'll say, 'My mummy has a divorce.'" They laughed over this, the raucous laughter of the desperate. Paddy said they should tell their father that she had put them in a reformatory and then he couldn't get them. They devised daring scenes to prove to each other how fearless they were. She thought to herself, In time it will all seem like a bad dream. She had forgotten normal life, never looked at the sky or the stars, and only occasionally bought a bunch of flowers, and then only because someone was calling. She ate automatically and afterwards would wonder what it had tasted like. Sometimes she stopped in her tracks to let the wind touch her face, as if returning to some carefree state. She thought that once it was solved she would be happy, but how the happiness would descend on her remained a mystery. There was a mistiness in her brain at all times and she marveled at the fact that she could work or make sense when people talked to her. Her brain never really let go of her dilemma. She was like a dog with a bone, and she used to say, "One day I'll bury this bone forever." On her thirty-third birthday, she wrote in her diary: "Stasis."

Walter went early the next day and took the eldest, Paddy, from his school. They were now in different schools because of the age gap. She collected Tristan and brought him to her studio, and so for the first time the reality of being separated from each other hit them. She rang her husband's house and Rita answered. She said that her son wished to speak with his brother. She stood in the room while Tristan talked to Paddy, and heard this stilted conversation, in which none of the things were said that he wished to say. He just discussed with his brother what was on television and how, at school, someone had stolen his pencil sharpener. Then, it seemed, he said good night to his father and promised to be a good boy. Later, she rang Paddy, who cried and begged her to come and get him.

"I want to be with my mum," he said, as if she were simply a messenger.

"Tomorrow," she said. It was always tomorrow.

"Tonight," he said.

"I can't," she said, ". . . I can't break the law." His voice went cold with her then, cold and pinched, because she was failing him. He said he had had fish cakes for dinner and Rita had made a very tasty semolina pudding.

In the weeks that followed, they stayed with their father. She realised that it was better that they be left together, because the night that her younger child was alone with her, he cried so badly that he had fits, and she had to hold him in a towel to steady him. Neither of them got a wink of sleep; yet he was eager for school the following morning, as if it was there and not with her that deliverance lay. She even wished now that she had not served the papers, and thought of cancelling the case, but her solicitor buoyed her along—"Keep your nerve, lass, keep your nerve."

Her husband sent reams of letters to undermine her. They came daily, often twice daily, through the letter box. She dreaded going down into the hall for fear of another envelope. The envelopes were always manila. Her solicitor said to be glad of them, because they were ammunition, and that with each bulletin he hanged himself more.

The day before the case was due to be heard, she did two things. She had her hair cut in a fancy salon, as she had been looking rather mopey, and she went to the courts to make sure she would find her bearings easily.

The buildings all around were a mixture of old and new: a stone church, a narrow, Tudor-fronted public house with a big Toby jug as its mascot, a tea blender's, and a modern bank. There was the sound of bells; they were pealing in the little stone church dedicated to the Royal Air Force. The church itself was closed, but she imagined a man in there dutifully pulling the ropes.

The courts themselves were grey and beige, arches and buttresses trussed with fat knuckles of carved stone. As she went up the steps and through the door and saw the sign ROBING ROOM, she felt awed. There was the vast tiled hallway, circles enclosing lesser and lesser circles, and through the long, leaded windows, the light came in pewter shafts falling slantwise on the massive portraits of judges and lord justices. There they were, in their red robes trimmed with ermine, and their absurd ringletted wigs, like little sausages framing the ponderous jowly faces. One such face would judge her on the morrow. The pictures themselves were so high up it gave her vertigo just to try looking at them. In a central glass cabinet was a list of the various cases, and she searched in vain for her own and her husband's name. Leading off the hallway through wrought-iron gates were the numbered courts . . . In one of them, she would be seated the next day, with her solicitor on one side and her lawyer on the other. There were also signs that said, POST ROOM, CLOAK ROOM, REST ROOM, and TELEPHONE, and she resolved that as soon as she heard the verdict, she would ring her few friends and the man she worked for, who by now was concerned for her. She was certain of a favourable result. Everything told her so: the Latin inscriptions extolling justice, the bells, the heartening holy bells.

As a spree, she decided on a doughnut and coffee. Everything was all right, the lawyer and solicitor were confident, and she looked better as she caught sight of herself in the glass case in which were antique garments that judges and lord chief justices had worn. She suddenly thought how odd it was that her marriage, which had started in such a dizzy and romantic way, should end in this cold, impersonal place.

A small miracle occurred that evening at dusk. Her husband telephoned her, his voice low and somewhat penitent. He would not contest it. He had decided that, culpable as she was, she was still their mother, and for the time being he could hardly deprive them of that link. She thanked him profusely, said his name as if no hostilities whatsoever had gone on. When she put the phone down she blessed herself, then rang her solicitor at home.

"Now remember, he's a man who changes his mind," the solicitor said.

She said not this time, she was sure of it, she could tell as much by his voice as by the very words he said. She said that possibly all the pain and the children's unhappiness had brought him to his senses. Eventually he believed her and it was decided that since the senior counsel had been promoted to silk, they could probably dispense with him and get the junior counsel to do the job, which now seemed straightforward.

"Save on the guineas," he said, and wished her a good night's sleep.

She had a dream that all did not go well. She dreamt that she was ironing the children's clothes, but ironed their limbs instead, so that their skins clung to the hot chrome. They simply vanished from existence, were ribbons of charred skin.

She got to the courts far too early, mooched about, and then withdrew into an alcove when she saw her husband arrive with Rita. They both looked flushed and excited, and Rita was wearing a very fetching beret. Immediately she ran to find a public phone to warn her solicitor, who cursed both her and himself for being so gullible and who vowed to bring a pistol.

The hearing was in Court Number 17. It was a small court and there were no journalists. Her husband was the first to speak. He spoke in quiet, considerate tones. He spoke of the tragedy that indeed had touched both parties and the shadow that had come to rest on his children's shoulders. He said that he felt fit to speak for his children, since they spent most of the time with him, and as he was lucky enough to have the services of a good Catholic girl, meaning Rita, he had tried to make home life as wholesome and as stable as possible. But that was something their mother could not endure, she who believed only in hysterics, in destruction. He cited a day on the common when Rita, he, and the children were having a harmless game of football, which their mother prevented them from having because she had felt left out. Yes, he added, she was left out because she could not agree with anyone and thought and lived only for her little self, her desires, her impulses, her advancement.

She would do it. No, she wouldn't. She was muttering. This she knew, not by her own hearing, but by the anxious glances of the people next to her. The young lawyer put his hand out to stay her. She was standing. Yes. Half up! Up. It seemed indeed as if the chair or the wooden bench had propelled her, as a moving swing-boat might. Now she had to do it, had to make them listen, even if listening was to cause her to lose all. She saw her husband cut short his sentence and look across at her, thinking perhaps that finally the madness he had attributed to her was about to unveil itself for all to see.

"I am thought mad," she said, addressing the judge. He was looking down at his desk calmly, as if deciphering scrolls in it. A silence then hung in the court as everyone waited. This now was her moment. A thought flashed through her mind of Judgement Day and how the designation to heaven or hell occurred in a mere instant. All the waiting at railway stations, the children's faces, their trepidation buoyed her up, and searching hurriedly in her handbag she hauled out the letters he had written her over the years. She read at random: "What infection, it can hardly be called thinking, makes you take for granted that your wellbeing is of paramount importance?" and from another: "Healthy growing boys will not be subjected to the emotional incubator of a vile, mad mother." She could hear one or two people around her gasp in disbelief as she read: "I will fight you. I will fight you my own way. Ill deeds beget ill deeds."

She became aware that she was crying, crying at the words themselves and at the fact of having to say them.

"Is that all?" the judge asked. He was looking at her quietly, in a paternal way, the gaze of a man who has seen many a desperate plaintiff, has glimpsed the reeking poisons within many a shattered homestead. She waved the pile of letters as if to say, "There is much more." Then she sat down and felt all eyes upon her. Her husband's face was blanched and livid, his jaw firmly set. She knew what the verdict would be; she could decipher it on the judge's face and in the hushed atmosphere around her. As she sat and heard herself being awarded custody, with provision for the father to visit them, she felt not the glorious surge of victory that she had anticipated but instead a great onset of sorrow, as if in the years to come the true consequences of it all would unfold and the heartbreak she had been party to would live like a ghost in whatever room, whatever country she happened to be in.

As she went down the steps she could feel that she was being followed. It was Rita, who had barged so quickly through the swing doors that they continued to open and shut of their own volition. A rash ran up her neck and was in patches on her face. The rouge and the rash mixed incongruously.

"You're a bad woman," she shouted, and with a jerking finger, "You'll pay for this . . . you'll pay for it, all your life." Then she ran back, helter-skelter, as if the malediction had to be put somewhere safely and she herself, batlike in her black attire, the custodian of this spurious curse.

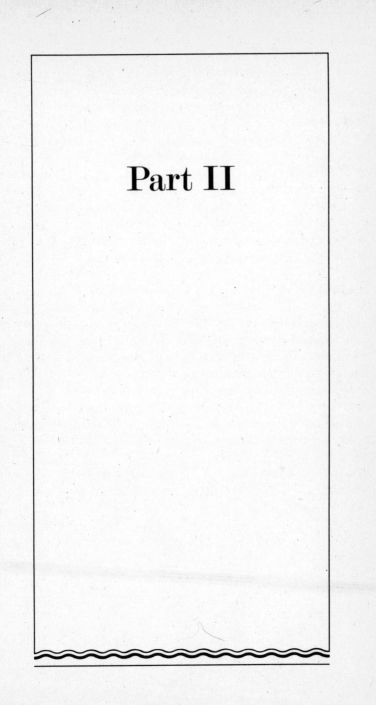

Part II

9

She rented a small Victorian house with a garden that ran down to the river. Most of the furniture was secondhand from a nearby auction room and the carpet from a warehouse, where the underlay was free. That first Saturday they went to the lane where the gypsies had stalls, to get bits and pieces. She bought a barrel for wood and stacked it with jugs, cups, saucers, a soup tureen, a cutlery box, and odd glasses, including some beautiful cranberry ones. Tristan put his hands on his hips, assumed a worried expression, and said plaintively, "What's worrying me is, who's going to pay for this big deal?" One of the luxuries was a lamp with a milky glass stem, inside which a mermaid was suspended. The woman who served her gave her a lace runner for luck.

"You take care of those little chaps and forget all about *him*," the woman said with a certain archness. She was a large, strong-featured woman with gold flecks in her eyes, and it being winter, she wore a woollen shawl over her shoulders. Her stall was freezing, and in between serving customers, she sat with her mittened hands by an oil heater. She told fortunes, said she would be able to tell Nell's at the end of the day.

"See what the crystal shows up," she said, and pointed to a drawn curtain that led from the back of the stall to a crammed cubby with two orange boxes, makeshift seats.

"I think I'll leave it," she said, too frightened to hear about either past or future, because she was living in this frozen haze, like the mermaid in her sphere of glass.

The woman saw things anyhow, saw the little house that they lived in, the path and the missing diamond in the stained-glass fan; saw much more, but did not voice it then.

Often at night Nell would dream that they had been taken and would rush to their room to find them sleeping, the bedclothes slung in all directions, their faces warm and infinitely delicate, like filament. Her mother had helped her with money until, as she said, she "got going." She had sent tablecloths and knickknacks along with cakes and eats. The boxes would reek of the smell of rich plum cake, with brandy or sherry douched over it. Even the postman remarked on it: "It's like Christmas." She put a slice in the greaseproof paper for him the next day, and so touched was he that he launched into a rigmarole about his first ulcer, then the world at large, especially football hooligans, how they were destroying the great name of England, tarnishing the name of King Harry, his solution being to put them all in a pound, strip them, allow them to fight it out until they were mangled or dead. Looking past her into the hall, with its little bamboo table on which rested a pot of African violets, he said, "Nice house, nice furnishings, nice lady." Nice lady! She had no idea how she seemed to others—did she look young, old, bedraggled? She'd certainly got thinner, and her hair drawn back severely made her look serious. It was as if she wanted to look like that, to atone.

Yes, the parcel or a registered letter from her mother arrived faithfully, the letters tugging at her. She would read about tillage, animals, and deaths, so many deaths. Often the ink would be a different colour towards the bottom of the page, a weaker colour where her mother had added water, and this, too, brought to mind the grim reality, money and so forth, her mother's plight; they had had to sell cattle to send the money for Nell to put down on the house, the ties deepening with each bulletin. Yes, her mother dilating on funerals, the size of them, the flowers, the mourners, including those who came from afar, the nature of the deaths themselves, the sudden ones and the lingering ones. Cancer was rife, taking root in every woman's body, cancer which her mother referred to as growths, the word itself being too shocking to express. Even women who lived up the mountains suffered from these mysterious growths, women who ate wholesomely, never touched a drink, and slaved all their lives. So it was a woman's ailment. Her mother often expressed the hope that they would be buried together. Buried? She was thinking of living, thinking in secret of a man who would come and whisk her to altitudes of happiness. This man had no features which she could describe, or as yet no name, but he was in the universe, waiting for the moment to materialise, the ordained moment. On such imaginings she got by. "I'll come back and see you one day," she whispered to the gypsy woman.

"I'd like to help you," the woman said. She meant it. There was about her something compassionate, something rooted, and Nell felt teary, missing the mother she had not had, who like the approaching man would vivify her dreams.

Proud of their possessions they hauled them up the crowded lane past stalls crammed with novelties: silver, gold, pewter, samovars, tea sets begging to be used, tapestries, rugs, and humbler things such as saucepans and wooden spoons, each stall a little repository of stories. At the end of the lane, as they waited for the bus, Tristan bought a slab of very white cheese, which he ate as if it were an ice-cream wafer. Sitting on the rim of the laden barrel, she felt an enormous surge of happiness, as if she was on the brink of a fresh life, what with voices all around, calling, joking; stall owners starting to pack up, youngsters sweeping the rinds and rubble of the day, women wrapping precious glasses in sheaves of newspaper, others making dates to go to this pub or that, and still another telling how she had had a shawl nicked when she turned her back; stories streaming in, like the sun itself, the stuff of life. The thing she must do is make new friends and banish the ogres of the past.

In the evenings she read manuscripts for the publishing house where she worked, to supplement her budget. Most were cries for help. One woman had hidden a letter in between the pages in which she confessed her unhappiness, told how her husband, who loved her very much, had thrown himself off Tyne Bridge, and was asking the world, asking any stranger, how this fatality could happen. A few of the novels she had been sent, too few, had that sacred breath of otherness that she believed to be essential.

"Can I have the blue glass bowl?" Paddy said, tapping her marriage ring. For some reason she still wore it. More atonement.

"What for?" she asked, surprised.

"My experiments," he said. He had brought home a fletch of frog spawn and by a method known only to himself was hoping to breed a unique species of singing frog.

"Of course," she said. Sometimes he looked at her with such need, a gaze saying, "Pay attention to me," and in those moments she knew that everything that had happened had marked him and made him needy. There were his years of asthma, his head clogged up, eyes watery, a smothered look to him, as if he were still inside her, gasping to get out. With him, her firstborn, she had always been more unsure, and he knew it. Perhaps it is always so. Moreover, he claimed that he discerned the moment when his brother was conceived, saw his father touch her, then lay her down on the sheepskin before the fire, a moment of passion after a journey she had made to her family, a moment of reconciliation and incarnation. Had she loved her husband then? She did not know. She did not know herself; her emotions were all tangled and she yearned now for a massive love.

"It's wonderful that your asthma has gone," she said to allay his fears.

"I still get it, but I don't complain," he said.

"Fibber . . . fibber," Tristan said.

"Buck Arab," Paddy said, and then words and accusations flew back and forth between them, like daggers, their tempers rising as they gave vent to these raw murderous feelings, looking at her from time to time for the moment when they might have gone too far, and looking also to see who was sovereign in her eyes. Often she felt as if she were being halved, each side of her ebbing, ebbing towards each one of them.

War games were the highlight of their week. On Sundays, friends from their new school would converge, carrying toy guns, catapults, or some sort of military garb. They clustered round the so-called armoury while they formed sides and debated whether they would fire blanks or real bullets. Then it was cries of "Charge! Charge!" with the house and the garden full of the rattle of artillery as they ran about shouting, "Keep down!" or "Cover," followed by a fusillade of sticks and stones.

Everything shook from their onslaughts. The stained glass above the hall door wobbled as if it might shatter and the bannister of the stairs became permanently askew. Even the cranberry glasses on the sideboard trembled and gave out an eerie, drawn-out tinkle. They wrecked flowers too, chrysanthemums, as it happened, planted by a previous owner. They lopped the heads off and tossed them like blunderbusses. The tawny colour of the chrysanthemums reminded her of her mother's Rhode Island Red hens. She would write to her mother that night, not one of those stilted letters saying "I am telling nothing," but a real letter in which she would describe the house, the path leading up to it, the rooms, the bits and pieces she had bought at the market, plus her mother's gifts, especially the bedspreads, pale green with candlewick roses.

That Sunday they had ordered drop scones, sausage rolls, anchovy toast, and chocolate pudding laced with rum. They had got the word "laced" from somewhere and were using it indiscriminately. Another word was "tippy." They liked the taste of drink and on Sundays they went with her to the pub garden when she had a beer. She thought it was a way of getting to know people, except that mostly people came with their own groups and those who wanted to get to know her were strays, especially a man with a patch over one eye who cadged drinks and talked about friends on the turf. The tea that she had so lengtheningly and lovingly prepared for them was downed in gulps, and so seriously did the nature of the game affect them that the hostilities were carried on, so that they sat on opposite sides of the long refectory table, sat as rival armies might, only to insult the other side and vow fresh carnage. Paddy tried to make peace and cited the fact that enemy soldiers across narrow boundaries and borders always made peace on Christmas Day and broke bread.

"Well, it's not Christmas Day, smartie," Tristan said, and his gang leapt up and banged their utensils to reaffirm their appetite for war.

By the time it was dusk, the game had reached a crescendo and the next-door neighbours had called to complain. Always towards dusk a greater frenzy possessed the children, because they knew that parents would soon be coming and that their adventures would cease. Their thinking, unlike her own, did not stretch to the next Sunday or the one after; they hollered and battled only for the moment. A neighbour rang to say the noise was intolerable and had caused his wife a migraine, so that Nell went out and begged them to go quietly. To appease her, they began to move like wraiths, creeping through the side door, ducking down the well of the stairs, their shouting replaced by a silent code, meaningful only to them. It was in this hush that he came in, her husband, tall, overquiet, and autocratic.

"So this is how they spend their Sundays," he said, pleased at having caught her out in such remiss.

"It's only a game," she said, removing her apron in a gesture of propitiation, or maybe even vanity.

"It's only a game," he said, and nabbed Derwent, a friend who was ducking out, ordering him to please send his sons in. Derwent was a very thin boy, with all the hesitancy of a doe, and her favourite because she knew that he guessed how frightened she was of her husband.

"A game today, an actuality tomorrow; what do you want them to become, gangsters?" he said, and then from his wallet he took a jotting pad to make note of something which she believed she would hear in one of the many bulletins that he sent, pointing out yet again how unfit she was to be a mother. The kitchen, strewn with litter, bits of breads, stones, chocolate crumbs, and some of the splinters that they had carefully shaved for their bows and arrows, did seem a wreck.

Paddy and Tristan appeared, their faces crimson from the excitement of the day, scare in their eyes. Tristan came first, as he always did, his grin slightly merry, slightly jaunty, saying "I am not going to show fear, I will not cower." Paddy lagged behind, afraid that he was going to get most of the blame as he was the elder. At their father's request they went with him to the front room, while Derwent sat at the kitchen table funnelling caster sugar with a little silver scoop. He collected it in the scoop, then let it slide in the hollow that he made between thumb and forefinger. His hands were filthy, but she did nothing to stop him. They were like two miscreants afraid to speak. Sometimes she went to the door of the sitting room to listen, but did not dare to put her ear to the door in case her husband opened it and found her out in something disgraceful.

Parents came and collected their children, thanking her, and then she went back to the kitchen, where Derwent scooped, and once for no reason ran up to her bedroom and without turning on the light put on some lipstick. She wanted to seem in control of herself. But Derwent knew better. He kept laughing to himself. He was happy to be spending the night with them. His mother had given birth to a baby, her fifth child. The baby was born in the afternoon and the phone call had come to the house about six. It was a girl and weighed just under seven pounds. She had told him it was a girl, but so busy was he with his campaign he did not appear to hear.

"What do you feel about this baby, Derwent?' she asked eventually, for something to say.

"Nothing," Derwent said, still mesmerised by the constellation he was making with the sugar, determined not to show his feelings. She knew from Paddy and Tristan that he was unhappy at home and didn't like his stepfather.

When the children and Walter came back into the kitchen, Tristan tried to assert his bravura by picking up a plate of leftovers and offering one to his father, which he declined. Then the three boys, unasked, set about clearing the table. It was their way of not wanting to be engaged in any grown-up conversations.

"They still have an essay to write," their father said.

"Mine is finished, he-he," Paddy said with a little show of rebellion in the way he bared his teeth.

"Would you like supper?" Nell said, trying to sound ladylike.

"No, thank you," their father said, and then announced to them, not to her, that he must be off. He put a hand on each of their shoulders and she felt a gush of pity for him, pity for their vacated bedroom and pity for the fact that he was perpetually the villain.

"They would like to go to the cinema with you some Sunday," she said, and caught sight of their little fists raised in mutiny.

"A boarding school would be more like it," he said, and assured her that he was looking into it; then from the bag he was carrying he took out a parcel and placed it on the table.

"These are second-rate," he said, and through the torn paper she guessed it was the presents they had given him for his birthday. One was an enamel mug with his name engraved on it and the other a canvas pencil case. They shrugged and tried to show indifference, but she knew that later on at night they would fret and perhaps wonder if they had been careless in their choices.

"Sometimes I could kill Dad," Paddy said after their father had gone out. She thought for a moment, then she ran. This was too much. He had moved faster than she suspected and she caught up with him just as the car was moving away. She shouted, ran, then tapped furiously on the passenger seat, and to her surprise found a woman there, a woman a little older than herself, hair parted in the centre and draped carefully over either ear, like cloth earmuffs.

"Excuse me, excuse me," she had to shout through the glass, and feared she could not be heard. The woman either could not or would not wind the window down, so he leaned across and very slowly opened it just a fraction, allowing Nell a sufficient aperture for her brow and eyes. It was like being muzzled.

"It's awful, awful to return their presents," she said.

"You call those presents," he said humorously. She wanted to say worse things, such as that he was a thief, owed her half the value of the house, never lifted a finger to support them, and yet assumed this high moral stance, but instead she found herself mumbling her grievances, then turning away.

Jocularity reigned in the kitchen.

"Spiv," Tristan said to Paddy.

"Toffee-nosed Etonian," Paddy was saying back.

"Dressing for dinner, Watson?" Derwent asked as he tossed spoons in the air.

"Might do," Paddy said and, turning to Tristan, said, "Fetch me my Garibaldi."

"Fetch it yourself, slave," Tristan said, and then seeing that she was close to tears he ran, clasped her hand, and in a much softer voice said, "Don't worry, don't worry." Perhaps it was the sight of the other woman that had provoked those tears. It was not that she wanted him back, but seeing him with someone else meant he was more capable than she of retrieving the pieces of his life. Rita had already gone, her parents dismayed by the fact of her living alone with a man, so that one day her sister who nursed in Birmingham came and took her away. She wrote them cards but never once included any regards or mention of Nell.

Unprompted, the three of them took it upon themselves to proclaim against fathers. Both boys gloated over the endless wrongs their father had done to them, raking up old scores, his stinginess about pocket money, his umpteen house rules, having to make toast for him, while Derwent scoffed at such trifles and said, "You think dads are bad, you should try stepdads," and taking the floor, he spoke with jubilance of his stepfather's grumpiness, his drinking, his shouting, his gluttony, his socks, his know-it-all-ness, and the way he closed the bedroom door when he went in there with Derwent's mother. With a snigger he recited from a valentine card that his stepfather had given his mother—"Seven years on, and still my queen!"

They made faces at the idiocy of this. Derwent's father was a television critic who watched television incessantly, so that if anyone stirred, or if a voice was raised, his mother had a habit of saying, "Ssh, Daddy's working." Having demolished fathers, they then got on to sisters, drips, and of course the new baby. The new baby was going to be called Clarissa. The three of them burst into untoward laughter and said they wanted to give Clarissa a good punch, and in the middle of laughing, Derwent blurted out that he wished to be part of their family and not his own.

"Yeah! Yeah!" Paddy and Tristan said, jumping up and down

with joy and asked her to show clemency for a boy who had to lay the table in his own house, who was never allowed to sit in his own sitting room, who had to help younger children, and who would probably have to burp the new baby.

"You can come as often as you like, love," she had said to him.

"That's not the same," he said, his little features sharpening.

"But you have a family, Derwent," she said.

"Yeah, but not like this, you guys love one another," he said, and looked her straight in the face with a gaze that was at once accusing and full of misgiving. He had pale grey eyes and was not a comely child.

"Don't be sad, you and me will go safariing later on," Paddy said, and Tristan, feeling excluded from this new bond, sat on the floor and began to grouse, saying that he hated school and hated geography and was probably the unhappiest boy alive. Just then there was another tap on the door and they all jumped, believing it was their father who had returned.

It was Daisy on her weekly ritual visit, which Nell had quite forgotten. She was an older woman with thin snow-white hair and rubber galoshes from which the toes and heels had been cut. She loved coming and said that the two sherries she drank were her treat for the entire week. While she drank, the boys made fun of her behind her back, touched her thinning hair and the headscarf that had fallen onto her shoulders, while singing under their breaths, "Daisy, Daisy, give me your answer, do. I'm half crazy, all for the love of you."

"I feel very spoilt," Daisy said, then sipped the sherry and ate the macaroons with relish.

"Daisy, did you bring the you-know-what?" Tristan asked, egged on by Paddy. It was an old military uniform with medals that had belonged to her dead brother George, and which she had promised them. They believed so strongly in George that they conferred with him, asked him questions about the fields of Flanders, the thrill of battle, and so forth.

"Goodness me, I must search," Daisy said, and put her glass daintily on the table for a refill, then changed the safety pin from one of her lisle stockings to another as a reminder not to forget.

They sniggered at her thin milk-white thighs, the part that was not covered by the lisle.

"Daisy, you're hopeless," Tristan said while she patted his fringe and said what a beautiful boy he was. It was the moment of her visit she relished most, flushed a little from the first glass and about to enjoy the second, off on a canter about her days as a model with the "Euston Road Crowd," recalling names of models and painters and hangers-on, blithe names like Dora and Bella; the names magically evoking the dash and vigour of those bohemian times as she wondered aloud where they all were and said to herself that one or two were certainly in Cornwall, yes, dotty old Cornwall.

"And who might you be, little chap?" she said, noticing Derwent for the first time.

"One of the family," he said, proud of his newfound prestige.

"Very thin neck, he needs malt and cod-liver oil," she said, and wondered aloud if it was time to go, though of course she would not say no to a third glass. It always happened: her hand just missed the edge of the table, and seeing the glass drop once again, she became flustered and exclaimed, "Oh bother, where have me eyes gone?" while Nell patted her shoulder and Tristan dutifully got the dustpan, muttering, "Here we go, here we go, same old story . . ."

The manuscript Nell was reading was set in the Swiss Alps. It was about a couple who wanted to adopt a baby but could never agree on the particular baby and therefore didn't really want to. It slipped in and out of sincerity, so that she found herself making notes furiously on her pad, asking this putative mother to show both her yearning for a child and her hidden revulsion, which made her so ambivalent. When the telephone rang she did not hear it for a moment, then did and hesitated, fearing it was her husband with fresh rebuke.

"Yes," she said somewhat hesitantly, and waited. At first there was nothing, then she could hear breathing followed by a succession of breaths, and not knowing what it signaled, she said in a high-pitched voice, "Who are you? What do you want?"

"Big cock," the voice said, then vowed to come right over and fuck her, because he knew where she lived and there was no point in her calling the police as he was seconds away.

"I'm going to do you, beaut," he said, and as she slung the receiver down, her elbow weighed on it as if she were holding down a writhing animal. As soon as she released the pressure it started to ring again, so she took it off the hook and put a shawl over it to keep herself from hearing the bleeps. Her whole being shook, but her mind became clear, purposeful, as she ran around the house to close the windows that had been flung open in the war games, bolted the front door, bolted the side door, and then switched lights on in the various rooms, calling at the top of her voice. Back in the kitchen she could not read but sat on the edge of the chair, alert.

"Who's that . . . who's that?" she said. It was Tristan, his face abashed, the cotton eiderdown bunched around him.

"Sweetheart," she said as she went to pick him up. His pyjamas were open down the front and his skin red where he had been scratching himself.

"The Baddie dream," she said, and he nodded. It happened again and again, and the only way for him to come out of it was to waken and to tell it to her word for word, except that the words came haltingly, and in between he cried or almost cried, even though he strove to be brave.

"I'm coming home from school . . . home to Pads and you, and the school is another school altogether, it's on the moors and suddenly it gets misty, all misty . . . and I know I shouldn't be on the moors and I start to run and I see a man coming and go up to him to ask him the way but he has no nose . . . and he has no eyes and no mouth either . . . a blank egg, so I run and I get to the coach and it's just moving away and I jump onto it and tell the conductor, who has his back to me, about the nasty man that I saw on the moors, and he turns and he says, 'Like mine.' It's the same man, it's the same Baddie, and I'm trying to come home to you and Pads, but I can't . . . my feet won't carry me.

"Don't tell Derwent," he said, suddenly remembering that they had a visitor, and then, recollecting that he heard her shouting and going around the house with a stick, he asked if it was to do with Dad.

"It was only playacting," she said, finding that with them, and on their account, she was fearless; her terrors got the better of her only when she was alone.

"Me mind Mama," Tristan said, reverting to being very young, and holding him she could feel his fear by his breathing, feel the quick galvanic little spasms; his heart like a bird trying to escape the confines of his chest.

"Are we going to boarding school like Dad said?" he asked.

"Not yet, not yet," she said evasively.

"When?"

"Not for a long time."

"That long," he challenged, and took his arms from around her neck and then drew his hands apart, putting great effort into it, the hands and arms going farther and farther back, emphasizing the distance, the never-to-be-filled distance until they were separated.

"Monkey," she said.

"You promise," he said, and tilted his face and cocked his ear for her to whisper assurances into. His ear was silken and the lobe squashed from where he had been lying on it.

"Meanies," Paddy said as he crept in unbeknownst to them. He hated those night conversations when he found them together, whispering and cuddling.

"Tristan couldn't sleep," she said.

"Neither could I," he said sourly. Rage and mistrust welled up in him. It was as if they had deliberately done it, to exclude him.

"I'm certainly in favour of boarding school," he said, letting it be known that he had been listening outside the door.

"We're not going to be apart," she said, and put her arms out, and though he did not want to weaken, he fell into her embrace, his nose repeatedly scratching itself on the sleeve of her dress, and now it was as if three hearts were thumping together. Half in anger and half in play they decided to box one another, and she had to remind them of her mother's phrase of being "good little chaps," knowing that the phrase as always would amuse them, bring back the summers, the biscuits, the glasses of homemade lemonade, and the night that Dixie came up to the bedroom and left her card under the bed.

"Will we go in the summer?" Paddy asked.

"Maybe," she said, and for the second time that night she carted them up the stairs to bed.

10

Emma towered above all the others; a creature of the forest, in her dark green seersucker dress and eyes green and aqueous, like eyes loaned from the bottom of the sea, and yet her quality was that of a fern, still, absorbent, a vernal thing. She had brought her violin in case Paddy and she decided to play a duet.

"Moron," he said, but that was only to conceal his delight.

"Hello Snail," Tristan said to her as he took her jacket and the soft bunchy present, wrapped in brown paper and tied with knitting wool.

Emma paused for a moment to admire the cake that had been made by a fancy confectioner's—turrets of piped icing and Paddy's eleven years in crimson on it. The little stack of birthday candles was beside it, to be put on at the last minute. Emma said that she would be very happy to help, as she knew from her mum that all mums felt left out.

"Thank you," Nell said. At moments she did feel them recoil, when they shut themselves up in one room or crouched together to look at television, feeling intruded upon if she came in, before she even spoke. Then there was that song that Tristan hummed—"She was there on the street, smiling from her head to her feet." Who was there on the street?

The party started off rather slowly. They stood in the garden in their good clothes, making remarks about the river, asking if it smelled, if the tide was coming in or going out, if they ever caught sight of any corpses or smugglers. The boys scraped the earth with their toe caps while guzzling the orange juice, which Paddy said had the merest soupçon of gin for verve. "Verve" was his new word. The week before it had been "amigo." He was treating Emma to a long-winded discourse about the river, basking in his role of historian as he told how Henry VIII breakfasted at the chambers of William Middleton, having called to inspect his kennels in Poplar, or how sailors were so superstitious that they always had a monkfish nailed to the mast as a safeguard against evil.

"You see that seagull?" he said, pointing to one and telling her that it was the ghost of a lighterman who had drowned and that all seagulls were ghosts of drowned people.

"That gives me the creeps," Emma said, and wrung her dress for comfort. Next it was about the prisoners, chained, in floating prisons, dredging all day long and with nothing more than a soup made of bullocks' heads and a burgo, which was a gruel of oatmeal and barley, for their supper. He was in love with Emma but didn't know it. Up till then Emma had been some nincompoop who kissed her mother at the school gates and was always losing her sheet music, so that he, Muggins, would have to loan her his. He often came back from Emma's house sneering about the awful gold tea trolley, her mother in slippers with rabbit trimming, telling that her ambition had been to play at the Wigmore Hall, an ambition she had bequeathed to Emma. Emma's father did not feature in these mockeries, since it seems he left home at six each morning, traveled to his office, worked fourteen hours, in the evening had two large gin-and-tonics, dinner, then up early to start for work to catch the stock markets around the world.

"Do you want to know a secret . . . the film we're showing is *Cat Ballou*," Tristan said, and Emma biffed him for spilling the beans, though it was too late.

"Rescue, rescue from this witch," he called as she put her belt over his lips to seal them.

At tea, Emma played mother. She moved among the boys, told them to behave themselves; she made the other girls pass sandwiches and pastries, made herself essential to every moment of it, even placing the candles at a more gainly distance from each other. The boys smirked at her and the girls nudged one another in pique.

"Now wish," she said, staying Paddy before he blew the flames out in a gust.

"Crikey," he said, and looked at the others, abashed.

Quiet reigned for the film, all of them sitting close together on a long bench, their eyes shiny and agog in the darkened room, their laughter contagious, and the box of chocolates soon devoured. When the reels had to be changed, there was a boisterous dash for the lavatory, but Emma stayed behind, musing over moments of the film, saying that whenever she saw a play or a film she felt dissatisfied with her own life.

A game was proposed later on, not quite as strenuous as their war games but which still involved dashing through the house, so that they were upstairs, downstairs, specters stalking through her kitchen, asking her if she had seen this one or that one, excitement mounting as the hunt came for the last two, they being Paddy and Emma. Paddy, knowing the safest place to hide, took Emma by the wrist and was dragging her off, except that she refused.

"Can't you leave me alone," she said quite testily. His hand dropped down as if it didn't belong to him or as if it were part of his sleeve, while he stood allowing her to go ahead and get caught, and then he turned in the opposite direction, quit the game, and went down to the river. Parties were like that. Later Emma came to Nell and stood by the stove with big tears in her eyes, saying that it was awful, awful, and that her life was ruined.

"Go down and see him," Nell said. Paddy was still on the wall, the wind inside his bright blue shirt, billowing it out, his new haircut giving him a grazed look.

"I can't. He wouldn't speak to me," Emma said, and left saying how wretched she was, how she hated herself.

It was dusk by the time all the others had gone, a nip in the air, torn wrapping paper everywhere, a few balloons adhering to the ceiling, and that crestfallen feeling that always succeeds hilarity. Paddy was exclaiming over a present, a surprise present which a very dull boy had given him. It was an expensive paint set and he said that he would do sketches of the river to go with his thesis.

"What did Emma give you?" Tristan said casually as he came into the room, his face covered in one of the hideous hairy Eastern masks that they had bought for the party. Around it were palm leaves which he had dipped in cardinal-red paint to emphasize the menace. Paddy held up Emma's present. It was a scarf, hand-knitted in the school colours, navy and red with fat pompoms. By the way he held it he seemed to ridicule it; then he let it drop slowly, slowly into the wastepaper basket.

"I kissed her," Tristan said, pulling off the mask. Either he was worried that Paddy might come to hear of it or else the disdain for the scarf made him think that Paddy really had no interest in her. Or else. Paddy said nothing for a moment, but his face went white and whiter, until it was like chalk, and then she could see that he was grinding his teeth behind his closed lips as he decided on what course of vengeance to take.

"Kiss her," he said suddenly, with great aplomb, and then added, "The whole world will kiss her, why not you." Again he was scurrying out the garden door and down towards the river, to nurse his hurt in the gloom.

"You're both exhausted," Nell said, loud enough for both to hear, so that she would not seem to be taking sides, and then, wrapping a piece of cake in a doily, she announced that she was taking some along to Daisy and that they were to behave themselves and mind the house.

A star kept trying to push its way through the inky cape of the heavens. At moments it glittered, then disappeared again, then struggled out, and so it was, as she walked along, a star appearing, reappearing, shining, faltering, its efforts so determined, its vanquishment likewise, and for some reason it made her think that if the star did not find a fixed place, her own life would be as futile, as floundering as that.

Daisy, who was bedridden, met her in her dressing gown, the thin gnarled hand small as a child's, eager to snatch what was given. This was how life ended, this famished existence, pithless, friendless, shorn. The one bar of an electric heater up on the wall looked down onto the bureau where a fox fur lay coiled, lifelike, its eyes a glassy knowing brown.

Like a child, she took the cake and the lemonade bottle of sherry. She could not talk; her breath was ebbing. It had come to this, just like the beginning—mouth, gullet, food, self, solitude.

"Poor Daisy is a skeleton," she said as she came in the back door and found Tristan with a duster, explaining that he had been giving some overdue tidying to his and Paddy's bedroom.

"Where is Pads?" she said then, using the pet name to show that all was well and that umbrage had passed.

"I don't know . . . outside," Tristan said. She went to the garden door and called, and when Paddy did not answer immediately, she thought to herself, He is carrying this huff too far. She called again, and then went out, her voice growing a little louder and a little more petulant, but when she got to his special perch on the wall he was not there and he was not crouching on the other side of the wall, where he sometimes went in order to give her a fright. She leaned over, calling, calling, but he was nowhere to be seen. The tide was out, the bank muddy and vacant, houses and flats from across the way like pyramids, wobbling, blue, green, and gold in the central pocket of water. The plash of some rowboats nearby made her jump, and even a bit of driftwood seemed deadly in the vicious moonlight. The moon had come out and furrows of stars pickled the sky.

"Paddy!" she said again, getting no answer; she ran towards the house, calling Tristan to fetch the torch. Paddy was probably crouching farther down behind some other wall, determined to make them suffer more, suffer over Emma, over boarding school, over sundry slights.

"Bring the torch," she said.

"Why?" Tristan said, but guessed by her voice that there was something amiss.

"Paddy's not on the wall," she shouted.

"Is he on the river?" Tristan asked, and then answered himself by saying, "He would get whacked if he was on the river." Now they both ran down, calling, their voices trying not to betray the urgency of their search.

"Where can he be?" Tristan said, affecting irritation, as if Paddy was hiding somewhere and could actually overhear them. But he wasn't hiding, he simply wasn't there. Where to go? What to do? She ran to the house and rang Emma's parents, thinking that he had probably gone to her. Emma's father said, "Too bad," and suggested she ring the police. She wanted to talk to Emma. If anyone could find him, it would be Emma, but her father said she had had a bad tummy and had gone to bed.

"Don't be cross when you find him," Tristan whispered, his way of saying, My brother is not drowned, this could not happen to us.

The police were helpful, took down all the details, and said that nothing of that nature had been reported.

"It's his birthday," she kept saying as they asked each question, her name, his father's name, Paddy's name and age, what he was wearing, and so forth. The policeman she spoke to could tell her consternation by her voice, said that they would get a riverboat at once, but it would take a little while to come up the river to her. For the next half hour she divided her time between the house and the river. Tristan was stationed by the phone in case Paddy rang or had a friend ring, while she kept going back out to catch sight of the headlights of the police boat. The dark water seemed to slobber at her strangely and the music from a white pleasure boat was gall to her ears. Paddy could swim, but as she kept telling herself, he might have swum too far and got weary and he might now be clinging under a bridge waiting for help, or he might have climbed up one of the neighbouring walls farther down, at that very instant asking people if he could please pass through their house and get to his mum. When he was frightened or ill he always referred to her as his mum. Soon the neighbours appeared. The next-door neighbour, folding up his hose, upon hearing her news became sympathetic, forgot the innumerable complaints he had made both by letter and by mouth about her boys' obstreperousness, was concerned, tried to reassure her by saying reasonable things, such as that it was normal for a boy to run away, that children were always running away and always found, and that the police had their hands full just keeping tabs on them. He cited a boy who had gone as far as Berlin. By the time the police launch whished about in the water directly opposite her wall, the garden was full of neighbours, the very same as if it were a party, except that the voices were subdued.

"Her son is missing," she could hear.

"Which son?"

"I don't know, her son," a voice answered back, and others arriving asked solicitously what they could do.

The inspector said they had picked no one up and they had not seen anything suspicious but would go on down as far as West-minster Bridge to make sure. He had to shout because of being moored out there and because of the spumes of water that the boat churned up, and she had to shout back, asking if his brother could go with them. The formality of the refusal struck her with fresh terror. The inspector said they never brought family on board, as it would be too distressing if they were to find a body. He was dead then in her eyes for a moment, out there will-less, weightless, flotsam drifting with the tide.

Inside the house, people waited and spoke in whispers. It was as if the worst had already happened, their panic clear when the phone rang and Nell rushed to answer it. It was a parent thanking her for the birthday, asking if a belt had been found, because Nigel had lost the belt of his sports trousers.

"I'll look for it later," Nell said, explaining why she was so concerned, to which the woman said, "Oh, poor you."

"We'll find him, Mum, we'll find him," Tristan said, taking her hand, and in some deference to courtesy she apologized to the neighbours for disturbing their Sunday evening with this. Her next-door neighbour and his wife looked at her sadly, as if they regret-ted all the times they had complained about the noise, because of his wife being an artist and because of her migraines. Now she stood there in her long plaits, rather like a schoolgirl, telling ev-eryone that that was why she would never have children, that that was why she advised her husband to ride the hack and save the hunter, because she could not bear to have children, who were bound to desert her.

"Now, now, Liz," her husband said, not wanting her to make a scene. A jogger whom none of them knew suggested to Nell that they have a turn in the park, and she went simply because it gave her something to do and because it postponed the worst.

Where the road swerved around the park a streetlight had gone out, and in the park itself the pigeons were cooing. The high wall was covered with bits of broken glass, which in the torchlight showed up like glassy fangs. The gate was locked for the night, but the men scaled it, asking if she would be all right, and by their question telling her not to do anything silly such as run out onto a main road. Behind her, cars whizzed by and she knew that all this, such as her standing there holding on to the spears of the gate, and the men inside looking, was merely stalling, was merely a way of prolonging what they would soon have to accept. Why had he done it? Was it Emma? Was it her? Was it his father? The thought of his father made her quake, the thought of having to tell him, of having to break the news. She could picture the telephone call, his voice probably calm, then angry, maybe even breaking down. No, it would not come to that. She began to pray. The first lines from several prayers fell to her lips, and then made-up prayers, the vow never to seek pleasure again. She could see them walking, the beam of the torch going hither and thither as if it were prancing about on its own, then trained on the trunks of trees, trees like a still-life battalion stationed along the riverbank. She thought she heard a cry and began shouting to alert them.

"It's Paddy, it's Paddy's voice," she shouted, but the men did not hear. Perhaps she had invented it, or perhaps it was a ghost cry, one of the seagulls. They went down by the line of trees and then she lost them as they disappeared under a canopy of dark leaves, the pencil of light charting hither and thither, and then they seemed to have given up as they headed back in her direction. About halfway, she heard one of them call, and though she could not hear him clearly she felt something had happened, something wonderful had happened, because the voices were loud, crisp, animated. She saw the beam of the torch was going up into a tree, the light spattering, their voices raised, then their hurrying back across the park carrying something, carrying him.

"Would you like a young boy for supper?" the jogger shouted, unable to repress his joy and his added joy at being the one to suggest they try the park. Paddy was handed over, and as he was placed in her arms she could feel his tears warm and gushing and feel the desperation as he clung to her, a clench that was as much rebellion as it was love. He was too tall for her to carry, but he clung to her all the same, and the clinging said, "Please don't say anything, because if you say anything it will destroy what is left for us."

Often she had prayed for a lover, but now she asked God that she never be separated from them, never, and that if so, her cup was full.

11

Virgins pale, pensive, limpid: others round-cheeked, saucy
wenches, some in flimsy raiment, others in sumptuous attire: sub-
limely immersed in their motherhood, one even going so far as to
kneel in adoration in front of her little sausage-like son, who lay
naked on a red velvet dais. Paddy and Tristan turned away in the
chapel on the hill, where they had journeyed to see yet another of
these Virgins, this time a pregnant one. The lights had fused in the
storm that struck as they drove in a little taxi, teetering off the
road; a bus full of tourists came towards them at a frenzied speed
and the taxi driver simultaneously blessed himself and swore.
Gashes of lightning rent the sky, sulphur and phosphorous zigzags,
strafing over the wooded hills, which were so dense they looked
like a vast continuous stretch of evergreen teeming with life. In
their sumptuous thickets mosquitoes hatched, adding to the host
that had gorged on them since they had arrived, especially at dusk,
when they had sat unthinkingly at a café table.

"Where is it, where is it we're going again?" one would ask of
the other, spleen in his voice, both resentful at being brought
abroad when a holiday with their grandmother was what they had
longed for.

"Arezzo," she said, and remarked not for the first time that it
meant either blue or grotto. They didn't care. They had sulked
since they arrived, put a hand over the postcards that they covertly

wrote, in case she glanced, as obviously they grumbled to their friends and more pertinently probably their grandmother, whom they believed they had betrayed.

She could not see the face or the expression of the pregnant Virgin in the dim light, but she saw the stance, which was sturdy, and the gash in her gown along the belly, a presage of the knife-like pain to come. She saw an aloneness, too, mother and child familiar yet distant, estranged from one another. Then she fell into an argument with the attendant, who refused to give her half-price for the children because she had not asked in the first place and he had already docketed the amount on his machine. Others watched while she pointed to them, said it was obvious they were children— *bambini*. The attendant looked on with scorn and did nothing.

In the next chapel they were a little more animated, because it was huge and they could prance about, while she went up behind the great altar to see the series of murals, which were blue to green to grey, the colours delicate as eggshell, delicate and frangible. The story of the murals was told in a booklet, how the seeds from the tree of Original Sin became the cross which Christ died on, despite the solicitude of Sheba. Suddenly the paint seemed to spatter and those beautiful enamel surfaces seemed to dissolve also, while her mind, the mind that had so unquestioningly—at least in a sacred precinct—believed in the purity of saints, now saw otherwise, as if all was amok, yielding to the hot and ravening passions within. It was something in Sheba's mien, a deference made all the more tantalising by the excruciating formality, the decorous stoop, by the gravity in King Solomon's eyes, black like his beard and the underbrim of his wide hat, but in both the frontiers of shame falling away as they yielded, without stirring, to the lasciviousness within. For a moment the tiles under her feet went liquid, her limbs, too, all dissolving, as the words came from somewhere, but where?— "Your groove a pomegranate grove" answered with "My love thrust his hand into the hole and my innards seethed there." She thought, Once long ago, I have lived this selfsame moment, this swoon, and thought how everything is known at birth, the lather of our begetting, known, then forgotten, blotted out.

In the town square, in the broiling sun, there was a rough clatter as shutters were pulled down, their shelved fronts like wooden washboards, rumbling, tumbling, then sealing off the shops and giving the street the gloom of early evening.

"Soup, beautiful soup," they chanted, fearing that every restaurant was closed. The driver followed behind, and as they entered a narrow street, a little backwater, she could hear them muttering afresh. There was a queue at the first restaurant, so they went along to the next one, down a passage, arriving at a café in complete darkness, with only cold things on offer. They drank mineral water and ate tasteless bread rolls filled with cured ham that was both too salty and too fat. Here, too, they conferred without addressing her. They spoke about friends at school. Emma and Lisa and Jane were now selected as subjects of sublime interest. A new swimming pool not far from their school came to fill a few moments further on, and then it was the return of their favourite television series in the autumn, a science-fiction program. The driver ate the roll she had just discarded, while the coffee, which she rarely drank, began to make her nerves jangle as she thought, We are on holiday, and it is a fiasco.

By evening the defiance had escalated. In the little pensione they sat on the bed, in their donkey jackets, refusing to take them off, each reading a book, pretending to be absorbed in it.

"Come on," she said, clapping her hands to rouse them.

"We're ready," they said. One said it, then the other. In mutiny they repeated each other's words and phrases exactly.

"You can't go to a restaurant like that."

"Why not?" they said again, in unison.

"Go and put on your good jackets," she said sharply, adding that she would not take such insolence.

"It isn't as if we're going anywhere posh," Tristan said, pointing to the shabbiness of the room, a dungeon with kitchen chairs and a few wooden knobs on which their best jackets hung idle.

"How dare you!" she said, looking at him, wanting to slap him, and seeing the first flashes of hatred for her in his eyes. It was enough to trigger off a rigmarole about her sacrifices, her marriage, her broken marriage, the way she worked, toiled, how they were indulged in every whim, Paddy with his train collection, Tristan with his stamp collection, and on and on; she even descended to the fact that at Christmas she had dearly coveted a brown astrakhan coatee and could have bought it but for them. They said nothing. They became like frozen figures into which her tirade passed, like dollops of paint. She thought she saw them smile, a smile that was half smile, half sneer.

"This is no laughing matter," she screamed, and went to clout them.

"We're not laughing," they said, ducking, their cowed expressions showing their disbelief at her unwonted fury.

"Are you or aren't you coming?" she asked.

"We're not hungry," Paddy said quietly, and Tristan nodded. She went out, carrying her shawl, the piece of finery in which she had imagined lounging with them in balmy squares, smoking a cigarette, drinking an aperitif, and talking a smattering of the language.

In the restaurant at the corner she ate salad and fish without knowing what she was eating and studied the postcards she had bought of the Virgins, wondering if the sitters had been virgins or mothers or fallen women and her swoon of earlier, in front of Sheba, filled her with scalding shame. Perhaps they had noticed, had been hovering. Some of her accusations hit her afresh, like splinters under the nail, words about their ingratitude, their selfishness, their insolence. She remembered, too, the glint of hatred in Tristan's eyes while still thinking that they would follow, except that they didn't.

The waiter opened her half bottle of wine and plonked it down, willing her to make haste. A queue of people stood at the entrance, and at one point another waiter came over and asked if she would share, but she refused, said she was expecting her children. She could picture them on the bed, still in their coats, eating crisps, veering between rebellion and remorse. The swordfish was like grilled rubber. The waiter cleaned his nails with a little penknife that hung from a cord around his waist, while she studied the menu, to choose something else.

"May I see the manager," she said, affronted.

"I am the manager," he said. She ordered a pasta, though she didn't really need it.

Vindictiveness oozed in her as she reckoned up the cost of the holiday and the discomfort of it.

"We're sorry," they said, standing to attention as she came into the bedroom, like young soldiers unsure of their drill.

"I'm sorry," she said, opening the paper napkin into which she had put the sweetmeats that she stole from a cake tray on the way out. They all spoke at once, blaming the heat, the storm, the strangeness, eager for reconciliation.

"I've been thinking," she said, and they guessed what was coming and went, "Yay, yay," jumping up and down with excitement. They would cut the holiday short and go home.

"It's not what we imagined," she said, slightly ashamed.

"It's not the Ritz," Tristan said, all his resentment now vented on the room, the stained carpet, the electric wires that gaped out of one wall, and mattresses with the dip of a sodden hammock.

"It's a dump," she said.

"It's a dump," they said lustily, taking her cue. But what to tell the woman at the desk, the woman who had surrendered this room after much persuasion and beseeching.

"We'll say I have appendicitis," Paddy said, doubling over to rehearse his agony and emphasizing it with a classic beating of the breast.

"We'll say it's a dump . . . a jolly old fustian Tuscan dump," Tristan said.

In the end she implied a bereavement, and what with the paucity of language, speaking mostly with sighs, she sounded convincing, so that they parted the best of friends.

Everything had yielded to a somnolence. The heat did it. The heat and the haze. The sunlit grass was like satin, blood-red poppies flung down on it like flowers on a quilt, but so airy they looked as if they were about to disperse again, while the mountains in the far distance seemed to be giving up their snowy undulations to the sky. Strange to see snow and sun at one and the same time. It was a very fast train and the countryside flashed before their eyes in quick, slicing images, villas with closed shutters, coral and terra-cotta, paint peeling off the walls, then field after field of sunflowers, some that drooped, like chastised golliwogs, others with centres quite black, devilish black, and a few still sporting their sun-saturated yellow faces, but most of them ripe and ready for harvesting. Then there were factories, long, thin, blond chimneypots belching smoke into a settlement of low squat houses, not nearly as beautiful as the shuttered houses, and then more countryside and fruit trees in neat rows like novice ballerinas, their legs spindly, as if the weight they bore might topple them over.

The carriage was full, young girls talking rapidly, their bracelets and vocal cords a-jingle, cigarettes exchanged regardless of a NO SMOKING sign—a red daub faintly reminiscent of a cross that ran slant-wise across a transparent cigarette, from which there came three plumes of feathery smoke. They didn't care. They were happy, boisterous. One of them had swarthy skin and a tumulus of dark hair, so much hair that, were she to lie down, it would cover the seat of the carriage like a drape. It fell everywhere, the cigarette smoke wandering through it, lingering in it, and no sooner would she pick up one haul of it, to toss it aside, than another had to be accommodated in the grip of a worn brown slide. She had a tic, so that whenever Nell looked in her direction, the girl seemed to be winking at her, as though she wanted to say something. She showed a keen interest in them, as if there was something particular she wanted to ask them. What could that be? As they shot through the gloom of the long tunnels, Nell could feel her boys' hands, or their feet, reaching to touch her, making sure, but then withdrawing as the scalding light re-entered. Her arms and her legs struck her as being an affront, whiter than she had ever known them, the humble white of separated milk.

The other couple were middle-aged, the woman studying a knitting booklet which had needles and a ball of wool on the cover, while the man kept coughing, then swallowing his spittle, like a syrup. From time to time the woman offered him a sweet, a miniature satin cushion, cocoa-coloured. Though at first suspicion reigned, later on, people began to smile as they watched the passage of the little motors which the children ran along the blue velveteen seat and up the steel window frame. Eventually the sweet tin was proffered and halting conversation ensued: the young girls listening with rapt interest and the girl with the tic asking if, when she came to England, she might stay with them, as she would be feeling fragile and would like to be near friends. Friends! Then her life story bubbled out of her, how she had a prince, but he was only an "interim" prince and had digestive problems and needed shirts ironed all the time, but that in England she would find a real prince and go boating in a punt. Writing down their address, Nell thought, I hope she doesn't come, but wrote it all the same and made a note of the girl's name, which was Francesca. Her friend took it in, with a kind of smouldering jealousy, and for that reason smiled a lot. Then more countryside, rich red soil that might have been dyed, the olive leaves frisky and silver in contrast with their trunks, which twisted and twined like witches in a writhe.

"Look . . . more golliwogs," Tristan said, pointing to another field of them, this crop heading in the opposite direction, so that the fringe of bladed leaves were like green bonnets on little bowing heads. His smile and the observation were meant to reassure her, to say that neither he nor his brother was any longer piqued.

The shutters were partly drawn so that the oblongs of sun came in sideways, in fits and starts, making inroads on the treasures in the room. Outside, dahlias bloomed, beds of them, too bright, too highly strung, too orange, an affront to the eye. On the wall was a *Last Supper,* Apostles all pensive and with a premonition of the sacrifice to come, the supper table in shadow, and always the black-green landscape, the green of cypress, imparting its breath and its gravity.

"I am at that time of my life," her host was saying, swiveling his wrist to include the paintings, the statues, the treasures, and the doddery servants, who were opening a little card table to place the tea things on. Their hands trembled uncontrollably, so that the cups rattled on their saucers and teaspoons struck against the china as if tuning forks were being tested. Yet with a flourish of authority he waved them across.

"Have a sandwich . . . do . . . do you good . . . Luckily you don't have to watch your figure," her host said, and drew his hand ceremoniously along his front to confirm his hidden girth. She took one, but only out of politeness. The bread was stale and the filling, which was a meat paste, was stale, too. They were sandwiches probably made for the previous guests and put in muslin for those who came next, such as herself. When she had phoned from the town he said that of course she must come to tea, his houseguests had left, gone south, and how lucky that he would have her all to himself. He was one of their authors, and sitting watching her eat, he smiled the thin, crepe smile of an old man in a beautiful house, whom people invade in the summer, whom he receives for some reason, habit perhaps. A sealed ring on his finger, a blood-red scarab, looked out at her unwelcomingly. He had nodded off. His droop reminded her of wisteria, fading wisteria, and she thought that it must be due to the blue of his eyes. She rose as if to go, to steal away, whereupon he rallied, opened those shuttered eyes, and said, "Yes . . . yes . . . you are doing such marvellous things . . . your boss has told me . . . you have a touch of the Sherlock Holmes . . . You divine the author's secret, then you do strange midwifery . . . Oh, you can't fool me . . . I know all about your skills."

"It's a beautiful room," she said awkwardly, ashamed of feeling so gauche and so ignorant.

"My dear mother, yes . . . my dear mother . . . She allowed my father to spend, but wisely . . . That is Isabel of Castile, who made a vow to the Virgin not to change her linen until Granada fell into her hands. And that black youth is Venetian . . . a scion of Othello perhaps . . . The wolf of course is Roman and the hangings are Flemish; now tell me what do you do, I should know, I should know . . . my memory is almost gone, I can't think what I did this morning," and his voice trailed away as he looked out at the dahlias and smiled as if he found something in their colour that regaled him. When she had telephoned him, she thought they might be able to spend a night or two in his house, delay the going home for a bit longer. She had left the children at the railway station, on a bench beside a withered miniature cypress, which had been donated by a bank, warning them not to speak to anyone and not to budge. Often in his letters this man had described his villa, saying it would make an old man very happy to see her fill it for a while, to hear her footsteps on the stairs, to gossip with her at night. Letters were one thing, reality another. As if guessing the secret purpose of her visit, he became quite awake, and looking at her with a startled expression, he said, "I rarely go down to the town now . . . I have so much to do here . . . Keeping servants happy is not an easy thing . . . worse in the summer . . . Of course, I keep the rooms shut . . . fifty or sixty rooms in all . . . yes, lots of rooms but not . . . easy . . . My dear, what a nice necklace you're wearing and how becoming." Then having satisfied himself that he had both disposed of her and complimented her, he drooped again, his chin lolling and his breathing very flurried inside the formal black suit that he wore. Had he put it on for her?

As she left he waved to her from the steps, the very old butler with the cataracts beside him, and though she had not asked if they could stay, she believed there was irritation in his expression and that he was saying, "Tried to cadge a room . . . Oh, how I hate these intruders . . . How I hate summer . . . and visitors, Bolshies calling up." Nevertheless, he waved graciously; they both waved as the taxi bore her away in a flourish of evening sunlight, every bush, every flower suffused with it, and her mind made up, that they would spend one last indulgent night in a hotel and go home prematurely on the morrow.

The light, as they arrived at sundown in the cobbled square, was of a melting splendour that gave to the blond and fawn façades of the houses across the river a muted look. They looked like doll-houses on the point of sleep. The river, which had smelt rank and looked so at lunchtime, was now a burnished waterway, without a single piece of traffic, like a river in an old picture book. On the church wall was a blue ceramic Virgin in a niche, and the bells which rang out were so soft-sounding and so liquid it was as if their peals came up from the riverbed to join the other bells which were ringing throughout the city. Evening. Evening. The air so warm, so tender, their fingers went up to feel it as one would a flower, but which flower? Three doormen rushed to take their baggage, while they themselves lingered, the beauty and the grandeur of everything gripping them, as might a sovereign presence. The distemper and the setbacks of the last few days were gone, and it was now as if they were being initiated into spheres of luxury and rareness, enfolded in a golden prism that would soon be blue, the hushed blue of night, of prayer time.

In their bedroom they marvelled at everything—floor and walls of matching veined alabaster; light switches which, when barely touched, gave off pencils and spigots of light; a refrigerator crammed with liqueur bottles, nuts, truffles, and even a pack of cards, which they intended to avail themselves of. In the bathroom, stacks of towels and dressing gowns reminding them of how spartan their own lives were.

"What would Granny say if she came here?" Paddy said, ever loyal, holding up several cream-coloured scallops of soap. Hearing her mother's name uttered in this palatial ambiance, she flinched and said that they must buy her mother something beautiful, rosary beads or an ivory replica of the Virgin, the Virgin in her solitary niche. Her mother had been understanding about the holiday, had said, "Travel broadens the mind," but underneath had been hurt, chafed.

When the waiter came with the tea tray, she allowed herself a little dalliance. He was handsome, somewhat reserved, not as gushing as some of the others. He had brought a rose, a slightly wilted rose, and seeing her, he made a big to-do, said it was not sufficiently *bella* for such a *bellissima* lady, and had he known he would have sent to his native town for the flower it was famous for, the Parma violet.

"Violets?" she asked, adding that she was under the assumption that it was ham that came from there, cured ham, such as one had with melon. She disliked herself for this bit of showing off.

"Ah," he said, touching his heart over his tuxedo, pressing it, as he longed, and made no secret of conveying, as he longed to press hers.

"The Signora is right . . . We have the ham, but we have also the violet . . . the chosen flower of Napoleon and his Empress Josephine."

"What kind of violets are they?" she said.

"Madame, madame," he began, and paused as if the revelation were too much, "they tremble . . . like a young girl when she falls in love . . . They are like"—and here he smiled and in a lower voice confided—"they are like to Juliet at the window . . . they are like to you, as I came in."

"Nonsense," she said, and laughed a little.

"But you are the more beautifuller. You are the girl and the woman in one," he said. It was too much. Tristan, who had been shuffling the cards, came and drew the curtain that divided the two halves of the room, drew it swiftly and with an emphasis, as if to shut out the impropriety. Hearing the rings jingling abruptly on the brass poles, she thought, Oh God, he thinks I have encouraged this waiter . . . and perhaps I have, and putting her hand out, she stayed his movements while telling the waiter somewhat authoritatively to go. It was while they were drinking the tea that he said it, casually, as if it had nothing to do with what had happened previously.

"If you get married, we could be your little page boys and wear white velvet breeches."

"But I'm not getting married," she said, affronted. Hearing such a solemn statement was what he wanted, both a delight and an elixir, but for that very reason he had to shrug it off, say that many of his friends' parents at school had been divorced and married again, and that in fact it was fashionable.

"Hey," Paddy said, looking up from the menu which he had been consulting, because of course they would go to the stately dining room for dinner.

"Hey, they have toad tail on the menu."

"You jest," Tristan said.

"I promise you they have *coda di rospo*," he said, showing it both in Italian and in the English translation on the page opposite.

"*Coda di rospo,*" they shouted in unison, and repeated it while they bathed and dressed, brilliantining their hair, then helping her with the little row of velvet-covered buttons that ran down the back of her dress, the little nuisance row of buttons which, as they conceded, were quite quaint.

As they went down the grand staircase, intoxicated with happiness, they paused to make the most of it, to admire this tapestry or that, this panel of tinted glass on which every conceivable fruit, flower, and allegorical couple were painted with amber lineaments, to touch the brass stumps of light, large as streetlamps, fixed to the pedestal of each staircase, wondering giddily about the history and origin of these things but not daunted, so that to any onlooker they were simply three people going down to dinner, precocious and perhaps even a trifle dangerously enchanted with each other.

12

Their boarding school was about eighty miles out of London and set among trees, with a view of the chalk downs on one side and of the town on the west. The town itself seemed dreary and spiritless as she and Tristan trudged around in search of a café. The one they found was the one she would come to know so well, because it was where parents entertained their children and partook of ploughman's lunch, cottage pie, or the vegetarian pancake. Tristan was in no mood to eat, kept worrying that they might be late, and lifted the sleeve of his jacket to consult his new watch every other minute. It was he in the end who had plumped for boarding school. His best friend had gone and said that this particular school was like a hotel, what with binges in the dormitory, surreptitious visits to the local pub, and trysts in the woods with girls. It was coeducational. She had already been told by the housemaster that there were no vacancies, but through a friend's influence she had managed to get an interview for Tristan. Now they had arrived and she was pacing a gaunt stone quad in two minds about whether or not she would be glad if he got in. Inconceivable to think of the house without them, their bedroom a ghost room, the long pine table vacant of schoolbooks at one end.

Their father had conceded to let them go there, not because he approved, but because since he had moved to the country his interest in them had waned, and he added as a parting shot that to be removed from her influence could hardly be to their detriment. He and Madeline ran a market garden, and his letters now gloated over his newfound happiness with this good woman.

Since it was vacation time, the school was deserted and her high heels on the stone steps sounded abrasive, so that frequently she turned round and apologised to no one. The place with its smell of floor polish and disinfectant felt chilly, reeked of rules and regulations, of a life where character and mettle would be ingrained into young people. How many in the next month or two would mope on that same staircase, sucking a lozenge or a stick of licorice, thinking, I will run away, I will run away, I will run away.

Seeing the headmaster stand in the open doorway looking rather awkward, she felt a stab of relief, believing that Tristan had not got in. However, when he sat her in his little study, which was painted a lugubrious green, she heard differently. Tristan, it seemed, had described their visit to Italy, added an imaginary visit to Vesuvius, where he depicted the lava as being slumberous. He also described the meal in which he and his brother were served an entire roast baby chicken along with a plate of chips. Although the school had no place, the headmaster would have to find one for such an exceptional boy, and she thought how she would remember forever that moment, this tall, rather shy man, whose legs were gangly and overlong, feeling ill at ease with her and sensing her own disappointment. All the time, and involuntarily, he touched things on his desk: souvenirs, photograph of wife and children, a miniature china tea set, and the little jug in which there were four different-coloured Smarties. It was the Indian measure for a drink and it was called a "jigger." He told her that. She was not sure now that she wanted her children to go, to consign them to a more ordered world, a world where the wildness would be squeezed out of them.

"There is his brother," she said anxiously. The headmaster flinched and looked away. Why did she have to be so insistent? He changed the little plastic disk on his calendar to give himself time to phrase his sentence, then coughed nervously and said there were no more places, there simply were not, and held up a sheet of paper crammed with the names of those on a waiting list. Outside, a huge chestnut tree glowed in the sun, the sun dancing off the dark, motionless leaves, and yet in this room there was no sun at all; there was only chill, and at home there was Paddy in a sulk. He had refused even to travel with them, said he had got a holiday job cleaning steps in a block of flats, and had begun to practise with mop and bucket.

"Dad was right," he said in an outburst. "You just want us to grow up and be snobs."

She saw rage in him, rage that wanted to defy and thwart her. She heard herself asking when his father had said it and in what context, and how could he, Paddy, believe it, how could he be so shortsighted? Then something checked her and she said rather sadly, "I don't think I am a snob, love," and he turned away, ashamed of what he had said.

Now, in the sunless study, Tristan was telling the headmaster that he couldn't leave his brother, that it would be a betrayal.

"But your brother and you will have to part one day."

"One day," Tristan said with a manliness that made it all the more wrenching.

"I can't promise anything," the headmaster said, but she knew now that he would relent and somehow a vacancy would be found.

Paddy's first response was to falter.

"I know I'll fluff it," he said, and as he said it she saw tears well up in his big grey eyes, which on occasions like this had the look of a sheep's.

"It doesn't matter if you do," she said, and added that if he did not get in, they would forget the whole thing about boarding school and both boys would go to day school and live happily ever after. Then, at other times in the intervening week, he felt quite buoyant about it, asked Tristan again to describe the grounds and the dining room, the quad and the library, where he said he would spend a lot of time on his river project. Together they swatted on maths and geography, his two worst subjects, and she cheered as he showed off his command of English. So certain was he of failing that he begged to be let go alone, promising that he would telephone from the station to deliver the news. His voice, far too loud and far too excited, told her what she had doubted all day, and so the decision was made, and the next few weeks were a flurry of preparations, what with buying uniforms, shoes, games things, a little boot-polish kit, and then having to sew name tapes onto all these new things. They were already planning the Sundays when she would be allowed visits and the weekends once a month when they would be allowed home. The nearer it got to the day, the fonder of her they became, no more huffs, no more closing their bedroom door and putting the DO NOT DISTURB sign on the knob, the one they had appropriated in Italy. They even professed an interest in the garden, helped her with the weeding, and buried coins to commemorate a momentous month.

In the train they all read while a talkative lady described a wedding she had just come from, a gorgeous wedding where the bridal flowers matched up with the ones on the straw hats, but how something upsetting had happened—oil got on her good coat and wouldn't come out.

"I was ever so happy until then," she said, staring at Nell while munching on a biscuit. A boy had wheeled a little moveable trolley into the carriage and they all had refreshments—coffee and biscuits. Outside, it was autumn, everything turning, bronzed sapling, scrub and treetop like the bright crests of the cock pheasants that were probably sauntering in the woods waiting for the gunman whom instinct had not taught them to hide from. She was afraid she would show her tears and almost did when in her book, *Anna Karenina,* she came upon a happy moment when two intending lovers began to skate together, skated nervously, courting risk in order to bewitch each other. The tentative happiness was what made her cry. She had to close the book and look out the window. In the novel the trees were decked in snow, which seemed like vestments, but through the window what she saw were the trunks of birches grey and spindly as if on the point of falling, and then the whole wasteland of gorse, angry, blossomless, winter gorse. She must not cry. In less than an hour they would be there.

A sign at the top of the long avenue said CHILDREN CROSSING, but she knew that there were no young children now. Her boss at the publishing house had arranged for her to stay with a colleague, a man called Hubert, who had a title and was widowed. The taxi drove slowly by a moat, then over a bumpy bridge, and then along another part of the avenue dense with laurel, leading to a court-yard with tubs of bright flowers. A purple Rolls-Royce stately as an ocean liner stood to one side of the open hall door, its fawn leather unblemished and the leather headrests without a mark. A servant, an older woman, met her in the doorway, confiscated her suitcase, and led her silently through a big hall and a dining room to a sitting room where a fire was already lit.

"Will Madam be needing anything?" she said in a deferential tone. Madam.

"No, thank you," Nell said, and her voice must have conveyed her apprehension, because the woman said, "I'll tell His Lord-ship, he's just bathing." So this was how some people lived: or-der, ritual, servants knowing their masters' every move, every moment defined as clearly as the stitching on the rustic tapestry that depicted lovers in a beautiful suspense. This was luxury such as she had not seen before. Often in London on Fridays she would see chauffeurs carrying out dresses on hangers, outfits in preparation for a dinner or a ball that evening, but this was more august, a shimmer of wealth, order, and tradition. First she stooped and smelt the roses. They were of all colours and they fitted so snugly into the low glass bowls that they looked as if they had grown there. Tentatively she touched the fat jeweled eggs in a brown egg stand over the mantelpiece. They were Rus-sian eggs, she had read about them once. Her own bric-a-brac danced before her eyes in comic succession as she wondered if the dress she had brought was fashionable enough. It felt as if she were treading on air, so thick and sumptuous was the corn-coloured carpet with its unbroken border of pale interlocked laurel.

She tiptoed for fear of disturbing the harmony of things. The papier-mâché drinks tray so laden, it seemed on the point of collapse, but of course it wouldn't, since everything here was ordained. Luminous table mats bore the names of casinos from all over the world, and from the wall a cryptic woman in a fur stared back at her.

Her boss had not mentioned her host's withered hand, over which he wore a black patent glove. This is what she noticed first, and then the eyes, which were sad and without lustre. His coming into the room altered it, the beauty now receding and his voice and bearing taking precedence. He was not distant or bristly, as she had feared; far from it, he was affability itself, chummy, as he escorted her to the settee.

"What about a little shampoo?" he said; then he plied her with questions, asked was she warm, was she chilly, if the journey was horrid, what of the young men, asked yet never permitted an answer. Suddenly she did not want to be there, she wanted to be in her own home, crying her eyes out. Unable to suppress her emotion, she described her last sight of them, like two little convicts with their luggage and their food baskets, braving their new world.

"You can let your hair down here as much as you wish," he said, adding how very becoming it was to see a woman weep like that, as most women now were harridans. Under his breath she thought she heard him mutter something about rosy human flesh, and looking away she thought him quite bizarre.

"Chin-chin," he said, sitting close to her. His eyes gleamed now with excitement as he looked up and down the length of her body, then admired her ankle-strap shoes. He had been looking forward to her visit, the highlight of his week. She contrived strategies such as that she was faint or that she had forgotten to give her children some very important document and must walk over to the school, and once there she would run away.

"It's so nice of you to have me," she said, straining.

"Pleasure," he said and then, pointing to the lawn, went, "Tch, tch," began to fume. He apologised for a ghastly strip of black plastic that was held down by stones, said it was simply not good enough for her first, her maiden visit. The lawn had been sacrificed, a man had come with prongs to scrounge it, to scrounge the old grass and moss and weeds and muck, then aerated it and spread fresh seed, but one naughty piece of lawn did not respond, did not take.

"I can't tell you all the muck that was in there," he said, glorying again in the word. She drank quickly. Not since her wedding had she tasted champagne, and now, just as then, she thought it was like chiffon that tickled. Seeing her guzzle it, he said he had opened a very good claret for dinner, as they were having game. Cook, he explained, was not Cordon Bleu but good at plain English cooking, and moreover, he had made the first course, a consommé with a dash of sherry and curry.

Her bedroom was a sanctuary—flowered wallpaper with bedspread and headboard to match and a dressing table replete with silver brush-and-comb set and a silver-topped powder bowl with pinkish powder. The cotton balls next to it were of various colours, and nestling together, they had, at a quick glance, the look of the Russian eggs. She was dabbing powder on her face recklessly when he came in, saying what an old fusspot he was, but he wanted to make sure that everything was in order, for instance, if there were enough hangers. Her black dress on its padded hanger looked idiotic and her stockings also on a hanger, seemed lewd. He ran the bathwater so that it would not be rusty; then, imitating the deference of the servant, asked if there was anything else "Madam would be needing."

"Nothing, nothing at all," she said, recoiling. The servant whom he imitated, and who had obviously unpacked for her, skulked by, too timid to look up.

As she lay in her bath she could hear the pigeons cooing and knew that they were the same pigeons her children could hear a few fields away. Already she was writing letters, receiving letters, their handwriting on the envelopes bringing them momentarily back. The pain had not started yet, it was waiting for the moment when she put the key in her front door. Presently there was the dinner gong, so in a fluster she got out, perspiring, half dried herself, got into her clothes with difficulty, and shot down the stairs, carrying her high-heeled shoes.

On one wall of the dining room there was a picture of a horse, solitary, bedraggled, standing in a swamp, and on the other side a painting of a woman, her knees and legs splayed, her dress pulled up over her face, either to hide her shame or to flaunt her desire. He came in as Nell stood watching, crossed, switched on a light to give a better view, and said, "Mistress Polly, parting her hairs," then went on to say the pleasure it gave him, how whenever he felt ratty he just stood and looked at her, talked to her, even made the odd suggestion. He had always coveted her; unfortunately, his best friend had also, and they had both pleaded with the same dealer, who of course would have liked them both to have had it, but finally gave it to his friend, who offered the higher price; yet the following day his friend was killed in his plane crossing the Alps.

"Bunny never was a lucky chap," he said as he led her across formally to the table where the jellied consommé waited. Dinner was sedateness itself, with the butler standing all the time by the long black sideboard, waiting to serve the wine or the vegetables or whatever, silent except when spoken to and watchful of their every need, as for instance when she spilt a blob of soup, he was there with a muslin cloth to soak it up. As soon as the main course was served, Hubert gave the signal for Daphne's plate, which was in fact a beautiful cut-glass bowl, one of a set that Daphne insisted upon eating from. Daphne, a yappy little fawn dog, trotted in, sniffed a stranger, and made for Nell's ankle. Daphne had been ill, had had diarrhea, and this illness and the cause of it and now the abatement of it were discussed in great detail. Then he thought fit to talk about schools, the schools his children had been to, and the school where her children were now spending their first night, while covertly she kept glancing at the clock, determined that she would excuse herself soon after dinner. As if guessing this treason, he said he had a surprise for her, a game, one she had never played before.

"I'm useless at games," she said.

"You'll like this one," he said, and from the way he said it he also implied, You will play this game, because you are my guest and you are indebted to me.

Moving away from the table, he scattered the cigar smoke that might impede her passage, said he loved his cigars as much as he loved his women and had asked his doctor when the time came to have a nice nurse put a big one in his mouth. They repaired to a red lacquered room, much cozier, as he said, where she saw her shawl folded neatly on a screen. In the dampened pewter ice bucket some ice shifted, allowing the bottle to stir, as if an unseen hand had moved it. The champagne was already open and he poured now not with decorum but recklessly. What had tasted like chiffon earlier on now tasted sour, and she knew that she must presently find a way to excuse herself. The game was a record he had put together, of mating frogs. Suddenly the room was filled with these loud, lustful sounds, which seemed to come not from the throat but from the belly, from the genitals of the bellicose creatures, each male tackling and topping his rival.

"He's calling, calling to his lady," he said, bending over her, the loose flap of his neck like a turkey's comb and his shirt front open to show a thicket of wiry grey hair. He was smiling. Was it not the randiest sound she had ever heard? What was it doing to her in her little black dress and her sheer stockings? He liked a girl who wore stockings, had no time for those twopenny tights. She could feel how stiff and priggish she must seem to him as he depicted a tropical scene, warm night, everything in heat—frogs, birds, beasts, skivvies, everything. She kept staring at her shawl to avoid his gaze, but she could feel his anger, or rather his petulance, getting worse. The game was simple. She was to give the frogs names and then put words in their mouths, the lewd words that spewed and farted from their bodies.

"Just like the bubbles," he said, puffing his cheeks and lips to imitate how words are depicted in a cartoon.

"I can't," she said.

"Oh yes, you can," he said, and whispered in her ear a little teaser:

Nymphomaniacal Alice
Dildoed herself with a chalice.
They found her vagina
In South Carolina
And scraps of her anus in Dallas.

"You mean you've never heard of a sharpener?" he said, disbelieving.

"No," she said.

"My my, what a cloistered life we've led," he said, explaining that it was what men got up to before they went into their lady's boudoir; then he took her hand and said to show a chap some pity, to get her Nell Gwyn side out and feel his map of Italy, with his long-cocked Sicily, and give it a squeeze. Now was her cue. Now was the moment to answer the entreaty of Mr. Frog.

"I can't," she said. "I cannot."

"Yes, you can," he said, and began to prompt, salivating on each word.

"We seem to be on a different wavelength," she said, overstiff.

"Then get on my wavelength . . . if you're fucking her, Jack, I'm fucking you fucking her, Jack, sort of thing," he said. She looked away from him, looked first at a jade vase which she thought she might pick up and club him with, then at the cream call-bell, which, bobbin-like, hung on a cord from the mantelshelf.

"I'd like to put a poker up your arse," he said as he led her in a sturdy waltz, saying that if talk didn't get her libido going, didn't get her knickers out of a twist, then a bit of a jig would. She saw the oak fireplace, the unchanging flames of the gas fire, the Chinese screen, her shawl, the champagne bucket in dizzying swirls, as he steered her angrily, wielding her this way and that, spinning her round when she least expected it, assuring her he was worth ten men, a fact she would yell to when he stuffed it into her.

"I know your kicks," he said, stopping suddenly and training a swivel lamp fully on her face, so that it glared like a headlamp.

"What kicks?" she said. The dancing had sobered her completely and she thought that yes, she would club him with one of the ornaments.

"You had three of them at Ronnie's sixtieth birthday . . . one in each loo and one on the stairs," he said.

"I wasn't at my boss's sixtieth birthday," she said.

"His club . . . our club won't have him back," he said, chuckling over Ronnie's shame.

"It wasn't me," she said.

"What's your name?" he asked then, eyes and mind wrestling with his blur.

"Nell," she said, and repeated it.

"Oh shit . . . I thought you were Samantha," he said, opening a drawer to consult a little notebook in which he had jotted some names. Ghastly mistake. Couldn't be more sorry. Would have to have it out with Ronnie or that slob secretary of his with the gargantuan B.O. Had written a little dossier on this one and that, and she, Nell, came under W for the Weeping Willow type.

"You will have to excuse me," she said, summoning an authority she did not know she had.

"Not even a pussy fart," he said with enforced mockery, unable to conceal his disdain at her attempts at standoffishness.

She lay on top of the satin quilt in her black dress and her court shoes, ready to bolt at dawn. She missed them then in a way that frightened her and would prefigure the emptiness to come. By living with them and for them so utterly, she had kept life at bay, but life in all its vicissitudes was waiting in the wings. For some reason she remembered a postcard that someone had sent her, of a sleeping girl lying on scorched earth, a lion of the same scorching colour approaching the girl, the still moonlit scene poised for catastrophe.

"According to Einstein, one may travel into the future but not come back. What a dizzying thought," Paddy wrote in one of his first letters. The children's letters vying with other to convey love, solidarity, and their burgeoning importance. Tristan had drawn a nine-banded armadillo in natural history class but found it difficult to finish because of the patterns on its armour. He had also discovered that human brains have bigger cortices than monkeys'. Did she like the notepaper, he wondered. It was made from the bark of the daphne bush according to an ancient process which protects the balance of Nepal's forests. A friend had given it to him and had also invited him to Nepal, an invitation he intended to take up. Meanwhile, he was very clever at scavenging, as he fitted perfectly into the dumbwaiter and crept down at dawn to nick grapefruits. They were for his friend Partridge, who never left his dormitory and was studying astronomy privately, kept a telescope under his bed. This information was "top secret" and no one must know.

Paddy had taken on volunteer work, was helping an elderly lady, emptying bins and putting coal in her scuttle, plus a bucket in the back kitchen so that it could easily be fetched. He had chanced on her the previous Sunday, weeping, and guess why, her family, her married son and daughter-in-law, had come to lunch but had just left, and sadly she was in her armchair disconsolate, her handkerchief sodden, ashamed to be seen.

"You would think," his letter said, "that her world had ended, but it hadn't, it was just that her family had come to lunch and left at four."

Tristan was tasting the joys of the local town, said he had mastered the use of chopsticks, fancied he would use them instead of cutlery in the future, and had had the good fortune to meet the oldest man in the parish, a man claiming to be one hundred and three, who said grandiosely, "I am the oldest man in the parish. Buy me a drink."

Paddy enclosed a poem which he had written about the stars, said the stars were people in their house, sleeping, with the lights on. Tristan went with another boy to the cricket pitch, where they spotted duck feathers and decided that two male ducks had had a fight and that one was killed, with only a wing remaining. It was touch and go whether or not he and his brother would engage in a similar battle. He was building a fortress to keep his brother out, for reasons which would later be disclosed. His brother was enemy number one. Their letters, which came in the same envelope, had added snippets of grudge, tirades against each other, but occasionally a truce was reached as they contemplated a binge on a pine-apple, which they would share.

For the Sundays she was to visit, they wrote lists, requesting marmite, peanut butter, Gentleman's Relish, tasties, to brighten their fare. On a little makeshift calendar Tristan marked off the remaining days until Christmas and hinted that he had a delightful present in mind for her but he was not sure if his budget would rise to it. It was an icon, a solemn face, enclosed in a silver niche, like a knight in armour.

13

"Call me Ned," the man was saying, gloating at the fact that she was in his shop, his humble abode, affording him the radiance of her presence. Her radiance had infected him. He could see it was a party as he piled the various purchases into a box, the webbed leaves of the pineapple on top like some sort of hieratic plumage. He totted the damage on the back of his hand, cancelling out sums that were already there and winking as he gave her a big discount. To add to her well-being, he said that he would drive her home, would not hear of her hawking all this stuff in her high heels and her good coat. It was a green nap coat that she had bought on the installment plan. There was a chestnut in the pocket, a polished and cocoa-coloured one that she had found on the street that had escaped the marauding children, clinging to its bristly bed.

"You can't bring me home . . . can't leave your shop," she said, almost chastisingly, because she could see that he was smitten. Life is all or nothing, either you are a grey shrew of a thing, a reject, or a human beacon that people stop to warm themselves by.

"It's an honour," he said, and opened and slammed the drawer of the cash register to give himself something to do. A distraught mother called through the open doorway to ask if she could have half a head of cabbage and Nell wanted, yearned to say, "Have the whole head, I'll pay, because I am happy," but the woman had fled. Other customers were more imperious, pinching the fruits

and asking the country of their origin. One woman made a big
to-do about the ripeness of the avocado pear, so that he launched
into a foolproof method of testing an avocado, said one finger
went on the white of the eye and another finger on top of the
avocado, to test the relative softnesses, and if they corresponded,
then "Bob's your uncle." He touched several of them clumsily. The
woman was so appalled that she changed her mind about her
appetizer, said aloud that she was going to have fish pâté instead.
He winked at Nell, and when the woman had gone out, he let it be
known by the merest curl of his lips that he had no time for such
people, called themselves ladies or toffs, but they were not ladies
or toffs like some.

"Saw you on the High Street the other day," he said.

"Me?"

"Yes, you."

"How come you picked me out?" she said.

"I didn't pick you out, you stood out," he said, and looked at
her with such naked admiration that she had to turn away. Hanging from the ceiling were strands of laurel and plastic fruit so
grimed with dust, so shrivelled, that she thought if a match was
put to them the whole place would catch fire. In his elation he
danced, trampling on cabbage butts and berries, saying yes, he had
picked her out and now here she was in his abode. He wore boots
such as countrymen wear, old, gnarled boots, black-green, that
turned up at the toes.

"Big party?" he asked then, unable to conceal the longing that
he felt.

"Quite big," she said. In truth, she did not know. Duncan had
said he would bring a few friends, make it a ceilidh. Just as she had
given up, believed herself to be outcast, along came Duncan, a
round blond barrel of a man with blue eyes and an amber smile;
Duncan, mesmeriser, drinker, and fallen cherub. He looked like a
labourer in a stockinette jersey that was too small for him, shouting "Bullshit, bullshit" to a woman who in a high quavering voice
was singing a plaintive song addressed to a young lover, bemoan-
ing his desertion of her, how he had taken the east and the west,

had taken the sun and the stars from her, and, she believed, was taking God from her.

As Nell came into the party, he smiled, handed her the wine bottle that he was drinking from, and said, "Transubstantiate, Sister." Sister. Soon after, he left, but on the way out handed her a crumpled matchbook, saying that she was to read it and then forget it. She ran to the bathroom and read, "Let us see the Northern Lights together"—underneath was his phone number. When she did ring him a few days later, he was puzzled at first, couldn't remember, then did. He was in the theatre and she could hear shouting and hammering in the background. He enquired where she lived, then asked if he and his mates could come for the bread.

All morning she had been busy. First the butcher arrived, delivering the goose, which she filled with two kinds of stuffing, potato and sweetbread, a recipe she had copied from a newspaper. Then out on the High Street with all the other shoppers, wanting to proclaim, to cry out, "Hey, hey, I'm having a party, my first party ever." It was as if the youth which she had never lived had been lying in wait and had come to possess her now. Where would it lead? A little afraid voice within her kept piping up, saying she mustn't be so extravagant, she must work doubly hard in the weeks to follow, pour herself into her work. Another voice said, "Live, live." Many of the shoppers, women of her own age or thereabouts, were fraught, women with wrinkles and sour faces, pushing prams and go-carts, as if not children were in them but sacks of coal. In the greengrocer's now she ordered prodigally, vegetables, fruits, candied fruits, nuts, a sheaf of flowers. The grey doom-filled days were behind her; she had even discarded certain items in her wardrobe because they reeked of despair, black veiling and so forth, mournful things. With his bare hand Ned cracked a walnut for her and held it out so that she could partake of the morsels. The severed walnut looked violated, brought a fleeting memory of pain, her own or her mother's, and this in its turn brought back her dream of the night before. Her mother came through the bedroom door, not as a living mother, but as a ghost in a blue flannel nightgown, identical to the one Nell herself had on, then slipped into bed beside her and said she would be always there, the silent onlooker at work, at play, or wherever.

In the van with Ned she was already running the rolling pin over the icing sugar to ease out all the little bumps, and she knew that in her kitchen in an enamel bowl the yeast bread was rising, each spore swelling next to its neighbouring spore, so that what had been compact like Plasticine was at this moment brimming over, a pregnant thing, pregnant as she herself was with thoughts of Duncan. The van seemed to be Ned's homestead. There was a tea chest with old clothes spilling out of it, on the dashboard his tea mug with the sign "Cancer," his safety razor, rags, bookmaker slips, a mirror that once had had shells around it, and numerous signs that read BACK IN FIVE MINUTES or BACK IN TEN MINUTES or AT THE BOOKMAKER'S NEXT DOOR.

When he saw her sitting room he became awed, embarrassed. The long refectory table and the long-stemmed cranberry glasses were too grand all together. He took off his cap and gaped at things. No, he would not have anything, he must dash. Hurrying out, he said that if she forgot anything she had only to pick up the "dog and bone."

All afternoon she worked, so that by dusk it was only a question of stirring the gravy and putting greaseproof paper over the cooked goose to keep it moist and consulting the mirror to make sure her makeup had not smeared. They were late. She had already had a drink and played the same record twice as she waited on tenterhooks for the doorbell. It was a song in which one man sat another man down to tell him that love is all there is. The singer on the cover had a ponytail and a sad, studious face. In a way it was the happiest moment of the evening, because in her mind she saw how it would all work, how he would stand next to her, how they would be shy, would become closer, simply because they were surrounded by all this furor and by his friends. She had not asked anyone that she knew, wanting it to be a party solely for him.

The room was like a chapel, duskly lit, flowers and candles everywhere, and a starched white cloth on the table. The flowers were jasmine, winter jasmine in big jugs, and in other jugs sprays of leaves, because of course with the wanton way she had spent, she had had to economise on something. In her bedroom there was a little bunch of snowdrops, a secret posy, the green edging of the petal exactly the same color as the drooping bell-like leaves. He would go up there with her for a moment, if only to kiss her once. All day she tried to stave off the thought and the tenderness of that kiss, and it was as if it had already happened, so that what was not yet realised existed as a memory, a tremor, and at the same time was a presage of something beautiful to come.

When the first peal of the bell sounded, she walked towards the door confidently, as if she were someone else, then felt rather taken aback to find three men there, complete strangers to her.

"Is this Duncan's gig?" one of them said.

"He's not here," she said a little brusquely.

"But it's his gig," the man said.

"Yes," she said, allowing them in, and as they trailed behind her she enquired where Duncan was.

"He's on his way," another said.

"He is coming?" she said, her voice that little bit nettled.

"Yeah," one of them said, adding that Duncan had gone to the pub to pick up a few friends and get bottles. He said the name of the pub as an added assurance. In the sitting room they sat close together, downing whiskies and talking amongst themselves in low voices about the show. It was *Gulliver's Travels*.

"When does it open?" she asked.

"Maybe never," one of them said, and laughed, and then they all laughed nervously, recounting the row with the producer that very day, Duncan telling him to get the hell out of the theatre, to choose his door, choose his window, the producer refusing to leave, then the two of them having a fistfight in the gallery, and in the end the ejected producer yelling, "You're fired, you're fired."

The next to arrive was a tall young man, very aristocratic, with a cigarette holder between his teeth. He introduced himself as Andrew and introduced the tiny man standing next to him as his fool. The stagehands knew him and were deferential towards him insofar as they broke off their murmurings and looked in his direction, ready to answer any question or obey a command.

"Where is Duncan?" he asked, his voice nasal and condescending.

"At the Elm," one of them said sheepishly.

"At the Elm. Shit," he said, and turned, grabbed his fool by the lapel, and started to storm out.

"I sent the car away," the fool said.

"How about some Pocheen?" she said hurriedly, sensing that if she was to lose Andrew she would lose Duncan, too, since Andrew was the pivot, everything about him spoke it: his arrogance, his motor coat, the cigarette holder, the sneer with which he addressed the others. He looked at her as if he just might insult her, then changed his mind and said, "Pocheen," and repeated the word with reverence, then waited while she ran to retrieve the lemonade bottle that was hidden in a pillowcase upstairs, a gift from the homeland. Holding the bottle to his nose, he smelled it, reeled back as if already intoxicated, and said in a slightly mellower voice, "This is it, gang. This is where it's at.

"Brain fuck. Total brain fuck," he said as he drank greedily from the bottle and wiped his lips to free them of the fire, his long legs in their fawn corduroy jodhpurs jigging out before him.

Next to come was Cissy, a loud-voiced, plumpish woman with orange hair, who seemed trussed into the velvet cat suit that she wore.

"It's the Styx," she said as she entered, then kissed them all, called them darling, and, looking askance at Nell, said half-mocking, "And who might you be, Cathleen ni Houlihan or Deirdre of the Sorrows!" Taking the glass that Nell offered her, she announced brazenly that it was her birthday and that she had just received the most divine present, simply divine.

"Not those," Andrew said, touching his own ear to draw attention to the hideousness of her plastic orange danglers.

"Revenge, darling, revenge," and she went on to regale them with a little incident that had happened as she was dressing to come to the party. She was in her bath when the doorbell rang. She'd called out of the bathroom window, to be told by an oaf that there was a delivery, a present for Mrs. Liddell, her own true self.

"Present from whom?" she said, becoming grand as she reenacted her hauteur.

"From her ex and the second Mrs. Liddell," she said, exagger-
ating the tone and lumpiness of the voice, then mimed putting on
her dressing gown, running down the stairs in her tootsies, expecting an azalea or maybe a crate of vino, and seeing in its basket of
straw this little skinless pink thing, this poodle, a few hairs on it
like flecks of cotton wool, and here she gloried as she described
how quickly she'd thought on her feet, thrusting the basket back
into the oaf's arms, saying, "Take it straight back to them," to
which he said he wouldn't like to think of what would befall him
or for that matter the poor little doggie. Before he could expatiate
on that fate, she had closed the door, and through the letter box
told him to take it to the fucking dogs' home or flush it down the
loo or take it anywhere he wished.

"Bitch. Mega bitch," Andrew was saying as he rocked back and
forth laughing, his boots with their very high heels clicking as he
raised them in the air.

"Life has made me a bitch," she said and, fearing that she'd been
a little too dismissive with Nell, looked at her and said, "Nice pad
you have here."

It was over an hour before he arrived, and then with a motley of
people.

"God save all," he said, and she knew that he was drunk by the
way he flinched. Having seen him only once before, and fleetingly
at that, she had not been sure if she was attracted to him, but when
she saw him for the second time walking towards her, his head
down a little, his smile so shy and apologetic, and his squat hands
reaching out in a gesture of conciliation, she felt her whole body
tremble with desire.

"Sorry, sorry, Sister," he said again and again, and squeezed her
hand. Then some of his entourage followed in quick succession
and she knew that the eager girl who tottered on exceedingly high
heels like a flamingo was his girlfriend. It was quite easy to see by
the way she sighted him across the room, picked her way among
the cushions, and clasped his hand.

"This is Nell and this is Sue," he said, obviously flustered, and to reaffirm her claim on him Sue ran her other hand through his hair.

Nell excused herself, said she would get them some food, and then in the kitchen languished, did not know what she was doing as she carved the goose and put helpings of stuffing onto plates.

"Listen, mate, you're not the only one," Cissy said, uncorking some wine and muttering that it didn't really matter much, since he couldn't fuck, wasn't a number-one fuck, simply a two-minute wonder.

"You're all heartless," Nell said, feeling now that her house, her kitchen, and her expectations were violated.

"Yes, we're all heartless, darling," Cissy said, and stuck her tongue out, going back with a bottle in either hand.

By midnight things had reached a feverish pace. She drank when anyone remembered to hand her a glass, and she could feel herself getting tipsy. Some came, others left, because either they were bored or they went to get more booze, and the telephone rang endlessly, so that she found herself shouting out, "Is there a Keith here? Is there a Miranda here?" and once she had to go upstairs to look for a singer who had locked himself in the children's bedroom with a Negress. His wife had followed, was in the landing, tottering in white fringed boots.

"Is my husband in there?" she asked as if she was about to cry.

"No . . . no," Nell said, and drew her away, said he was in the garden, she had seen him go out in the garden with his guitar.

In the sitting room, Andrew lurched towards her and said what about Irish coffees, where were they? She didn't know. Her eyes were on Duncan and Sue. They sat close together, Sue with her hand inside his pocket, her body rocking rhythmically to simulate the pleasure she was giving him.

"It's vile . . . vile," she heard herself say, and Andrew followed her, grabbed her by her lace collar, and said that yes, he could see that she fancied Duncan but that she was to put it right out of her head, period. It sent blasts of iced nausea through him. Duncan had been married, had had a wife and kids and all that shit, and it had gone wrong, putrid, like it always does, so she was to put him out of her mind and out of her crotch.

"We're soulmates," she said.

"Bog-road soulmates . . . but not body mates," he said, turned and called into the room, saying it was time for them to split. Some thanked her, some didn't; others picked up bottles in which there was wine left, while Sue shook Duncan to waken him up. Since she had left the room he had drifted into sleep, in shame perhaps.

"Wake up . . . wake up, baby," Sue was saying, her hand under his stockinette jersey as she tickled him.

"Let him sleep," Nell said, seeing in it a glimmer of victory.

"Like hell I will," Sue said, and began to pummel his body. So this is how it would be; they would both be there while he slept and both be there when he wakened, like the women at the foot of the Cross. The room looked as if a herd had passed through it—plates, cushions, and records were strewn all over the floor, the ashtrays piled with ashes, cigarette papers from the joints they had rolled, and, incongruously, a florin which someone had left as payment for a telephone call.

"Baby, baby," Sue shouted at him, but he simply turned and buried his face in the folds of the loose velvet cover. She tried coaxing him and then, realising that it was useless, she took a pen from the side table and wrote a message on the back of his wrist, then gathered herself into her black voluminous cape and left, saying she hoped that they had not made too much of a mess.

"Shakespeare was wrong," he said, his lips coming awake but his eyes still closed.

"Why?" she said. She had sat all night, not touching him, not once, so near that it felt like touch.

"It's not a stage . . . it's not 'All the world's a stage' . . . it's a dream stage," he said, then opened his eyes and looked around to see where he was.

"They've gone," Nell said as he surveyed the pillaged room, his eyes taking in every detail, even the little clocklike petals of the jasmine, and then looking down at his hand he read the scrawl,

"See you tonight, shmuck," and dropped his hand, saying, "Bullshit, bullshit.

"Do you forgive me?" he asked, his voice very gentle.

"Forgive you what?"

"For all that garbage last night."

"Do you remember it?"

"No . . . not much . . . I remember one thing, though . . . one thing," and here he put his hand out and touched her cheek, eerily delicate for a man with such sturdy hands, the forefingers flat, spatula-like; his father's hands, as he said. They were to see the Northern Lights together. He remembered that. Already her mind was on stilts, thinking, When, where, and yippee. In supposed jest but really to get nearer to him, she covered his face with her chiffon scarf, to shut out the dawn light, and gradually their hands met, then clasped, the insides of their fingers softly feeling, softly finding out, as they rocked back and forth like children. First he talked nonsense, said the usual nonsensical things, then less so, as he stood up, flexed his muscles, walked about, looked at her, looked at her books and her records, and then looked back at her, with such tenderness, and astonishment that he had found her among the dross. What he tried to say was not easy for him and not customary for him: "A total fusion . . . flesh and intellect . . . I want to think with my balls . . . correction . . . with my every-thing . . . I want to feel you . . . I want to know you . . . no broken ends . . . no explanations . . . the summa of love," and here he became sad as he asked the porous air, How the fuck do you sing summa and what key is it in?

Taking strands of her hair and twisting it into tight plaits, he pulled it, so that it rasped at the roots, and told her that they must not fall in love.

"Why not?" she asked.

"Because I'm stuck and I'm trying to unstick," he said, and kissed her, and in the doing, he could just as easily have said, "I love you," because the kiss was from somewhere deep within him, a deep, solemn, aching kind of kiss.

After he had gone she drew the curtains and fell into one of the longest, sweetest sleeps she had ever known, then wakened in the afternoon, spouting a line from a dream—"It all depends on the music and the modulation." He had said, How do you sing it and what key is it in? They thought alike. Suddenly remembering him, she thought how, when he held her, the clasp had something of the fervour of her own land, ancient, turbulent, and beyond pity.

14

Night, dark night, the landscape outside the bus window like a night sea, endless, featureless, except for the bushes; unwieldy shapes that looked like animals in a strange land; a silence throughout. Then towns with high turreted walls, battlements, and farther along shacks, in which men sat in biblical robes, the light from the braziers showing their taut faces, their loping mahogany limbs; women behind veils, veiled; the goats asleep and out of sight, oranges in a crush on the ground, oranges to trample like rotted potatoes. The earth was brown, red-brown, and ochre, sinuous, winding, barren, the building also of earth; houses and landscape all of a piece, a strange parched land. There were cacti, too, dark now by night but turquoise by day, paws splayed together like prongs, a pronged welcome and an emptiness that prefigured the vastness of the desert, the desert whose spectre haunted the landscape and crept inside the bus, making the lining of her jacket that little bit colder.

"Sand and silence and us," Duncan had said. What a long way to go to consummate their love, their stuttering embraces. He had said many things on those mornings, those selfsame mornings after the parties, when he wakened flinching, asking where had all the flowers gone, and held her, his grasp so strong, so compact that it was like being pressed and imprisoned inside a pod. The parties, the sprees had become a regular Saturday-night event, with strangers, friends, hangers-on, people telling her she had been an Aquarius in a previous life, people throwing the I Ching to fathom their destinies, others bent reverently over the felled mirror to take their lines of cocaine as if it were Communion, and she, too, entering into it all, living at last, breaking the fetters of duty and propriety that had held her down till then. She even looked different, more daring.

In dreams there were warnings which in daylight she ignored. In one dream she saw those selfsame people, their papier-mâché faces turning to an ochre powder and her kitchen in flames. It was all for Duncan, Duncan in whose presence she felt elation, heard utterances that kept her hopes agog. She flirted with others, one doctor in particular, liked his Christ-like expression and his smile of mockery towards others, acolytes who sat at his feet and listened to his ambiguous pronouncements—Life is a fountain; life isn't a fountain. He and she had exchanged lines of Baudelaire, the sick flowers that to them took on all the beauty and stamina of health, infusions of thought between them, the tension of his body on hers, prone with desire. "Odalisque," he had whispered, and she smiled. She had put her children elsewhere, put the minute-to-minute contemplation of them aside, almost like putting something, an ornament, high up on a shelf, knowing that it is there but that it is out of sight. Their letters became more enquiring and in their separate ways more suspicious. Why hadn't she been the previous week and was the problem with her landlord sorted out and had she forgotten that she was to send a change of underclothes, and so on. Yes, she had forgotten. Then an outburst from Paddy—"I am a pauper. I have only one pair of frayed pyjamas which I have been wearing for three weeks." Tristan had got a timetable of Sunday trains in case. Yes, they suspected.

"How to paint skies," Duncan had said on those mornings when they rocked back and forth, saying nonsensical things as he described the desert in Arizona, the sheer fucking formidableness of it, and then the toy theatre that he had made from matchboxes as a child. The desert and the theatre, his two passions.

"We mustn't fall in love," he said often, and she pretended to agree.

"Where will we sleep?" she said, a thrill in her being as he proposed the journey to Morocco for a few days.

"We'll sleep in the sand . . . I'll make a sand castle over you," he said, and kissed her to seal their tryst. She did not tell her children that she was going away with a man, said it was something to do with work, and saw by their eyes that they disbelieved her. It was in the café not far from the school, a wet Sunday, their wool duffle coats giving off a half-wet sour smell. At other tables there were other children and parents, and everywhere there were little huffs as needs were voiced.

Half awake in the bumpy, trundling bus she saw the corrugated shacks on the outside of the town, biscuit boxes with families before a brazier, their faces lurid in the flames. It was raining. The rain had followed her. Duncan in his own room now, the attic room, the navy-blue blind drawn, the dark tassel soft as a bat hanging limply over the ledge, his unpacked bag on the floor, half unzipped. Oh, the lurch, the relived lurch as the Customs officer studied his passport, then said, "Can you step to one side, sir," holding on to the passport and them both knowing at once that probably it had expired. First, Duncan smiled his ready smile, tried to ogle the man, said a temporary visa would do, anything, a piece of headed paper; then he scowled when he saw he was getting nowhere, resorted to his bullshit tirade, said they were all the same fuckin' bureaucrat bullshitters, and walking back through the turnstile, his blue canvas bag humping on his enraged back, he muttered to himself, then turned and said, "Keep the home fires burning, Sister."

She went on ahead, a bit downcast, a sinking such as in childhood, when you are promised something that does not happen but you wait, wait long after, believing that it will. This was different—he was coming, he was.

At the hotel all was commotion, people spilling out of the coach, crumpled people shouting out their name or a description of their luggage, porters in long robes darting about tending to these clamours, a certain glinting canniness in their eyes, eyes that narrowed like pincers. Pathways were lit with lanterns leading to the various bungalows scattered throughout, and in one of these she would set herself down, set her luggage down, and wait for him. In a way it was more exciting to have come on ahead, she would welcome him to their abode, their temporary home before they set out for the desert. They would find nomads down in the town, make friends with them, barter with them, because, as he said, "Only two fucking fools would venture into the desert alone."

The hotel lobby was sumptuousness itself, a series of dusky salons, the light from ovoids of brass, colanders of light shedding on tables and carpets and on dried skins that hung from the ceiling, like gigantic flypapers, while all around a gaggle of voices shouted their needs, asking which bungalow and if their fires were lit and if there would be supper. All seeking, seeking; she, too, except that she maintained a kind of meekness. If he were with her now, he would squeeze her hand and she would not be so apprehensive surrounded by these know-all voices and ravelled skins with the ghosts of the animals they once were immanent in them. The porters' smiles were both ingratiating and cutting.

Her own bungalow was a distance away, at the end of a crescent of low pink houses, each house and balcony smothered with swags of bougainvillea, its purple more vivid because of the artificial lighting. Did she have to be so far away from the reception, from the hub, from the salons with pickled light and hanging skins? For a moment she thought of rushing back and asking for a room closer, but instead followed obediently. Two men walked very rapidly ahead, one carrying her luggage and the other bearing a huge tray with a cloche over it which contained her supper.

Her room was a palace, the low bed like a fairy dais under the canopy of ceiling painted in festive colours, and everywhere bowls of fruit and bowls of roses, then the same colanders of light giving a dusky glow, the whole effect like stepping into a painted caravan. Logs and kindling were piled on the hearth, just like at home, except the kindling were twigs, thin as whiskers. The two men left, and once alone she began to gabble, as if Duncan were there, and ate her supper walking about. Her terrace showed onto a field, beyond which was a range of dark mountains that looked unearthly, like another kingdom, a region of Hidden Spirits. The closed red petals of the hibiscus flowers jutted like the beaks of birds, but were soft as the finger of a glove. She touched them, she touched everything, walking about knowing she would not sleep, would not rest until he arrived.

In the morning the mountains were white, a sheer white, as if salted, and in between the crests of salt she could just see vents of blue. These mountains were waiting for him. The gardens blazed with colour and chirruped with birdsong. Bougainvillea hung from the trees in great boastful dips, and the birds swung from it, asserting their gaiety. The birds were everywhere—calling, screeching, swaying, some picking the feathers of their offspring, others raising their rears to squitter, and everywhere a riot of song and colour, a glut of nature in contrast to the thin bodies, the unfed faces, and the procuring eyes. Workmen in long blue-bleached robes raked the field free of cut grass, and as she ate her breakfast she watched them. The litter, made of sacking, was on four poles and a man thin as a pole stood sentinel at each corner. They worked in silence or near-silence. She gorged. She ate things she had never eaten before—fruits that were sliced like bread, pancakes soaked in a sweet viscous syrup.

Once the men had filled the litter, they carried it across to a cart, where a young boy held the reins of a donkey. Glad of his moment, he let out some sort of yodel and set off at a gallop, except that the donkey's forelegs got bogged down in the wet field. The rain had ceased now and in the brilliant sunshine everything trembled; small drops of rain on the saucer-shaped leaves like melted diamonds. She had a moment of doubt, but cast it aside, like throwing crumbs to the birds. Yet in the gardens she felt on edge—the foliage too luxurious, too clotted. The stamen of the Easter lilies she saw as the sulphurous tip of a match waiting to be struck and the palm fronds were Spanish combs ready to scrape scalp and hair. Waiting. She must wait the way nature waited. He would arrive at the same time of night that she had, make the same bumpy journey on the coach, see the barren land and feel its chill, see the bushes and the paws of cacti, allowing the strangeness to sift into him, so that it would be as wanderers they would meet in their little caravan.

*   *   *

The town looked quite different in the morning, showed up in all its glaring poverty, no castles, no grand emporiums, no vista of steps leading to pyramids, but a humble coral-coloured mosque in need of paint and a marketplace with a pitiful array of household things. The narrow streets were crammed with men, men picking their steps between the puddles, their shins bare and bony as they raised their garbs. Veiled women stood behind trestle tables, selling things, mostly dates, brown, off-brown, and caramel-coloured dates, a host of flies on each batch. Occasionally one of the women shook a plastic rattle to disperse them; from there they gathered on a neighbouring box of dates, only to be dispersed again at the sight of a customer. Everywhere there was a hunger, a fasting in the eyes, and a knowledge that this fasting would not end.

When she stopped to buy toothpaste, the woman tried selling her a saucepan and some Brillo pads, and rather foolishly she began to explain that she was in a hotel. Young boys hung about, insisting that they were her escorts, promising to get her souvenirs at special prices. She didn't want souvenirs, she didn't want these escorts, but as with the flies, she had no sooner got rid of one incumbent than another popped up smiling his habitual smile. They all looked alike. She hated herself for thinking they all looked alike.

"Fill you eyes . . . fill you eyes," they would say in some attempt at bravura or maybe flirtation. She saw brass lamps and hangings (humbler versions of the ones in the hotel), Koran cases, bags, pouches, skins bristling in the heat, giving off a faintly foul smell. She saw knuckles of amber that she longed to hold, or to gnaw. Owners stood in their doorways holding their prayer beads, giving and receiving silent signals from the boys who clustered around her. It was divined that she would like to buy a carpet and so carpets were unrolled, threaded scrolls, zigzags, mythological creatures depicting wars, love, and barbarity, rasped in the sunlight.

"Tomorrow . . . tomorrow," she said, thinking how she would walk there with Duncan, proud not to be alone, free of their pestering.

"Not now . . . not now," she said, weaving past them, and yet soon after, she allowed herself to be pushed into a shop which was crammed with objects, mostly silver, the whole place having the solemn silver hue of a church with leaded windows at vesper time. The owner was so thin and so transparent it was as if every morsel he had eaten had been wrested out of him, yet his eyes danced with glee at the possibility of bargaining. She found herself bargaining for a Koran case. He explained the procedure to her. She was to quote a price, he would suggest another price, and after much debate they would meet somewhere on the raft of bargaining. She had not the heart for it, she wanted to pay what he asked and have done with it. It was a flat Koran case with enamel on the front and a hinge up the side which would not yield. She would give it to Duncan, it would be her first gift to him. The blue lozenges of enamel seemed to slither as if they were going to melt in the glare of the sun, disappear back into the silver chasing. The bargaining was endless, entailed drinking cup after cup of mint tea, her having to admire other, costlier cases, have necklaces and pendants held before her, and even an invitation to come back at sundown.

On her way back to look for a taxi in the square, she saw three things which gave her the shivers. First she saw a young man bargaining for the dead head of a goat, a black severed head with eyes which were brown, wide open, and trusting. The jet-black hair looked silken, girlish, yet the young man dangled it like a rag, waved and shook it at the vendor, who was obviously asking too much, and then dropped it with vehemence. Farther on, on the blistering cobbles, there was the foetus of a fallen bird, a shred of yellowish near-flesh, drying in the sun, and nearby a beggar with only half a face, flies lazing in the cavity. How could she wait on love when there was suffering such as this? How could she not wait on love when there was suffering such as this? In the small taxi she sat back, appearing to be calm, and waved to people in their shacks, knowing that it was ridiculous. In the grounds of the hotel a young boy told her that there had been a message for her. He was the same boy who had brought the fresh supply of roses and for a small tip brought her extra ones. He was nicer than the others, more amenable. She ran to the desk, wondering what this message would be. The manager was in an inner room consulting figures, and as she called out to him, a telephone rang, which he picked up languidly and spoke into at length. Coming out, he looked at her askance, as if the idea of a message was a fantasy on her part.

"*Communiqué*," she said, to which he shook his head and then put a phone on the desk thinking she wished to use it. Suddenly, in halting French, she asked if she could go on the coach to the airport to meet her friend. "The coach is *complet*," he said with such sternness that she dared not plead.

Over at the pool she stared down at the water, and beneath it at the tiles, which seemed to sidle about, breaking free of the thin lines of cement which sagged like bits of wet rotted string. People sat reading and sunbathing, many of them milk-white like herself, but none as restless as she. HAMMAM—BATHHOUSE. Seeing the sign she decided that she would have a hammam, be beaten with twigs and at least pass some time. The attendant was standing outside on tennis balls, exercising the soles of her feet, her body swaying back and forth with the ennui of jelly.

"Hammam," Nell said, pointing to the sign above the door, but still the woman chose not to understand her. She thumped the sign to emphasise her need. The attendant did not like that, seemed appalled by such urgency, and took her time before getting off the tennis balls to fetch the little-used pack of ticket stubs from inside the door.

"Why?" Nell asked, impatience welling up in her whole body.

"*Bientôt*," the woman said.

"Why?" she asked again, and eventually resigned herself to going back over the stepping-stones and through the garden, whose beauty now was suffocation itself, made her itch, then through the endless succession of salons with their foul-smelling hangings, to the desk to get the ticket. A young girl in a purple outfit gave her the ticket and said she hoped she was enjoying her stay. It was their serenity, their insouciance which galled her most.

In the hammam she lay on a burning board watching the steam run down the walls and form rivulets on her body. The floor itself sizzled. She had gone in in her bare feet and had had to go back to get clogs, which didn't fit. There was no one to help. The board was burning her. Stationed against the wall were three buckets which should obviously be filled with cold water, waiting to douche her, but this was not happening, as the attendant had left. Lying there in the heat, she tried to imagine their lovemaking, felt only trepidation, nagging fear that perhaps he did not desire her, that he desired others—those brittle, blond creatures who trailed him, followed him to her house, but whom in the end he eluded by falling asleep. Yes, he always fell asleep and thereby remained with her, and the sight of him on her sofa, in the lamplight or in the dawn, brought to her mind the heartfelt line of a song about a hero "wrapped in white linen" as if love for her was bound up with death. These were dark thoughts and not to be countenanced. Only fear made her baulk, and once they were together she would open up. She had only to think of the hibiscus and its surreptitious unfolding.

"*Entrez*," she said to the tap on the door. It was a young girl with a telegram on a tray. She knew what it would say before opening it, yet entertained some mad hope, some dreg. In the steam she could not read the print easily and had to step outside, where the girl put a towel over her at once.

CAN'T COME. MADE TWO PROMISES BOTH TO TRANSPIRE ON THE SAME MOUNTAIN, she read, and looked at the girl, thinking that from the heat and this news she was going to faint. What time did the coach leave for the airport? was what she heard herself ask in two languages.

"Soon, madam, soon," the girl said, and was gone.

Taking another towel and her clothes, she ran after her, to catch up with her to beg her to help her pack, because in this state she would not be able to do it herself. Instead, she found another young girl who wore a white apron and cap and was obviously from the kitchen, and of her now she begged, showing such dementia that the girl looked at her with slight shame, a shame that said, "You are not a woman . . . you must bear your pain in silence, in reserve . . . the way we bear ours."

"Can you help me?" she said, promising some money, and together they hurried back across the grounds, where all the birds seemed united in one stoical chorus and the word they seemed to say was "Philadelphia." The girl packed slowly, obviously shocked, though uncomprehending of her mad tirade on the phone as she asked when the telegram had been delivered and where it had been lying all day and why she had not had it sooner. Then she slammed the phone down, repeating what the manager had just said: "Unfortunately, madam, we are only human and we erred."

The girl was looking with wonder at the clothes, her makeup brushes and the Koran case, looking at them keenly as if she coveted them, and though she wanted to give her one of them, she couldn't do it, her heart had congealed. How she hated those mountains now, cursed them, mountains that she had seen rosy at dawn, then blue with salted crests, and now growing black, a black haze over them, because night was coming on and she was leaving them forever.

The bungalow was billed for seventy-two hours until they found a replacement.

"Shit, *merde*," she said to the manager, who merely waited for her to sign the traveller's cheques, and then carefully, methodically, he pressed a stamp on the green sheet of paper. As she went down the steps to the waiting coach, a young boy rushed after her with a bill for the hammam.

"No, no," she said, berating the pokey little room, the ill-fitting clogs, no attendant to wait on her, and the telegram, then as she remembered its suddenness, its brutality, beads of sweat and tears ran down her body. The boy stood there motionless, just waiting to be paid. Finally she took the money out and flung it on the ground.

"*Malade*, madam," he said, and looked at her without pity. *Malade* indeed. She slunk into the back of the empty coach and on the journey now saw barren earth, thorn-strewn with flocks of goats and sheep like skeletons from the Old Testament, and women bent over their weeding as if they had dropped from their mothers' wombs onto the very parched stretches of land that all their lives they would be tied to. How could she weep at the loss of a lover? She hated such weakness. It was as if she had learned nothing and still believed in transubstantiation through another.

*   *   *

Duncan's house was in darkness, a pile of mail on the hall floor and milk bottles on the step. At the theatre where he worked, no one could help her either. Stagehands who had been to her parties shrugged, said they hadn't a clue. He was missing. He often did that. There had been trouble, part of the set had collapsed on the opening night and the play was postponed. She wrote him a note, which she handed to the doorman and then retrieved. It was far too supine.

Then it was on to the several pubs in the vicinity of his house. In some of them she stopped and drank. She drank vermouth, and after two or three she was flushed with the notion that he would walk in. The drink did that: it brought him nearer, even allowed her to have conversations with him in which she said she understood what his other troth on the mountain meant and yet forgave him. In one of these places the barman, who was young, talked to her and gave her free drinks. He was fresh from home and thinking already of going back for Christmas.

"Home," she said. Every day she put a greater distance between herself and her past, believing that if she could forget it, she would be cured of this devouring loneliness. Yet something about the barman's voice, his eagerness, the way he already envisaged Christmas Eve—the candle in the scooped turnip, neighbours dropping in—made her long to be part of it. He had his ticket already booked, a cheap fare on the night boat.

On the third evening after she arrived, she knew he had news, knew by the beam on his face. Duncan was in a dive that was closing down. A builder had bought it and was going to sell it for offices, so a few of Duncan's pals were holing up there, finishing up all the drink.

It was in a basement in Leicester Square, dark as the Catacombs. He was at a table with three men, and they were all dazed. He squinted as she came in, as if he did not recognize her. The rain on her green nap coat and on her hair clung like a halo.

"I was just passing," she said, knowing that she should not have come.

"Been to any good parties?" he said, as if she were some casual acquaintance, or the barmaid, and then added that parties were the *axis mundi.*

"Axis who?" one of his friends called out. He was a big man with a strawberry face and startled eyes.

"Shut up, Ahab," Duncan said, and asked her if she believed that the axis mundi that ran through the cosmos connected heaven to earth and earth to hell. He was hard, like flint.

"I got the telegram," she said sheepishly.

"You did?" he said, excited, as if it were something pleasing. "Which mountain?" he said, then laughed, adding that it must be Dante Alighieri's purgatorial mountain, since it was not the mountains of fucking Mourne.

"Bollocks," the man with the strawberry face said.

"Duncan," she said, as if by saying his name softly she could induce him to look at her, to answer her. "Could I talk to you for a minute?"

"Talk. Shit," he said, a wounded look in his eyes, blue eyes that strove to tell her something, something he could not remember because it hurt too much. That was the worst thing—she was there to befriend him, and yet he was repelled by her. The big man reprimanded him, said it was no way to treat a lady, and, rising, dusted one of the kitchen chairs with his cap, begging her to sit, offering hospitality. She sat, thinking, If I wait, Duncan will melt; something in him will soften, and it will be like before. A man she knew named Andrew was among them, lolling in his motor coat and so hazed he thought she was a dancer and kept calling her Vicky. The third man was very young, very affable, and seeing her nerves, he tried to make up for it by pinching a stuffed fox that was on the counter. It was an old, frowzy fox and in jest someone had draped a tea cloth over it, so that it mimicked a waiter or a waitress. The whole place had a look of abandon. There was a stack of cutlery in an empty refrigerator tray, along with a ball of uncooked pastry that had gone mouldy. A hand-done sign said DRINK NOW AND AVOID THE CHRISTMAS RUSH. Another read THINK IS NEWS AND THINK IN LOOS. There was bric-a-brac on the upper plywood shelf—an accordion, a shillelagh, and some black pots—reminders of his and her upbringings, and unwisely she referred to them.

"Bullshit," he said. Everything about her vexed him. To think that once he had written in purple on her tablecloth: "To love someone is measureless . . . yet we try."

"That's a fancy yoke," the young boy said, pointing to an oblong glass case in which there were some pitiful relics of grandeur—a lace napkin, some bone-handled cutlery, and a dinner plate with matching skin-plate.

"It is," she said, swallowing her tears.

"Place your order: bacon, egg, black pudding," he said, smiling at her. With a stick of chalk he wrote her order on a blackboard that was wedged into the crook of the fox's arm.

Not knowing how to get up assuredly was what prevented her from leaving. Everything in her seemed to have frozen as she stared stupidly—at the fox; at an old-fashioned poster for beer, which featured roses and a lit cigar resting on the edge of a table; then at Duncan—like someone immobilized.

"Don't fucking look at me like that," he said. Her eyes moved to a slot machine; it was unlit, but in the dim light she could make out patterns of raspberries and oranges and lemons, quenched now, but at the mere click of a button all could gleam again, simulating a garish gaiety.

"I'll be off," she said, and with some spurt of courtesy, or perhaps it was relief, he rose to see her out. Her body, aching for him, almost collapsed onto him as they staggered out.

"I'm no use to you, babe," he said as he stood in the doorway, with the bruised look of a boxer, saluting passing people with a "Hello, goodbye."

"Why didn't you come?" she asked, barely restraining herself from touching him, touching his hand, which was inked. He felt it and moved away, and she saw the goodwill leaking out of him as he mettled himself.

"You're a cave woman," he said. "Ball and chain, chain and ball."

"All women are cave women. They have to be," she said.

Then he flinched, a flinch so painful that she thought his temples might just split. It was painful to see him touched by some traces of love but touched differently to her, and watching, she thought, Don't say it, don't think it, don't even form the thought, because he is already stamping it out, which he was. A soft whistle to prove it.

"Would you sort of wave to me if ever we meet?" he called as she hurried away.

The rain had stopped, but lugs of water deep enough to sail toy boats in swished in the gutter as the buses and cars sped vengefully past. The city sky was spinning itself into a winterish lilac haze, prettier by far than anything in the street, which was a mad gallop of feet and faces, a newspaper vendor yelling some significant event, yelling unintelligibly, as he tried to thrust folded newspapers like javelins into the hands of the passing throng. She did not want to go back to her house. She did not know where she wanted to go, but it was not home. Cold city. Black city. Void.

You walk around Leicester Square and you see slabs of food through windows; you see ketchup and wounded faces, cracked faces, avid faces, sharks; you turn into a side street and you see litter; you see an old radio disembowelled and you turn back and go down the main thoroughfare, thinking you will take your place among the crowd, you will not lurk in side streets; you see the newspaper man again—or is it his double shouting and jutting the folded javelins of ephemera into passing hands—and you see a sign above a theatre and an arrow leading to yet another theatre and you think, Gold, gossamer, the spell of make-believe. You go past the theatre and past a seedy rifle gallery where people, mostly men, are whiling away the hours, and you see in their faces the shreds of their unlived aspirations, and then a bisection offers two streets—in one menus, half rained on, beer froth, a balalaika in the distance, faint, like a shell held to the ear; the other street nobler by far, with a huge stone gallery in the process of being cleaned, part ashen, part charcoal, and then a church, with steps that you could ascend, but no, the thing is not to settle but to walk, to keep walking, sometimes to halt at a shop entrance; you read signs about cut-price cruises, then more ketchup and varnished Minnie Mouse tables, and on a whim you risk the pedestrian crossing and plunge out with the multitudes, who seem to have somewhere to go. Above all, you walk, and you mutter to avoid the rattles and conscience of house and home. Cold city. Black city. Bustling city. Void.

15

But this was morning, morning in which loneliness and hesitation were going to be wiped away, the autumn flowers fresh and moist as if just sprinkled, the winter creeper—periwinkle it was called—like drizzle over the rockery, the last of the roses lording it, blithely. They were flowers and creepers then, but later on they would become creatures, breathing, murmuring, miaowing like cats, and much, much later the rose petals would tumble down her body, in a wild wanton cavort. She could cancel it, but something stopped her. What that something was, she could not say. The auguries were bad. There was her dream, for instance, simple, breathtakingly simple. In the dream she was a little girl endeavouring to walk or run herself out of existence, through meadow, marsh, and bog towards the horizon, beyond the edge of the world, into where she designated heaven. Heaven. She was on her way to school in the dream, satchel braced across her shoulders, all the familiar sights—stone walls, gates, milk pails, cabbage heads turquoise and mottled with slug holes, the near and not so near barking of dogs, and the voices of people saluting or growling at each other. It happened just beyond the old workhouse, her brain came tumbling out of her skull and landed on the roadside next to a clump of dock leaf, a small grey shirring thing. People converged to look at it, to speculate on what it was. Some thought it was a spinning top, and soon they began to dance on it, great clodhopping footsteps and yodels of mirth. She could hear its whirr, because although she was brainless, one strand of thinking was left to her, mindful of the calamity that was happening. At moments the brain, endeavouring to escape the stampede, the hobnailed boots, and so forth, flew up into the air, spiralled, but someone caught it, some pair of hands collared it and returned it for the rustic frolic. The dream told her everything and yet she ignored it.

As the doctor came in, she saw how pale, how remote he was, and she longed with all her being to embrace him, as if his paleness and his coldness could be warmed, irradiated by her ardour. Instead, she took his coat, led him to the sitting room, and, pointing to the rocking chair, said he might like to sit and look at the river while they chatted. It was quiet on the river, one of those lulls; a few tugs being trailed along, swans in all their stateliness, and the water itself with a brackish colour to it. Perhaps they could discuss the wisdom of what she was about to do. He had shown her the testaments of others, garbled, fragmented, grotesque bulletins. One man described eating his own teeth, chewing them with their shreds of gum attached but getting nowhere. Another described a skeetering tobaggan ride: winter, whizzing down a winter slope and coming smack into the bark of a tree, meeting it with such an impact that his forehead received pieces of moss, bark, and so forth, these impedimenta stuffing themselves willy-nilly into the cavity of split forehead. When he went home to be nursed, his mother, who was scrubbing a floor, stood up, slapped his cheek fiercely, and asked what craziness he had been up to. A working mother in a council house in Aberdeen simply did not have the time for catastrophe or for moss. Yes, there were testaments of those people who had made the journey and there was her dream, and yet she sat, managing a little smile while he administered it to her from the phial. It was colourless and tasteless. Yippee. It would have no effect at all. How could it, a colourless, tasteless nothing. She would go off to sleep like a child. Blanketstown Tram. She would have done the thing without having to do it, and he would love her or at least grow closer to her, creep into her bed beside her, take her silently, oh so silently, but with such intent, and then slip away again and be the doctor that she saw once a week to have the molars taken out of her brain.

She knew that he desired her, sensed it the moment they met. He had been brought to one of her parties, eyes large, shiny, miscreant, as he looked about and said, "It's not like London . . . it's like . . . it's like Russia."

"It's like Russia," she said back.

He followed her around, and when they sat together they were already a little smitten, quoting Baudelaire and his sick flowers. He would be the decipherer of her angst, the seer who looked into the fevered but oh so juicy crevices of her being; he would fuse with her, his albatross whose eggs were sweet, and yes, they would make a mad journey together to the heart of the forest, the elixir vitae. They sat, exchanging those moribund flowers, shivering, their eyes meeting, the bones of their knees, the flank of their thighs, the pillar of their shoulders, all touching, all supporting each other, like fallen trees in a forest which entwine as they fall and prop each other up. His wife came in from the garden and threw a glass in her face, then flounced about asking all and sundry to consider the humiliation that she was made to suffer. No one replied, since everyone knew that she had tarried in the garden with the seducer, a man whose boast was that he needed very little in life, his *raison d'être* was simply to stroke pussy, any pussy, English, European, Oriental, black; to stroke and tease and re-stroke and watch the woman break, the face going into a million contortions, the wild succession of yodels, so that she was only cunt, everything else a painted façade.

"Pay no notice . . . pay no notice at all," he had said with regard to the flung glass. She didn't. She sat, knowing that she was one with him and he with her.

Sometime later he went into the garden and lay down in the dew, to revive himself. People stood over him, made jokes, wondered if he should be covered with a blanket or if he should be left to sleep while his wife, who was now the ministering wife, asked herself what she was doing married to a drunkard. There was a setback before they left. He couldn't find his keys.

"The Witch has hidden them," she said, looking at Nell, then stormed around the house looking for them. He looked, too, looked under chairs, put his hands beneath cushions, looked in his wife's handbag but could not find them. His wife turned his pockets inside out, and coins and toffee papers fell onto the floor. His pockets had holes in them.

"Has she sucked your keys as well as your cock?" she asked, and tapped his body smartly as she searched it. Eventually the keys were found in the garden, where he'd been lying.

When she saw him in his consulting rooms the following week, he was withdrawn, his fretful expression saying, "Can't you see I am involved in an inner dissertation," yet by the next week he was all laughter, splitting with laughter, and the following week expounding his tenuous, silken sutras. He had replaced Duncan or the need for a Duncan in her affections. He was the precursor who would bring her to herself. Not once did she admit that what she sought was her own ruin. Not once do we admit.

But she was doing it now, or about to do it, embarking on this escalation, this vertigo, that would bring them together. Watching him pour it, she felt that she could still save herself. Yet, like nectar she took it, drank it back, believing she would be spared. It was not long before it began to work. A lurch, inside her brain, as if blood were either being poured into it or tapped from it, or both.

"Doctor," she called, but the words came out in a splutter. Then she looked up and saw that he had become a rat; he was Dr. Rat, perched on her velvet prayer chair, his bristles bristling rhythmically, the face however still human, the white features like a papier-mâché mask above the furry tuxedo.

She stood up to go to him, or perhaps to run from him, but fell and believed herself to be falling down into a hideous, oozing cavern. She was on the floor, her parquet floor, crawling, then felt his bristled arm drag her along. The room revolved like a big wheel, and she was powerless within it, pitched hither and thither, the terror growing as the room, the cave she was in, began to bulge, then contract, so that even as she was being hurtled, she was also being swallowed. Prayers and curses in an awful conjunction shot out of her, but were not heard. He was saying something. What was he saying? His voice a murmur in the midst of many voices and the room itself a sucking sea. Her chaise longue reeled on its buckling casters and received her like a groaning corpse. He had thrown her onto it. Her sight had gone, too, the eyes full of a viscous stuff, so that like a blind person she put her hands out to fumble for her bearings. Then the visitations—faces, mouths, a pair of floating lips complete with porter-foamed moustache and Dr. Rat dancing to his own esoteric reveries. She made lunges to get to him, but fell back each time. Men, women, freaks half man and half woman, and sundry animals began to pant and stalk over her. Then came the seducer, the long black whisker that jutted from his nostril getting in the way of the botched copulation that he was trying to effect. Angels looked on. They had clung to the curtain pole, their sussurations quick and gossipy.

"Bring me back ... bring me back," she howled. He paid no heed. The cries that she sent to him were like broken masonry falling about the room. He was in his own trance, but paused for an instant to say something. She was to breathe. Did he not see that she was submerged in this swamp and that breathing did not come into it? She heard her clock chime from the kitchen, such a pretty chime, a memory of certainties. That was the worst of it. The world she had been hurtled from and longed to return to was just there, a shaving away, but an eternity away. She was going down, down into the deeper circles of it, it now becoming a hell, the flames fluctuating between flame and blood, so that she was roasting one minute and chilled the next.

"Oh, the bastards, the bastards, this is how they do it, they dampen you so that you don't cook to a cinder," she said, though of course the words came out as a slobber. She could taste blood, just as she could taste fire; her mother's maybe, or her mother's mother's, or a more distant matrix. He was hauling the big gilt mirror across the room, then holding it in front of her so that she could see herself. Her face was contorted, purple, and her eyes fleshy sockets. Why was he showing her this raw besmeared creature?

"Go away ... go away," she said to herself, and then a greater swoon took hold of her and she went into a deeper chasm, calling on God, shouting God's name, cursing God for her mad mad history. A bit of her, it must have been a hand, yes, it was a hand, reached towards him, but he was not there, and instead she gripped the wing of the chaise longue in order to be saved. The wood was soft, almost liquid, and as she clutched it, she felt herself to be the smallest, most insignificant morsel alive, no more or less than the ribbony shred of existence that she once was. It would last forever. Forever. She begged. Her hands and eyes sent myriad messages to him. Only he could save her, if only he'd choose to, but he did not choose, he danced, allowing himself to admire his glacial features in the mirror that was now propped against the wall. He was joyous, mournful, happy, sad, caught up in an amethyst haze, Narcissus bewitched by his own meanderings. The father-shaman-son-lover that dallied with her was not with her now.

There was a moment when she thought the worst was over, because she was aware of having a body, of bodily things. Her inner thighs were damp. Had she peed? Had she disgraced herself in front of him, him for whom she dreamed rose essence? Attempting some sort of apology, she found herself hauled back again into the dungeons—voices, flames, freaks, making mayhem with her. It came and went. Vignettes of her room, and then the denizens, going out to places that were too far to come back from, like those creatures in legends, transformed and banished indefinitely.

She knew it was over as soon as she became conscious of her breath. She thought of both lungs as little oranges expanding. It was a short jerky breath, but still a breath, and she smiled at the faithfulness of it and said, "I am alive . . . I have returned."

"You see now why they call it a trip," he said, the faint inscrutable smile on his face as he mused inwardly.

"It was awful, awful," she said, horrified by his remoteness, his aplomb. He was looking at his watch.

"How long was it?" she asked, at the same time feeling her bones to make sure that they had not dissolved.

"Five and a half hours," he said. She would remember that, when the bill came a week later.

"Am I over it?" she asked feebly.

"I think so," he said, and suggested that she call a friend, announcing that he would soon have to go. A photograph of Paddy looked earnestly at her, a proud, lonely, angry little boy in an off-white rough-knit sweater. It had been taken under the arch of an ornamental door, and framed as he was by white stucco, he had a patrician look. She wondered aloud if it would be a good idea to telephone her children. He couldn't say, it was not something he could give an opinion on. He could do nothing for her except take his leave. She did not see him out, her limbs were not sturdy enough, but after he had gone she got down on her hands and knees and went all around the room saying hello to each object as if she had been away for a duration, which she had. Spire, transpire, perspire, she heard herself say. Where did these words come from? Why did the seaweed matting look so green, and why was it pulsing? The long sheets of glass in the bow window seemed to shudder within the stout white frames. The glass was the green of gooseberries, gooseberries such as she had once eaten in an orchard.

She went out to see the flowers. Some were beautiful, some threatening. The rosebuds were little fingers, fingers poking at things, the colours much more ravishing than she had ever remembered. Colours and petals pressed on one another, leaching. She longed to be in the country in a meadow, the swards warm and high, someone beside her, cradling, cradling her. It was all she wanted. If he had held her, she would not be in fragments now. There was a sunset, tributaries of red and so forth, but it was too far away. Maybe her children were watching the same sunset. She could picture them in fancy costumes, distant from here, their voices not their own voices at all but lilts, the mingled lilts of dead children. Children.

The telephone rang. It was dark and perhaps it had been dark for a long time. The evening had gone by, and now this black instrument was recalling her, with its queer arresting sound. She felt apprehensive about holding it, as if it might be soft and sinuous like a panther, but no, it was a telephone made of Bakelite and without sinews. She blurted into it, not knowing what she was going to say.

"Cut it off the carpet, cut it off the carpet," she said.

"Sorry," a timid little voice said, and rung off. It was Paddy. He had not recognised his mother, his own berserk mother. It rang again, almost immediately, and Paddy was asking very formally to speak to his mother.

"I am your mother," she said.

"Mama," he said. She could feel the shock in his voice as she tried to push herself into some semblance of normality.

"Cut it off the carpet," she said again, to let him know that she had said it previously, though it was devoid of meaning.

"What's wrong, Mama?" he asked.

"Just a little joke," she said.

"I only have a minute," he said. "I've put all my coins in and Norrie is waiting."

"Who's Norrie?" she asked, as if that could save the situation.

"Oh, a boy," he said, and then blurted out the reason for his calling.

"I am financially embarrassed," he said, his words stilted because of his guilt. Then she heard the first pip, and his voice very concerned now shouting, "Mama, Mama, please tell me what's wrong with you ... Is it Dad?" and then they were cut off. She held the black Bakelite thing for some time, as if his voice or even Norrie's would trickle through. Then she tried dialling the number, but the digits began to slide into one another, so using the corner of her handkerchief damped with spittle she began to clean the circles and the dust-grimed digits, believing that was why she could not reach anyone. By the time she did dial the number there was no answer, as they were all gone from the quad, up to their dormitories. For a while she stood there willing that someone ring her, that a voice, any voice in the entire world, would spare her a jiff. Then she did it, knowing of course that it was what she had intended to do all along.

"I've lost my marbles," she said to Dr. Rat, who did not relish being disturbed.

"I did it for you," she said tenderly, so tenderly that he must feel it, he must yield to it. He said nothing. She could feel him cogitating and she prayed that he might come over for an hour, just an hour, to see her through the tail end of it, to bring her back, to steady her, to say in a quiet voice, You are all right now, you have come back from hell. That was what she wanted, what she waited for. He said nothing, nothing at all, and soon the line went dead.

"Bastard, bastard," she said, visiting every vengeance on him, vengeances such as she had not known were in her, the secateurs of her thoughts cutting him where it mattered most, a poker, rose-red and with a dusting of ash, to gouge his eyes out, a cloven hand to disfigure the Christ-like face, to strip it of its grace, so that he would not be desirable again. "Bastard." Every cup and jug that hung from the dresser repeated it after her and jigged convulsively.

The words wrote themselves. They larrupped out of her like paint, spewing walls, ceilings, and mirror, the mirror in which he had shown her her tortured self. "Dear Mother," it began. The dear seemed comical under the circumstances.

Dear Mother,
    Brickbats and tiles, say the bells of St. Giles. I was with cousins of yours, distant cousins; they thought I would be pleasant and not the mope I was. I was a pest crying all the time, so that they sent me out for walks, and passing that restaurant, getting the bisto gravy smell, a terrible hunger gripped me, not just a body hunger or a mouth hunger, but a mind hunger, a longing for you, made all the worse when I saw cakes, like princesses in their ruffles, sugared and decorated, some with coconut, some with fine icing, some with chocolate flakes, and the smell, how can one forget it, it was more than a smell; it went right down into the taste buds, through them, into the flesh, the weltering flesh. I could taste the coffees or the coconut or the vanilla or whatever, without the satisfaction of it, and going back to the cousins sooner than expected and being made decidedly unwelcome, I was put to do some household chores, making beds and so forth. I wrote you a letter which spoke of my misery but didn't know how to post it. I was not resourceful enough to find a post office and couldn't ask them for a stamp. They made remarks

about me, imitated my snivels, my accent, asked if I was not going a bit too far.

"I want to go home!" I would say.

"I want to go home!" they would say.

As a result of their having been so cruel to me, a bicycle outing was proposed as a sop. One of the girls—there were three in all—one of them suggested that some evening she and I go to the outskirts of the city on an expedition. They did, you see, try to be pleasant on occasion, to make up for having been so sarcastic and so mocking, and hence the bicycle ride, a perilous passage through busy streets, to the outskirts to look at bungalows, pebble-dashed bungalows, named after seas and rivers and cities in Italy and so forth, ordinary abodes with ordinary gates and chip-stone paths, and she remarking from time to time how pretty it all was. She also stopped her bicycle to crack an egg—can you believe it—in case she got weak. She had brought a few eggs in a basket and now cracked a raw egg and swallowed it directly from the shell. I was disgusted. She was keen on some man. I'd overheard her and her sister talk about him, talk about the mesh of hair on his chest, and probably she wanted to look healthy for him. She had a pasty face but could look good at night, in lamplight. Her beauty surfaced in the evening.

On that bicycle ride there was a distinguished look to her, in her dark purple tweed and a brooch that looked like crystallised violets, which I coveted. From time to time she would ask very sweetly if I was enjoying myself. She could be sweet, they all could when they wanted to, but one never knew when that would be. It was out there it happened. I felt the saddle damp, but there was no rain, and then I felt my legs damp and thought I had wet myself from the fear, what with the cars and buses and lorries that roared past us. Luckily she dismounted. I thought it was to crack another egg, but no, it was a breather, and also for me to see the electricity plant that had been recently installed. Presently I found out. To stand and look at this electricity installation was one of the stupidest things I could have imagined, since we knew nothing about it, but for me it was a chance to investigate this dampness. I slipped my hand under my frock, brought out the fingers, and saw blood.

"Jesus, blood!" I roared. She saw it and couldn't believe that I didn't know what it signified, that you hadn't told me, prepared me, couldn't understand the hysteria. Oh, it was real hysteria. I wouldn't move. I stood, legs glued together, to try and stop this awful flow, and looking at the saddle, I vowed that I would not get on it for anyone or anything, not even her, who I knew would bully me.

First she resorted to kindness, solicitude, said that we would go home and get napkins, the shop ones, not the ones you use, but I refused, repeating that I would not budge from there. Then she tried to be sensible, said it was natural, a big moment, and that I was a woman now. Again she wondered why you had not told me. I had of course seen your napkins in the bowls of water, put there to soak, the water blood red, like the oil in the sanctuary lamp, but otherwise carnal. I did not know what gave them that hue, what butchery had gone on.

So there we were beholding a ridiculous electricity station, two or three miles from the centre of the city, and I simply refusing to mount the bicycle again and she talking twenty to the dozen now, imploring. I was not afraid of her. I was beyond fear or, rather, had entered into a penumbra of fear from which there was no escape. I believed the blood was flowing, flowing wildly and weirdly out of me, and that if I moved the flow would lead to death, my own death and a memory, oh yes, a memory-death of something long before that had to do with your blood, to do with you and me. It came to me then that you did not have the heart to bear me, and it has come to me now. These things are incontestable, the source of our wisdom, the quick of our pain. There is always another, a darker secret beneath the surface of the secret we unearth. God speaks in strange ways, does he not? I wait for you. You.

Sometime around dawn she skulked out into the street, crept under houses and gardens that all seemed like fastnesses, all bleached white, like houses huddled in a seaside town. The dew on each bit of garden and each wooden gateway gave them a silent, sealed-off look. It was all sea, her mind likewise. The cars, many dilapidated, lay like sullen beasts, parked grumpily and butting into one another. Had she met someone, she might not have posted it, but she met no one, just saw the swath of a cat's tail, lifting and lowering in some sort of bestial trance, then posted the letter, regretting it even as she was doing it, yet exalting in the realisation that this would sever them forever.

16

At the midnight shop she knew that she looked hussyish by the way a man turned away from her in dismay. It must have been the lipstick, the bold fillet of red which she had applied on her way there and was no doubt smeared. The young shopkeeper was busy bringing in the things which had been on display outside—buckets, dustbins, yard brushes, and fertiliser in white plastic bags with a picture of a bog land on the front: a bog land fringed with green rushes, a loamy backward place.

"Can I help you?" he said to her, holding the handle of a broom as if it were his staff. He was a tall, thin, conceited young man who wore leather thongs on his neck and on his wrists. Usually his mother sat like a Buddha at the cash register, her small eyes animating whenever she touched her fingers to the till.

"Eilert Lövborg with vine leaves in his hair," Nell said to the young man, the words tripping off her lips.

"Excuse me," the young man said.

"Eilert Lövborg with vine leaves in his hair," she said more flirtatiously. He must know Hedda Gabler, the Colonel's daughter, with her tantrums and her hauteur.

"You want a cigarette?" he said.

"I wake renewed by death, a shepherd's coat thrown over me," she said, throwing off the raincoat that she had put on over her shoulders. Yes, he was beginning to see. He followed her to the back of the shop and watched as she hid behind the ribbon-like straps of plastic that fronted the long refrigerator, at moments peeping out and saying, "Boo!"

"Where's your ma-ma?" she said rather tartly.

"Upstairs in bed . . . she has troubles . . . Uterus," he said.

"Uterus!" she said, and shrieked with laughter, tempted to tell him what she was thinking, which is that she wanted to come, to come in his shop, to come all over the comestibles, over the yard brushes and wheelbarrows, to come all over him in his Hamlet black, to come all over the world. She could see semen, she could taste it; it shone, it frothed, it glistened, it was everywhere except in her.

"You know that song," she said, still laughing.

"Which song?" he said. He was trying to keep some semblance of steadiness because of the occasional customer that came in. Two tramps stood in the doorway and begged for a bread roll, but were refused. No Saint Francis of Assisi he.

"The song about the pretty boy," she said.

"You find me pretty?" he said, and smirked.

"Very," she said. "Very, very pretty." She would seize him, take him as soon as he put the catch on the door and pulled the blind down over the window that was chalked with prices and slashed prices. He was what she wanted, heaven-sent or hell-sent, his thin eel-like body, his mean close-together eyes, his conceit. Then he lit two cigarettes and, before handing her one, blew the smoke directly into her face, saying by this gesture that, yes, he understood she was a streetwalker and was willing to go along with it.

"Do you mind my stubble?" he asked her then, looked at her, saw the answer, and pressed her against the edge of the refrigerator, his body flush with hers.

"You want fucky?" he asked. Yes, that was what she wanted. She wanted him to shut shop and take her, saw herself as bog hole wet and slushy, bog hole which he would ride and stampede like a mountain pony. She could not wait.

"My math-her," he said, and lifted his weary hazel eyes towards the ceiling.

"She won't know what it is."

"She will know. Everyone knows what fucky is," he said, and snickered. She did not want him in her own house—the floor, the street, anywhere, but not her own house. Her own house had seen enough madness for one day. He saw her hesitate, and mindless now of the risk of customers, he put his hand shovel-wise over her crotch and said that he was very good at making the womans happy.

"How come?" she said.

"I make them happy . . . I make them crazy . . . First I eat their pussy like cake and then I lick it and then I make them grovel," he said, pinning her, until she had agreed to let him come home.

In the garden he chased her round and round, then laid her down on the wet earth, took off her stockings and knickers, and put a rose inside her, shaking her wildly so that the petals dispersed, asking her to tell him when she first fancied him and what it was she had most fancied about him, his skin or his eyes, or the way he dressed, or his hair. In the bedroom he looked at her clothes, her possessions, asked if her jewelry was real or plate, opened the wardrobe, took out a dress of hers, and then put the green glass necklace into her mouth, making her gnaw on bead upon bead, as a baby might.

"Put it on," she said, referring to a dress that he had taken out. It was her best grey dress, chiffon, with cut velvet patches and a sash. The excitement which she had felt even half an hour ago was dwindling. The paroxysms, the orgy that she imagined when she ran there to solicit him and came home across the road cleaved to him, refusing to let go, even as he bent to get the key from inside the geranium pot where she kept it and was foolish enough to let him know of it. But now it was different; she was able to see things clearly, herself naked save for a long necklace, the beads of which were like a baby's rattle, see him in her dress, looking girlish, desire waning with each second, as she longed now only for privacy and for sleep. How could she have strayed this far?

"What's happened?" he said. He sensed the change in her, the cooling; possibly her eyes no longer shone with the feverish glitter, and she was not talking so rapidly or so disjointedly, talking about Saskia, the second wife of Rembrandt, describing the golden

sleeves that Saskia wore, that Rembrandt painted, sleeves like cor-
ridors leading to the richness, the goldenness, the Saskianess
within.

"Eilert Lövborg with vine leaves in his hair," she said airily. If
she could keep to the same words, the same gibberish, she could
keep the momentum, make him believe that what she had felt
when she first sought him out was still true, rampant within.

"Talk fucky to me," he said as he knelt above her, and she
looked at him, frightened, believing that if she did not go through
with it, he might become vicious.

"I don't even know your name," she said.

"Me, I am called Boris," he said.

"We don't have to talk now, Boris, we can just make love," she
said coaxingly, yet felt herself stiffen, as if frosted, but went on to
deceive him with the lewd words he longed to hear. All, all, belying
the housewife in her nightgown, a calico nightgown that he had
asked her to put on, to afford him the pleasure of tearing it off
again. He was feeling cheated and he said so. Where was the she
that had frisked with him in the garden, played tag, lay down and
allowed him to stuff the rose petals into her, while she said these
fucky things? Where was that she?

She claimed to be there and gave a little shiver to simulate fresh
desire.

"Am I the cat's pyjamas?" he asked with a leer.

"You're the cat's pyjamas," she said, and smiled.

"Suck my cock," he said sulkily.

"In my own time I will," she said, manifesting a confidence
that she did not feel. He liked that. He said he liked a woman
with spunk and that it was true that they were not in such a
great hurry and that he might smoke a cigarette. Rising to fetch
some, he urged her to cover herself, not to go about the house
naked, in case neighbours should see in. His puritan streak
struck her as absurd.

"I'll have a cognac as well."

"There isn't any."

"Bring me whatever booze you have."

*   *   *

In the morning she felt strange, aghast, as she recalled moments of the previous evening: going there, soliciting him, all that talk about Eilert Lövborg and the vine leaves in his hair.

"As you sow, ye are like to reap." The words, as if on a sampler, swung into vision, stitched by an unseen but all-seeing hand. Who was that? She could guess. The woman to whom the mad, irate letter had been sent. She was holding an egg on a tablespoon, to see how quickly the water evaporated. He was fussy about his boiled egg. It was to be exactly three and a half minutes. He did not like it hard and he did not like it soft, he liked it the way he liked his women, a bit of both, and here he winked. The clock had stopped from the battering she had given it the night before, after she had telephoned Dr. Rat.

"You had a good time," he said.

"We both had a good time," she said, having a presentiment that he was going to ask her for something. She hoped it was not money. She would give him the candlestick that he had admired or else the red ashtray of Venetian glass. All she wanted was for him to be gone now, and the memory of him, too, knowing that at night when she came from work she would scour the whole house, banish all traces of him and hence her transgression.

"May I bring my girlfriend?" he asked.

"No."

"You'd like her . . . she is understanding, she do licky . . . then we have a threesome."

"I don't want a threesome," she said, shrieking; then collected herself, not wanting to offend him, just wanting to leave in good grace. He took her hand and kissed it then, but she knew it was a kiss in order to press his suit. He had something to ask, a favour, a very big favour, and was asking only because he liked her and because she liked him and they had had such a good time. Could he spend a week, he and Olga? They were in a squat which they had to leave and had found another squat, but could not move in just yet. The police were on to them and Olga would be deported unless she could hide.

"She can move into the shop."

"My mather," he said, irritably.

"My children will be home soon," she said. He had seen photographs of her children. He believed in their existence, their holidays, but in the meantime might he and Olga have a bed.

"It's impossible, Boris," she said.

"Just a few lousy nights," he said sulkily.

"Not here, not here," she said, consternation in her voice, in her eyes, and in the way the egg wobbled in the tablespoon.

"You are all the same . . . all you rich womans, you are all the fucking same," he said, and went out without even starting his breakfast.

17

The flowers were looking at her as if to remonstrate. They were tulips, a column of them in a large pot, a gift which an author had sent her in gratitude for the work she had done on his novel. They were yellow, and as she nodded to them she could swear that they were turning slowly in their pot of clay, slowly swivelling, so that each one for a moment gave her its undivided gaze and attention, and she gave her attention back, studying the cavity of the large yellow cups, with the little transcription of jet in the centre of each one and stamens forked. Around they went, slowly, slowly, until it was the turn of the one two-tone flower, the scarlet and yellow, which had folded its little foolish petals like wings around the green stake which had come with them, in order to keep them upright.

"Poor thing . . . you're wounded," she said, and reached to free the two petals from the wooden stake. No sooner had she done it than they reverted, and impatiently she ripped them off and laid them on her pile of papers. There were six in all and the scarlet rims were like threading that had begun to ravel.

"What's got into you?" Jan said, and peered with her narrow sluggish eyes. She was a podgy girl who shared the office with Nell and groaned about her rights. Her rights were the desk near the window and a saucer of water next to the gas fire to save her cat from the fumes. Her cat and she had been brother and sister in a previous incarnation.

"Whims," Nell said . . . "whims." To her the flowers belonged there, guardian angels of the secrets beneath them. She had kept on the slashed grey chiffon dress, the witness of her debauch, and over it she wore a long navy cardigan. Something made her keep the dress on; it was not love or liking, it was not loathing either, it was some stab at defiance, a newfound jauntiness. To crown it all, she had a love bite.

"Is that ringworm?" Jan said, peering at it, then squirming.

"You know what it is," Nell said, and playfully hid it with a long switch of wet hair. She had allowed herself to get soaked on the way to work; she had stood in the street and opened her mouth to the rain, drinking it in, thinking it a presence, a whet to her lust. In the pleats of the dress she could still feel it, cold, shivery on her bare thighs, an aftermemory of him, the delicious chastising thrill when he claimed he wanted to take her again, take her as if he had just picked her up in the street; sent her to don high heels and a mackintosh. Yes, maybe she would seek him out again and put riddance to these pinings for Duncan.

"WP is in today," Jan said ominously.

"So he is," Nell said. She knew, because his black umbrella was outside his office door. WP, P for Pickwick, was at the far end of the long corridor, in his oak sanctuary, his reading lamps shedding a steady, pellucid light, his books and papers sedulously arranged, a tetchiness towards whoever entered to disturb his slow meditative way of reading. A peer in his realm, with exquisite judgement, able to marry commerce and art. But in him, too, there was a flaw, a skeleton. This stern man, so highly thought of, formal, capable, successful, punctilious, had taken a mistress and received phone calls from her at least twice a day, lovey-dovey mush, according to the senior telephonist, who had served him for years. Not only that; he took her abroad, took her to book fairs and conferences and, horror of horrors, considered leaving his wife, his staid wife, who did charity work, his governess, his erstwhile stalwart, who had started him off. Now he did not need his wife, he needed Miss

Flight. Miss Flight, herself a career woman who nevertheless liked satin undies and very high heels, and who spoke in a feathery voice, as if she were stroking people with her breast feathers, but was quite fierce in her opinions and in her design; would collar him in the end. Oh yes, beneath that flutteriness was a second governess, far more concealed, a schemer trussed in her satin undies and her silk culottes, cooing inside them, her auburn hair perfectly coiffed and sometimes propped with tortoiseshell combs, but in a haphazard way, as if they had just slipped onto her head, so that all, all was miraculous camouflage.

Miss Flight attended the weekly lunches which were held in the boardroom that adjoined his sanctuary, lunches for authors, foreign publishers, editors, and on these occasions Miss Flight shone, as she took time to talk to both men and women, though the latter was only an expedient. She managed to linger for the extra "cuppa" with William, who flinched with nerves and excitement as soon as she said aloud, "Are you going to throw me out or are you going to give me a last cuppa?" and always the other guests made themselves scarce. Miss Flight had let it be known that she had only to lift a finger and William was helpless, a blob, a jelly. On one of those afternoons, the brown panelled door shut, its baize backing sealing off all sound, Miss Flight and William, unable to resist the brazen enticement of clandestine sex, said to hell with propriety and had a romp, and afterwards her knickers were found, dove grey, almost new, elasticised across their satin midriff. A cleaner found them under the table, where, in passion, they had been tossed by one or the other. Everyone eventually learning of it, endless debate followed among the office staff, so that there was tut-tutting, prurient whispers, laughs, staggers from the old ladies in the mailing room who had never heard such a filthy thing. The debate was this: Why did the flighty Miss Flight, who arrived with the knickers, leave without them? Why did she venture into the maw of Great Portland Street on a wintry day, down a long, raw, treeless, inhospitable thoroughfare, unless it was to go to some other swain, or perhaps to wear her shame in the taxi, her badge of recklessness, to dwell on it, luxuriate in it, like some sultana; to sit back, to loll, smoke perhaps, stretch her thin legs in their mauve fishnet and think, I am that much nearer to my goal? William, on the other hand, at the same time, had resumed work, resumed being William, his voice crisp, unimpeachable, as he pressed the bell for his four o'clock tea and digestive biscuit.

Yes, all knew of it, but very few thought any the less of him, although scrapings of pity were gleaned for his wife, the woman who did charity work and wore plain skirts and Cuban-heeled shoes and had often met Miss Flight at functions and had had conversations with her, each perhaps thinking the other to be stronger, because strength was all that counted in this contest over William. To be fucked under the table or not fucked under the table, but sedately in bed with "Did I hurt you, darling?" was routine, as routine as the digestive biscuits with his four o'clock tea, because this was a world where such things were recognised; they were calls of the flesh, more or less condoned, until the cleaner, Bea, short for Beatrice, held the offending garment on the end of her mop and said, "Wha's this, then, a hanky belonging to his dicky bird?" She also tried them over her apron and found them to be scant.

"WP wouldn't want to see you in that attire *and* barefoot," Jan said in her most affected voice, a voice that she had picked up in the theatre, where she worked as a press liaiser before coming to the publishing house. She always called herself a liaiser. She liaised about everything, food, drink, her summer holidays, and all day on the telephone she liaised with journalists, extolling the virtues and madcap habits of authors in order to get features written about them or have them paraded on television.

"He shan't mind what I wear," Nell said, also adopting an affected voice. As she turned to her task of reading, a rash of fervour and impatience possessed her. It simply would not do. These butter-wouldn't-melt heroines with peach skins and voile dresses gave her the pukes, as did the flatulent lore about castles and the effluence of steamy words that revealed the sexual twitches underneath. No. No.

> Goosey goosey gander,
> Where should he wander?

Upstairs and downstairs,
And in my lady's chamber.

She added in the margin, "You're in heat, Mrs. Gilbert, hence the vapours in your prose."

To Daphne Winterton, who loved castles and wrote endlessly about them, she said, "You would do better to introduce us to your front parlour and your china dogs, and why—because you know them, whereas you have perceived nothing of the intrigue, the blood, the clank, the ghost-stained stairs, the tumuli of warm corpses."

To the next author she was tender, indulgent. It was a woman called Millie, who said she had waited weeks to pluck up the courage to send her story. It was a synopsis of her life, the tale of an unmarried mother in Victorian England whose sweetheart was lost in action, whose illegitimate child was born in an institution, and whose life then was a round of service in big houses, nursing old people to their deaths. So many old people, so many death rattles. She asked for a ghostwriter, said her story was too near to her to tell it. To this woman, Millie, Nell wrote: "You have to be near to it to tell it, and then you have to go very far away from it to give it that enchantment that distance bestows, the infallibility of the gods. Imagine it, Millie. Imagine it like this . . . It is morning in your cottage in Somerset; your clothesline billows with a nightie, bloomers, a tea cloth; you have emptied the ash pan, filled the scuttle; buds are just beginning to fatten, and you think that the woods beyond will soon be a carpet of snowdrops, then primroses, then bluebells, so airily blue, mirage for the eye, a fillip for the heart, but . . . but the man you have waited for, call him lover, call him husband, call him bridegroom, call him what you will, he is not coming. No, Millie. We know that. You and I know that. We know that there will be snowdrops, violets, white violets, too, but the bridegroom has gone past your gate. Perhaps he died in the war, or perhaps he didn't, maybe he married someone else, your double, or emigrated to Australia, where he shears sheep and now and then has a stabbing thought of you; but he is not coming, because there is no second coming. So, Millie, take the little motif from under your pillow, or from under the linen that you keep in your oak chest, where the wood-lice scramble, and give it away, then sit with your story, your rich, raw, bleak, relentless story, the one you are so near to, too near to, and moisten it with every drop of pain and suppuration that you have, until in the end it glistens with the exquisite glow of a freshly dredged pearl. You may decide to set it anywhere, in any season, any location—an orchard, a city street, a cave—because with language you can dare, you can ruminate, you can pillage, you can weep, you can conquer, and the wonderful thing is that no one else can do it but you. It is as fundamental as motherhood, but the seed is within yourself. 'How?' I hear you ask. Simple. The sperms are the moonbeams and sunbeams and shadows of every thought, half thought, and follicle of feeling that have attended you since your first breath of hardship. Think only of big things, Millie, big, sad, lonely, glorious, archetypal things."

"You're not listening," Jan said as she tried to peer over her shoulder to see what caused such muttering, such fluency of the hand.

"Scram," Nell said, but was subjected to a bout of gossip.

"Anita got fired. Donald fired her, did it by letter, hadn't the guts to do it in person, all David's fault. Yes, he put the boot in, once his wife found out, his wife went to a Tarot reader and, would you believe it, the cow spilt the beans, told all about David and Anita, and now Anita in a mobile home, no job, no David, ghastly, ghastly; a single parent at that."

"I'm a single parent," Nell said.

"And you spoil your children," Jan said, adding that not only she but *tout l'office* concurred, seeing the way she brought them to the summer party, let them sip drinks and make edifices of all the spare glasses to play "Humpty-Dumpty had a great fall" with.

"Would you like to know what we did last night, me and my chap?" Nell said, shocked by her own overtness.

"I expect I'd die," Jan said, believing that it was Providence which, at that moment, had caused a messenger to appear with a portfolio of photographs which she was waiting for.

It was Nell's turn to get lunch that day. Something about the gleam in Jan's eyes, the little swallow of victory, unnerved her as she went out. The first sandwich shop was crowded, fat men ordering fat overstuffed sandwiches; at the second shop, the queue extended to the pavement, so she went farther on, to a more select delicatessen, and got two pieces of quiche, yellow, fluffy, eggy quiche, which they heated, then packed separately in pale yellow triangular boxes. While she waited she drank a Coca-Cola, and it seemed to her that the beads of her tongue could taste every single synthetic ingredient. Everything was at once sharp and metamorphosed. The drink, itself becoming one with the warm bubbles of blown glass, the meniscus a dipping mouth. How long would it take to wear off? Would her mind ever be fully hers again, or would it unhinge and fail her at unexpected moments? Had she bartered with the Devil? Yes, she had. Dr. Rat was the Devil; they had each desired each other with an avatar's frenzy, as if each could suck the vitals of the other.

On her desk the tulip petals were rearranged and Jan was humming.

"Telephone message for you," she said, waving a scrap of paper, adding that it was a gentleman who simply said, "Hello . . . goodbye. Hello . . . goodbye." No, he hadn't given his name, and she added tartly that if these blokes, bounders, or whatever don't want to give it, why press them.

"What kind of accent?" Nell asked blithely, because she knew it was Duncan.

"Bog," Jan said, and bit into the body of the quiche, saying that it would not be enough and where were the trimmings? He had rung from a call box.

"How do you know?"

"Because I heard the pips," she said, delighted by her skill at figuring it out.

Since the day he had got rid of her months before, in that dingy public house, they hadn't spoken; there had been no tidings of him, but quite often her phone had rung and had been put down, especially late at night. She knew in her bones that it was he, that she was on his mind, that a link existed between them, and that even these speechless phone calls were a sum-

mons to her. Often she felt him at the other end of the telephone, on the point of speaking, his nerve giving out, then
imagined his slinging it down, with a "Bullshit." Why was he at
the airport? Perhaps he was going home for a funeral. Odd that
she should be dispatching him, when in fact she was soon to go
herself. At any rate, he would be restored to her, and thinking it,
she walked about clutching her cardigan, hugging herself. The
manuscripts on which she had written her invective or her en-
couragements felt warm, as if they had just come out of an incubator, like little baby chicks.

"Why are these warm?" she asked.

"Why is the Pope a Catholic?" Jan said as she searched about in
the triangular plastic for spare crumbs of pastry and fastened them
with an index finger on which there was a piece of grimed sticking
plaster.

"Have you touched them?" Nell asked, and she could see the
envy stirring, mounting, see a face to which triumph was giving a
torrid blush.

"Think you're the bee's knees," Jan said, and bending to get the
saucer on which the water had dried, she told the gas fire, "We're
all artists, you know . . . but we don't brag about it."

"What are you talking about?" Nell asked.

"Looking down your nose—toffee nose—at these poor women,
trying to make a few bob . . . or let off steam."

"You've made copies of them," Nell said, realising now why the
pages felt warm.

"Retract that," Jan said, her face twisting with rage, and grab-
bing her knitting, she stormed out of the room, said she was not
going to put up with calumnies, was going for a walk, and when
she returned expected a written apology.

"Miss Marie Antoinette," she said. Each word soaked in bile.

I pray God that I'll never be like that, Nell thought, seeing a
moderately young woman in which only two attributes reigned,
greed and spite.

A vexed flare of the nostrils was reiterated in the thin stony
smile. She stared down at his mementos—a silver-mounted wine

cork, a photograph of his wife as a young woman, the house in London, a house where Charles Dickens had lived, and her own handwriting, wild and importunate.

"What would you have them write?" he asked, pointing to the sheaf of papers.

"Their guts," she said.

"Their guts," he said, and laughed a bitter laugh, yet conceded that she was right. He had something to add to that. When the time came and the world was to be treated to his memoirs, he would not give of his guts either, though he was as tormented as the next man. She didn't smile or didn't try to curry favour, it was too late for that.

"I suppose you despise me for that," he said, almost bitterly. He need not suppose that she didn't, since the whole office despised him for the way he strung two women along, couldn't make up his mind; even his ninety-three-year-old mother despised him, said, "Choose, William, choose one or the other . . . for pity's sake, choose." The thing was, he couldn't, he was like the camel in the fable, halfway between food and water—when he went forward, his thirst was met, and when he went backwards, his hunger was met, but never both. He looked at her so earnestly, so pitifully, and she thought she must make it as easy as possible for him.

"Will you give me a reference?" she said, smiling a weak smile so as not to make him feel too bad.

"For what?"

"For . . ."

"Good God, no, I'm not that stuffy . . . though I may seem it," and to prove it he took a whisky bottle from behind a leather-bound dictionary set, winked, poured large measures, and, with an archness that almost made her weep, said, "Here's to the next twenty or thirty or forty years."

He kept walking, partly because he was restless and partly because he had waxed sentimental, recalling the first day when he had met her in the lift by accident, this eager girl who had come in off the street to look for a job, had not even an appointment, and was pumping him for ideas. Yes, he remembered that first day and how he had been bewitched, as indeed any man would be, and she thought, How strange, he does not see me as I am at all, he sees some other, he sees freedom, he sees confidence, he sees bewitchment.

"And I've never touched you," he said with a strange, boyish innocence, a boyish nostalgia, and as if to make it respectable then, he said that if ever she needed him, if ever she was in trouble, she must come to him, she must count on that.

18

The phone was ringing as she came through the door a few evenings later, and she ran to it certain that it was Duncan. Had she not envisaged this, the tenderest of returns, his standing before her, contrite, his eyes with that beautiful heartbreaking flinch, eyes that reminded her of bits of blue ceramic stuck into the soft pebbledash of a country house to give it colour? Instead, it was a voice from home, a woman, Maisie, a neighbour of theirs. Bad news. Terrible news. Her mother had died suddenly, that morning, after feeding the chickens and the sucky calves. Died on the flag, fell down across the steps, gashing one side of her neck and jaw.

"Did she die from the fall?" Nell asked, at once assailed by the vision of the prostrate woman.

"No, love . . . her poor heart gave out," the woman said, and launched into a spiel, how her mother had been to Mass that very morning, had saluted people on her way out and bought a loaf of fresh bread, which she never had a bite out of.

"Her poor heart gave out," she said again.

"I killed her," Nell said, but there was no one to overhear it.

They were waiting for her: her poor demented father was waiting, her mother's remains were waiting, everyone was waiting. In her mind there ran a host of excuses, because she dreaded going—if she saw them she would break down, admit to her crime; yet limply and obediently, she heard herself say that she would catch the early-morning plane, and it was in this fractured state she travelled and was met by the driver, who mashed her hand in sympathy and said, "Sorry for your trouble, missis."

Her father fell over her, groaning, shouting, calling her darling, saying, "Darling, we lost the best friend we ever had." But that was not so. There was enmity between her and her mother, between her mother's effluvia and her own. The only way to come through it undetected was to sing dumb, to say nothing. The house was damp throughout, walls and windows were damp, and in the lavatory the strong smell of disinfectant made her retch. Her father waited outside for her to rejoin him. She was all he had now. A helper had put a green bow around a new roll of lavatory paper. Out of sight of him, she talked to herself, told herself to pull through, to pull through, not let the bejeebies show. They could reoccur at any minute, a face peer out of a doorknob, the floating eyes staring at her with unwonted grief; her mother's eyes? Once she found the letter, she would confiscate it and keep it till her old age, because she could not read it now.

In the kitchen there was a bustle, women making sandwiches in preparation for the mourners, who would come in after the remains were brought to the chapel. They referred to it as "remains" and not as her mother. They had put a gauze scarf around the wound, Maisie had told her that. The sandwiches were egg, flavored with mayonnaise and bits of onion. In the chapel men mashed her hand to convey their sympathy and women's embraces were crushing. "Sorry for your troubles," she heard hundreds of times, but they did not know. No one knew but herself. She was the criminal who had to pretend. The chapel, too, had its own signs of dereliction. There was an old crisscross bird's nest hanging askew from one of the rafters and the flowers on the altar were pitiful, just bits of evergreen. The wreaths on the coffin were mostly artificial, plastic configurations, a mimicry of what flowers should be, without life or breath, trumpets of death. A cold send-off to a woman who had had no warning.

Later the mourners sat around the breakfast-room table chewing the sandwiches and condoling, each one pleading with her, as if she could in some way resuscitate them. They plied her with questions, endless questions about shops in London and the prices of food, and she answered routinely, her eyes taking in all the features of the sad room: the grate without a fire but with a heap of ashes over which cigarette butts were flung; dust congealed on the buttons of the corduroy-covered bed chair, scums of it on the picture frames; and letters everywhere, but not the one she wanted. She must find it, she must. Every time she stirred, someone made her sit down; they engulfed her, they needed her cheer. One admired the fitted dress she wore and another said, "There was no need to gild the lily." She thought that if they had had the merest inkling of her transgressions they would lock her up, which is why she must go home immediately, invent some emergency, be deaf to the entreaties of her father, who was begging her to stay.

Her father drank his tea from a saucer, dipped a currant biscuit in it, and kept groaning; neighbours tried to hush him, reminding him of the good years, his wife a queen, their beautiful house, their harvests, his wife a daily communicant, the chutney she made. A rug was put over him to comfort him, a rug which he threw off like a rearing colt. He needed a doctor, an injection, a tonic, anything to take him out of his misery. He roared. He roared as an animal might, refusing to stop; the women took turns clamping their hands over his mouth, saying he was going too far, too far altogether. "Pa-thet-ic," one of the neighbours said, a pedantic man who wanted to talk to Nell. He had written an archaeological history of the parish, had sent it to her to read, but without success. She had not acknowledged it.

"I'm so sorry," she said lamely.

"Oh, we're nobodies, nobodies," he said, appraising the cut-glass cruet.

One of the women put a crushed sleeping pill in her father's tea and made him drink it, so that not long after, he began to droop, and they carried him upstairs to bed, undressed him, save for his flannel drawers, and laid him out on the side of the bed which was nearest the door.

"Poor creature, poor man," Maisie said, reading his plight from his shins and the state of the room.

"Will you stay the night?" Nell whispered to Maisie on the landing.

"Don't be afraid, darling, your mam is gone to God," Maisie said.

"I want you to have her lizard handbag," Nell said. It was a way to keep Maisie for the night, because she loved style, even though she never wore it. She tried to duck out of it, said she would be back at dawn before they wakened, back with warm scones.

"I'm afraid," Nell said.

"Afraid of what, love?"

"Afraid of my father," she said, and Maisie thought a moment and winked in collusion.

In bed, the damp oozed out of the sheets and eiderdowns, so they had to get out and dress themselves and get back in again. Maisie made her go with her to the lavatory while she did wee-wees. They were both askew now.

In bed Maisie told her own sad story. Nell's mother hadn't talked to her for nearly a year. It was over a spoon, a missing egg spoon. Her mother had loaned a set for the ploughing-match dinner, twelve spoons in a box, a purple box with a faded velvet lining and a little recess for each spoon, except that one got lost, had probably got thrown away, emptied with the skins, and could not be found, though Maisie herself searched high and low, even raked the ash bed, and in the end sent a youngster back with the eleven spoons and no note. Her mother was bucking, said it was daylight robbery, and did not speak to her again.

"I wish we'd made up," Maisie said, sobbing.

Across the landing they could hear her father's cries; the whole house was crying, and soon the dog joined in from his burrow under the hedge. He had refused food and milk since the woman of the house went. First it was a low sort of whine, then it swelled, rousing neighbouring dogs for miles around, who answered back and soon began to run from their own lairs, their barking frenzying as they got nearer and nearer, and soon they ringed the house, first fighting, then barking in chorus: an anthem for a dead woman.

Not long after, the sound of a car, brakes coming to a terrific standstill, and a banging door.

"Cripes, it's the doctor," Maisie said. They had called him earlier in the evening for her father's fits, only to be told that he was away and might not be back for the night, was at some card party or other.

Nell saw him from the top of the stairs, his big red, beaming face and his body swaying proudly, a love swain in a wide fawn suit that was stained and crumpled. His spirits rose as he caught sight of her, dressed as if for travel and her hair still pinned up.

"Gorgeous . . . gorgeous," he said.

"He's stocious," Maisie whispered under her breath, and ran to tell him that they didn't need him now, that Nell's father was sound asleep. He refused to go, said he wanted a chin-wag with Nell, and Maisie, ever beholden, slunk away, thanking him for coming. Taking Nell's arm, he marched down the hall towards the kitchen, where he knew the stove would be on, saying that he never thought when he got up that morning that he would be sitting down with her that night.

"Ergo, it was meant," he said, and searched for drink, knew where the tonic wine was hidden and where the cut glasses were. He sat back, gloried in her presence and the lucky chance that brought him, swigged the drink, and talked of urbane things, races he had been to, hunt meetings he had been to, even a damn cup he had won, which was on the mantelpiece at home.

"I'd love you to see it," he said proudly, and remembered how as a young girl she had craved sugarplums and how one day he had brought her a basket, red sugarplums, soft and squishy as Turkish Delights.

"You were crazy about me," he said, nudging her.

"Was I?" she said, embarrassed. She remembered often saying recitations for him and another man when they were tiddly and then pestering him in the autumn for the sugarplums, and she was ashamed of it now.

Did she know that his wife was dead? His dear wife, his darling Annie? She knew, her mother had said so. So she knew everything? She nodded as he recited the saga of his falling in love, yes, falling in love with a young chit of a girl, and now they had a child which the young girl passed off as her married sister's. Woeful. Woeful. Love was a terrible thing, made men daft. What was love? he asked her then, his pale eyes in mid-expression between tears and laughter, as if a lewd thought had possessed him, which perhaps it had, because he asked rakishly, Where does it reside, is it in the backside? All of it, as she could guess, made him unpopular, made for enemies, so that young pup of a doctor, a locum, had moved in, stolen his practice, and here he wept as he remembered that decent people such as herself and her family trusted him, knew that he was of the old brigade.

There was no stopping him. His chair came nearer and nearer, and she knew that soon he would touch her, fondle her knee. His eyes were full of tears now; they were like jellyfish floundering about in their bloodshot sockets. He was shaking. He was shaking from drink and desire, luxuriating in the onslaught of memories, the innocent memories like the sugarplums and her arch recitations, the later memories when he went off the rails. What was his meat now? Shambles. The young one was playing around, oh yes, deceiving him, playing around with a forester, in the forest. Every day he went to his wife's grave, or certainly every other day, and pleaded, said, "It's the same fucking story, Annie," and then he put his hand on Nell's and asked her for God's sake to comfort him, because he was running on empty. Three or four times he said it, as if he enjoyed saying it—running on empty. His mind stretched back to the very first day when he rode into the village on his bicycle, newly qualified, without a penny but rich in ideals, yes, ideals. He had come to the parish long before the cottages, the factory, and the pebble-dash bungalows were built, when there was only the workhouse with its boarded windows and the town with its handful of people whom he had come to save, meaning to wipe out every disease, every fucking disease there was.

"Like an Apostle," he said, then reached for more drink and repeated his recent blow, how that very morning he had found a gift under the young one's bed, a gift that was not from him, a pair of fur-backed gloves, no less, which she denied were hers, expressed bafflement as to how they came to be there. But everyone in the parish knew; his dirty linen was being washed in public yet again.

"Do you get my drift?" he said, pleading, pleading. Yes, she knew what he was saying, knew the blunder of his life and how completely helpless he was, like a machine she had seen earlier in the day on a walk, an old mowing machine that had broken down and was left there to sink into the soggy ground, moss and ivy throttling it, its few spears up in the air defiant, grotesque. Yes, she knew, but she remained stiff as the artificial flowers on the coffin, stiff and calcareous.

"What can one do," she said, her voice matter-of-fact, not the voice he craved. He repelled her, and he knew he repelled her, grew more tetchy, saying wild, inappropriate, suggestive things.

In the end she had to ask him to go. He stood up in umbrage, staggered, said it stood to reason, she being a city person now, had better fish to fry, no time for them, no time for him, a country doctor running on empty. "Oh, tooraloom, tooraloom," he said, and danced to a vicious tempo.

Next morning, after breakfast, she decided to do a thorough search. It was somewhere. She had searched in the ashes, but there was no trace of a charred letter, only ashes and cinders and fawn cigarette tips.

"Can't you sit?" her father said, seeing her stir.

"She's looking for her darling mother," Maisie said, to keep the peace. She believed that if she found the letter she would know by the way it was folded or crumpled if it had killed her mother. Also, she clung to straws. Perhaps her mother did not understand it, perhaps it was too high-falutin' or the writing was illegible, vowels and consonants slithering off the page, like knitting coming off a needle. She did not remember signing it, so that it could have come from anyone. She did not remember posting it, but post it she had, afterwards went to a midnight shop and flung herself at Boris slattern-wise. This was the dissolute side her children did not know, must not know. They were thinking of her now in the classroom, missing her maybe, in dread she would not return. Her father was by the fire asking alternate things, if she would stay with him or if he could come back with her. One or the other it had to be.

"We'll see . . . we'll see," she kept saying. She was rummaging in the holdall now, the holdall that held everyday clues to her mother, time-worn clues, bills, recipes, a small credit note from a drapery shop, mortuary cards of friends with rending photos and rending verses. They, too, would choose a mortuary card for her mother and dispatch it to friends and mourners. There would be a tombstone, too. At moments he discussed it, a tombstone that not many would see, because the grave was on an island where there remained the ruins of a monastery and a stone oratory from the tenth century. There was a plaque telling this and the names of the monks who had fasted and prayed there. The butcher hired the grazing, and so bullocks romped and fattened there. She could be buried there herself in due course; there was a space for her, next to her parents. The thought made her quake.

The post was delivered around ten o'clock, that she knew, that she had found out. Her mother died at around eleven. She had gone up to feed the hens and the calves, had come down and died on the flag, the top half of her keeling over a step like a tilting statue. That she knew.

"Was she upset about something?" she asked, feigning inno-cence.

"How would I know," he said, citing a ravaged man who had gone out to count cattle and had come back to find this heap, this pitiful heap, her skull half open and the dog there, beside the blood, moaning.

In the dresser she found pots of jam and apple jelly with mould on them and letters of hers, earlier letters, pinched, discreet. In its way the other letter had groped for truth. But who wants truth? She thought she had come upon it in the orange bowl with the mesh top, because of spotting a royal-blue envelope. But the thing was, all her envelopes were that royal blue, imagining them to herald gaieties.

Perhaps it was upstairs. Opening the hot press she let out a scream as she caught sight of an animal, a baby fox, that looked at her before vanishing and by its glare said, "You have killed your mother . . . you have slaughtered her." When she found the gifts under the towels she felt a gnawing pity. They were gifts for her and her young. They were handmade wallets with their names on them. The thonging was too thick and the leather was not soft, but they were gifts. She saw as well bottles of blackberry wine with screw-on caps and for an instant, unnerved by the fox, pictured the lanes and briars in September, her mother kneeling, looking for blackberries, picking the sweet juices of the countryside for her.

It would be under her mother's mattress, that was where it would be. She ran, found the crucifix, the one her mother slept with and held in the crook of her hand in times of tribulation, found a letter from an old friend who said she was going blind, yet whose children had deserted her, showed not an ounce of pity. She saw bloodstains, too—one huge bloodstain that had formed the shape of a fish, and lesser ones, spatters. She could taste blood then, feel it going down her throat like a warm, rank cordial.

Suddenly she looked up and saw red streaks in the sky, red streaks that for some reason brought tears to her eyes, as if something beautiful, profound, and sorrowful were being explained in this silent tableau. Beneath the red streaks was a swath of purple, gently hazed, trailing, a lilac chiffon dropping down to a basin of grey-white that filtered into lonely invisibility. A stray beam of light that passed over the knob of the brass bed then gave her the shivers, as if it were the gasp of a passing soul. She had never dwelt on death, had shrunk from it, but knew from her prayer books that on the very spot where the soul is separated from the body, judgment is given. She should kneel down and talk to her mother, follow her soul's route, ask forgiveness, say a prayer, but she was unable to; she fled from the room, genuflecting as she went.

"What the hell are you doing upstairs?" her father called.

"Nothing . . . nothing," she said as she trotted down. His temper was on the boil. He could not understand why she lived in England; he had gone there as a young fellow after his pleurisy, thought it the most godawful friendless place he had ever set foot in. She was to take her mother's jewelry, did she know that? Yes, she knew. She had found the tortoiseshell casket with the few trinkets, trinkets that had once seemed priceless, a square black ring with a diamond in its centre, another ring with a cream-faced cameo. She thanked him. She was a child masquerading as a grownup. He was a child, too. Her own children could not be mentioned, they were rivals for her hand. Again she started in on the questions about her mother's last hours.

"Holy Jesus, you have my heart scaled," he said, and stood up and with his fist swiped the air, which he would have beaten with his ashplant were it to hand. Afterwards he had to have a spoon of his tonic. Maisie had arrived with the freshly washed linen, and the sight of it along with the fresh smell was wholesome—as if all bloodshed had been washed away. Maisie had brought his clean shirts, clean handkerchiefs, and bolster case. Like a magician she undid the knot of napkin, allowing warm buttered scones to come tumbling out. Maisie was humouring him as she knew how. His missis, she claimed, had had the biggest crowd ever to the chapel, broke the record, had had up to a thousand, not including cars and bicycles. The postman had counted them. Maybe she would ask the postman—yes, he would know.

"Do you hear that?" he said to Nell. She heard it. He was willing her to hear it, so that he could ask her again if she would stay or if he could come back with her. Knowing she was going to refuse, he cried and wished himself dead, said he had always been an orphan, a foundling, and seeing him so pitiful, so shorn of love, she put out her hand, to let him hold it, to bask in the comfort of it. More than anything she wished that she could love him or even delude him into thinking that she did.

"There . . . there," she said, allowing him to pummel her hand, to infer from it tenderness and solidarity, and moved as he was by this, he redescribed coming in the gate, seeing her poor mother and thinking she had fainted from the fasting or had ripped a varicose vein on a bucket, going to her and picking her up and trying to give her back her breath.

"Oh, the creature, the look on her face, the growl on her mouth," he said, and enacted picking her up, and then as he broke down, she saw that he loved his wife with a raw, violent kind of love and that this was the only thing that he could cling to. She would have liked then to have poured her heart out, to tell him how afraid of him she had been, his shouting, his boots, the very click of the latch as he opened the door, and to tell him her abiding fear, which was that all other men, no matter what their character or their voices, were shadows of him, whom she was afraid of, and because she was afraid of them, she was unnatural and beholden, an outcast from the very intimacy most craved. Her mother had never been a go-between, perhaps out of fear, perhaps out of something darker. Near as they all were in their bristle and in their enmity, they knew nothing at all about each other's deepest, most wretched feelings, and shrunk from the contemplation of them. Only by living inside these cages and growling at each other as animals might could they manage at all.

"I'll stay a week," she said. It was all she could say.

"So it's the bare road after that," he said as he looked through the damp, darkened window at the creeping dark beyond. He would take to it. He would walk to houses and public houses, retrace old paths, haling people at crossroads or in their cabbage gardens to tell the story of his wife's sudden death, his consequent loneliness, and then he would drink with them or drink without them, and before a year was out, he would be beside his wife in the isolated graveyard over which the bullocks romped.

"What's that?" they each said, and gaped, too frightened to stir. It was Maisie who ventured first, crossing to open a door in the room across the hall, the best room, the shrine, full of china and ornaments. An oval gilt mirror had fallen to the hearth on its face. It fell because the cord was brown and rotted, but occurring as it did that night, and with their minds centred on death, the shattering had an extra, terrifying significance. Maisie went to pick the shards up, laid them on the table with a solemnity, as if the mirror, too, were a corpse, and said with some semblance of cheer, "I'll glue it together."

By their eyes they told one another that the haunting had begun—three people united by the selfsame fear and separated by starker ones too terrible to admit.

19

Something about the house was different. She sensed it as she stepped from the taxi. The gate swung at an odd angle and not the tilt at which the postman always left it. Also, there was a light from upstairs, a light she had not remembered leaving on. In the hall, her heart leapt with delight when she saw her children's belongings in a heap on the floor. They had surprised her, stole the march on her by coming home a day early, probably told the headmaster a graphic story of their grandmother's untimely death. "Yoo-hoo," she said as she flung her suitcase next to theirs and hurried up the stairs to find them. Their little faces, their beaming, their slight apprehension at having come a day early, she could already foresee, and thought that once they were in her arms, she was safe again, safe from all the vertigo and madness of the last week.

A woman in a short black slip appeared on the landing. She was thickset, with glasses, and the slip looked far too dainty on her; the scallops of lace above her knees looked absurd.

"Who are you?" Nell asked. For some reason she was not afraid, she was affronted.

"Me . . . I am Olga," the woman said, and added that she was the friend of Boris. Then, seeing Nell's fury, she put her hand up in a gesture of apology and retreated back into the children's room. Nell's first thought was to call the police, but then she decided that she and her children could fling them out. So he had the effrontery to break in, thought he could blackmail her because of one profane night.

"Where are my children?" she asked brusquely. There was a silence and then Boris called out insolently, "They have gone."

"Gone where?" Nell asked, thinking that possibly they had gone to a sweetshop for a stock of sweets and comics, or perhaps to a neighbour, a family of young boys whose father dealt in second-hand cars and whose mother was a bit listless.

"To their friend house," he said.

"Listen . . . you get yourself and your madam out of here." She shouted it. The expression on his brow was one of irritation, as he did not like to hear his girlfriend spoken of so. He came out, tying the front buttons of his very white shirt, the starched cuffs dipping over his hands like napkins. The fact that they were both in a state of undress made it worse, more flagrant.

"Welcome back," he said to her with a slight smile, and coming down the stairs to greet her, he touched the fox collar of her coat, wagged it, and began to tickle her chin. It was her mother's coat, brown velvet with fox fur trimming. She had taken it out of duty, meaning only to wear it for the journey.

"You get out of here," she said, hating now every feature of face and body that she had, but a week ago, so brazenly procured.

"Not so fast," he said, smiling a sly, confident smile.

"Yes. So fast," she said, trembling at his gall.

"We leave Sunday . . . that is our plan," he said, drawing the shirtsleeve to his mouth so that he could fasten the cuff links with his teeth, except that Olga was hurrying to do it.

"We must go soonest," Olga said, and in her unease stood so close to him that her body seemed both to be shielding his and to be melting into it.

"We were no place to go," Olga said then to her, tears starting up in her large, baffled eyes, which looked stupid in their spectacles.

"I'll call the police," Nell said.

"Don't be nervy," he said, certain that she would recall when he had used the word previously, when he had carried her across the road, her whole body in a swoon. Everything about his smile, his expression, the cigarette in the corner of his mouth seemed to be saying, "I fucked you, left, right, and centre, and you're not going to get rid of me now."

"Thieves," she said, her voice much too shrill.

"Excuse me," he said, with an added frown, and his expression now was one of effrontery, as he debated if he might become rough with her, teach her a lesson.

She almost hoped he would, to give her anger an outlet. Often she had dreamt that her husband had moved back into her house, refusing to leave, claiming it as his own, and the frenzy that it engendered was now being transferred to them. He closed his fist, appraised it, as if he might strike her, but presently thought of his own position and decided to paint an august picture of his origins, the family *Schloss*, huge tracts of land, hunting grounds, the furs and jewels his mother had once proudly worn and had had to sell in order that they could flee their own country. Far from being thieves, they were the ones who had been robbed.

"I don't give a damn about your *Schloss*," she said.

"We best to go," Olga said, and took off her glasses so that Nell could see the fear in her moist, frightened eyes.

"I thought you fancied me," he said to Nell with a sneer.

"You thought wrong," she said, and looked at Olga to disavow this vile insinuation.

Then, deciding on a last-ditch strategy, he began wagging the fur again and said, "Olga will give us nice massage . . . you and me . . . and then we have drinks and some fucky . . . Heh-heh."

"I don't want massage," she said, her voice betraying her panic, and then, pointing to the door, she repeated, "Out . . . Out." He thought on it, shrugged, said yes they would go, since she was such a shrew, but it would take them several hours to pack.

"Where are my children?"

"They have gone to their friend," he said, and went towards the bedroom, his hand patting one of Olga's buttocks as if she were his prize cow.

Out on the street she met neighbours coming from work and of each asked, "Have you seen my children . . . By any chance have you seen my children?" Cars were being parked in a fret, gates were clanged and lights came on in several front windows. She knew each house, knew its little peculiarities: the Canadians, for instance, who always had a great stock of wood in case they should light a fire; the righteous people with a poster in the window—this week it was DIABETES, THE DEADLY DISEASE. Then there were the bohemian family who left furniture and statues in their garden; once even an upright piano had been left there for a whole week. The first Christmas tree was already up and decked— squat balls, the size of tennis balls, garish bobbins of red and green. They would get a tree on the morrow. She knew a market where the young trees came fresh from the forest, each tree in mesh, a taper which, when hauled out, swagged like a tassel. Christmas. That was a word to hold on to and to fill with all the distractions that she could muster. Her mother had left her money, a little windfall.

Smoothing the notes, pound notes and larger ones, she was at first too ashamed to count them. They had been put in any old way, folded, not folded, some in a clump, others stained or with handwriting on them, all secured with a rubber band. They were in an old evening bag, whose amber clasp had disappeared, leaving a rusted jutting screw, and as she sat on the bed with it, the little oblong beads of jet fell off and danced on the white counterpane. Her name was on the envelope but nothing more, so that it was impossible to assume the emotion which lay interred in them. As with many a thing, it remained unfinished. Her father in a last effort to appeal to her said there would be more money, as he would sell the homestead and live with nuns. In the end he was glad to see her go, having settled on his raw pain and his raw revenge.

Her children were not in the car dealer's house, had not even called. The mother, pale and abstracted, with a purple blotch beneath her right eye, went into a yarn about the stairs being too narrow, one thread of stairs being loose, so that she tripped, hoover and all. The baffled shame of a beaten wife. Nell knew that sometimes she left him and had been found in such disparate places as an all-night cinema, a railway waiting room in Dorset, and once a shelter for the homeless. She had come from Dorset; her family had been weavers there.

"They've probably gone to the park," she said cheerfully.

"The park is closed," Nell said, pointing to the ghastly blue sodium light that made their faces spectral.

"So it is," the woman said, asking why she thought it was summer, why she had got the seasons wrong.

On the footpath Nell looked up and down, certain that they were about to appear, that this looking, this longing, would swing them into sight. She would have to account for the visitors, apologise that their bedroom had been invaded while thanking her lucky stars that they had not found her in her own room alone with him. She thought of going to Emma's house, but it meant venturing out onto the high street and crossing a road, and that she could not yet do. She was certain that in crossing that road, or indeed any road, she would be run over and mangled, and die a stranger, in a city of strangers. She would ring Emma's house, and surely they would be there, having tea and toast, making light of their setback. Back in her own hallway the first thing she did was to take off her mother's coat, feeling that it was not lucky, feeling that all the tribulation it had known resided in it and was imparting itself to her now. Then she listened to see how far along Boris and Olga were with their packing.

While opening her suitcase to get her cardigan she spotted the note. It was on the back of a letter, in Paddy's handwriting and signed by both—"We came home but you were not here. Two people were here, strangers. We have gone to our friend in Wales who has a pony farm. We won't arrive for six hours." She ran, taking two, three steps at a time. Why hadn't they told her? At what hour had her children left? Were they driven from their own house? Her tone so enraged Boris, so undermined his pride and his role as swain, that he made to strike her, but Olga took his arm and muttered to him, said sweetish things to calm him, and called him Kermit, Kermit. That was her pet name for him.

"We pack we pack . . ." Olga said as Nell followed them up the stairs and was appalled to see the clutter in the room—bags, cardboard boxes, trunks, even an old pair of velvet curtains on a brass curtain pole.

"I am not going to ask you again," she said.

In the kitchen she set about making herself some tea and vowed that the minute they had gone she would go up there and scour the place, remove every trace of them. It was then, as she put a match to the gas, that it happened. All she knew was that glass was flying, jagged pieces of glass from the window, flying in all directions, followed by the crackle of explosion. She screamed above the noise, and as they ran into the kitchen, she saw him question Olga, then strike her vehemently across the cheek and shout, "Cow . . . you stupid cow . . . what have you done?"

"Get an ambulance," Nell called, but as she put out her hand to reach them she fell in a blur to the floor.

The dregs of the city seemed to have converged in the emergency ward. There was a man bleeding profusely from the temple, who seemed not so much worried by it as by the fact that no one had witnessed it. Run down he was, by a van, and the taxi driver a few yards behind hadn't seen it, didn't want to.

"See no evil, hear no evil," he said to the room. They were squashed in together on a long bench, Nell next to Olga, who held a towel to the nape of her neck and said words of solace, the few she knew in English; Boris standing over them, going out to smoke or take a mouthful from his lozenge-shaped hip flask. He had given Nell some. It made her woozy. She needed to be woozy. Bits of flying glass had got into her neck, and her hands and face were badly burned. On the hands Olga had smeared Vaseline and in the neon light of the waiting room it had a strange glisten to it. Her face was burnt, too, and with her good hand groped for the blisters, prodding them while knowing that she shouldn't. Another of the incumbents, a woman, just trembled, her lips and cheeks moving of their own accord, as if they desperately wanted to say something of dire importance, which they probably did. Still others had the spiteful, haunted look of the relegated, showed no injuries, and looked as if they had come in simply because they had nowhere else to go. One very young man who was laughing to himself cowered inside a grey wool blanket. A couple who had quarrelled and had hit each other with flowerpots were now making up, kissing and saying babyish things, once or twice making to leave, except that they were prevented by a nurse. She was a young girl who looked into the room from time to time to make sure that no one had stirred. She particularly scrutinised the kissing couple. The woman wore no stockings although it was winter, her legs and pink arms were chapped with chilblains.

"You won't let go," Nell said repeatedly to Olga. She believed that if Olga let go of the towel her neck would simply swivel off. "I sorry ... I forget ..." Olga said, and again and again repeated how she had gone to make his lunch, had turned on the gas, and how he had called her back upstairs to make the love. With her fingers, her sighing, she was doing everything to atone, talking and ministering. Boris had gone twice to the Sister in her glass booth to ask if they could be given preferential treatment, because his friend was in shock, only to be told that everyone in Emergency was in shock. A secretary had taken all the information when she arrived, her name, her age, her maiden name, her profession, Boris asking all the while what the fuck use it was, wanting to know these things.

"You won't leave me," she whispered to Olga.

"I stay ... we stay," Olga said.

A man came in shouting that he would kill them all, telling them to move up, to make room for him, did they not know who he was. They squeezed together, the whole party united now by this worse menace. As soon as he sat, he launched into a tirade of curses, taking advantage of each face or each pair of frightened eyes to vent his rage. To herself Nell kept saying, "My neck will not come off ... My face is not disfigured," while feeling her breath in the ventricle of her throat as some strangling thing, a thread, a white thread, for some reason. Olga had a cure for this also. "Now we breathe ..." she whispered, and together they breathed—in, for a count of four, hold the breath for a count of four, and then breathe out. With each breath Nell felt she was sinking into a greater decline and thought how fitting that she should die within a week of her mother, that retribution should come so soon. Olga, who understood only part of this tale, kept telling her to say, "Good morning, sir; good morning, madam; good morning, St. Nicholas," whenever fears of any kind threatened her. Yes, her abiding fear was the obvious one: that Boris would one day leave her.

"I can no have the child," she said sadly, but without rancour.

The elderly doctor who saw Nell flinched, disliked her hysteria, her ridiculous phobia about her neck coming off, and became even more tetchy when she mentioned the drug she had taken and from which she was still askew.

"Just be still . . . Mrs." he said, pulling the towel away, looking at her neck, then shining a little torch on it, then shouting to the nurse who was assisting him to put the towel back, and going to the phone. His alacrity alarmed her far more than her own nightmares.

"Could I speak to Dr. Dow's secretary . . . Oh, Deborah . . . it's you . . . Yes, it is Emergency . . . I can't say . . . but it looks a bit nasty, so we must move fast . . ." As Nell heard him, she rose to say that she couldn't go to hospital yet, not until she retrieved her children.

"You do . . . goody gumshoes," he was saying into the phone, avoiding the gesticulations that were being made to him.

"I've got to go to Wales first and get my children," she said as he put the receiver down.

"You're going to hospital and you're jolly lucky to have the best surgeon in the business . . . top of his field, Anthony Dow," he said as he sat and penned the letter which she was to take with her.

"For how long will I be in the hospital?" she asked, and the tired Asian nurse just looked at her and shrugged and said that was up to the doctors.

20

Christmas Day was in a small hospital room, where she was recovering, sitting up in bed, a brace around her neck, so that she
moved like a wooden puppet. Her stitches were coming out soon.
Much to her surprise she loved her little room, loved the view of
the back gardens, the nurses coming and going at all hours, nurses
of all kinds, cheery, sullen, brusque, each with her little nylon cap
pinned at a different angle, as if to convey her individuality.

"Merry Christmas . . . Merry Christmas." She had heard it since
dawn and snuggled under the covers, longing to return to sleep
and the placenta of her dreams. She had been dreaming of a rose
bed, a small rose bed crowded out with the bushes, one which
Tristan had put in, and she had said sweetly to him that it was the
wrong bed and they were too close together. In the dream he
looked a little crushed.

"Merry Christmas," she heard again and again. The fair-haired
young nurse whom she liked was struggling with the cord that was
supposed to lift the cloth blind but never did, so that either the left
or the right side dipped down, carcass-like.

There was special breakfast. Besides the usual toast and honey,
she had received a little chunk of Christmas cake in a wrapping of
cellophane. On the icing was a silver ball, and this for some reason
brought back another dream, one in which a baby had been born
to her, slightly deformed, but alive, oh yes, alive and asking ques-

tions. The two features of its face she remembered most clearly
were the eyes and a little tongue. Both were purple, the eyes small
but liquid and the tongue like a violet nib off which the ink
dropped, the ink which was speech. The baby said its first word.
It was the word "echo." It then asked what that word meant, and
she tried wrongly to explain, said it meant a fox, or the lowing of
a cow; it meant country things, but that was ridiculous.

"Your son phoned later on, last night . . . said he was sorry you
got cut off, but to tell you that the pet they are thinking of acquir-
ing is a pony and not to worry." They were spending the holiday
in the pony-trekking farm along with other children whose parents
lived abroad. They had been told about her operation by the ma-
tron and it seemed had taken it well. The first time she phoned
them, she felt frightened, as if they might say something cruel, but
no, they had asked very solicitously about her health and if she
was all right and if she was eating enough. They both used identical words, but neither said, "We came home and you were not
there." Still, they knew it, it hovered. Paddy had said he was
earning extra money, "mucking out," and Tristan told her his
pony had run away with him but that he took it in his stride and
fell quite merrily.

The second phone call was on Christmas Eve. It was arranged
that she would phone them at a certain time. It was just before
supper and she hobbled down to the office, hating when she caught
sight of herself in a mirror: her whole body stiff, ungainly, her face
marked. They were excited. Tristan had just won the jackpot from
the fruit machine, won a great haul of money, and was worried
that while he was talking on the phone, other boys, rogues, were
picking up the coins and hiding them in their socks or under their
beds.

"The money has rolled all over the place," he said, his voice
flushed with excitement and with nerves as he deferred to Paddy,
who also said he had to dash so as to assist his brother and act as
broker. Before ringing off they told her that they were thinking of
getting a ———, but she had not caught the word. A pony! Where
would they graze a pony?

"Here goes," the nurse said, holding up the red paper cracker, contorting her features in mock trepidation at the deed which she was about to do. Not long after, Nell was sporting a pink paper hat, looking at a picture of clover on her little pot of honey, and thinking, Will they forgive me . . . in their heart of hearts, will they forgive me? She had been foolish enough to ask several nurses, and opinions varied. Some said that quite honestly they could not say, others said that they themselves could not do it, and one very stern nurse who boasted about being up at six before she came on duty to mind her babies and leave feeds for the day said of course it was wrong. Nell believed that it was this young nurse who had set a madwoman on her, a dark-skinned woman from the kitchen who came into her room shrieking, telling her to repent, because Satan was in her, in her belly and in her eyes. It was one morning during that lull after breakfast, when the nurses were elsewhere, down in the operating theatres or having a tea break, and this eagle-faced creature burst in on her, hands like claws, voice high-pitched, calling, "Ora . . . oracle . . . oraculemus."

"Who are you?" Nell said.

"Ora . . . oracle . . . oraculemus," and she laughed as she sniffed out the environs of the bed, the foul bedcovers, and the sinning body beneath it. Like a little genie she had grabbed the emergency bell and pocketed it. Who was she? She was the one who routed Satan. She had been sent there. Her voices told her. In a strange guttural language and with a terrible anguished expression she searched the length of the body to find the seat of sin. Railed about his stench, then nabbed him, chased him, collared him, and squeezed him like a louse, this Satan, squashing him with her long nails, which were soft as a web. Then, peering under the bed, she shouted some more, stood up, took two little metal rods from her pocket, rods that jigged towards each other and made her mutter more. Before leaving she produced a book of hymns that was stained and tattered. Nell was to copy out each hymn and sing it, and in the singing she would find her way back to God.

"I'll have you reported," Nell said without blanching.

The woman looked at her with a strange, venomous glee and jumped as her metal rods had jumped, gaily and unconcerned.

"No one will believe you," she said, and curtsied before going out.

So the day stretched before her, a long, quiet Christmas Day, misty weather and her brain misty, too, from the tablets they gave her to sleep. Her surroundings were by now as familiar as the lines on her hands or the pencil marks on the wall behind her bed, crazed squiggles by a previous occupant. Outside, a playground, the slide with the worn seat, school windows with frames painted a mustard yellow, tall trees, London plane trees which did not have the ramble or lassitude of country trees but were still trees, thrusting right down to the roots and clayey tentacles of themselves. She did many things to avoid thinking, stamped on each thought as if stamping flies. Anything not to break down. She would look at the trees, the slide, the rosebushes in the back gardens, bags of fertiliser, wheelbarrows, the humble impedimenta of suburbia, and think, I am on the mend . . . I am on the mend. The surgeon had been extra kind to her because of her dementia. After the operation she had screamed, could not be quieted as two nurses held her and one clamped a hand over her mouth, saying crisply that patients far worse than she, patients who were dying, would be unnerved by the hullabaloo. They sent for the surgeon, thinking perhaps that he would be more severe. At first she thought he was a chef because of his white coat and his white hat and told him to please go away. He sat with her, talked in a low voice, and asked her what was it, what was it. At first she could not tell him, because to say it was to relive it again, but gradually she described how in a waking vision she had just been home, yes home, up the avenue, over the high grass and the thistles, past young trees and old trees all lambent, and how at the doorway she was met by a man in livery, who admitted her. In the vestibule she saw the most beautiful collection of robes, laid out as if for a ceremony, scarlet, wine-coloured, with gold epaulettes, emblems of sovereignty; yet when she lifted one, she saw a severed head and next to it another, both freshly hacked, dripping, so that she dropped the garments and ran from the carnage, but running was no use, because she knew, yes she knew that these were her own people mauled and ritually sacrificed. Within the welter of it all, she had shouted out, "And still, the house gleamed as the world must gleam to those who are entering, before the vessels burst their ravenous bounds." He said it was only a dream, the aftermath of anaesthetic, that many people saw and heard strange things. He envied her, wished he had such transports; his was just the same old exam dream, and even that was fading. She was to think of getting better, because he wished it, the nurses wished it, everyone did. Life was fun. Life was to be enjoyed. Her life was ahead of her, a bright tapestry.

"Thelma, peel me a grape," he said then, for her amusement, impersonating Mae West: Mae in her high heels and her décolletage, treating people like scullions.

"Thelma, peel me a grape . . ." He said it two or three times, until she laughed.

The big strapping nurse who came to take off her bandages teased her about him, said that most likely he would steal away while the turkey was cooking and pay a surprise visit.

"He'll be with his family," she said, and for some reason she hoped he wouldn't come; she wished him there with them, joking, presiding. Something so good and mild about his manner made her want him content. As the bandages came off the nurse hooted with delight, said how beautifully the wounds had healed and how soft the new skin was.

"Skin like a baby," she said, then fetched a basin of water, and for the first time in weeks Nell washed her hands. She felt playful, a sensation from some far-off time, hands in a stream or in a rain barrel, clasping, letting go, hands swishing and paddling, alone, or with another. Which other?

"What's the happiest moment you've ever lived?" she asked the nurse.

"Crikey . . ." the nurse said. What a question. She couldn't say. They were all mostly happy, happy in different ways.

"But there must be one."

"Yeah . . . when the parsley took."

"Why the parsley?"

"It means you'll hold on to your man," she said, her laugh and accent deepening into the rich Northern burr of her childhood.

"So who's the man?" Nell asked, and in reply was told a riddle, that to ask was like "gathering grapes from thistles."

Boris and Olga came after lunch, glided into the room, looking radiant. They had been running and moreover had decided to leave London. Boris walked across to look through the window while Olga stood close to the bed and handed Nell a gift in crinkled tissue paper. It was a brooch, a leaf of marcasite in which there was an inset of ivory, which had darkened over the years. It was her grandmother's, on her mother's side, who had vanished in Prague, had been rounded up along with a sister and two brothers.

"You shouldn't," Nell said, overwhelmed.

"She should . . . stupid cow," Boris said, and laughed, because stupid cow was rich, since many women needed massage around Christmas, women in Belgravia and St. John's Wood and as far up as Highgate, women with husbands, women without husbands, randy women all alone in rooms, needed their tummies flattened. Then, to prove their affluence, Boris took Olga's leather drawstring bag and held it upside down, so that the coins rolled along the floor, and then he made Olga get down and pick them up while he kicked her amiably and she whimpered, "It hurts, Kermit . . . it hurts, Kermit," as she did the circuit of the room. Soon, they were going abroad, first to Bali and Indonesia, then on from there to Australia, where they would become beachcombers.

"London is ugly . . . ugly," he said, and made a face to emphasise his distaste, adding that the places where they had been squatting were not fit for animals. Strange that there was no rancour, none at all, but they were not quite real to her, though she could see their blushed faces and even smell the cachou smell of Olga's breath as she pinned the brooch to the collar of her nightgown. In a way she wished that they would go. Her mind was too frazzled, and when she thought of her brain, the image that cropped up was of telephone wires under the pavement, tangled, weevilling into one another, so that men had to come along with pincers to straighten them and snip them apart.

"Snip . . . snip," she said as she saw Boris look at her and think how barmy she was, barmy and old, with old, unshining, sapless eyes.

It may have been the light, yes she believed it was, the soft melancholy light of a winter's evening touching her to an extremity of feeling.

"Dear Mother," she began again. "There are moments in which you appear tender, like a snapshot melting, tinged with beauty and grace, imparting the same vague sorrow as when one sees an old man or a young child at a farmhouse, staring, the child waving but not sure if the wave is seen and losing heart in the middle of it. You would come down from the yard, your hands smeared with meal, a few eggs in a can, but never enough; they would be dunged and covered in meal and the one above all others that I remember is the shell-less egg, soft as any placenta, its bruisedness a resemblance of us. If only we could have imagined ourselves into each other's depths. If only!"

She folded it again and again, thinking she would go back one time covertly and leave it on the grave, a shredded flower.

It was dark when she saw the figure in the doorway and for a flash believed it to be Duncan, her wandering bard. Only when he spoke did she realise that it was the porter, and then she turned the light on, to find him in his suit, ready to go home, but bearing a gift, a bowl of fruit—grapes, strawberries, and kiwis. He had put a paper napkin under them so that they sagged, and like a courtier he proudly placed it before her, muttering, "Do you good . . . do you good." He had seen her earlier, had caught her crying when he came to ask her preference, brown meat or white meat of the roast turkey, found her in her nightgown rooting in the wardrobe, looking at her clothes and her money to make sure they were still there, holding up a plastic vase in case she got flowers.

"Do you good," the porter kept saying, not knowing where best to place his offering. A letter he brought had been in the wrong pigeonhole downstairs. This indeed was Duncan's handwriting —at once childish and assertive. Inside, a picture for her. It was as if he had taken a bottle of red ink, poured it over the flimsy paper, allowing it to make its own sweet, zany, barbaric course. Underneath he had written—"For you, tonight, the blood on my sleeve and the love that I've left." The postmark was from Arizona. So he had gone to his desert, gone without her.

"Strange," the porter said as she held it up. Most likely he had been hoping to see robins or a jingling sleigh.

"From Arizona . . ."

"Arizona . . . that's a long way," he said. Yes, she could picture him, his eyes sand-mad, sunsets like footballs of fire, but no matter how hard she tried, she could not picture herself there in the emptiness alongside him.

21

The fields rose up in a gradual swoop towards a line of trees, and the light was so clear that up there above the branches she could catch sight of a moving thing, a buzzard, a pair of buzzards, black, hovering and wheeling over the cropped treetops. Everything so still, so calm, and so ordained. Everything seemed beautiful, as it must be to those who have just been given a reprieve. A friend had loaned her a cottage for the remainder of the vacation, and sitting as she did, very quietly, she looked at the fields on one side and through the opposite window at the woods, tall, towering, each branch attuned to every shift of wind, so that when a storm was due they creaked, and when it struck they swayed and heaved like creatures seized. Deer grazed in the field in broad daylight, and sometimes they lifted their haughty heads and stared across. The crop planted there was soft, feathery, like cress. A haven. The kitchen walls were green, the chairs a lighter green, with some gold scroll on the back as a decoration. The Christmas tree was her own handiwork; green branches wound with isinglass and dotted with tiny bulbs, gauze arms, gauze limbs, a woodland Buddha holding its breath. There were paper roses, too, white, with an edging of crimson, and a cloth angel at the top.

Each day she had walked and met the country people, all of whom saluted her, talked to her, one woman confiding that she didn't like Virginia, the owner of the cottage, found her stuck-up, because she didn't mix. A forester led her up a slip road to find the holly with the berries on it. The ground underfoot was wet and loamy, his stick squelching into it as he chatted, told her that he was called Greg but that it was not his real name. His real name was Angus, but he answered to Greg; it was the only thing he answered to. Born and bred in the locality, he identified each tree, each hoof mark, each bird call. She saw a hemlock tree for the first time, brought back by a Lady Sophia from the East fifty years before. The lords and ladies, he said, had strange habits and weren't always lucky despite their money. His mother had worked in the Abbey as a junior maid, getting up at five to light the fires and heat the irons in order to iron the gentlemen's shirts before they went riding. The Abbey had burned down. He pointed across to the turretted grey ruin and the one wing which remained, a low storey, like a cloister, leaded windows ivied, wintry, ashen gloom.

Staying out of doors shortened the time. She walked and talked, thinking that she must not suppose how they would greet her; she must behave as if she had seen them yesterday and not as if a passage of weeks had expired. The trees were sombre now, armies of them, with ventricles of sky between the trunks, the sky a saline blue, and she thought, When I don't see these blue gashes and when I don't see the trees distinctly, then it will be time to turn back.

The dark steals in on each and every feature, each skein of it as precise as dawn but the reverse of dawn. The earth and the briars grew indistinct, and soon it seemed as if it were her own sight which was deserting her and not the night itself coming on, the soft circumventing cloak of night. At moments she lost her way, strayed into the wood, then back onto the path again, then downhill by the stream, which in the dark seemed to gurgle more recklessly. She could not see the stream or the floats of weed that lay on the surface of the water and brushed it like tender brooms. Everything was a spectre now: briars, bushes, old compost bags that resembled whitish corpses and trees imprisoned in cages of mist.

They would probably see a change in her, some aging perhaps, some aftermath of shock, but they would not say so, they would put it away for a future time, the way we do when young, put away what we must later look at, a look that often so appals us; it is as if our eyes are flung into a bath of bleach and henceforth stripped of every soft solacing image. The owl had already begun its battle cry, a cry in which pity and rage were wrought into the same single note, coming first from one direction, then another, as it darted through the woods.

Walking towards the cottage she heard them and ran up the flight of steps to greet them.

"You're here . . . you're here," she said, expecting them to run to her as they had always done, but instead, they waited on the threshold, paused, the distance being too much, the constraint too great.

"The train was earlier than you said," Paddy told her. He looked older and rougher, and both of them looked unkempt.

"I meant to be here to pay the taxi," she said.

"We paid," Tristan said as he ran his finger over various objects to acquaint himself with them.

"Isn't it pretty?" she said, and then proudly, though shyly, she turned on the switch so that they would see the little stencils of silver light on the tree and see its beauty to full effect.

"Who sent the cards?" Paddy asked.

"They're not for us," she said abruptly, and clutched them lest he might daub them. They were for Virginia, who was on safari in Africa. One depicted horses, nags, standing in a snowy field staring at one another across a snow-topped fence, their shanks deep in snow and their expressions sad. The second was much more elegant, greenish horses in a green paddock, being led out by stable boys, while the gentry waited for the carriages. The third was of Big Ben faintly outlined in a column of mist, which bore no resemblance to the monument she had gone to see on her second day in London and had stared up at, unable to muster any excitement. It had seemed so tall, the decorative parts too far away. All around, the Houses of Parliament and the black-and-gold ironwork had struck her as imposing, having the weight of history without the hum of life. The flag posts bare of flags looked like thin white-robed postulants.

"These are just tokens . . . your real present is in the envelope," she said, handing them shoe boxes which she had clumsily wrapped. She saw them look at each other with a glance that was both mischief and shame, mischief because they were pleased at what they were about to find in the envelope and shame because they had been so reserved.

"Open them," she said as she went across to put on the kettle and get the Christmas cake which she had won at the hospital fête.

"Is Mama better?" Tristan called.

"I went a bit bonkers," she said, to try to make them understand.

"You're not bonkers," Paddy said, and gave her a startled look that said, Don't utter such nonsense, that is not how a mother should speak.

"You were just in a brown study," Tristan said tenderly, and then, as if he might ennoble her with it, he handed her an oblong packet with the name of a Chinese restaurant in Chinese lettering. Where it said *To* and *From* he had written her maiden name and his own name in full. It was a calendar of bamboo, and on its pale wheat-coloured surface, two young pandas were gorging on lush leaves of bamboo.

"It's lovely," she said. It bore the name and telephone number of a restaurant in Wales and the hours when orders were taken.

"They gave it to me," he said, somewhat abashed, as if to apologise for such a gift. Paddy's was a tablespoon, its front rim worn to a knife edge where it had scraped the leavings from many a saucepan.

"Do you know what I dreamt?" he said, and went on to tell her, "I dreamt that we met Emily Brontë and I said, 'Excuse me, Emily Brontë, why did you write only one novel?'"

"And?" Nell said, putting the thin lip of the spoon to her lips by way of showing how thankful she was.

"And then," he said, waving his arms, "she danced away in a white shroud." How she longed to kiss each of them, to kiss them again and again, but she daren't. The screech owl intruded upon her longing, the same sound, jarring, relentless, out there in the dark, perched now in some tree, digesting its prey or affirming its indignation. They listened, waiting for each repetition, each pause, and suddenly Tristan suggested that they go out in the woods, go "nargling."

"It's too dark, pet," she said, pointing to the pane of glass that was itself a sheet of darkness, like a river.

"But here's a torch," Paddy said, picking up the one she had set aside for their arrival, meaning to meet them with "Yoo-hoo" and "Mind the step" as they came up the pink, wavery steps which in daylight looked like kidneys.

"A little adventure," Tristan said. It's what they wanted. In the woods there would be no hesitations and no wonderings, there would be the reunion, she dreamed.

Out there they feigned fear of beasts, yet hoped that some animal would spring on them and imagined the glassiness of deers' eyes staring into theirs, the deer that she sighted each evening as they bounced through the garden, their startled expressions and grey-white rumps all that she saw, since they moved like meteors.

"Ssh, ssh," one or the other said as they slipped on fallen boughs or got caught in a thicket of briars, each claiming to be blinded, their shoes squelching, their socks sodden, while they asked the moon to please, please show herself. At moments clouds passed over the moon's face, quickly, then were whisked away to be replaced by the next batch and the next, like creatures paying their respects.

"We're sorry about Granny's death," Paddy said, regretting that he had not posted the card which he had bought for her as a Christmas gift. It was a prayer called "Desiderata," which advised people to go placidly, which poor Granny hadn't, and what a pity that she had not received it in time, or it might have saved her.

"Poor Granny," Tristan said, trying to sound both sorrowful and grown-up.

In the darkness and hiddenness of the woods they had found each other again, found the mislaid tenderness and the little scraps of news that had to be exchanged about this and that. The woods with their unseen menace made them cling and gabble as they defied the dangers and marvelled at a sky of stars that had come out. Sometimes stars are content in their own bright sockets, but that night they shone with an added verve and an added intensity, as if they were chattering one to the other, across the reaches of sky, and how pleasant it was to wonder what these stars were saying, what euphoria had got into them.

"Stars are like the people sleeping in their houses with the lights on," she said, recalling the poem that Paddy had sent her.

"I have lots more to show you . . . better ones," he said.

"And *moi*," Tristan said, and started on about a story he had written, "The Good Mother Heberdeen," who lived on the edge of the moor and helped people, helped shepherds and travellers to escape the Nasty Brigands, gave them jam, a special jam which she kept in red jars with a sealed top and spread on scones for them. Once they tasted it, they turned into other shapes and levitated across the misty moors. With each description of Mother Heberdeen, her knuckles, chicken meal under her nails, her scones and the magic jam, Nell saw a picture of her mother emerge, and thought they must never know; if they knew they would take her mother's side, they would turn against her, and fearing it more than anything, she gripped their hands and in the knotted dark began to chatter, recounting snatches of things, jokes, hospital meals, country superstitions, like some mummer who believes with sound it can efface what must not be said. Her energy quite prodigal as she strode with daring buoyancy.

"Mam-ma!" they said, delighted by the sudden levity.

22

"The thirty-first," he said without emotion. He was a little man with a dry, barking voice, his knitted hat far back on his head and his eyes darting, eyes used to assessing everything in a room. As he sucked behind pursed lips, she believed two opposite things: that it would not happen and that of course it would happen, because she had willed it, wanted it, and conspired towards it.

"The thirty-first," she said, but without conviction. He saw this. It was obviously a common reaction, people pretending to themselves that they were not in ruin. He took out his diary and remarked that it was seven days, a week hence. She had had three final notices but had refused to acknowledge them. She gasped, wondered where would she go, said thoughtfully that nobody could do this to her. These were remarks he had often heard before and was as impervious to as if she had just said, It's raining. There were hostels, there were boardinghouses, rooms to let in the daily paper, no end of possibilities.

"That's bunkum," she said bitterly. To that he looked away at an old tug making its dozy passage up the river. A boy wearing an oilskin stood at the helm, looking through field glasses. Surely there was something she could say in order to get a breathing space, to make it a month at least, by which time she could borrow. No, a week was a week. All he was doing was his duty. The world was founded on business and that alone. Of course, there were satisfying things like gardens and furniture and children, but business was business.

"I was ill," she said feebly.

"Illness can topple the best of us . . . can and does," he said dryly, and he looked away from the river directly at her as if to say, When are you going to believe what is already a *fait accompli*?

"I can get the money," she said.

"Well and good," he said, then gave her his card and added that there would be legal fees, of course, but he would be glad to countermand the order, and the landlord would be happy, too, having always liked her, though she was an unusual sort of person. Otherwise, the thirty-first. Strategies, all improbable, flashed through her brain. She thought of people she might appeal to, but as each name came up, she dismissed it again. She thought of her father, but knew how it would fuel his hopes. She thought of her boss and of the moment when opening his heart out he had said, "Darling, you have never asked me anything, but you must know that you could." She couldn't. Simply couldn't demean herself. She had only to think, to sit down and seriously think; the entire city throbbed with money, the opulence of gateways and pillars and balustrades all testified to it. In hotel lobbies where the chandeliers were never quenched, men sat down and fervently discussed money. It was everywhere. It was palpable. It was like reaching out to touch a tree; she had only to reach and it would materialise. That thought soon spent, she considered going to a moneylender. On no account would she be wrenched from her rooms, her garden, her perch by the river where she sat and saw the slanting lights, so myriad, pillars, floating edifices, down there in the underbelly of the river, and the foghorns hooting in the distance like solitary seabirds. She would tell herself each night, before going to sleep, that the answer would come in a dream. It must. It must.

She had not been to Freddie's house, though he had invited her twice, but cancelled twice, cancelled on the grounds of flu. Freddie, who specialised in Oriental and Byzantine silks, lived alone in a large house and was something of a recluse. He had come to her parties with Duncan, tagged along; saw that she, too, loved Duncan and pitied her for it. They used to have little chin-wags in a corner, he and she, he telling her how he had sailed close to the wind once, a boyfriend who had done something unspeakable, though he did not say what. He loved theatre and opera, talked eagerly about both, described rare moments he had seen— transcendent moments—great Hamlets, great Juliets, a theatre set for *The Cherry Orchard*, where the trees, of white linen, eventually took on the flutter and wander of blossom. He described the opera house in Milan, seeing Maria Callas come on stage, a hush, a tense, waiting chamber, a high priestess who might, if she chose, turn her audience to stone or salt. He knew the finest hotels, the gardens, the best suites, had sat in the room where Wagner wrote part of *The Ring* and slept in the castle in Austria where Rilke had composed his seventh elegy. Yes, Freddie used to tell of these glories, and when he travelled he often brought her back a post-card, an *Annunciation* full of solemnity, from Padua, or an *Assumption* from Verona, where the Virgin was like a concubine propped on some buxom cloud. Of all the gate-crashers he was the most courteous, admiring the glasses or the new pole screen, touching the corn jars, saying, "You have good taste . . . you have an eye."

They lost touch, but Nell knew where he lived and decided that she would go there and ask him straight out and that he would not fail her. There were steps up to his house with pillars on either side, pillars freshly painted in cream, a cream that was tinted, like cream mixed with strawberries. His laundry box was outside, and the two ornamental bay trees had just been hosed. The door had two bells, and feeling lowly, she was tempted to ring the bell marked NURSERY. When he came to the door, he said, "How strange." He had dreamt of her recently, dreamt of her in a carriage where the horses had run wild, broken through a cordon of spectators, and how she clung to the shaft and was assumed into heaven. Of course he remembered her, remembered her wonderful parties, remembered the night she dropped the goose on the kitchen floor and he and she had got the giggles as they picked it up and put the various pieces back in the roasting pan to give them a crispy look. He remembered the guests that had quarrelled, guests that had got drunk, Duncan of course, and the poet or the would-be poet who insisted on reciting his own verses—"And the green-eyed whore, in the red-eyed dress," he began; "Stalks the tundra of my waiting groin," she continued. They laughed. Yes, it would be all right.

He was probably wondering why she had come and why she was trembling so. She refused tea, because she got the distinct impression that it would be a bother since the kitchen was in the basement and his daily had gone. The room had the impersonal aura of a small museum, one of those rooms where a famous person's effects are kept in a state of gloom, roped off from life. A bronze torso of a man stood in the window, like some sort of guard, but instead of eyes, the sculptor had put gold leaf in the sockets, so that the stare was beyond human comprehension, like a mummy's. She should have asked straightaway. There were flowers everywhere, sheaves of them in tall china vases, wildflowers and cultivated flowers, giving the effect of a garden, and to break the ice she went and smelled them.

"You always used to have beautiful white lilies," he said.

"Well, not now," she said, thinking it a perfect cue, a way of saying, "I don't give parties anymore, as a matter of fact I'm skint and I'm going to be evicted." But she didn't say it then; she hesitated and balked, the way a young greyhound balks when the trapdoor is opened. They spoke of Duncan, his wildness, his madcap friends, the black singer who had joined a cult, shaved his hair, and chanted in Oxford Street with members of his sect. It was in all the papers. They talked of the weather, how ghastly it was, how grey, how possibly it would snow, both agreeing that they would welcome the little flakes the first miraculous hour or two, the mesmerisation when snow first falls. There was constraint between them and she wished now that she had said yes to a cup of tea, because it would create a little distraction, a little hubbub. On the far wall there was a painting of a sandy road leading to a hill, making her ask aloud what lay ahead.

"It's a very happy painting," she said.

"Yes, it's very soothing," he said, and added that it was a bargain, since it had trebled in value. He spoke of fluke in the art world, how some artists, first-rate ones, went down in value while others soared. Then she admired a tapestry, all its threads a dim bluish grey, so that in the distance it looked like mist, mist from which figures were dimly emerging. Its companion, he told her, was in the Louvre. He got out a book to show her the other, almost but not quite identical. The birds—ostriches, she thought— were grouped differently and had a more vacant stare.

"The Louvre" was all she could think to say. To pluck up courage she went to the bathroom and in there addressed herself in a round Italianate mirror with plump little cupids clinging to the rim; then, turning, she looked into the lavatory bowl, where in the veined, stippled, cream-white china she read the name W. Crapp & Sons.

"That's a very funny name in the lavatory," she said.

"Isn't it," he said. He had moved a bowl of flowers, probably because they had been too near a radiator and might perish. The radiator let out occasional burps.

"Did somebody send you the flowers?" she asked.

"No . . . nobody ever sends me flowers," he said, a little pee-vishly, but she knew that he was not peevish at heart, because he had told her a story once of how much he loved his mother, his mother so beautiful, so remote, like alabaster, and that then one day as a great treat he went in a car with his mother, a huge, old-fashioned car, from London to Brighton, plaid rugs over their knees, a picnic basket on the front seat, and his mother allowing him to snuggle near her, so that he could not only smell her per-fume but smell the way it lingered in her clothes, changing and being changed by the different fabrics, so that on her scarf, which was chiffon, it smelt quite different from the smell of her astrakhan cuffs. His mother, he told Nell, always dressed like Anna Karenina and always took a lover. Lydia was her name. No sooner had they got there than Lydia, seeing the choppiness of the sea, decided that it was time to go home again. They did not even get out of the car and the picnic remained untouched. It was because he had told her that story and wept a little that she had a special fondness for him, and felt brave enough to approach him.

"I love your house," she said with perhaps too much flattery.

"Yes, it is nice . . . but I don't know how long I can afford it," he said, and she gasped, believing that he had guessed her intent.

"Freddie," she said urgently, "I've come to ask a favour, it's terrible . . . I've come to ask you for the loan of five hundred pounds." She could not have foreseen his reaction. He went quite pale, drained of colour, and began to cough—dry, involuntary coughs—and then he clutched a velvet cushion from the sofa arm-rest and said that any other time he might be able to let her have it but that he had just loaned a huge sum to his profligate cousin.

"Family," he said weakly, and she knew that she had done something awful, something that he always dreaded, and that her asking hurt him as much as if he had actually parted with the money. Then he began to sneeze, was seized by a bout of it, trying to say, " 'Scoose me . . . aschscoose me . . ." Clutching the cushion, he doubled up, as if gripped by pain. She alternated between hating him and pitying him, and she thought, If he could do it, it would be wonderful for him, and she also thought that she had made him wretched, that after she left he would have to lie down, that he would probably lie down all day, and later he would ring someone, not his cousin, relate what happened, and say people had no shame now, none. She rose to go, saying that she should not have come, that it was importunate, and then somehow to redeem herself, to make it excusable, she said that she would send him a change of address.

"Oh, poor you," he said, quite concerned now, asking where she would go, and as she pondered this, he was quick with sug-gestions: the evening paper, *Lady* magazine, maybe go a bit out-side London, somewhere like Barnes, which was leafy and bound to be cheaper. She could see the fear in his eyes, his drained eyes, which had little cysts on the lid; a fear that perhaps she would ask again or linger, and she thought bitterly, Five hundred pounds would not alter your room or your life one iota, and yet she despised herself for having come and for reducing them both to such ignominy.

"I must call my aunt . . . she had a nasty fall," he said, as if the summoning up of a relative gave him a cloak of decency. His aunt lived in Kew, chose it so as to be near the tropical plants, and had had a rose named after her, a purple rose.

Walking down the street, she imagined him pacing, grinding his jaw, and saying, "Why should I . . . why the hell should I . . . I don't see why I should," then ringing someone, a chum, and describing it down to the tiniest detail, how she had arrived with her woebegone look, kept admiring everything, gushing over everything, then sprung it on him—"Five hundred pounds . . . five hundred pounds . . . She must be mad, Pollyanna time . . ."

She walked, not knowing where she should go.

23

"I'll never slip up again," she said to them, thinking what a contrast to their glee and dizziness the day she was granted custody of them, to their war games each Sunday, which now seemed to have happened in another era altogether, a more rosy era when she herself, though she did not realise it, was pregnant with hope—daft, young, indeterminate hope. Here she was, on the floor, wiping up pools of water on the very eve of her departure from her own house. Pipes had burst in the bathroom, in the kitchen, and in the downstairs hall, so that she was running hither and thither from one place to another, with floor cloths to soak up the water that came gushing out and overfilled the bowls which she had laid under the pipes, there not being enough space for a bucket.

They had come in, pale, truculent, a look of protest in the eyes, the flecks of snow on their duffle coats like sodden grains of rice. What shame had she wrought? It was week-old snow, and in the garden the black bushes and the treetops poked their way through, so that it looked like a torn counterpane, whereas on the ground itself, it lay in thick untrammelled piles. She had not gone out there, nor would she; the farewells were already done. The path from the front gate was perilous, as Paddy said, becoming quite officious, adding that someone, meaning her, should have sprinkled salt on it. The neighbouring paths had had that sensible service done to them. At moments like this she saw traces of his father in him. Ah, wouldn't his father rejoice now at her fall. "I thought we wouldn't tell your dad just yet," she had said. They couldn't see why not, since he would know sooner or later. Terse letters were exchanged between them, and Madeline had sent them a junior encyclopaedia at Christmas, with both their names on it. Yes, when sorrows come, they come not in single file. By their expressions, by their grudge, they showed their fury, along with tart rejoinders, supposedly to the air. They could see it coming. Parties. Cigars from Cuba, no less. Moreover, where were those wooden boxes with sliding tops in which they had been packed? Paddy enquired. They would serve as pen and pencil cases in his now penurious state. Pointing to two urns filled with shrubs, he asked, "Are we taking these?" A bird was pecking on hard red berries, and wise to the futility, she pitied it.

"They're going into storage," she said without any concession. How dare they not sympathise with her in this, when they had been with her in all else, in every breath and hesitation of their joined lives. Was she not entitled to make mistakes, have longings and hungers that in her own way she sought to appease? No one was just a mother, a vassal. Those galas had been for a reason, to stave off loneliness, to find friends, which of course secretly meant *the* friend, the lover, the bridegroom.

"Storage," Tristan said with a sting. He was more openly cutting than his brother, thought he could get away with it better because of his erstwhile charms.

In fact, storage was a fairly humble affair, an address she had found through the local newspaper, run by a man who kept a small amount of stuff in some sheds in his garden. He was due later that day with his van. Arguments then arose as to which of their belongings they would store and which they should bring back to school.

"Just like gypsies," she heard one say to the other in the next room, where they had gone to dismantle the train set, put the tracks carefully in boxes, put their toy soldiers in wadding, and take down their posters. All the while she could hear them talking in low voices that she was meant not to overhear. She shouted that there was food on the table, hot toast and Gentlemen's Relish.

Food, the great binder. They didn't want it. They'd had crisps on the train. They were going to have it—that was her ultimatum to them.

She was still mopping up the water and thought that, as it gushed out, it had an animate quality, like a patient coughing blood or green bile onto the floor, onto the rags, onto her memories. It had all been for Duncan. To win him. Of all the nights, the one in which he'd called unexpectedly had thrilled her most, called with two producers, and because there was no largesse, she ran to a restaurant at the top of the street and bought wine and a hamper of things, pâté, shellfish, cooked veal—a feast to pamper them, to keep them captive, like Odysseus in the clutches of the Sirens.

A million other follies, such as going to an antique market on Saturdays to buy something to deck herself with. First it was a necklace, a long necklace with pale violet stones that looked as if they had been rinsed in violet water and old-fashioned suede shoes with diamanté buckles which, when she stepped into them, allowed her to be someone else, a contessa perhaps.

Then it was a dress, a period piece by a famous French designer, something she could sell again if she must, as the young assistant so tactlessly said. It, too, was purple, with lace fluting around the collar and a lace bib down the front. There were footstools and cushions; there was a three-branched silver candelabrum, its insouciant arms like a tree, on her windowsill, beckoning, beckoning.

Many of the things she resold. She had brought them to an auction room and, like others in the same boat, stood at a counter, sheepishly took them out of their newspaper wrapping and waited while an assistant came and examined them, looked for flaws or chips of any kind. In the case of the dress she was told she would have to wait until the costume expert came back from lunch to make sure that it was not a fake.

"It's not a fake," she had said, chafing at the fact that she had to be there at all. The man next to her had teddy bears, a whole family of them, and, if anything, seemed more fractious than she and showed it by refusing to put out a cigarette, which a porter had asked him to do. It smote her to think of her little gilded sofa being banished to a shed, likewise her books, her bed, the prayer chair, and the mother-of-pearl table to which she had given the fancy name of Zena.

She had found lodgings in a large house in Chelsea. The owner, who was crusty, assured her that he let out some of the upper rooms simply to keep them aired. She had been recommended to him through her boss, and she saw at once that he was a miser, saw by the fact that he was busy with his paper knife, slitting used envelopes for memo pads, and felt it by the funerary note in his voice as he inveighed against everything, noise, neighbours, the working class. He was an interior decorator, but that, too, as he told her, was a fading business, taken over by charlatans and spivs. His reign had been.

"I'm an artist . . . an artist," he kept telling her, while stroking his little poodle, which seemed to have some sort of disease, its skin through its thin coat pink and flaky. Though galled at where she had exiled herself, she kept up a perfect pretence, enquired about cooking arrangements, the other lodgers, if guests were allowed, and even then, even then, believed that deliverance would come.

As she squeezed the cloths, then emptied the basins and went back to her task, she thought that perhaps she had always wanted this downfall. Money or the lack of it had caused such grief in her parents' life, and the bills which lay like warrants on the dresser, stuck in behind plates, appeared before her eyes now, reminders, with her mother exclaiming, How in God's name would they manage, and her father saying in Jaysus' name to stop persecuting him.

While she was emptying the bowl, a pipe in another room decided to divulge its quota of rusted water, and going in there she saw that her beautiful Afghan rug was ruined, its little blue whorled border a daub. It was in answer to her piercing cry that they came. Seeing her and seeing it, they could no longer sustain their hostility.

"Poor Mumsies," Paddy said, and touched her arm, and Tristan followed suit, and now they knelt, all three, squeezing bits of rags, and they said consoling things, such as that everything would be all right and they would chip in, sell their toy soldiers, leave school, do holiday work, rent a cottage in Wales. Rash and inspired schemes fell from their lips, their hands unconsciously repelled by the brown ooze and the slush of the water, but doing it all the same, and that was what mattered. *"Plus ça change,"* Tristan said solemnly, as into the cold uncarpeted space of the hall, a large envelope fell. They jumped, each probably thinking that it might be a reprieve.

"Congratulations . . ." Paddy read aloud, telling her that according to the said document she had been specially chosen to receive a free gift.

"What is it, love?" she asked.

"A secateurs with which to cut the stems of your houseplants," he said, and waved a booklet which contained pictures and flowing sentiments about cyclamen.

They laughed then, the pent-up laughter of anxiety, the laughter of people who have been estranged, and glad of this abandon, they laughed loudly, shrilly, exuberantly—eddies of laughter everywhere, issuing out like the burps of water; laughter on the mirror's front, on the hairy underlay which needed cheering, along the bannister sheer from their sliding; laughter in the old fire grate and lurking in the corner where the new occupants, whoever they were, might catch some hint of it, like a whinny; laughter that was loud, oh yes, loud and feverish, but not quite friendly, laughter that said, "How bitter it is . . . how bitter life is"; but laughter all the same.

On her first evening in her new lodgings, she sat by the window in her room on the second floor and took stock of the street below. The lodging house, imposing, double-fronted, and painted a dun yellow, looked out on a narrow street of tiny brick houses, cottages really, brightened by white or cream stucco. It was a little enclave, not rich, not ostentatious, but well loved, each house with its windowbox and its purtiness. Mercifully, there was a view of the sky, a ligament heaped with, at that moment, some clouds, pink compilations that looked fetching, chaises to lie upon. To the right of these pretty creatures she could see a statue of a woman, a white plaster woman with a tiara above her head, not resting on it, hovering, in some sort of miraculous suspension. Far from being downcast at having lost everything, she felt elated, felt that these clouds and this rising woman were a sign to her, a challenge and a reminder that she was a woman, too, that her hopes had not died, had merely been put to sleep and were waiting to be ignited by some new, some magic intervention. Yes, a chapter had just begun. Who has not thought the same; who, when every link has snapped, has not imagined redemption, some lifeline materialising from nowhere, and, sighting a few luminous pink clouds, has not declared them to be castles in the air?

Is this not the last fervent hallucination against futility, the skeleton of famished dream?

Part III

24

Many were out that blustery Sunday, and for a variety of reasons. Some to pass time or allow their children recreation in one of the parks, to swing them on swings, plonk them on rocking horses and slides, and say, "Yes, Mummy is watching," in answer to their voracious claims: "Watch me, I'm brilliant . . . I'm brilliant." Others came to canter on horseback, at considerable expense, up and down a stretch of upturned gravelly topsoil, within earshot of buses and motorcars, thereby annulling the sweet illusion of countryside. Still others came to visit friends in their homes, to eat pork and crackling and three kinds of veg, and then to sink into the swamps of their sofas; relatives went to visit the sick in hospitals and nursing homes scattered all over the city, dying people or merely sick people propped up sullenly on wrought-iron beds, their eyes towards the door, eyes waiting for the familiar face, the bunch of carnations, the box of sweets; an inferno of coughs, growls, and stares, the stares silently deducing who would go first.

Yes, many were out and about, defying the March wind, which, true to its record, was cutting. It tore at things. It ripped the petals of the primroses, made mince of these little hairy creatures with their butter-yellow-ringed centres; sent pages of newspaper skeetering along the towpath because people from passing motors threw sections about, sections that were too dull or too commodious for the lazy grip of one citified hand, and so from the ground criminals or royalty or strippers stared up at one for an instant before the flimsy leaf of newspaper dashed off in search of some more secure lodging. But it was late now and most were heading home, the last scurry to savour the end of the Sunday, to bask in it before the beginning of the working week, the grind.

Nell did not hurry just yet, drew back with a shudder, as the motorists, also mindful of the passing day, began a lively vendetta with one another, tearing up the centre avenue that runs through the park, careless as to whether a child or a rider might be crossing in the dusk.

She would go home soon, or quite soon. She had come out to allow Paddy the house to himself. Yes, it was like that. Not open war but estrangement. It was his year before university and he was attending a crammer before retaking two subjects, English and maths. He would have liked his own flat, as he often said, but was stuck with her, as he did not say but which they both knew. When does a mother become an incubus? It was not the first time she had asked, nor would it be the last. She had asked it, mulled over it in the years as they grew away from her, sometimes in a burst, sometimes then an intermittent relapse of tenderness, a freshly found compliment, saying, "You look nice," but more and more this aloofness, spending time with friends, roughing it with backpacks in foreign parts and coming home nut-brown, a tan which they were proud of but which she believed coarsened their features. Sometimes a little gift for her, a plaque or a poster, and sometimes not. There had been girlfriends, of course, those who stayed overnight, often secretly, a great hush-hush going up the stairs and not coming down, but she knew because there would be an earring on the kitchen table or a hairbrush or a perfume spray in the bathroom.

A few who stayed quite openly and did not want to leave dallied, sat on the sofa in the morning, and begged by the acceptance of endless cups of coffee to be let stay. Oh, she knew why and she understood why and she pitied them for their clinging, but saw the mistake.

Meg was one of these. Meg short for Megan. Meg with long

black satiny hair, which she drew over her face, web-like, to hide from people, because hide she did, her principal communication being with a cigarette, always one between her lips and several on her person, loose cigarettes, and her spare hand cupped permanently to take the ashes in case she should be scolded. Meg had replaced Emma in Paddy's affections, although she was not nearly so vivid, not nearly so striking, more a waif. Emma had got her comeuppance, made herself too available and had to be discarded, the very same as the pompom scarf she had knitted for him was discarded, high up in the cupboard where old suitcases and broken tennis rackets were dumped. Nell consoled her as best she could, the morning it happened. It was a Sunday, summery, and Emma in a chiffon dress, a slightly absurd attire, standing in the street, by the lamppost, next to Paddy's chained bicycle, waiting, yet deliberately refusing to look up, not acknowledging the series of welcome tappings, staring with a false security, a close-to-breaking smile, waiting for him to appear. His bicycle was his trademark, secondhand, something thin and blemished about it, the mudguards painted white, the handlebars a scratched metal, and a jaunty saddle which he had recently acquired. When his saddle got stolen he put a printed sign on his bicycle which said, HOW WOULD YOU LIKE IT IF YOUR ——— WAS STOLEN, and had drawn an oblong for a saddle. She didn't like that, said it was an infringement. "An infringement of what?" he had said. "Privacy," she had said, and he turned away.

Emma knew his moves, knew that on weekdays he went to his crammer and on Sundays he went for a swim. She was still beautiful, but something had gone, her preen had gone. Nell heard that, once, in her boarding school, Emma had gone down to the lake with the intention of drowning herself or half-drowning herself, having taken a bottle of wine and sleeping tablets, which she had pinched from the infirmary. She had had to be pumped. Paddy had told Nell so, but without a flicker of emotion, refusing to see that it might have anything to do with him. Several times, Nell tapped on the window and still Emma did not look up, remained in her see-through dress as if posing for a camera.

They were in another house by then, a cottage, not so spacious as their house on the river but their own; their own, as she often said.

How she had hated being in lodgings, hated the poodle that smelt of pee and the landlord with his thrift and his paraffin heaters who was always spying on them, hated her neighbor Rachel, who talked all the time about "Mother," how she and Mother had met the Queen's equerry, or how they had dreamed of having a cruise, or how Mother had deceived her about her illness, kept it from her, to make the pain of parting that bit less. The three lodgers, Rachel, Genevieve, and herself, never ate together, and met on the stairs, carrying their trays, embodiments of grumpiness and shame. All had known better days and believed they deserved a better fate. The lustre and daring of her dizzy gatherings used to possess her with a kind of gall, as she saw the rooms, her former rooms, festive, little night-lights in red pots up the length of the stairs, her brain and body in a transport waiting for Duncan. Time magnified the thrill, the gaiety of these events, time opened up the rooms as if double doors or shutters swung apart; rooms as for sacrament, at once holy and profane: sheaves of flowers, the night-lights in deep red little pots, not only to show the way, but as a come-hither to some orgiastic rite. What dreams she had fostered then. Even for the mad spate of a week envisaging Dr. Rat leaving his nut-brown wife and following her up those red-hued stairs. A memory, too, of velvet cushions, goblets threaded with gold, cranberry glasses that seemed to have the essence of the fruits secreted somewhere within them, the berries on the surface recalling a kitchen garden in summer with the soft clusters of limp berries dawdling on thin cane. She had wanted heartbreak, yes; by choosing him she had wanted the love that lives on half-sentences, half-promises, the aftermath of broken chords. What saddened her was not just the pain, not just the excruciation but the malady deep within which wanted it and would possibly always want it, as if love were a dispensation denied her. Her paradise was to be outside, imagining, looking in.

He had died suddenly, of a stroke, in Canada. Died in a theatre, his chosen milieu, or, rather, keeled over in a theatre and died soon after in a big hospital. Spoke Irish as he ebbed away. There was a girl with him. There would be. The girl, Nancy, wrote to her and said she intended making a film of her lover's life. Her lover's life! She had enclosed a list of names to whom she had also written, famous names, and to each made this brouhaha about her lover, suggesting that all would agree, would they not, that he was an exceptional man, a Renaissance man. Yes, Duncan had wanted death, had walked to it as purposefully as people walk to work. In a friend's house the previous New Year's Eve, he had written in a guest book: "Life is a habit of walking and talking, I have a habit of walking towards death." He had written to her from that house that revelled night, written to say he missed her; he was at present on cloud number 999 while a woman of uncertain age with a gloriously mournful voice was outside the window singing "Red Roses for Me." He was buried far away. For a while Nell was convinced that he would appear to her, that it would not be in her bed at night when ghost and ghost thud are imminent, but in daylight, in a café perhaps, or on the street, sidling up to her, and that he would tell her something significant, something amazing about life, or about death, and that in some strange way all the barriers between them would have passed, by virtue of his death, because over there he had discovered their affinity.

"Put that in your pipe," she said to Nancy as she held the letter to a candle flame and saw the crepe blobs of ash as birds fluttering around his soul.

25

The morning she learned of the change in her fortune was the second most affirmative in her life, the first being the day she was awarded custody of them. It came in a business envelope with a solicitor's name on the back, her father's solicitor. He had written to her after her father had died, had sent an inventory of all that was owed, a pitiful and chastening list, which included fees to barbers, butchers, a stud farm, and several hotels. It seemed that she might be liable for further debts while the farm was being sold and death duties paid, but instead she learned that she was to receive a sizeable sum and that it would be payable by the end of the month. With what pride she led them to their new abode, did not reveal what the surprise was, merely got special permission for them to be allowed out and met them at the station in a chauffeur-driven car, with a gift for each of them on the back seat, gift vouchers to get themselves togged out, in folders that bore their initials.

"Emma is out on the street . . . She's been there for an hour," she said as she went to Paddy's room to waken him. Sitting up, blinking, he asked what time it was and feared that he would be late for his swim. That was another thing: he slept late, he stayed out late and slept late. His excuse was that he was growing, still growing. They were at variance about so many things, clothes, food, films, girls. Tristan had even ventured to a brothel on his travels, the previous holidays, had sought out the red-light district in the big town and was being admitted, until the madame noticed, then pinched his cheek and called him "Poussin . . . poussin"—little chicken—and sent him away with advice to come back in a year or so.

"What would you have done if," Nell asked, too embarrassed to finish the sentence.

"Gone up," he said nonchalantly, and she longed to ask if he would have known what to do and so forth, but of course did not and could not ask. That was the thing. These hesitations springing up, multiplying. Their housemaster had given them talks about sex, showing them slides from nature, slides of insects and butterflies, but what they knew or did not know was uncertain, until his girlfriend, Tracy, announced she was pregnant. She phoned from America, asked urgently for Tristan, and hearing the news first he was staunch, then cried as she had not seen him cry since infancy, when bested; then he steeled himself and withdrew into a shell. He refused to eat, refused to speak, sat by the phone and snarled when Nell spoke to offer advice or sympathy, and eventually he turned on her and said, "Can't you let me do even this much alone."

A week passed and Tracy was not pregnant. In the aftermath of hearing it, and the relief of knowing that he would not have to be a father, he became jocular, as did Paddy, and they joked about fathers and uncles and were merry with her now, agreeing to go to a restaurant, an Italian restaurant where the owner gave them complimentary liqueur, a sweet transparent syrup with a coffee bean in it, and macaroons, the thin tissue paper of which, when lit, soared to the ceiling like feathery mantles.

"Father, have a Grisstick," Paddy said.

"Oh, *molto* thank you, Uncle," Tristan said, while they wondered skittishly if it would have been a boy or a girl, Tristan moreover vowing to teach Tracy a lesson when he next saw her, except that she did not return to the school, her parents deciding to send her to an "all girls" in Maryland. That was the way of it. Parents all over the world in a dither, having to admit that their children had too much licence, too much rope, and yet beholden to them, as she was that Sunday morning, calling Paddy again and again to come to Emma's rescue and fearing a sulk as he emerged, pulling on a sweater and yawning the vindicating bout of yawns.

"Back from your rustications," he said to Emma with open sarcasm, as she put down her embroidered bag. It was plain to see that his affections were not only dead, they had gone sour. He was asking brusquely why she had left the farm where she had gone for holiday work, spoke to her in crisp terms, as a parent might, said if she wanted to be a vet, a farm was where she should be. She did not want to be a vet, she had changed her mind and wanted to be a dancer.

"You're too tall," he said without a scrap of friendliness, and so they sat at the kitchen table in this semi-sulk, Emma gazing at him, willing to do anything so long as she was not turned away.

"The farmer and his wife went to bed at nine o'clock . . . I was miz," Emma said.

"Good for you," he said. He might just as well have led her upstairs and opened the door above the wardrobe proper and shown her the discarded scarf, emblem of her discarded self. Most probably he had told her it had ended, but the tedium of the country had irrationally renewed her hopes. She waved two tickets, which she had been given for a concert, a group from Mali were to play in Glastonbury; she had chosen it because it was mystical.

"Glastonbury!" he said; he could just have easily said fiddlesticks.

"We're to bring tents," she said, her enthusiasm leading them out the door, onto a train, cups of tea on the train, holding hands, lovers again, because had they not parted bitterly once or twice before and found that they were inseparable? He was adamant, he had studies, he had grinds, and soon had an appointment to swim with an instructor who was teaching him to dive.

"Just this once as a goodbye, Pads," she said in a babyish voice that must have been the voice he thrilled to, when they first fell in love, or after they had fallen in love and he would hawk her violin from venue to venue. He was not to be cajoled. If anything, it made him more abrupt, made him rise from the table, automatically look at the wall clock, and tell it, not them, that he had to be at Porchester baths in fifteen minutes.

"Can I stay a bit longer?" Emma asked Nell, her eyes filling with tears.

"Of course," Nell said.

At first they didn't talk at all, Emma merely accepting a mug of tea, then another, then a gin; tears huge, like pendants, dropped onto the table or plonked onto the newspaper.

"He asked me to marry him the first night we were lovers," she said eventually. It was not said in accusation but in shock, because no matter what the rejection, she had clung to that utterance; it was her brief, at school, at home, in the country, wherever she happened to be. Now the simple realisation had dawned on her and she knew that nothing could temper it, she had just heard his goodbye.

"I'll kill myself," she said in a quiet tone, a quiet, dry tone in contrast to her tears, and then tumbling into a rawer denizen of desperation, she began to tell of her father, her poor father and his affair, his one and only affair, and her mother learning of it and telling him that he had to get out, out; that they had cut a deal and he knew what the deal was, but he broke it. She recalled her father packing one Sunday afternoon, then knocking on her bedroom door and asking her sheepishly if she would have tea with him sometimes, then his leaving—his clothes on hangers, his clock and his Wellies in a basket. Then a foretaste of their future—the empty house, the television turned on (it was *Oliver Twist*), and her mother banging things. But before an hour had passed, a shocked, blanched shell of a man reappeared in the doorway, knocked—because he had not taken his key—staggered in, crying, and without any preamble told them that his mistress did not want him, had turned him down, and there in the hall, he knelt and begged like a child to be let back, to be reinstated, promising to be faithful, to be on time for meals, to be a family man. His humbling of himself was too awful, and the shame of it somehow reflected her own shame now and yet allowed her to understand his suffering all the more, a suffering she could do nothing about, because he had settled for that which he could not endure. Half-dazed, half-broken, she asked if life had to be like that, asked how people like her father or even her mother kept going, put a brave face on it, went to parties and remembered anniversaries when their hearts were dungeons? How? How?

"They just do," Nell said, and repeated it.

"Have you ever been like this?" Emma asked, looking up with the pleading, sorrowful look of a creature who thinks it has known the worst and in some part of itself luxuriates in that sorrow and thinks, I am a woman now.

"Let's go for a little walk," Nell said, remembering those several desertions of her own, each succeeding one a mad replica of the other, heartbreak, that no house, no room, no confessional could contain, and how when it was at fever point, she used to walk the city, thinking she could leave it somewhere, leave it in a little green hut in Battersea Park that overlooked the river, leave it at a deserted taxi rank, or outside the shop that imported Spanish tiles, their glazed, refracted blues, totems of baked and sunnier climes. Once she was so askew she even thought she could leave it in a launderette and see it whirl around in a grey muzzle of suds.

26

The house was in darkness as she came in, calling Paddy, eager to
tell him that she had got some flowers on the way home, Casa-
blanca lilies, his favourites. The vendor at the corner was taking
down his canvas awning and humming to himself as he placed the
unbought bunches into long, perforated boxes with the word HOL-
LAND stamped on them. Not only was he willing to serve her, but
said she was to have whatever she fancied, for a couple of quid,
and then he armed her with this great bunch.

Turning on the light in the kitchen, she saw that indeed Paddy
had risen, had breakfasted, because there was a mug on top of a
plate and the remains of burnt toast, the burnt crumbs infinitesimal, fine as the sand in an egg timer, only charred. Also, his coat
was on the bannister. So he had not gone out. So often now did she
know his moves merely by his belongings and his bicycle.

"Paddy . . . Pads," she called, going up the stairs to his room,
the unwrapped lilies like a babe in her arms, and being so proud
of them, she opened his door without knocking, a thing she made
a rule never to do. He was cross-legged on the floor, still in his
pyjamas, with a blanket over him, sunk in thought or in prayer.

"What are you doing?" she asked, astonished.

"Nothing," he said, and confirmed it with the split word "Nothing." His voice was different, and although she could not see his
face, she was certain that it looked intense.

"What are you doing, Paddy?" she said, this time a little more anxiously.

"Laying ghosts," he said, but without raising his head, and then continued his chant.

"What ghosts?" Her voice now was high-pitched. He began to laugh. It was not a normal laugh and it was not a friendly laugh and there was mockery in it.

"Are you making fun of me?" she said, a little too tetchily.

"Not at all . . . I am masked forevermore," he said formally, his voice faraway, like a voice fogged by ether.

"You're on something," she said.

"Mother," he said with exaggerated restraint.

"This is craziness," she said as she switched on the light and crossed over to stare into his face, dumping the flowers onto the unmade bed. His eyes were very large and wistful as he asked her if she would be kind enough to leave the room, since he was in the middle of a Zen meditation.

Of course, she had not been blind to his moods, sometimes so tender with her, other times so remote, still others shamelessly dismissive, saying, "Yeah, yeah," and then those peculiar messages for him on her answering machine, code words—"Did you get the A," or "Have you got a rush," and his always having a plausible answer for them. The answer was that Paddy, who should be studying, who should be alert, was sitting in the middle of a room, murmuring some foreign chant and telling her that if she did not leave he would have the unpleasant task of throwing her out, a thing he would rather not do.

"Don't you dare," she said, and bent towards him, a venom in her stoop and in her voice that she scarcely knew she had. He saw it and flinched a little, his face now growing quite pale as he tried to reason with her, and his way of reasoning was to say something so incomprehensible that she thought she would strike him.

"By seeing only the circles and the lines we miss the galaxies."

"Oh, Jesus," she said, embracing him with a hold that had at once terror, rage, tenderness, and protectiveness in it. She knew that she must not estrange him, so she knelt and said as calmly as she could, "What is it, love, what's gone wrong?"

"You've got a yellow nose," he said, fingering the pollen from the lily and then studying it as if it was of great importance.

"I'm frightened for you and I'm frightened for me," she said without rancour.

"It's one of those worlds," he said, but there was fear in his eyes, the selfsame soft hurt in them that she had seen once before in his youth, when some hooligans had stopped him on the footbridge across the river and asked him if he had got a light, and he had said innocently in reply that he did not smoke as he was too young, and then their pounding into him, five of them, knocking him to the ground, kicking him, taking his fountain pen and his comb and threatening to throw him into the river. His eyes had the same stricken look, a look of someone mauled by the enemy, except that she was the enemy now.

"How long has this been going on?" she asked, and remembered so many clues: his being late for everything, the state of the house if she went away for a weekend, lavatory paper in bows all over the pictures, squiggles on the telephone notebooks, her shawls in disarray.

"Fiddlesticks," he said, then turned to a figure which existed in his reverie and said in a cold voice, "They do bug you, don't they?"

"Yes, they do, and they have every right to bug you, and they are your parents who pay for you, watch over you, worry over you, and I'm one of them and I will not see you go down the drain," she said, each word delivered with a ferocity that brought spittle flying.

"Oh . . . cut it off the carpet," he said blithely, recalling the night of her own mad transport, years before, when he had rung from school to ask for money and did not recognise his own mother's voice, so far gone was she, on some scaffolding of her own.

"You mustn't go under, Pads, like I did . . . yes, I did," she said, touching the fold of the blanket where his arm would be, to reach him, and in the softest, most confidential voice that she could summon told him that they were a team, that he and Tristan and she were a team who loved each other, sustained each other, and that her purpose was not "Thou shalt not" but to help, as his equal, as his friend.

"Mumsies," he said then, feeling her desperation, not by her anger but by the abatement of it, and assuring her that he would not do anything silly, that he knew what he was doing and that fasting and meditation led to altered states and the opening up of the rich seam of the unconscious. She herself could benefit from it, could become happier, healthier, by making a friend of her demons.

"Healthier?" she said.

"Dare to know—Siggy Freud," and he looked at her with a kind of weary wisdom.

"So you have had drugs," she said, looking at him earnestly, so that no lie could escape from his lips, and responding to it in the only way possible, he admitted that most young people had a smoke and that, yes, once at school before a dance he was shy and his friend Jeremy had said, "Do you want to turn on?" and then both going up to the stables, pretending they were going with oats for the girls' ponies, having a few puffs and as a result being swells at the dance.

"It's just a bit of grass . . . you can grow it in the window box," he said, putting his hands out now both to make light of it and to welcome her into his mystic state. In return, she offered him the flowers to smell, and still in his half-reverie, he nosed his way into them as he once used to into the wardrobe of her clothes, he and Tristan playing grownups and dancing waltzes with her.

"Were you that shy at school?' she said, thinking how animated they had all seemed in the quad whenever she called, envying them the rapport which they had with each other, boys and girls joking and tussling. Having a steady at school was very important, he told her. Once you had a steady you had arrived. It meant that you went into dining hall with her, you went around the grounds with her, you held hands in front of teachers and pupils and therefore let it be known that she was yours, your princess.

"I had to fight for Boda," he said, allowing thoughts to sift slowly, sweetly into his brain. She could feel the reserve, the delicacy of these thoughts, and knew that the harsh words of a few minutes earlier had been dissolved.

"How about us going out to dinner, to a nice restaurant?" she said.

"Fab," he said, and then helped her up, her knees snapping like dry kindling.

"I'm getting old, Pads," she said.

"No, you're not," he said in a voice all tender.

"I'll ring and book somewhere nice," she said, and went off to do that and to make herself presentable.

When the doorbell rang she jumped, as they were expecting no one and there was rarely a delivery on Sunday, rarely circulars, or a youth, himself dim-sighted, coming to sell dishcloths for the blind. For one giddy moment she thought it might be Tristan, that he might have got the Sunday off and that all three of them would celebrate. It was Jock, Paddy's friend, the friend she liked least and whom she believed to be at the root of this waywardness.

"Oh, Jock," she said, trying not to show her resentment.

"How do you like my pants?" he said, then lifted his thigh to show orange trousers, iridescent, clinging.

"Very smart," she said, intending not to invite him in.

"Where is the Boy," he said, at which Paddy opened the bath-room door and called out in a voice flush with friendship, "Jock . . . the Jockser . . . come up."

"You didn't go to Australia," Nell said, having heard from Paddy that Jock's family had arranged for him to go to a sheep farm where he might mend his ways, having crashed cars, been expelled from three schools, and once been arrested for shoplift-ing. He assured her that though his parents had Australia in mind, he himself had developed a well-timed tenacious bout of pneumo-nia. In fact, he was staying put in the old country and was about to start a business, finding country pads for the rich who were too dim-witted to find them themselves.

Outside the bathroom door she heard Paddy ask, "Who's going to be there?"

"Just us and Steve and Lindy."

"Who's Lindy?"

"You know Lindy!"

"No, I don't know Lindy."

"You know, the girl that looks like she was in Dachau."

"I'm a bit nervy," Paddy said.

"You'll sail through it, you'll sail . . ." Jock said, and at that she opened the door and saw Paddy's ire at her doing so and Jock's amusement at the ridiculous hat that she had donned to go out. It was a black hat with a cockade of black feathers, a hat for a funeral really and not for a dinner.

"I think you've lost weight, Mrs. Steadman," Jock said, and asked if that was not so. She reminded Paddy that she had booked the table and with tempered enthusiasm asked Jock if he would like to join them.

"Another time, another time," he said effusively, as Paddy explained to her that Jock and he had a date, something arranged aeons ago that had gone clean out of his mind, someone's birthday party."

"Whose?" she said, daring him.

"Daphne's," he said, and she knew of course that he was lying, but then she could not accuse him of lying in front of his friend.

"Bit of a night out," Jock said, raising his thigh to study it, as if mesmerized by the glow.

"Do you take drugs, Jock?" she asked, her voice thin and unassured, her temper mounting.

"Oh, Granny takes a trip," he said, smiling at Paddy, then corrected her, saying that the way to ask was not "Do you take drugs?" but "Do you do drugs?" With great persuasiveness he said not him, he took the odd pill for hay fever and night-nurse to curl up, but nothing funky.

"I wouldn't want Paddy to," she said.

"Pads is a big boy now," he said.

"He is also my son," she said, no longer wishing to hide her asperity, at which Jock gripped Paddy's elbow and said, "On our bikes, boy wonder." They eased past her on the stairs, Jock bemused at the fact that, but for pneumonia, he might now be shearing sheep in the outback of Australia.

"It's quite cold, so take your coat," she said to Paddy, her way of saying to him, "Although I have said something sharp to your friend, it is not intended for you."

"I rarely feel the cold," he said, although she knew he did and wore a vest even in summer.

"Don't you," she said, again meaning to convey something intimate, something exclusive.

"And the way it snows," he said, his voice so vague, so charmed.

"It's not snowing, Paddy," she said firmly.

"When I am rich I will buy you a beautiful Russian shawl," he said, and closed his eyelids to allow for a seraphic smile. Part of her hand held the door latch, to follow, to run after him like a fishwife, but the other part knew that it was in vain; she knew by the haste with which they left, the hurry in their stride, the gabble of their voices once they were free of her.

Left alone now and looking through the curtainless window of her upstairs sitting room, which looked out on an identical window, with a ruched blind, she had the entire evening to ponder it, to suppose where he might be—some dark room, as she imagined, with blaring music and cigarette smoke, Jock master of ceremonies, Paddy getting frightened or perhaps skittish, then the transport, him losing his mind as she had and like her unable to return, but gasping, gasping as one gasps at the definitive moment of birth and death. Yes, many hours to toss and turn, a sequence of events that she would never know, no matter how hard she tried, believing that it was then, that Sunday evening with the lilies still withering on the bed, it was then that the rupture had come.

She lay awake until he came in, but come in he did, and creep, so as not to waken her. It was almost five.

In the morning she was affable, felt it the wisest thing.

"Nice birthday?" she asked.

"Tops," he said.

"Jock is a funny one," she said, a little sting in her voice. He wouldn't hear of it—Jock was highly strung, a bit abrupt with people, but his best, his closest friend. If one crashed on the motorway Jock would be there to pick up the pieces. Lunacy. Lunacy, she thought, yet asked politely about the birthday and if there had been a cake, and inwardly shivered at hearing him describe it, its flavour, its filling, its icing, and she thought, He has now entered a labyrinth of untruth where I will never find him, and worse, where he will not find himself.

After he left she decided to search his room, to pillage. She thought that when she did confront him, as of course she must, her evidence must be foolproof, and she also thought that this was the first time she had ever really betrayed him. She opened drawers, looked in folders and old wallets, and opened his precious little memorandum book, which contained a plait of hair and the unfinished story of the Thames. "My River," it was called . . . and ended on a childish note: "And now, dear reader, I must desist, as I hear my favourite sound, which is the tunes from the ice cream van playing, I believe 'The Swedish Rhapsody.' " Jock's letter made her shake. It began:

Dear Chick,
    Any illogicalities in this missive may be attributed to the fact that I'm pissed, not football hooligan rollicking, but squiffy on Asian lager. I'm knackered coz I've done so much s——ing. Also have had elephant treks, rafting expeditions, meeting Anna (squawly Sue's mate), seeing razor blades, milk shakes, and Sherman tanks emerge from the uterus of a young girl, much to the surprise of the accompanying goat at a dodgy nightclub. I'm living, man, and think all studies cock . . . poppycock . . . not a bad pun for a naughty boy . . .
Your ever loving,
ever faithful,
Jock

As she read it, she was seized with the impulse to ring him at his grind, or ring Tristan, or ring his former headmaster to ask what she should do. At work she tried writing him a letter, made five or six attempts, trying to steer a course between reason and concern. She did not want his life ruined. Could they talk? Could he tell her why he had come to this? Did he hate her? Would he see a doctor? Each attempt so feeble that she tore it up, while thinking that if he didn't mend his ways, he would find himself in some gutter. In the end she decided that she would break it to him at dinner, tell him that she had rooted through his papers and was concerned both for him and the company he kept.

"Don't worry . . . I know what I'm doing," he said, but the look on his face was fear coupled with resentment.

"Our minds are all we have," she said and somewhat pompously quoted Sir Arthur Stanley Eddington—"Mind is the first and most direct thing in our experience: all else is remote inference." He agreed. He agreed with everything, said they must talk things over, but unfortunately he had to dash, because it was his night for rock-and-roll and he had entered a competition with Chrissie. They had come in second the week before and were all set for the biggy.

"Let me come with you," she said, and thought in all the years with her parents, with her husband, even that time with Duncan, she had never been quite so beholden as this. From where she sat, in the confines of her kitchen, with a bit of unfinished fish on her plate, he was sinking, not in water but in mire, where his mind, like her own, could meet its end on a street, mangled, run over, in bits.

"Not tonight . . . we'll be a bit nervy," he said, and kissed her sweetly, chewing a bit of parsley as he went out, then called blithely to remind her of a programme on television, so that she would not sit and pine.

Scarcely had he gone than the doorbell rang. She felt certain that he had returned, contrite, that he had come back to say, "Come on, doll up . . . of course you can come, of course you can watch." A strange girl stood quite helplessly, unable to utter a word. Her dark hair had henna lights in it, so that when she stood under the porch lamp strands of it sizzled like threads of spun sugar. Hearing that Paddy had left, she whimpered, looked at her shoes, which were ankle-strapped, and said she didn't know where the gig was, couldn't remember. In the sitting room she sat with her head down, waiting for Paddy to ring, refusing the offer of anything, and from time to time occasionally gave a slow and vacant smile, as if fearing to be chastised or accused of some wrong.

"Did Paddy know you were coming here?" Nell asked.

"I think so," she said vaguely. She was in a blur, lost in her own world, but now and then saying something complimentary, probably so as not to be thrown out.

"You have the same taste as me, you like candles," she said.

"Yes, I like candles," Nell said, and awkwardly stood up and lit one. In fits and starts she got it out of her, that her name was Christina, that though she had been there last Monday she wasn't sure which end of Oxford Street the club was. Then came another long bout of silence and more of her history, which was that she shared a flat with a girl called Sarah, and that Sarah was much better since she got engaged to Craig, who was in India, but that it was all right, because they wrote every day.

"Yes, she's much nicer," she said, withdrawing into herself again while wondering about the time.

Suddenly she was breathing very rapidly, as if she might faint, and her face went the colour of chalk.

"Are you frightened about something?" Nell asked.

"You have the same taste as me," she said again, her eyes glued to a chair, as if she were seeing some prophecy in it.

"Are you in a panic?" Nell asked.

"No . . . no . . . very good about that . . . never get in a panic," she said, then stared at the clock, which was chiming the hour of seven. Then she wondered aloud how old Paddy was and, yielding to a rapid agitation, jumped up, said chocolate munchies, said she was strung out, said she had to be in North London, Highgate, mentioned a patisserie; chocolate, munchies, must, must have, left, right, centre; presently she was gone, leaving only a tissue in which there were some curled orange rinds.

27

"A visitor," Paddy said proudly, and pushed the animal up the step towards her. It was a stray dog which he held with a corner of his grey neck scarf. He had found the poor beast wandering around the tube station, going hither and thither, trying to squeeze through a turnstile, desperate to find its owner. No one paid it any attention, simply kicked it to one side, so that he in sympathy stopped and said, "Good boy . . . good boy," whereupon the dog latched on to him. To compound matters he had correctly guessed its name. He said the first name that came into his head, which was Charlie, and Charlie yapped and licked his hand, answering to what must be his new master. Charlie was a half-breed, a spaniel and something else, something of the wolf.

"What will we do with him, Paddy?" she asked, a bit startled. She need not have asked. She already knew. Charlie was being given a tour of the house, his new home; Charlie was being lifted up to admire the pretty little walled garden outside, where no doubt he would leave his traces.

"What will we do?" she asked again. She did not want a dog and did not consider herself at home with a dog, especially this whelping stray. Charlie guessed her intent, because each time she looked at him he opened his mouth to show a mound of rhubarb-coloured gum and long, discoloured teeth.

"He's vicious," she said.

"Now, Charlie, don't be vicious . . . no biting . . . mustn't bite your new mother," Paddy said, putting his face to Charlie's snout, to which Charlie reacted by giving him a little nip.

"He's vicious," she said, but he would not allow it, said that it was simply that Charlie was blinded from his long hair and could not discern friend from foe. Charlie would have a haircut. Seeing Paddy open and close the blades of the scissors, Charlie decided to throw himself upon a rug, to roll and reroll and writhe on it in some sort of rebellious rite, and in every sense to show recalcitrance. It meant that Charlie had to be lifted, then carried and placed in a corner where she was to hold him and where, in the lowliness of his crouch, she felt treachery.

"Hold him . . . you're not holding him firmly," he said, managing, just, to catch Charlie by the tail as he made for the door, eager now for the relaxed, scissorless atmosphere of the street. This time Charlie was wedged under a chair, while huge dollops of fawn and brown hair dropped onto the floor like tassels.

"You're taking too much off," she said, as patches of Charlie's skin met her eye with a sort of ambivalent pity.

"It'll soon grow," he said, adding that the important thing was to make Charlie clean, make Charlie trim, to deflea him, prepare a little supper for him, and of course allot one of her kitchen bowls, which would now be known as Charlie's bowl. Furthermore, he had to be photographed so that they would have a picture of him were he reckless enough to run off again, were he ever given to the wanderlust.

"Smile . . . both of you . . . smile," Paddy said, taking a quick succession of photographs, her face inclining towards Charlie, who was of two minds whether or not to snap at her. Charlie was their child now, which meant they would have something to talk about and to be united by. Moreover, it allowed her a moment to ask if studies and so forth were going well, and thereby to ask covertly if he had given up his bad habits. He said that yes, everything was hunky, and what was more, his tutor was convinced that he would sail through his A-levels and that next year she and Charlie would be photographed in the august precincts of university grounds.

28

She was upstairs in a bus when she spotted them brightly clad—
Paddy, Jock, and several others in an enclave, next to a mock-
marble public convenience, pigeons hovering around them,
skidding over their faces, mirage-wise. It isn't . . . it can't be, she
said. Jock was in an orange toga and Paddy was wearing a black
hard hat with the name of a champagne company printed in gold
lettering. The bus had moved away, so she jumped up, ran to the
back, hit the emergency bell, and then, indifferent to the death that
might befall her, leapt from the moving bus and came very nearly
a cropper as she weaved into the gutter, in the path of a furious
cyclist. Walking towards them, she passed the black man who had
made three littered steps and an archway his foothold. He was
black through and through, his face smeared with black oil, his
hands covered with black leather gloves, and his body in a black
full-length overcoat. She knew him by sight. He stood behind his
empire, a metal trolley full of rubbish, which each day grew vaster.
She had never dared look him in the eye, but she did now, and saw
dark, hating, unrepentant eyes, staring out at a world that had no
time for him, no place for him, eyes that said, "You have done me
wrong and you will pay for it." His body was utterly still, like a
statue, the arms immobile inside the long black mantle and the
head covered by a smeared trencherman's hat.

She waited a second before crossing the road, both to alert

Paddy and to brace herself for it. Coming close up to them, she felt awkward, unnerved. Some of the girls were topless and two had silver hair which stood up as if cemented. Nearby, on a bench, some drunks beholding the gaudy intruders were torn between laughing at them and driving them away. The day was scorching. The sun made even greater mockery of the dyed hair, the shaven glistening heads, and the paints with which some of the girls had streaked their faces. They looked like night creatures, creatures of the forest, the sockets of their eyes ringed in dark arcs of ritual purple.

"Paddy," she said, crossing to him and trying not to sound too solicitous. It was for a moment as if everything were motionless as he looked at her in stark disbelief.

"Josie," he said, using her middle name, speaking coldly, as if she were a stranger. A girl in a brocade bodice came and told her to hoof it, as it was their pad and they didn't want no oldies.

"This is a private party," Paddy said, and doffed the champagne hat.

"Yes . . . we're having a bit of a party," Jock added, and held up an empty beer tin, feigning largesse. His eyes, which she had never studied before, were green, a hissing green, the colour she imagined a satyr's to be. A Scottish boy in tartan trousers which had been slashed grabbed her arm and said, "Are you lost, missis?"

"That's my son there," she said, pointing to Paddy, but the boy refused to believe her, said to tell that to the birds.

"He is," she said aloud, and some of the girls began to sneer and grumble under their breath.

"You wouldn't disown your mother," she said to the Scottish boy, who laughed and said that he had, but he wouldn't do it now, 'cos he felt marvellous, blood marvellous, that it was better than booze or sex.

"What is?" she asked sharply.

"Shut your gob, Glasgow," one of the girls said.

"You see that little green man," he said, endeavouring to reach up to the pedestrian crossing, which flashed red and green alternately. He was trying to jump up to touch it. He was worried. The little green man seemed to have no willy.

"He's got no willy," he said, and pleaded with his mates to hoist him so that he could make sure. Two of the girls offered to lift him, and reaching it, he shouted out, "God's truth, the poor little bugger has got no willy."

"This is insane," Nell said to Paddy, who was deeply engaged in a dialogue with a pigeon, which he held in his hand. The ground was covered with grey-green pigeon shit, some fresh and some like dried lime. In the heat, a few wallflowers that had been planted were giving up the ghost.

"Go away," Paddy said savagely.

"I haven't seen you for days," she said, and by her voice and by the catch in her voice and by the urgency beneath it, she was also saying, "Don't do this to me, don't, you are my son, you cannot do this, you cannot be so cruel, except that you are."

"Florence," he began, as from his pocket he took a guidebook, which he read from, and, in order to be heard, stood on the low kerb of wall, allowing his audience to convene around him and, as she believed, to exclude her.

"Florence the Divine gathers within its boundaries every form of beauty, lying between the hills of the Arno valley. Idealised by a diaphanous amber light, it mixes art and life gracefully under the town's heraldic signs of the red Turk's cap lily."

"Choose your window," the Scottish boy shouted to one of the drunks who tried to interrupt the speech.

"The Guelphs supported the Pope while the Ghibellines were partisans of the Holy Roman Empire . . ."

"Up the Guelphs," someone shouted.

"Is that where we're going—crikey," one of the girls said, and smiled.

"Yes, sweetie," Paddy said, turning to her, and then, resuming his stance, read out how Savonarola the Dominican was the antithesis of the Florentines, who were artists and high livers, and in 1497 to punish them he organised in the Piazza della Signoria a bonfire of the vanities in which wigs, musical instruments, and books of poetry were burnt.

"A bonfire of the vanities!" two or three shouted, and Nell, unable to restrain herself any further, pushed her way through them and said, "You realise you could get into trouble here, all of you."

"Who's she?" the girl in the broderie anglaise blouse asked. Jock, who had been biding his time, said that if they were to get into trouble, what about the drunks with their meths and their cans of strong brew?

"But alcohol is legal," she said weakly.

"That's what my mum and dad say," another girl piped up, and started mimicking her mother's voice: "Did you say Thursday, darling, yes, Thursday, Wheelers . . . splendid . . . yes, we did . . . We did . . . the same thing only the other way around, almost twenty years ago . . . just after the war . . . number five was conceived there, at the foot of the Atlas Mountains," and her friends laughed because they knew this familiar patter in which she described her mother and her own lousy conception. To round it off, she told Nell that no, she did not get on with her parents, she did not admire the gin-and-tonic gluggers, and if asked what was the most boring thing in this world, she would say Sunday lunch at home. Ugh.

"No, I would not have asked you," Nell said, and turned to ask candidly what they thought they were doing.

"A huge energy field . . . Can't you feel it?" a young man said, and told her that if he wanted to, he could jump on top of any passing bus or vehicle.

"You'll all end up in the clink," she said.

"So . . . we'll all end up in clink," a girl said, and added, "Will someone tell her to leg it."

A young man, blond, with reddish-blond eyelashes, took it upon himself to be mediator. He said that he could see how disturbing it must be for her, but that she must see also. What was it she must see? Why were they so antagonistic? She had not harmed them.

Conceding somewhat and with a little smile, he said no, that she in particular had probably not harmed them, but that harm had been done; she was looking at a group of charged, gifted, alienated people, who in one way or another had lost their way.

"Why? Why?" She was shouting now.

"Who can say why," he said sadly, and then looking away from her over the roofs of the buildings and the roof of a car showroom he said sagely, "There's so much beauty and so much shit . . . too much beauty and too much shit."

"Here, here, Barnaby," some of the girls said while the Scottish boy called out that he wanted to poo.

"I told you to have a crap this morning," Jock said; then gripping a flap of the trousers and tearing it more, he led him to the Gents, where two drunks stood, vainly, requesting an entrance fee.

She thought that she would try one last time, that she would say to Paddy, nicely, solicitously, that if they all went indoors it would be better, as they would be less conspicuous, less endangered. People had come to stare at them, others darted by in disbelief and unquiet.

"Come home and I'll give you all a picnic in the garden," she said, ashamed of her own appeasingness.

"Can't . . . we're going to Florence," he said quite gently, quite excited by the fact that on the morrow they would see the famous *Pietà* which Michelangelo at the age of eighty had left unfinished.

"*Pietà*," he said aloud.

"*Pietà* means pity, Paddy," she said, almost crying.

"I know it means pity," he said, and she thought she saw something break in him, but Jock saw it, too, and taking her arm as if he was also going to escort her somewhere, he said, "Mrs. Steadman, may I say something to you frankly?"

"Sure," she said.

"Don't you think Christ and his Apostles were on something?"

"No, I don't," she said.

"Come off it," he said. "How could they walk on water and make loaves and fishes and all that shit if they weren't on something?"

"Those were miracles," she said, and they all laughed; they laughed loudly, their laughing a signal to the drunks who, upon hearing it, being infected by it, laughed also, and it was like being in the middle of some zoo, where all the creatures, human and animal, were mingling in mad, mindless, baying collusion.

"What's the joke?" she said, incensed.

"Come on . . . let's split," Jock said, clapping his hands, and though in various stages of daze, they rallied and began to collect their effects—rucksacks, bags, beads, a skateboard, and a metal trolley with two items of shopping. As a last plea Nell turned to Natasha, a girl she knew, whose sister Amy had been in a motor-cycle accident.

"How's Amy . . . is she all right?" she asked.

"She's fine," Natasha said petulantly. What was so awful was how they all mistrusted her.

"When will you be home?" she said to Paddy, catching his coat sleeve as he went. He was wearing his worn green tails and a vest.

"Anon," he said, but airily as he walked onto the road with the others, careless of traffic, careless of hooters, careless of a bus driver who leant out the window and shouted torrid abuse at them.

"To the bandstand . . . to the bandstand," they chanted.

"This is madness," she said to Jock.

"You luck in and you luck out," he said viciously. It was a phrase she would never forget.

"You're the bad apple," she said, staring into his eyes, which danced with rage, a rage which she believed was vented on her because of the love she bore Paddy, as if it were a disease, an affliction.

"I'm a dark person," he said coldly, and then remembered that he had something of import to tell her vis-à-vis motherhood. He had a parable to tell her.

"I don't want your parable," she said, but he insisted. A friend of his, a young man, was dying, or "passing over," as they say in some circles, and his mother was sent out of the room at the last moments, and why was his tribulating mother sent out of the room? Answer—because she never once made her son laugh and she wasn't going to do it just then, as the curtain came down.

"I didn't know that people like you existed," she said in a hoarse whisper.

"Spirit ancestor," he said, and winked; then like a Druid took to the street, where three successive lots of traffic lights, weirdly biddable, glowed green to hasten his way.

* * *

"Have they gone?" a voice called, half childish, half dazed. It was a young girl who had been sleeping in the triangle of grass just beneath the wall. She was wearing a denim skirt which was slashed at the hem and an orange necklace with whiskers of black that crawled insect-like through the fat, transparent beads. As she stood, she shook her wheaten hair to bring herself to her senses.

"Yes, they've gone," Nell said.

"Rats," the girl said, and looked about, trying to guess where they had gone, then asked for a fag, then wondered where the nearest telephone was. Suddenly she was petulant, said they would not have gone without her, especially Big Celia. Big Celia should not have done that to her.

"Did they say where they were going?" she said, growing more impatient and throwing things out of a satchel as she searched for an important address.

"Florence," Nell said.

"Florence . . . that's wild," she said, and chuckled at the thought of her headmistress, a Miss Stow, being told that. She was a boarder at a girls' school near Ascot and had got out that day on the excuse of the dentist. It had been a doctor the previous week and a bereavement the week before that.

"Talk to me, butterfly," she said to a white butterfly which giddily fluttered about, skimming the dead wallflowers and the sagging heads of the drunks. She followed it about, her hands cupped to grasp it. At first she was amused, then remembered that her friends had deserted her and said again and again, "Where the fuck are you, Big Celia . . . big fat Celia." Her mood ranged from childlikeness to frenzy as she strutted in front of the drunks and asked for a light. One of them, one of the younger ones claimed to know her, stood up and said, "Hi, blonde." Yes, he knew her, he had seen her in World's End.

"Dumbo," she said, and told him to get lost. He insisted he knew her, had had a few jars with her.

"I've never been in World's End," she said, taunting him, then applying some lip gloss.

"Bitch," he said.

"Pig," she replied, causing the other gallants to rise and rally with him, make jokes about her knees and her matchstick thighs, not to mention the little skirty that was from a charity shop. The confrontation had sobered them a bit and they would have liked it to escalate, except that Nell dragged her away, towards the station entrance, where the black man was now perusing his cortege of rubbish with infinite care.

"Who are you?" the young girl asked.

"I'm Paddy's mum," Nell said.

"Oh, he often talks about you . . . He tells stories about you," she said.

"What kind of stories?" Nell said.

"You know, family stuff . . . how he and you and his brother went to buy a castle in Ireland and it was full of bullocks and doodahs."

In the artificial light from some rustic lanterns, with seascapes of Naples behind iron grids, they sat drinking coffee, the girl with her back to the window, smoking, then at moments drawing the cigarette away and training it on a box of window plants that looked so dead, so motionless, they might have been made of rubber. They were fern and tired cacti on which settlements of larvae lay, motionless as well. The entire café, with its iron girding, had the look of a prison, yet people sat there, came there, saw it as a sort of refuge, especially the regulars, who chatted to the waitress. The young dark waitress stuck her tongue out and circled it teasingly each time she took the men's orders, whereas with women she was more formal and said, "Yes, lady." The gold or semi-gold bracelet above her elbow rasped in the heat, and the smell was of frying oil. On the row of houses opposite, scaffolding, wherever the eye fell, and behind green mesh men looked like allegorical figures in shadow. A window of naked models, porcelain-faced and with ginger wigs, freaks, with hips thrust forward, seemed as real as the motley group who had departed. Where were they? Where would he surface? Silently she asked it of all the near-moribund people around, lost souls who hid in bed-sitting rooms and in the afternoon emerged for tea, believing something singular awaited them.

Pandora, for that was the young girl's name, went to the bathroom twice, and the second time was much more voluble when she returned. She asked Nell to please, please not pass judgement on her, because that was what parents did, that was parents' gig.

"I wasn't going to," Nell said, and hesitated in order to account for herself, but Pandora had already begun and with a hectic spurt of energy was telling why, why she did it: the adventure, the danger, the very first time, getting out of school on an excuse, on a train with Big Celia, a guy in Bayswater with a clubfoot, haggles over the money, then off to a little hotel pretending to be meeting Mummy; Big Celia preparing it in the loo, bending down, the ritual, the terror, first nothing, then wow, the glow, the belly warming up; out on the town, floating, nicking things, saying "Piss off" to authority, then going to someone's flat or someone's parents' flat and all getting into bed together and watching yourself screw, watching yourself screw boys, or girls, but none of it mattering, because it didn't hurt, it didn't get to you, and looking at Nell brazenly and with a determination to be grown-up, she said, "That's why we take it, because nothing hurts, not boys or the curse or your best friend dying . . . nothing hurts . . . especially love . . . Love doesn't hurt." But she was unable to keep up the charade, and her eyes began to fill with tears, eyes that were now like pale fruit drops staring into Nell's eyes, which were also full of tears, older, more bashful tears, and in a flourish of kinship they shook hands. "We're all part of the same planet . . . We're in it together," Pandora said solemnly, her hand like a little china hand grasping Nell's, kneading. All I have to be is a mother to them, all of them. They need me, Nell thought.

But wisdom comes too late.

29

His language was babble, at moments comprehensible, then not. He was talking both to Charlie and to her. To Charlie it was "Marry, thou art a noble dog," and to her it was "Rescue, he needed his mummy to rescue him." "Don't lift the lid . . . don't lift the lid," he repeated, holding the crown of his head as if it were being mashed. He had run into a spot of trouble. He had met a sage who wanted to drill a hole in his forehead, to give him the third eye, according to an ancient Eastern tradition.

"Just here . . . just here," he said, pointing to the spot between his eyebrows and frowning a little tetchy frown as if mimicking anxiety.

"Me say no no . . . Me run home to me mummy," he said, placing her hand on his forehead.

"Don't lift the lid, promise you won't lift the lid," he kept repeating.

Gradually she got it out of him that he had been with friends, new friends, and that this stranger had come to give them mind expansion, to trepan them. It meant enlightenment. It meant discharging all the old pus and bourgeois inhibitions, dispensing with the "I'm-all-right-Jack shit." He had been chosen to be the guinea pig. His forehead was the one which was about to be drilled. He described then the sage in his robe, opening his kit bag to get out his drill and the various fixtures, rummaging for the finest one, since only the best would suffice. As for the third eye itself, there was no description of it. Nobody enquired if in fact a hole would appear, gaping, lidless. Nobody took his side or said, "Poor Paddy, he's scared," and nobody had the good sense to ask where this man had come from or who gave him such licence.

"Jesus," she said, and patted him again. He escaped, simply because he started to vomit, was sick on the instep of one of his bodyguards, Jessica, who was furious. In the loo, where he had been allowed to go to rinse off, he escaped through a tiny window onto the roof of a shop and, by tapping a skylight, alerted, then frightened, and finally appealed to an older woman who was eating a slice of cake and drinking a Coca-Cola. "I'm safe . . . I'm safe with my mumsies," he said.

In the weeks since she had accosted him and his friends, he seemed to have turned over a new leaf, sitting with her in the evenings, reading aloud from the play he was studying, getting her to read bits to him, too, so that in turn they were Lady Wishford or Mrs. Fainall or whoever; promising also to sweep up the garden or hang shelves or do anything she wanted, play his part in the domestic chores.

"Marry, thou art handsome," he said again to Charlie, refusing to take off his overcoat, removing only his tie and saying, "Me wants me long johns," then complaining of the cold. A coin that fell from his pocket he retrieved and put in his mouth, sucked on it as if it were a lozenge, and resisted, playfully, while her finger searched his gums to get it out.

"It's no laughing matter, you could choke," she said as he murmured, "It tickles . . . it tickles." Charlie fought to defend him in this tussle and for his heroism was allowed to hop into bed, be a St. Bernard.

"Get me your nice shawl," he said, speaking of the frayed cocoa-coloured shawl that was sometimes a chair cover, sometimes a tablecloth, and once upon a time a shawl. As he held it he counted the fringes, said they were like catkins, and remembered a time long long long ago in Ireland when he fell asleep in the hay shed and everyone forgot him and he almost missed his supper. He said nature was the only healer and that he was not alone in that supposition. Alexander Pope had said, "Those who are most capable of art, are always most fond of nature." Moreover, the tree that Samuel Palmer had painted was a replica of the tree in the Garden of Eden. It was in Kent. He requested a tisane and sugar cubes to dip in it, to suck the way he had sucked that nasty penny.

"That nasty penny," he said, and wagged a finger in vague admonishment. She did not reprimand him or ply him with questions, thinking only, He's at home, he is safe for now, for now, as she sat on the end of the bed and heard him vouch that he could taste every single grain that comprised that beautiful cube of sugar and how it was a pity to melt it, but that melt it one must. "Marry but you have a pong," he said to Charlie, and fanned the air with the tail end of the shawl, ordering Charlie to go out onto the landing until this noxious whiff had evaporated and then come back in again. He had a request for his mumsies, too. Would she read him a story? Would she read him the sad story that he liked, the one about King Tristan and the two Isoldes? As she went to find the book, he took the telephone off the hook, obviously fearing that his friends would telephone and call him a coward, a scab, a traitor, whatever. To make light of it, he put the receiver to Charlie's snout, and she found him prompting Charlie to say, " 'Sdeath they come—hide your face, your tears, you have a mask, wear it a moment . . ."

"I think you should sleep," she said.

"I'm too afraid," he said, and tapped the book, gave it a few impatient smacks in order for the story to begin.

"So Tristan being wounded was cured by Ysolde and on his return to Cornwall told the King, who asked for her hand in marriage. She was married to the King but still loved Tristan and saw him illicitly, and when this illicit love was discovered he was banished from the palace and went away to fight great battles in Spain and Brittany. In this last place he met with Ysolt of the White Hand, whom he married. After many more marvellous exploits he was wounded, a wound so deep it could not be cured, and so he sent to Cornwall for Ysolde to come and cure him, saying that if she consented she was to hoist a white flag on her ship as she approached. She hastened to succour him, but Ysolt of the White

Hand told him that, yes, the Queen's ship was coming with a black sail, whereupon he fell on the rocks and split his brains out and died, and as soon as Ysolde arrived and heard this she flung herself upon the corpse and she too died, but of a broken heart. Her husband buried the two in one grave and planted over it a rose-bush and a vine which so intermingled, their branches grew so that no man could separate them."

"And so ends my story," he said with tears in his eyes. Why had he wanted that story? Was it because of his brother?

"Maybe . . . maybe," he said to Charlie, who was now gazing at his master with a rapt stillness. True, his brother and he had grown apart. They were not enemies but somewhat estranged. His brother and he still had some battles to fight, but deep, deep. He claimed to remember when his brother came into existence.

"You tried to kill him . . . you poured a papier-mâché bath of water over him."

"Not then," he said sadly, "but when he first materialised . . . when the seed entered," and he looked at her steadfastly, as if she were not his mother at all but someone to whom he was telling this story while he fiddled with the tassels of the shawl and allowed Charlie to lick the sugar on his lips, saying that once upon a time he saw a lady and a man together, entwined together by the fireside, and that they embraced, and though he ran off, because he knew he should, he knew that it was no longer a question of him and the lady and the man, but that another had stormed their world, a rival. To combat his jealousy and his rage, he had overturned the vase of sweet peas, then trampled on them, made shreds of them. Afterwards the punishment. His father had put him in his pink high chair, strapped him in, and made him survey the sight of wet carpet and trampled flowers, not to mention an overturned jug.

"I shouldn't have allowed it," she said, remembering vividly his being strapped in and his expression when she peeped from the other room, his searching with his eyes, his eyes rolling in every direction to find out the time perhaps, or if someone, herself, might be coming to his rescue. His eyes so full of hope and hurt.

"Of course, although we are enemies we are of the same tribe

... my brother and I, and we would defend each other against alien attack."

"Ssh ssh ... you'll sleep now," she said, and pulled the quilt over him as he snuggled down and said how lovely it was to be tucked in by his mumsies, just like long ago; his mumsies, so omnipotent that she could tell the rain to patter softly or the moon to dim its lamp; she could send him into the sweetest, deepest sleep with her words, and her arms, which always smelt of custard powder. After he dozed off, she sat there watching, watching his body and the twitches it made under the covers, still frightened, and she thought that if only she could put a spell on him then, if only she could send him into a long room of sleep, away from the perils that he spoke of, if only she could be omnipotent, as she had once seemed.

30

She was beside a flower bed, looking down at the first crocuses, two frail little ribbony things, mites that had sprung up. The city was not yet awake, not the sound of a single engine and not yet the soft throaty half-sounds of the pigeons, though she could see them shuffling around in the ruminous limbs of the fig tree. Leaves that were upright held drops of water, like little hourglasses, and elsewhere the clay and the rosebushes were damp. He came out to tell her that he was leaving. He was quite grave about it, said grown-up things such as that they needed a break from each other, neither having realised until the row the night before how wound up they were. He apologised for his own part in it.

"I'm sorry, too, Paddy," she said, which was also a way of pleading with him not to go. He was going. He was leaving London, making a break, away from the bulldozers to the calm of the country—rabbits, pheasants, gurgling streams, orchards, the dappled shade; the quintessential world, as he called it, twice. He had been on the phone to his friend Stefan and they had both agreed that he go there for a bit. Stefan was an older friend, married, a stabilising influence. That and quintessential were his key words.

"But what about your crammer and university, Paddy?"

"I'm not cut out for university . . . the groves of Academe," he said, and flinched.

"Give it a chance," she said, doing everything now to erase the
spleen that had shown its vicious face the previous night.

"Don't force me," he said.

"I'm trying not to force you," she said simply, reminding him
that he could go to university, get a degree, and then commune
with nature, the dappled shade and so forth. She begged him to
think on it.

"I can't think just now," he said. "I can't concentrate . . . I can't
even read a book . . . I can't can't can't," he added feverishly, then
opened his mouth very wide and said he was having a breakdown.

"No, you're not," she said, frightened to hear him use the word,
but he shook his head and insisted that he was and that there was
no stopping it. It was an avalanche, it just came, it took over, it
swallowed one up.

"Oh, sweetheart," she said, regretting every moment of the row,
the ugly things she had said to him, his insolence, his savagery
towards her, lumping her in with all the other smug, self-satisfied
parents, then her rounding on him, saying that he was happy
enough to eat her food and drink her drink and take her money for
crammer, for drugs, to lavish on his top-notch friends, who had
trust funds but who never carried money; no, like the Queen they
never carried money.

"Are you getting at my friends?" he had said.

"Users . . . users all," she said, asking him to cast his mind back
and think when a friend of his had brought as much as one daisy
or written as much as one postcard to say thank you for supper or
the weekend. If he was going to demolish her and her ilk, the
consumer society, then he was a consumer, too, and so were his
fake friends.

"I can see that I have overstayed my welcome in this prison,"
he'd said, viciously gleeful at having secured his exit at last. But
now it was a different thing, it was two people unnerved, unslept,
who were trying to patch things up.

"What is this breakdown?" she asked.

"I can't describe it . . . except that it's *v.* painful," he said, and
looked down at the two little crocuses and said, "Are they lilac?"

"Has someone let you down?" she asked.

"That, too," he said, and she remembered his terror the day he kept saying, "Don't lift the lid," and it was now as if the lid were lifted, flapping up and down, his sanity in jeopardy. He said no one had any idea how knotted he was and how confused, and by the way he looked at her, it was as if he wished her to stand on tiptoe and look into the cavity of his mind and see the crags there.

"Is it Clarissa?" she asked tentatively. Clarissa, his ex-girlfriend, had disappeared. Clarissa, whom everyone called Puggy and who loved being called that; Clarissa, who arrived most evenings on her bicycle, eager, demanding, always with a sheet of hotel paper on which she had written pert summaries of films they might go to—"For interesting teenagers or sexy adults"; "Small budget film with considerable elan"; "Family fare." Hearing this read aloud Nell would think, She knows how to get around men . . . she knows the ropes. Clarissa spent her days in a gymnasium that adjoined a smart hotel, and in the afternoons she sat downstairs and wrote letters to her friends and read the film critiques in the hotel papers, then had tea, which she put on anyone's bill, any room number that came into her head. If he voiced the slightest opposition to any of her suggestions, she turned on her heel and said he didn't have to go with her as she could always go with her brother. To this he said, "Pugs," touched the lightly rouged point on one of her cheeks, and repeated, "Good Pugs . . . good Pugs . . . what would *you* most like to see?" Now she was missing and mutual friends believed that she had bolted with a famous pop singer who spotted her in the hotel lounge.

"She doesn't want to know," he said, and the earnest way he said it made it seem so finite, so brutal.

"Don't leave home just yet," she said, and looking at her, with his unslept eyes, the little red veins like hairs in the whites that once were a marvelling blue-white, he reminded her that when he was young she had always quoted him a proverb and he was now asking her to abide by that proverb, which was that "a good heart always gives a little extra."

There was nothing for it but to help him pack, to try to be

cheerful, offer him knickknacks, since he was quite sentimental, and ask if they could keep in touch or have dinner from time to time.

"As often as you want," he said with a new largesse. Now that the break had come, he felt free of her clutches, free to offer the gift of friendship. The taking down of the suitcase, removing a strip of tinsel that had clung to it, the opening of one latch, then another, putting shirts and sweaters in, all these actions were happening to someone in a daze, or rather to two people in a daze, two people listless from the fever of the row that had both shocked and drained them. He had promised to come home the previous night, because it was his birthday, but instead the rack of lamb, the savoury stuffing, and the Brussels sprouts had dried on a plate which was kept heated over a saucepan, while friends phoned intermittently from pubs trying to locate him. To them he had also promised the favour of a dinner. Around three or four she had met him on the stairs, punitive, in a nightgown, the very image which she vowed never to present, tackled him about how selfish he was, how careless, how he couldn't keep the smallest promise, how different friends had rung, all without a vestige of manners, and though at first he merely ground his jaws, so that she could just hear his teeth crack, eventually he had told her to shut up. He was not selfish and mendacious, he would not have it said; moreover, he worked harder than she ever gave him credit for.

"Like hell you do," she said bitterly.

"You want to call me a liar."

"I haven't called you a liar."

"You want to call me a liar."

A catalogue of grievances on both sides was aired, and even as she heard them or voiced them, she thought how muddled it all was, how far removed from the nub of the matter, which was that the love they once had, the sweet vital reserves of love, had vanished, disappeared like those streams that go underground without leaving a trace.

"What about Charlie?" she said.

"He's coming . . . aren't you, boy?" he said, and Charlie, realising that something unpleasant was afoot, got up and licked them both, first his master, then her, as if to say, "Be friends ... be friends."

"I've got quite fond of him," she said, which was about all she could say without breaking down completely.

"City of Bells and My Heart" they heard, in the interval of the chamber music on the radio. It was a Russian poet's cry to a fellow poet, and it spoke to them so piercingly, so succinctly, that she still thought it was being recited as she heard them go downstairs, Charlie's excited patter, the swoosh of his tail, louder than Paddy's tread, then the closing of the front door, softer than at any time, as if to close it at all was a death.

"City of Bells and My Heart," she said again and again in an endeavour to repiece the moments, embattled moments which at the time she could not endure but which no doubt would return to shame her and to startle, as when upon opening a shutter in winter time, a host of sleeping butterflies come rising up. "City of Bells and My Heart" ... she said again and again waiting for a cue, a voice that would carry it on.

31

Looking down at the beautifully tinted map was to be brought summarily back there, so that she was not just seeing the names of towns and lesser towns and rivers with their ample estuaries, she was seeing and smelling all: the grass banks glutted with dock, the hot smell of nettle, cows at evening time, pendulous, moving en masse and as if in a ritual of discomfort, their udders mutinous. Above all, she was seeing in the wavery purple-red lines that divided two provinces the varicose veins on her mother's shin, raised, purplish, madly gurgling. All because of looking at the map which lay on the kitchen table, the glass newly broken and Kim's little note: "I break, sorry."

"You break, sorry," she said, vexed, and put it down, because the slivers of glass, which lay like a jigsaw on the towns and rivers, eased apart, giving off dust and infinitesimal splinters.

"You break, sorry," she said again, while in her mind she began devising little punishments for Kim, for being so careless; Kim, a small Asiatic creature, open as a lotus, given to laughter at everything, believing it stalled punishment; Kim now the butt of her anger, her spleen. Yes, ever since he'd left, ever since that morning, she had felt filleted and slowly but inexorably was joining the Brigade of the Vexed.

"You break, sorry . . . shit."

Yet a few weeks later, coming out of the frame shop, she heard herself say, "Oh, Kim, look what you've done for me . . . look what you've done."

She saw him first as he emerged from the artist's shop carrying a tin box of paint. It was his beret she recognised and the slant at which he wore it, a thing he copied from the Breton man who delivered onions on his bicycle, always drunk and pressing for a cognac. For a moment she hesitated, but he had already seen her and came to her, beaming, jaunty, showing his precious purchase, paints for his evening class. He had taken up painting and went two evenings a week, sat in front of his easel and painted a model or a milk jug or fruit or whatever. It was weeks since he had left home, and though they had talked on the telephone, coming on him like this had something propitious to it. Moreover, he was glad to see her. Under the streetlight he showed her the paints, lozenges of colour, lickable, edible, the reds and blues the most enticing, the white very stark, like the makeup on a circus clown. Yes, he had taken up painting and loved it, found that these forays with colour were wonderful, gave him a freedom, a purpose. He could not tell her how pleasant it was to assault a canvas or to paint a few daisies on an enamel plate.

"Like Kandinsky," she said.

"Not quite," he answered, and smiled. She could scarcely see his smile in the streetlight but could tell it from memory, deferential, both shy and thrilled when attention was bestowed on it.

"I came to have the glass put back on the map of home . . . Kim broke it."

"How is Kim?" he asked, not feeling staunch enough to ask how she herself was.

"She misses you . . . She says, 'No master's ironing for me any-more.' "

"Master," he said, and chuckled, and then remembered that Kim didn't like Charlie, hid from Charlie, and put the hoover or a chair between herself and Charlie's snarls.

"He bit her," Nell said.

"Only a nip," Paddy said, and promised that he would send Kim a card. As in his letters, he repeated how satisfying it was to be in the country, doing manual things, chopping wood, thinning cabbages, milking (he had learned to milk), and as she soon saw this was a preamble for him to say solemnly how unhappy he had been, how everyone had suffered from it, especially those near and dear to him, a matter for which he would have lasting regrets.

"Sweetheart," she said, but nothing more.

Twice in a letter he had asked her to visit, mentioned the family, their new baby, a hammock under a tree where the baby slept, various other features of a house which was next to a stream so that one wakened or slept to the sound of trickling water. He had got a bit high-flown about this trickling water and had called it a threnody.

"I will come soon," she said, and then he kissed her, a warm kiss, and as of old said scoldingly, "I hope you are getting out and about and not being too much of a hermit." As she followed his shadow among all the others, she had to bite back tears of warm happiness.

The pavement seemed to spring under her feet, and at moments it was as if she were in a conveyance, being borne along, waving, waving, because she felt so elated. A chance meeting, better, far better than anything sought. She remembered his smile when he saw her and the rush with which he came to her, the excitement over the box of paints, and then that bit of scolding which was a mark of affection, too. Sighting all the people, she thought that she must smile at just one of them. They were young and old, lame and fit, men with briefcases which they wielded like dispatch boxes, young girls walking briskly, their heels on the cobbles like smart hammers; others chattering, men darting into pubs, people by a bus stop jostling each other as a bus came into view that was already overflowing, so that those who jostled had now somewhat shamefully to rejoin the queue and look down at their feet, disgruntled. To whom could she tell her surprise? To whom could she say that of the ten million or more, crammed in nooks and corners and boardinghouses and grand houses and even palaces, of these ten million whom should she meet but her son, her son who had been restored to her, who had even said as they parted, "I'm a good boy now . . . I'm clean." Clean!

Farther along she saw a seated figure on a bench and thought, I will talk to this poor stray. It was one of those streets that sidled off into nowhere, just a crumbling brick archway and a dark passage that led to some warehouses. Behind the bench was a half-ruined brick church, its windows smashed in, the gates locked, and the grounds full of hawthorn trees just coming into bloom. She would go there and tell this figure. She pitied all those who hurried and jostled and didn't smile and didn't see the hawthorn, the pale, soft constellations of blossom that were soon to shed. The figure, a woman in ragged clothes, had a headscarf pulled forward over her face, the face well concealed. She was muttering to herself. Her shoes were stout country shoes and her stockings fell down around the calves of her legs. Her hands, which had the splay of a spade, were opening and closing as if mashing clods of earth. A country-woman.

Nell resolved that after the first few awkward words she would ask the woman about herself, would listen to her and give her some money. It did not turn out like that. The muttering, which was low and incomprehensible, heightened to something other, something distinctly unwelcome, venom in it. A stream of curses came out, followed by the slinging of a satchel which the woman had at her feet. It was a school satchel made of canvas, and when she aimed, she struck out with the open buckle and swished at her opponent, shouting, "Off . . . off . . . with youse . . . all of youse . . . living Jesus . . . Holy Paul . . . Off by the blood of the Blessed Sacrament . . . Leave me in peace . . . I'm a lady . . . more than you are . . . you're shkin through your clothes." Then, in a parody of grace, she bowed and bent towards her assailant, or what she thought was her assailant, to recite something she remembered from her schoolbook, a torn page that perhaps was in her satchel.

"O Dun Dealgan, thou city of my sires, thou shalt receive a Red Eric for the many battles thou hast fought and won."

Then drawing back the headscarf, to emphasise her prowess she said formally, "Yes, madam . . . I bless the people who bring me down."

Nell shook in disbelief, in freezing terror. It was Rita, Rita almost beyond all recognition, old, a reject with frizzy hair, smiling, because somewhere she realised that this was a woman she had once taken up cudgels against.

"Rita," Nell said. Hearing her name called out gave cause for another bit of jousting with the satchel, which, sickle-wise, beat the air, as if she were beating briars aside to make way for a herd of cattle. At the same time she wished shite and scutter on every passing soul, on their citified shoes and their citified hose.

"Rita," Nell said again.

"Breach of promise . . . breach of promise," she said then in a hoarse but gloating whisper, a thousand treacheries real or imagined contained within it, and she stuck out her tongue gleefully at a woman she had once cursed and still cursed perhaps, in the flounder of her being.

Then she was gone. Her shouts rose, subsided, then rerose, the cracked shouts of an intemperate woman; it could just as easily have been a man, lacerating himself, fighting a crazed, useless battle in the vast equivocal maw of a city. A common occurrence, but in Nell it struck terror. From this baulk, this unwonted scream, this boiling rage, she had fled. But how long can we hide from that which forms us, which is the very mucus of our being? The memories die away or are put down, the road rushes on, rushes with an increasingly frenzied speed, as in our variety of clothing and disguises we are in turn husbands, wives, lovers, enemies, friends; but always sooner or later we are brought back to the dark stew of ourselves and the ancestry before us, back to the midnight of the race whose sins and whose songs we carry.

She ached for one of those songs, for a figure, any figure, to stand before her and sing one or hum one; for Paddy to appear and sing the way he used to at Christmas, his eyes shut, the theme of the songs almost too much for him, as now and then his voice quavered and the words, words such as "List for a while to a blind Irish harper," or "Only five nights in Ballygrand," had unleashed sentiments that threatened to engulf him.

She thought it to be a vision, but no, there he was on the steps, leaning backwards and looking up at the stars as if he was counting them. He had not gone indoors, as he was afraid it might give her a fright.

"Paddy," she said, startled.

"I decided to spend the night, if that's all right," he said. And again she marvelled at how all his old ways and his willingness had been restored to him.

Over dinner he sang, because she had asked him to. She did not say why and did not recount the meeting with Rita, as it might unnerve him, since Rita had not liked him and had always put him in the wrong. The warp and hurts of that time would come flooding back, to no avail. He sang two songs, the two that she liked best, and it seemed to her in her red panelled room, with deep blue glasses that were like chalices, and his new haircut, which gave him a clean, countrified look, like a peeled willow, that these were the most plaintive and yet most affirmative songs she had ever heard and that of all their moments together, even the giddy gosling moments of his infancy, none was so sweet or so lasting.

"If ever you needed me . . . you'd say so," she said, but without touching, without reaching.

"And vice versa," he said.

She would repeat those words later, take them out of her mind to look at them, like a young girl with a little hoard of wedding cake, taken out and consulted after dreaming, mindless of the fact that such trifling is in vain. The words, so very simple in themselves, were stitched into her.

Part IV

32

Cold! The cold took root in her then and grew. Yes, deep things are cold, cold within and cold without, like the centre of a sea rock which, even if you split it, dynamite it, retains its innate coldness and breathes it throughout. Merciless, heartless, feelingless cold, the cold of aeons that has a knowledge of itself but no way of altering itself and perhaps no wish to. But people are not rocks, nor should they have to be. People are people. Yet her heart had gone to gristle. Her heart or that bit of her that felt and kissed and communicated had changed inexorably. How to banish that cold, how to even warm it a fraction. The shock was like something she already knew. Perhaps it is birth. Perhaps in birth the chill of our lives unfolds before us in a cold, uncomprehending tableau. In the first slippery uncharted moments, when the link is severed and the dark moist hush of an insideness is exchanged for the vast inhospitality of a creaking world, we know death. In birth we know death. And now in death it was as if she knew birth, her own, or his, or both, because the water, the inscrutable voracious water, had taken him and others. Yes, death stalked the city that night, stalked the city like a great water wolf. The river—sheer, ruffled, grey, brown, black, and khaki—took them into her inhospitable bosom. Why? Why did the river want them? For what?

All her life she believed that she would have a presentiment if a mishap should befall either of them. Her bones would tell it. Her bloodstream would tell it. Every follicle of hair would stand on end. Often in the past she had half imagined such a thing, indeed on occasion went with the delirium of it, upon hearing of an accident in this street or that, on a motorway, or a leafy lane, and had waited and the wait seemed both necessary and ludicrous. She knew the ropes. A policeman, or rather two policemen, came and knocked on one's door. She had heard that somewhere. Yet as the taxi driver rattled on about an accident, young people partying, she had no intimation of anything, just felt glad to be going home to sleep. It was a Saturday. Party night. A pleasure boat had collided with a tug and many were drowned or drowning. She felt a flash of dismay—a mockery of the sadness to come.

When a mother sees two policemen at her front door, she knows. She thought it was Tristan, was certain that a truck or a lorry had gone off the road in Turkey, where he and his friends were spending the summer on relief work. It was Paddy. He was one of the young people on the pleasure boat, and as he was still missing, they had to legally inform her. Missing. Missing is not dead. When a mother knows, she does everything to unknow. She goes to her bedroom to dress. She discards the old stockings that she had been wearing in the daytime for a new pair. God knows why. She says, This is not true, this is a false alarm, testing her last reservoir of strength. She puts on powder, hurriedly, then returns and, as on any normal occasion, offers brandy or tea. They say it is better to get moving, to get back to the scene, since all the force are needed.

She sits in the black van with them, and slowly and solemnly recites, as if it were his own chant, the words of Christ in the Garden of Gethsemane: "O Father, if it be possible, let this chalice pass from me." Missing is not dead. She says that aloud to them and adds how providential the night, since it is so still, since there is scarcely a wind. They recognise that undertow of hope and look at each other with eyes in which she believes there are recesses of non-hope. She cannot see their eyes but she can see their fidget. They have already been there, they have already seen bodies crawling out senseless, unable to grasp their whereabouts, asking, "What happened ... what happened?" They have heard the screaming, the disbelief, the shouts of crazed, incensed people, and they are not in the business of doling out niceties. She has not seen it yet. Now she does. Ambulances bursting from the entrance steps, their lights whirling round and round but no siren sounding, ghost machines. Inside, commotion, delirium, people who had been inches from death asking, asking. Each voice higher than the next, voices charging each other across the room. Has Alex been found: Found. The word both urgent and wan. A girlfriend has lost her boyfriend. She calls his name, shouts it. He does not materialise. She runs, the double glass doors almost swallowing her. A man has lost his wife. He stands, a sodden picture of despair, with a blanket slipping off, saying quietly, "My wife . . . my beautiful wife." A younger man weeps for the woman he swam with. Where is she, where is she? He describes how they held hands, tight, tight, until in the end she slipped away from him, eluded his grasp. Was she dead? Was she still struggling?

This is the young man who could tell her the only thing she needs to know. This is the prophet of doom, whom she will meet one day, when all is confirmed. She is sitting quietly, sitting with herself. She is afraid of these people. They pace, they are quiet, then at moments give rein to some outburst. This night has dislodged their reserves of sanity. Nurses who go about with forms and thermometers and blankets are told to piss off. It has the insubstantiality of a dream, but it is not a dream. It is a raw, raucous, unashamed confrontation with life or non-life. The names are shouted incessantly. Samantha and Sue and Paul and Jeff. No one says Paddy, as if no one knew him but her. Outside, the sirens screech with animal intonations. Inside, coffee, cups of coffee, a voice asking for someone to put another spoon of sugar in, sloshing it. Paddy, where are you? She has been told to sit and wait. She will be informed the moment there is news. Rumours bob up the way she imagines, cannot stop herself imagining, the faces appearing on the water. His face. His alone. A body has been found eight miles upriver at Hammersmith. A woman's. Not a man. Not him. Should she go to Hammersmith? Did drowned bodies follow one another like shoals of fish? She must go somewhere. Paddy, where are you? She has been told to sit and wait. They know her name and her son's name. They are on a document. Many are weeping, wishing that they had not been saved, claiming that they do not want to live if their comrades are dead. Their teeth are chattering, they shiver, their features slavered in black mud and ooze.

"Where's my mates . . . where's my fucking mates?" a young man shouts as he enters. His head is gashed and the blood streaming down his face has black rivulets in it. He is telling everyone how cold it is, how cold and how stupid. She runs from there and down a narrow footpath where people are milling around a posse of police, shouting names, asking if such and such a one has been found. It is dark and deathlike, everything in mayhem. Police and rescue workers like shadows, giving and taking orders, their voices tense. The river is calm but black, a black pit which everyone dreads. Calm black swishings of water. Looking at it for the first time, looking at it steadily, she thinks it cannot be. He is not in there. He has swum ashore, he is somewhere, he is one of the dazed people in a blanket, covered in mud. He is asking someone to telephone her. He is. He is. She hears the tide, its slip-slap against the lifeboats, and she thinks, You have not got him. The chains, which go clank-clank, tell a different story, however, a death knell and the line came, how could it not—"A current under sea picked his bones in whispers."

A young policeman loses control, says how the hell does he know what one boat was doing crashing into another. Sirens fill the streets, and she thinks that if Paddy is still in the water, which he must be, those sirens will be a clarion to him, a reminder that everything is on the alert, everything is being done.

"Oh, Paddy, we are coming to you, we are coming," she said, and going over to an officer she asked if there was any way they could light up the water more, give hope to those who were still struggling in it. For some reason he thinks she is a journalist and tells her to shut her trap. She screams back, screams that she is a mother.

"Why isn't the water lit, the way it's lit for a Jubilee or a Coronation?" she says, and he looks at her with a kind of murderousness and says that those who are still down there have had it by now. She lets out half a cry, a short, unearthly, broken cry. This figure, this totem of authority, wishes them dead. She does not know why, but she knows it is true, and for a moment she is with the others in a rasping feud.

"Bastard," a woman says to him. A match is struck, and the flame, which soon expires, shows how feebly searchlights could penetrate the infinity of black. Unknowing it then, for a fraction of a second, caught up in the blaze of confrontation. Bastards. Bastards. How helpless they all are, helpless and wild, clinging, with a retina of hope, non-hope to a canvas of crazedness. Questions being pelted. Why is it taking so long? Are any found? Where were the lifeboats? The lookouts? A senior officer tries to calm them, says that they are doing everything they possibly can, that any bodies that are still in the water will be found. Found. There is that word again. She asks him if by any chance she can go to South-wark in the police van, since others are going. He looks at her with all the candour of a man who has to refuse and says no, that it would be better for her to go back into the hospital and stay put.

In the hospital she sat next to four youths in blankets, not asking them anything, just listening. Each had the same story, and had to tell it, the same hideous story, a party, a night out, balloons, a bar, a disco, new friends, old friends, some going up on deck to see the spectacle of the city at night, St. Paul's, skyscrapers; others onto the dance floor, hilarity, then suddenly colliding, a crashing sound, the boat going to one side like a drunken whale, toppling, every-one plunged into a black hole, a black flood, the water pouring in, the deluge all over again. They all knew it. They had been through it, and yet they told and retold it to one another because they had to, because they were wet and frozen and delirious and waiting for their friends to be brought back. At moments they are united. A family. A shocked, stricken, bereaved family, a vast family, each mindful of the other, solicitous, offering a shoulder, a hand, an ear, and then at other moments they are separate, each thinking only of their own, their own at the expense of all else. Life is like that. There was tea, coffee, orange juice, the occasional attempt at a joke such as "Been to a party, Chas?" She smoked. She hadn't smoked in years. The tobacco and the smoke itself tasted foul, but it filled her mouth, and for those minutes that was all that mattered.

A group who are silently weeping hold one another and rock back and forth in grief, like children in a pen. A boy and two girls. They have lost their mate. The boy jumped in the water to search and had to be hauled out. They rock back and forth, like women in labour, giving birth to their grief. Each time they smoke they give her one. Sometime later the girl looks up and screams. She is afraid it is not true. It can't be true. She looks down, she covers her eyes and asks them, Jesus, to look up. It is him. It is Justin. He has been found. Or has he? Is he a spirit? He walks towards them in his slather, with a strange dazedness. He is holding half a rubber ring. They get up. They all embrace, four friends, lost for words, unable to speak. They don't believe it. A miracle. Then they do believe it. They cry. They kiss. He cannot speak. He cannot say how he swam ashore. He holds up the bit of black rubber, refuses to let it go. Sucks it like a soother. It saved him. It. Then one of them speaks, one of them says that they are going to get out of this hellhole, drive in his little banger, get booze and get fish and chips, ring everyone they know, and give the party of their lives, a party that says, Welcome home, Justin, welcome home. She shrinks away from them. The young girl knows why. She is still one of the waiting ones. There is nothing to be said. They cannot swap with her. Were she the lucky one, she would not swap either. It is as primal as that.

What she must do is give Paddy strength, send messages to him, urge him, tell him to kick, to kick, not to give in. Her breathing quickens with it, and it is as if she, too, has entered the water. Then she pauses and says, "Turn over on your back, love, and float." She does this unendingly, because there is one thing which she cannot unknow. It is this. Some are trapped in the sunken vessel, were caught in a downstairs suite; corpses side by side, or cleaving to furniture. The vessel cannot be brought up till daylight, when a toll will be taken. He is not among them. She is certain of that. He got out, crawled out and swam, and is making his way, is holding on to a raft, is on a little bit of beach waiting to be picked up. He is that seagull he loved to read about, who flew higher than all the other seagulls, up into the lonely altitudes, and hearing herself say, "Seagull," she shrieks, glimpsing the maelstroms ahead.

33

Another day. Parents. Relatives. Police. Waiting for names to be called out, in order for people to go into the morgue and identify their own. Bodies in glass cubicles under sheets, bloated, puffed, disfigured. All prey to the same lunatic fate.

"Oh my God," she said to the woman next to her, as the policeman lifted a sheet and she saw what was not a resemblance of a face but something grey, prehistoric. She does not know if it is a boy or a girl. The hairline is black and eerie, an eerie streak like a charcoal line. She has gone in unbeknownst, to mettle herself, and now she turns away. He has not been found, he and another. She goes back to the chapel of rest, where mourners sit silently, too silent by far. Praying to a bare altar, a bare God.

A mother and a father sit fingering the one black rosary. Not long after, a man comes and speaks in a whisper to them and says yes, it was Jason, their Jason; he recognises the two back fillings he had done the Easter before. In his hand an envelope with the X-rays of the teeth. They confer. The father goes in while the mother sits in the chapel praying, a paragon of strength. Suddenly the silence is shattered. A woman's cry. A mother insists that the girl they have shown her as her daughter is not her daughter Fiona, is not the white maiden, and that no one can tell her so. Fiona is not that lump of disfigurement in there. The policeman tries to reason with her, says she had been warned, advised not to go in, at least not to go in alone.

"I got to, hadn't I," she says, lashing out, saying it was clear that they were all drunk on the boat, except for her Fiona, who had never touched a drop in her life, and was sacrificed, sacrificed for what, scoundrels, brigands, drunks. Looking across at Nell, who is looking at her aghast, she screams and says, "Who do you think you're looking at," and Nell shrinks into the corner, hoping the whitewashed wall will absorb her. The woman, while discussing her Fiona, is also holding jewelry, bracelets, a jingle of bone and silver, the finery that Fiona wore. How unfair that these and not the humans can escape the ravages of the water. He had no jewelry, but a tattoo, and she wonders if this discolours.

"Oh, please, God, let him be found," she keeps saying over and over again to herself, so that she does not break down. It replaced the terror in her mouth and her windpipe. For him to be found now is all that she asks. She is beginning to lose hope of his being alive. People smile now and then, as if to say, "We are here, we are all here, we are in this together." In the makeshift refreshment room, things are heated, embattled. A small group have already started to rally, to press about, fighting for their rights, for compensation, for lolly. She cannot join in. She cannot even be incensed. She says it is too soon. She says, "Who can tell what happened in the water in the dark. A hundred versions will be trotted out and a hundred excuses, and still there's the mystery of why a tug rips into the side of a boat, batters her, and within minutes sends her down.

"Now you listen," a woman says to her, but cannot think what to say next. Rage and grief are battling in her, and her eyes are like wounds from crying.

"I am listening," Nell says, and the woman throws back her head in a hateful grimace and says she knows exactly the lawyer she'll go to, exactly the shark who will fight her cause. A friend encourages her. Cites shipowners with untold wealth and villas in Spain. It seems odd, inappropriate, considering how close they are to the morgue, how the depths of their feelings are just waiting to be met in there.

*   *   *

At midnight a detective came and asked her to go home and get some sleep.

"I'd rather stay here," she said.

"It's orders, ma'am," he said, and she knew that he hated saying it, because it meant that they had more or less given up. The tears that had been lying in wait came then, unheralded, unannounced, in a burst. She was sobbing. A desecration. Before that, she had merely cried like others into her sleeve or into her handkerchief, but this was torrents. It stunned the few mourners left into silence. She had allowed the truth to seep into her. The truth was that she would not see him again. It was worse than death. It seemed to be above and beyond death. A rigmarole then of how he would not walk through the door, or ride his bicycle, or run a comb through his hair again.

"Squeeze my hand . . . just squeeze my hand," the detective kept saying while the tears poured out of her, baths, basins, buckets, reservoirs of tears that seemed hot and life-giving as blood. The blood of death as opposed to the blood of life. Why her? Why her? Why him? Why them? The words flew out like pellets. Telling them how he believed that seagulls on the river were the souls of dead lightermen. Seagulls. She thought a little brace of them whizzed about, beating the air, then vanishing. She had gone that far.

"You're all right now," the detective said.

"Yes, I'm all right now," she said, and remembered that during the outburst he had told her that there was a pamphlet by a famous specialist which described death by drowning, how beautiful it was, not a painful death, happy, a kind of ecstasy once the body submitted and allowed the water in.

"Could you find it?" she said.

"I'll try," he said, and helped her towards the swinging door.

Outside, everyone gone. Her banshee tears had sent them scarpering. Nothing but statues and the shadows they cast. Iron men, iron women, iron horses, and an iron Boadicea. Fawn buildings and fawn clock tower like fairy fortresses inside those selfsame oblongs, tipped with gold. To think that here they had come one Sunday to see the crimson splurge of power: carriages, horses, mace bearers, standards, a glittering parade which they watched from the towpath and the boys ate a whipped ice cream. The lights in their proud hexagonals were burning dimly, beautifully, speaking not of catastrophe but of enchantment, of the time earlier, a few hours earlier, when a group of exuberant people set out for a party and perhaps one or two of them even noticed the hexagonal lamps in their gold basketing, emblems of revelry.

"Where are my friends now . . . where are my friends?" she yelled, hand and arm going up wildly to hail a taxi, missing this one and that, crossing a road, recrossing, waving an overnight bag, Paddy's bag, with a few of his childhood effects in it, to put beside him, to keep him company, a little tobacco tin and a Hunters fob watch which her father had given him but which never worked.

"You looked as if you wanted the airport," the driver said, and slammed the window up.

"No . . . I want home."

"So why did I think you wanted the airport?" he said grumpily.

"I want home," she said weakly.

Home. Once she was there, the doorbell would ring or the phone would ring to say he had been found. He would be found and the kiss or the clench, or whatever it was, would be exchanged between them. She would not quake at the cruel metamorphosis, oh no, her son was her son, a little image locked inside her, inviolate, the way he had once roamed and kicked inside her womb. And to keep that image company she gave him the voice and the recitation that he had when he was four or five, his voice like a toy xylophone saying:

> Pam pam pipe
> Plum jam
> Ten bob
> Tip-tip, Peter all the way

She would bury him. She would bury him as best she could. His friends would come and there would be flowers, lots of flowers; it was, after all, summer, high summer, the time of the hollyhocks and the Canterbury bells, and she would have a little party, and then what? Then was a blank in her thoughts, a wall, so to speak, in which memories would be placed end to end, increasing and multiplying like stacks of books. But first he must be found and then he must be buried, because that was fundamental, because earth and not water was the kindest, meetest resting place. Why did she so fear water, water from whence he came, the waters of herself, her own being, as she in turn had come from her own mother, womb of waters, known and unknown, nourishing and leeching, giving and taking back. She kept picturing earth, little slants of earth, little mounds, graveyards with things growing out of them, anything, daisies, moss, anything.

The driver was not going fast enough and not going the most direct route and was determined that she suffer the indignities of his last fare. Foreigners. Zulus. Couldn't breathe with the four of them in the cab. Under her breath she kept upbraiding him, but did not want a contretemps. If one vexed word was exchanged, she would break down and maybe run from the moving vehicle.

So for three days and three nights she held on to that hope and believed that the moment they could not trace her was the moment they were ringing to say he had been found, and for that reason she lived in transit, from her own house to the pier at Westminster, to the morgue at Southwark, policemen turning away from her in embarrassment and herself being understanding, overunderstanding, so as not to rattle them, because they, too, were testy, disgruntled, and unslept. She felt so alone. No father, no Tristan, and as yet no word, so that she ran to another venue, to her office, where everyone was offering to do something, but what they offered was of no use to her just then. All the time, though, she insisted to herself that he would be found, she had a scraping fear that he wouldn't and that this would be the deepest, the most unfinished hurt of all, a hole inside her that would grow bigger and stockier and uglier each day, so that she cursed the God whom hitherto she had implored so passionately.

34

That night, that drive, that dawn, that mouthful of toast, the blond girl who screamed at her because of the way she described Paddy, every detail, his eyes so very mixed between blue and grey, like chip stone, only softer, and his few freckles and his beautiful hands like a pianist's, and the girl telling her for fuck's sake to belt up, because her boyfriend had beautiful hands, too, and they were to be married in September. That was that night or the next, and dawns, merciless, drained of light as dawns are, and her own house for an hour or two, for no reason, then a dash to Paddy's flat, where she should have gone sooner but couldn't, and going up the stairs, becoming petrified in case his girlfriend Penny might be there. Penny was not there. Penny was in Spain training to be a potter. Paddy had moved to a flat, to sort himself out, as he put it. Climbing the last bit of steep stairs, she remembered how he would have opened the door by then and found her puffing and admitted that he puffed, too, when he hadn't been to the gym, and oh, madness of madness, she thought, He has not died, these policemen are mistaken, askew, he is here, he is here either asleep or awake, and the door will open from the inside. Lucky that he had given her a key. They had exchanged keys. Another sign of trust. Charlie came towards her with an abject, frightened look, and all she could say as she patted him was "You haven't peed, Charlie, and you haven't done number two," and saying it she thought of their youth and Dixie, her parents' dog years before, years that now seemed blithe compared to this inferno. Charlie licked her a lick of thanks, relief, and imprecation. He was hungry. He needed to go out. In the front garden she stood a few yards away from him, disowning him, in case a landlady or a caretaker tapped a window and shook a fist. He took his time as he squatted under a lilac bush. He was nervous, overnervous. His tail and his hind legs shook uncontrollably, but nothing came, his eyes fixing her in case she stirred. The lilac bush was withered. Fobs like used lavatory brushes. Some rotting smell. What happens to a body in the river? She must look it up in a book. No, she mustn't. Charlie staggers to one spot, then another, does dribbles, then gives up.

Upstairs she begins to go through Paddy's things. A diary with entries and little mottoes to better himself. What would he have been? A teacher, she thinks. Yes, a teacher of man, his conscience always smiting him, and his pity, pity for those who had not. A teacher of man. There are birthdays. Her birthday is there, too. She is not left out. A motto—"The lapwing cries loudest when far from its nest." Why that? Beside the diary are his three pipes and a stack of pipe cleaners, then a photograph of Penny in a pair of shorts, looking so young, so vulnerable, not the needy Penny she knows. The child that had been mentioned was not. Was not. What happened, she would never know. The curtains she gave him are drawn. He drew them before he went out that night. Yes, they are there, and the armchair, the wooden armchair that he got off a skip, and a beautiful lapis bowl, the one beautiful thing in the room. She must get some of his clothes because he would be cold, shivering, and that meant madness was taking root, because clothes are for the living; a habit is for the dead, brown, grey, or off-white. Going shyly to the bedroom she tiptoes, knocks as if he were there with Penny, traces of them there, and opening the wardrobe door she cries at not having given him more money, because his clothes are so sparse and so pitiful. There are some secondhand suits, a stack of sweaters, and three gaudy ties, probably birthday presents from friends. His sanctum. She does not touch a thing, or rather touches them by way of a little glide of the fingers, and goes out. It was a mad dash to a shop to get Charlie some sliced ham, which he ate on the street, in a twinkling, and then tried to eat the greaseproof paper which she was still holding.

Another journey, another taxi, people she had never seen in the anteroom, waiting, muttering. Different people from the times before, new recruits, hopeful, despairing. The others had all gone home, were in their houses now, facing it, cursing, seething, because who is ready for death? In the morgue they are each caged in a shaming silence. Couples in a double cage, alone and together. Why the stoicism? Why the silence? She asks in vain if her son has yet been found. The policeman simply shakes his head. She says, and her voice becomes quite coaxing, that he might well have been and not been recognised. She says something ridiculous about a credit card; he did not have his on him, as she found it in his flat. She begs him to let her have a peep. He does. In there, three lots of people are standing before the raised sheets and doing what can only be done, which is to nod and renod in hideous believing disbelief. Only three corpses, three of the last. Neither the living nor the dead seem to breathe. It is a room without breath, the coldest she has ever been in, and although she goes out, it does not leave her. Outside, someone gives her a rose. They know her by now and they know that the waiting is almost coming to an end. It is a white rose and it smells. It is a girl who gives it to her. She does not know if she knows the girl, but she must, because the girl invites her to a cremation.

"I don't think I can," she says.

"Do you good," the girl says. She's Jackie; she has lost a girl friend. She was a hairdresser. She was invited at the last minute. Invited to do someone's hair in a posh flat. She did it so nicely that the woman said, "Join us," and she said back, "I was meeting Rosie," and the woman said, "Rosie can come, too." It was as impromptu as that. They sniff the rose, they cry into it, they tell each other their own first names and the names of the two who are gone. Paddy and Rosie. Rosie and Paddy. It is like a valentine. She tells Jackie that, yes, she has another son and that he is in Turkey, that he has gone there with his friends to do relief work, but that she has not had him alerted, not yet, not until his brother is found. That will be the time to tell him and have him brought home. She does not mention her husband, the man to whom she has not spoken in over a decade.

35

Charlie met her and licked her with joy and mounting need. She opened sardines, had one herself, and put the rest on a saucer, wondering if the very yellow oil was too rich, pouring it anyhow, and saying things to Charlie, practical things, desperate things, Charlie licking the plate so clean it shone and then kicking it, putting his paw into the central hollow to demand more, not the least bit grateful, growly, so that she sprinkled sugar on the clean plate and said a few conciliatory things. Did Charlie know? Yes, Charlie knew, because that night Charlie started up his own incantation, his own wake, his own subhuman howl. First it was from the kitchen. She was wakened from a clotted sleep. She had taken half a tablet, cut it carefully down the centre, because of wanting not to be blurry on the morrow, yet wanting sleep, even ten minutes of sleep, for her mind to be borne somewhere else, to be assuaged, even if it meant a different nightmare. The phone would ring and she must not be so asleep that she could not hear it.

The nice detective had promised her that the moment the body was found they would summon her, no matter what the hour. He was Welsh, friendlier than the others. He had not yet found the pamphlet, but he assured her that he remembered the line written by the neurosurgeon, the line that said the sensation was ecstatic once the water entered the lungs and the body gave up the fight. Wakened instead by Charlie, with a howl that had a human plaint in it. Her own hysteria speaking back to her but animalised. Charlie knew. He missed his master. He went around smelling shoes to locate his master. He smelled shoes and Wellingtons, he did not give up. Down to the kitchen to give Charlie a telling off, whereupon he skulked, became silent, except that as soon as she went back to her room the howling started up again. This time she thumped with the broom, the two ends of the broom, the worn, wiry twigs, and then the handle as a parting shot. She put her winter coat under the jamb of the door to shut out all sound, because sleep, sleep she must. If she did not sleep she was in danger of going mad. Her upstairs department was sizzling, on the boil, as if a current were going through every single cell. No use. He started again. She dragged him into the garden, thinking it was that, but it was not that; then in the kitchen coaxed him with an old biscuit that she found, a damp biscuit, ginger. He spat it out. He was not taking this. She left him again, but the howl that started up bit into her brain, and hurrying back full of vengeance now, she simply said, as if he could comprehend, "Charlie, I've had it . . . I've had it." His teeth marks on the rungs of the chair told her what she already knew. Charlie was rebelling, Charlie was unmanageable, Charlie had to go. The teeth marks on the chair, her chewed coat, the ravelled grey-white threads, all too much.

Barely seeing the streets they drove through, traffic lights, a slice of river sauntering, either upstream to disgorge its prey or downstream to do an identical thing. How can one plead with water? It is never there, but fleeing, fickle, inscrutable, cunning. How well she knew its colours. She had lived by it. She had loved it once, claimed to have been moved, oh so moved, by its harmony, its colours, its sheers, its ruffles, its greys, its currents, its debris, and so on. Paddy had loved the water, too, had made a little logbook of it. Just as there is a little logbook of life, so also there is one of death. She had found it when she went through his things. Read it, read, "People will tell you that it is not lucky to see the river life destroyed and that as a result dead lightermen are haunting all the old wharfs and docks in the East End, in the guise of seagulls. I am inclined to believe it. I am young, you see, and there is a proverb which says, 'The younger you are, the nearer you are to the fairies.' " Didn't look at Charlie once. Barely seeing the streets, skimming, the dainty lace-like girders of a bridge an affront.

The building was a smearish colour, mud brown. A man going by with his dog on a leash shouted, no animal of his would set foot there. Inside, baying. A great swell of it that rose and dipped and rerose like the swell of a foaming sea. Multiple baying. Then individual barks, individual cries, saying, "Find me . . . come along down to my little cubby and find me." She shouldn't be doing this to Charlie. It was to Paddy she was doing it. Passing the cages was the worst. Some yapped. Others stared in silence. Redemption in silence. Some dozed in aluminium basins, and everywhere fresh and not so fresh shit. Charlie's temperament, Charlie's teeth, and Charlie's hair were all subjects for discussion. Then it was by herself while Charlie was brought off to be examined and vaccinated. Did it hurt? Of course it hurt. Everything hurt. In a little room which adjoined an empty café she struggled with a form. Where was her heart? It was gone. It was murdered. It was with her son in the bed of the river, trying to find him, two hearts missing, the way people miss in dreams. It was in a sack like a dead animal, bleeding, the blood oozing out of it, senselessly. The questions were routine. Her name, her occupation, how long she had known Charlie, and if he could be trusted with children. Staring at her from the wall a newsletter about a dog called Patch who had been badly treated, abandoned twice, and twice brought there, where he made a miraculous recovery. In the end Patch had found a good home and it was the owners of the good home who wrote this eulogy after his death. Why was she doing this? Only because Charlie howled, a howl that cut notches in her.

36

Back to the chapel of rest, glad to be with others for a moment, or a fraction of a moment, escaping her own operatics. She let them weep with her, cling to her, say the most rending things. Secrets blurted out. Parents who hadn't seen their children in years blaming someone else, such as friends, friends! Everyone was beginning to crack. Parents and grandparents and brothers and sisters and stepbrothers and stepsisters all attesting that they could not go on. Hope scooped out of them like bits of their insides, their guts, their gizzards; lives that thought they were booking a holiday or going to learn to drive or to plant roses, were heading for a joyride of permanent mourning. Everything slashed, every plan and half-plan, and every dream. They gave her strength. While she was with them she did not think how she would tell Tristan, how she would break it to him. She thought something, such as "You do not know yet, sweetheart, you can laugh, you can joke that little bit longer." Had she her way, he would never know, he would live in ignorance of it.

"She was my morning's light and my evening's lamp . . ." A mother who stood in the pulpit kept saying it, her voice dramatic, measured, calling her daughter in various intonations. Catherine was her name. It was as if Catherine might appear. The name flew about the rafters, as a sparrow might. Catherine was not one of your high fliers, far from it; Catherine would lay down her life for others, and did, as a nurse in a city hospital. Services and cremations everywhere, in the city, in the suburbs, all over the country. Young people having stabs at gaiety, short skirts, blouses like those worn in a bullring. The draped and decked coffins a far cry from the cold consignments of flesh in the morgue.

People were nice to her, invited her to services and cremations. A young girl with a great swath of unswept purple hair stood up and began to talk rapidly, began to shout, "We're not going to take this tragedy lying down . . . Catherine and Dom and Henry and Samantha and Rosie and Sophie and all of them are probably laughing up there, asking us to stick together, to be friends, to be faithful, because we are a family now. Father Thames, the bastard, has brought us together." At that, she broke down and recited all the names again and went across and picked some of the flowers off the coffin, giving each flower or bouquet the name of a best friend, until someone led her away, linked her away with "Come on now, Becky . . . let's go outside . . . Becky."

The vicar praised those who had come to mourn and those who had died. Talked of the necessity of fun and how no one must fault these young people, stressed the fact that they were not to blame and the skippers were not to blame either; all, all were blameless. Then a psalm, then "Lucy in the Sky with Diamonds" and a short reading from *The Little Prince*. A man had given her that book once. A lover. Finnish. It came to her that if she was to make love the frostbite of death might be taken away, even momentarily. She had heard it somewhere.

A rare and sparkling morning of it outside. Church grounds immaculate, everything pruned, summer bedding in, an air of festivity. Balloons on railings swirling and a convoy of motorcycles ready to take young passengers to the crematorium. Air inside the silver skins of the balloons, stretched, as if about to wheeze. Laughter. The young seemed better able to face death, were more heroic about it. She must rally. Some people were again talking about compensation and lawyers and the whole gamut of justice and retribution. She couldn't say. Her brain was porous, swishing with the sound of waves, like a cistern leaking in her. The day before, a woman had given her tranquillizers, had given her a few in a handkerchief. They had a queer effect. Dislocating.

The plots in the cremation grounds were minuscule. Midget slabstones, as for a dog's grave, and midget messages, a single yellow iris in a Lucozade bottle. Oh, the paucity of it all. They had to queue. A service was still going on inside and a sermon of much the same ilk. Resign oneself to God's will. Why? Why? In the motorcar a woman kept telling them how she had heard the news, how it was dumped on her from the television. She had thought that her daughter Amanda was in Amsterdam on a tulip farm, but no, she was in London, whoring, and had changed her name from Amanda to Ruby. Why was she with such people? By your friends ye shall know them. "Deceived us . . . deceived us rotten." Amanda did not get on with her stepfather. Both headstrong people. He refused to come to the cremation. Stayed at home and lit a fire, even though it was a warm day. Revenge. Another mother in jeans, grumbling because of being kept waiting. The fact that she was in jeans seemed wrong, seemed inappropriate, worse when she tightened her belt to show how dishy she was. A young man, a very tall, sepulchral-looking young man, stepped aside as if to pray. Had the look of Hamlet. Seemed stunned. Everywhere shock and those outbursts, and now the woman taking the white belt of her jeans off and using it to hit, to hit out.

37

"I mean, darling, everyone has a night, you have a night, Joe Smog has a night, everyone has a night or two." This was Dolly, a thin woman in an orange wig; Dolly in her sad club, drinking vermouth and boasting. But what of it. In the midst of death, life. Better hear this than talk about inquests. She had gone in there by chance, saw the faded velvet curtains, wine bottles crusted with candle grease, a bird cage with budgies. It was an artists' club. Everything shabby, faded, the relics of a daring bohemian past. Several drawings of nudes, photographs of boating parties, and the menu for the evening meal chalked on a blackboard. After the service she decided not to go home with them but walked instead, walked as far as Soho, thought she might go to a cinema there. No one stopped her, no one said you can't come in. The young man was busy, going from the bar to the kitchen, where he seemed to act as chef.

Dolly was at a table having her usual, vermouth and soda, and glad of a natter. A story, real or perhaps not real, her Black Prince, a night that was not your statutory night in the sack but a night on the altar, yes, on the high altar of love and fucking. How she gloated, how she warmed to it, pressing closer to Nell at each saucy admission. Herself a little cuckoo, put in her cuckoo clock with a smack-smack, and told to wait there because her angry prince had vanished. Had smacked her, oh yes, made her black and blue, and she deserved it, naughty, naughty, doing a Nancy on stage with others, nothing on, not a stitch, only a powder puff, but that was the way of it: you dangled your powder puff and you curled your finger and you waggled and you wiggled and you said naughty things and you got paid. Black Prince in a fury, a writhing rage. Tracked her down to the strip joint, jumped on the stage, belted the stagehands, brought the curtain down, and dragged her to his premises, where he gave her the once-over, told her to stay there and not stir. Where did he go? No idea. Maybe a walk by the waterfront. It was Sydney. Yes, Sydney darling, in the good old days. Came back looking like a god, a great he-god, glistening, with a plan. He was going to give her a gift such as she had not had before. Yes, little cuckoo could come out of her cuckoo hole and preen. He was going to give her his country, its songs, war songs, love songs, hate songs, and he was going to give her forests of rain, until she was herself liquid, and he was going to feed her the fruits, the luscious fruits after rain, pack them into her, the papaws and guavas, then beat the drum, oh yes, beat the drum of her little harlot's arse until it smarted, because he was her prince and he knew how to love, how to fuck, and this was her night, when the angels looked down from heaven and up from hell at this man who had decided to give everything to this woman. "Took me all night, darling . . . took me until I thought, I am not of this earth . . . I am floating . . . I am flying, I am laughing . . . his little cuckoo crazed . . . tossed about . . . Calling for more . . . more cock . . . more man, more prince . . . dancing, singing, writhing, buggying, buggering . . . in me . . . inside of me . . . possessing . . . possessing. Heaven . . . Heaven." Her eyes blazed, like oranges on a tree in the dusk, as she remembered how he had said goodbye, because the night had been his farewell gift to the cuckoo who worked in a strip joint. She had known her Black Prince and she would not forget it. When she was gaga and toothless in some dump in Essex or Kent, she would remember her ecstasy, yes sir, the high altar of love and fucking, and she would boast of it until they put a clamp over her lips. In the midst of death, life.

Better, better far than going home. Nell wished that they had rooms and that she could stay all night, stay indefinitely.

Hated going home. Into her dark house. Into sleep and into dreams. Searchlights in her innards and men shouting, shouting what? Then a cold white ship, a liner onto which guests were coming, la-di-da people, oodles of them, with parasols and hand-bags. Famishing. "Hold on till I plug in the fire," she called, not wanting them to shiver, not wanting to be inhospitable. The electric plug going soft in her hand, soft and warmish, turning into a wet tea bag. The people higher up at work clubbed together to send her to a health farm. Thought it might help. As soon as she crossed the threshold she knew she must leave. It was all too bright and hygienic, that and a smell of grapefruit. She fled. She went to Paddy's flat so that she could not be traced. She slept on Paddy's bed and thought he might appear to her. In a way he did. A dream, a salve. He came alive in it. It was a strange place, a square bathed in warm golden light, a southern town, yellowish walls, turreted, sun pouring down. A beautiful girl in leopardskin trousers and high leopardskin boots in attendance. Penny waved to her. Had an errand for her. The errand was to go to Paddy with a message, to search him out in the monk's room where he burrowed and where he was praying for guidance. He was to come to the square, the golden square, where he would receive instruction. He agreed. In the dream he looked thin, emaciated, but he smiled at the news of his release. Then it was the next day, it was morning and the white chairs were stacked on the round white tables, their legs ungainly. He arrived clean-shaven in praying robes and a shirt, a white shirt that was threadbare at the cuffs. He looked around to meet his messenger, the woman in leopardskin. Instead, Penny appeared and moved towards him, radiant, then laughing, because she had played a joke on him. They danced in the square. The pink stone of the cobbles was dark where it had just been splashed with water, and the music came not with nighttime heartiness but in a trickle like a flute heard across distances of mountain. They danced between the tables and chairs, danced beautifully towards a sign which read TIVOLI GARDENS. She wakened almost happy. She would write to Penny. She would write and tell her this dream and by telling it say, "It means we must be friends." She posted it to Spain. They could bury the hatchet. There was no child, the child was a blind, and there was no Paddy, Paddy was among the perch, the roach, and the slippery eel, but as she had to keep saying, free of them now, free of all predatoriness, adrift among the algae and the slapping vegetation.

Then at home, on the windowpane, a sign, galling, galling. Its appearance brought on by the steam. In a blur of grey, in a fog of steam came his initial, P for Paddy. Pasta boiling over in a saucepan. Long strips of it dyed green. A great splutter on the stove, spitting and hopping, beads of water jumping about like translucent insects, the kitchen all foggy, fogbound like a river late at night. His handwriting, his particular little squiggle. Jesus Christ. She crossed over to it. It was a P. She hoped it might be an O, but it wasn't. He must have sketched it in once while she was cooking dinner, one of the evenings that was either amicable or testy, sketched it in where it lay concealed and needed only a bit of steam to show up again, apparition-wise. She ran her finger along it, tracing it slowly, while at the same time not wanting to blot it out, and thought that if anything can reinvoke the dead, it must be this. An afterbirth of hope.

Then she rang someone. The bereaved were told to ring each other at moments like this, to ring for counselling, co-counselling. The woman she rang was livid, calling all journalists scum and newspaper proprietors worse scum, millionaires, making packets out of tragedy. There had been an article implying that her son was gay, that he lived with a young man, that they had had wedding vows, a wedding ceremony, that they were going to adopt a baby. Lies. Total lies. Garbage. She was going to the editor on the morrow. The next woman she rang told her to see a spiritualist. It was the only thing. It did wonders for people, it brought peace of mind. There was a place in Belgravia. She would find out the hours and they would go together.

The pasta tasted like glue, or porridge that she had had in

Scotland. How long ago was that? Too long ago. "They're peeing on us from a great height," the first woman on the phone had said, and suddenly Nell laughed a mad laugh, remembering him and Tristan peeing on each other from apple trees and shouting, "Bang bang, you're dead, I'm not dead," vying with each other as to who could pee longest and say the most scalding things.

38

She had found it easily in Paddy's diary under F for Father. He was in a home. Had lost his marbles, or some of them. She'd lost hers, too, but not the ones that enabled her to forget. Memory weevilling into her every minute, a fresh issue of pain, picking, like the hook of a crochet needle, drawing blood. Awful journey. Monotonous. Fields, more fields. Cows. Cattle. Lines of washing. Towns with their miserable little chimneypots. Signs for life insurance. Paddy had made a will and left her everything. Big houses with gates. More fields. Like going across the steppes of Russia. Had brought a book to read. *Light in August*. Sad stubborn book. The deep kind of animal sad. Arriving at a neat little railway station that had won a prize. Hanging baskets and things. Out in the street affable, smiling faces. Away from the rat race. Recognised her as a stranger in the town. Tea shops. White scones and clotted cream and barley sugar in twists. Big geranium in the conservatory of the nursing home. Biggest geranium she had ever seen. Gigantic. Clawlike. Bright orange. Flaming orange. The colour of life. Of fire. White is the colour of death. Baxter, one of Paddy's school-friends, had said that. Had written her a soulful letter. The names of those missing had been in the paper. Had tried to be manly. Said life had changed a bit since they last met.

Letters that were meant to console did the opposite, squeezed the sap out of her, and the image she had was of a mangle wringing water out of old clothing. Baxter's second name gone from her, but not his face, pale, somewhat sepulchral, his shirt always outside his trousers and a lisp which got the better of him in argument. Loved Paddy but didn't know it. Lost his temper one day with Paddy, over a word. A house party in Scotland. Hostess all briary and agitated, pink-hued, like a bloated marshmallow. Windows rattling, old, pimpled, gooseberry-coloured-glass, rotting frames. Storm outside. Hedges and bushes trying to take off. The Three Graces daubed with moss and bird shit, curls copious, fetching; their little rears tight as twopence. Baxter with his own bereavement. A child that he and Pandora were having, for all of twelve or thirteen weeks, scooped away. Pandora like a moth until she cried, then not like a moth, becoming raw and pink and skinless, like those young worms that venture out onto a road after rain and get squashed. Penny there, too, insinuating herself, the shiny plait of her dark hair, the rope that Paddy held and milked with his grey I-am-falling-in-love eyes. Baxter and Pandora at wordless war. Pandora drunk on sherry each evening, drunk, then fluent on the subject of parents who cared only for themselves and screwing, screwing each other, then screwing others, and dragging each other down into the sewer. Mummy better at it than Daddy. Daddy with only one floozie, a Miss Buchanan who worked in Skin Care, Mummy going the whole Lady Chatterley hog, in the woods with her gamekeeper, out at dusk in her kilt and her stalker's hat to gun down a few rabbits, staying out until the dinner gong was rung, then rushing in, dumping the bunny rabbits, their bloodied fur aglisten, dumping them on the draining board for a slave to skin and gut, undressing on the stairs, so happy-looking, so fucked-looking, peeling her woodland attire off, until, on one of those evenings with the soup getting cold and guests flustered, Daddy decided that Mummy had gone too far and slapped her left right and centre, and Mummy not caring because she had had such a good time of it, such a long-drawn-out sated time of it, in Daddy's woods, and Daddy pelting her, half in fury, half in lust, because Mummy still had that pale-faced, shepherdess appeal.

Of course there was a good side to Mummy, too. Mummy said

God forgave everything, and wasn't that nice of Mummy. Then back to why she drank and why she smoked and why she couldn't bear to be alone and why she couldn't bear to be with others either. No use anyone saying that an unborn infant didn't know, because she knew it knew. Couldn't bear for Bax to kiss her or touch her. Anyhow, he hated her, said she shouldn't have done it, even though they had both agreed. Reliving it. How she went to the nursing home all cocky, made phone calls to friends, then getting cold feet in the lift, getting the wobbles, the nurse saying it would be over in no time, except that it wasn't. Waking up and feeling awful . . . bloody and sore down there . . . but it was not blood and sore, it was it, something gone, a little thing, without trace. For some reason she thought of it as mesh made liquid, like gunge in a liquidiser, her own blood which she had shed, but not blood alone, morsels of flesh in it, the whole caboodle wrapped up in sheets of newspaper and put in an incinerator, but not gone, hovering. She could hear it at odd times, a little mewl, a little "It's me." No friends, only Paddy. Paddy came to the nursing home with a pot of African violets and listened, listened.

Pandora phoned from Florence. Had gone there for a painting course. Said, "Pads was Jesus Christ to some of us," then broke down and asked if Nell would like her to come home. Said she would do a death mask of his face and that Giorgione was her master. Got cut off twice. Each time her voice more askew. Said young people were dying all over. The world was in transit. Discos were morgues, places where people went to shrug off death and couldn't. Said again that Pads and Nell were her best friends, her best best friends. She walked around Florence thinking of nothing, only his face, his pullovers, his smile. Baxter more controlled, said Paddy and he had gone down pit together in Yorkshire, went about half a mile underground and then into a coal seam forty inches high, just the two of them. Had talked down there. Had talked about life and things they must do. In a P.S. he reminded her of Aphrodite coming out of the sea, then apologised for being a bit stoned.

Others wrote also. A girl who did group therapy with him wrote a poem:

It was only a dream that I had a son
Who grew so fair and tall.
It was only a dream that I had a son
Once so frail and small.

A cleaner from his school described how he had visited her after she had a breast removed and asked to see the wound. Tributes from his teachers. Getting to know him through his friends and thinking, I have Tristan . . . I have Tristan . . . I do have a son.

Sympathy somehow worse than rebuff. Sympathy too terrible altogether. She'd do anything not to go up those stairs and meet their father, anything. Slight hitch—he was in the toilet. She must wait. Made a bolt for it. Ran down a passage, through a door, into a narrow passage, and found a white door that slid, like a trapdoor. Near-naked woman by the lavatory bowl, looking in at it, laughing, boisterous laughter. In her shift. Legs like candles, spent candles, white. Age and death. Youth and death. Nurse saying, "You can come now, Mrs. Steadman . . . Your husband is ready." Worst would be over in an hour. Stand up to him, fight back, if he should say, "You left me," or, "You destroyed them," or, "It's your fault that he went there." Needn't have worried. Man in pyjamas, vacant, vacant, sitting upright on bed. Shadow of tyrant he had once been, who had exchanged a "love, honour, and obey" rigmarole. More metamorphosis. Breathing lightly and staring. Staring. She had to sit. A waiting white chair said to her to sit, and she said back to it with the little gumption that remained in her, "I am not here . . . I am not here . . . I am not sitting down . . . I was never married to this man . . . and I do not intend to apologise." Geranium downstairs bursting with life and rage, clawing the glass roof. A waiting taxi. Freedom only two staircases away. His mouth was moving to say something, the something not coming, the sympathy for his son, for surely he must have read the telegram that she had sent, he must know. Lips squashing, unsquashing, then stretching out like rubber bands; a sound of sorts, but no meaning to it. Lips pursing, nearly saying it but not, not yet. Man in the bed across showing no such rectitude. Roaring like a jackass. A roar she well knew. Father, husband, mother, all mingling in. Better take the bull by the horns, but not yet. Lips still struggling, like mauve trodden-upon fruits. Eyes very sharp, cross, nails that dig in. His son and his not grasping it. She had said it clearly, very clearly. On the bed beside him a pen and pad. Maybe she should write it down. No, that was too awful. His eyes looking daggers at her. He knew. He was about to pontificate.

"Do you sleep?" she asked.

"I slee . . . eee . . . eee . . . ppppppp"—the words going wrong like mince. Awful. Getting out the gifts she'd brought. Shades of love or would-be love. Which? Flowers from the station. Red carnations sunk in a white haze of gypsophila. Red and white. Not lucky. She would leave what Paddy left her to Tristan. Tristan would save her. He had before. His birth had saved her when she was in the dumps, his little kisses, the teeth he cut, the teeth he lost, and the sixpences she put in eggcups as a reward.

She had brought flowers and a bottle of pink champagne. Impossible to think they were once married. Unrecognisable, and yet recognisable by that sneer, that disdain. Otherwise a stranger, a stranger with parchment skin. No trace of his other self, his gallant self, his dash. When do changes happen. In sleep. In waking life. Both. They had stood together, proud to be married, a ceremony in the sacristy of a church while a priest grudgingly tied the knot. Workmen as witnesses. Paddy kicking away like blazes, saying, Let me out, let me out of here. Born a few days later. Her firstborn. Always felt she was too afraid, afraid of his fragility. The little well in the crown of his bare head giving her the shivers. Two lines of bone opening and closing like a mouth, saying something.

Still, she tried. Got the pepper the day he put pebbles up his nose. He was crawling then. Thought the stones were boiled sweets, brown cushions or acid drops. She ran and got pepper so that he sneezed, a weird, hilarious succession of sneezes, and then she hugged him and then delivered a bit of a scolding that he was impervious to. Rascals. They were his, too, his and hers. But they feared him. Sitting more upright, he was telling her slowly but determinedly that he refused hospital food because it was poison. Each word, each bit of word taking an eternity to get out. Had to be wrenched out. The tongue and the purple lips struggling with it, the voice box wan.

"Paddy got drowned" is what she heard herself say, calmly but bluntly.

"You got drowned" was what she heard back. A smile. Vengeance even in absentia.

"You . . . got . . . drow . . . ned"—a smile within a smile, in the recesses of blur. Man opposite deciding to shout louder and louder for nurse, nurse. The worst was said. His eyes, both tortured and torturing, wished to nail her.

"No . . . Paddy . . . not me."

"You got drowned," he said, triumphant. The speech quite quick, quite clear, the meaning, too. The hate he had for her was like a pilot light, waiting not for extinction but to be relit. She hated him, too, remembered a whole nest of wrongs, yet more than anything she wished that they could throw a crumb at each other, they who never had. Why did they mate? What stars had caused such a strange conjunction? What now was the fresh bafflement in his eyes? Hearing others go down to tea, she rose to fetch him some, but once outside she knew she would not cross that threshold again.

39

At first it seemed to her that he was breaking, spilling in her arms, his sobs punctuating the little things he said so as not to seem too broken. He had gained some hours. The difference in time between Turkey and home was a difference of hours. At moments she thought he was going to retch. She held him. He held on. It was a clumsy embrace. He would have come sooner, the very instant it happened. She should not have borne it alone. She should not have had to bear it alone. Did she know the people who had given the party? Of course not. Sorry, sorry. He should not have asked that. He would not ask anything else. Questions were cruel. Everything was said to comfort, to augment, to show solidarity. He had gained two hours and that was something. He had brought gifts. He did not say for whom apart from her. There was a goatskin, dappled, luxurious, a brown that had endured the scorching heat of the animal's life so that it was almost black. She laid it on the stairs where they sat and made plans. Plans of a sort. He would go to Paddy's flat and move the things, give them for a jumble. Paddy had a little insurance policy. He could have it. He didn't want it. He didn't want anything.

"You could live there if you wanted . . . my pet."

"No . . . I'll stay with Mumsies." In every syllable, in every thought, in every fresh bout of grief he grew closer, snatching at the fringing of the rug for comfort, his other arm shielding his eyes from the light. A window smothered in creeper, each leaf of it purling in the heat, looking in at them. He enquired about the summer. It had been warm, though not as warm as where he was. He had eaten a lot of yogurt, grown fond of it, to his surprise. Been invited into houses out in the wilds, dogs following the truck, big dogs with muzzles leaping up; the women in the houses veiled, veiled and spinning. Got drunk with his friend Andy on his last night in Istanbul. Met carpetbaggers, many, many carpetbaggers, in one tavern after another; got home somehow, paralytic. His pockets full of cards, business cards, the exotic Byzantine print bearing the name, address, and complimentary swirls of numerous carpetbaggers.

"Where's Charlie?" he said, looking around, ready to whistle.

"Charlie . . ." she said, flustered, and knew that he knew before she had even started the sentence. Charlie's crying had got to her, bitten into her, as she said, adding the word "banshee" more than once. He did not say, "How could you," but suddenly a brute determination seemed to spring up in him and he shook with hate.

"I couldn't sleep . . . I was going mad," she said, and tried to have him imagine the house empty, the hoping, the ebbing of hope, and then Charlie, and then Charlie. It seemed a long time, too long, as his tongue sought words to annul the spleen that had just entered him, but finally he said he would go straight to the dogs' home and find Charlie, no matter what.

Find him he did, so it was home and truce of a kind, as Charlie pattered around, much quieter now, much more subdued, almost speaking to them, so happy was he to be back, so abjectly happy, so grateful, licking even she who had consigned him to exile. The tick under Charlie's ear had to be removed. She fetched her tweezers and watched him filch it out, deftly and with love, the whiskers first, then showing her the little fat squat belly of blood, Charlie's blood, that had been the tick's homestead for the week. Charlie mewled with excitement, relief, showed not a trace of venom as she held him. Then he was ensconced in the bath, a thing she would normally have objected to. They took turns soaping Charlie. She thought, Tristan doesn't hate me now. It was a passing thing. Later he poured boiling water onto a soup plate, dunked the tweezer in it to sterilise it.

They were near. They would hold each other up, be the props of each other. She did not know then that he, too, would go, yet feared it, believed it might be her crying at night, crying and crawling along the floor, beating the carpet with obscene fists, to break free of her pain, to exorcise it. She did not foresee, either, the change that would take place in him, once it had sunk in, the inwardness, the guilt; did not know that he would not shave for weeks and would not eat and would not talk or be talked to. Neither of them dreaming that it would be Penny, sailing thither in her barge of fertility. After she had sent Penny the dream about the Tivoli Gardens and appropriate condolences, she got a letter back, a tight, pursed message ending with "I knew him better than anyone in this world and still I didn't know him." To say that to a mother. Between Penny and her a guillotine. Sealed the night of the much vaunted pregnancy.

She had gone to visit them, Paddy and Penny, installed in an attic flat in Primrose Hill, pine furnishings, joss sticks, Penny's tennis shoes dyed pink. A family dinner was how he had termed it. At first, Penny lurking in the kitchen, behind a beaded screen, doing nothing, just standing there, something soft and violet and stealthy about her. Later, Penny chopping carrots deftly as she sat on Paddy's lap, drank from his drink, and went chop chop with her sharpened vegetable knife. A different Penny with him, silken like a flower, black and scarlet, an anenome. Different again when she spoke on the phone to her friends, eager, excitable: "You didn't. You must be joking . . . My God, you said that . . . What did he do, faint?" With Nell, serpentine. A strange, cruel, "Don't pander to me" glitter in her dark licorice eyes. Disappeared in the middle of dinner, went up the ladder stairs to the "nest." Paddy trying to pretend it had not happened, launching into a rigmarole about a man who got a parking ticket while he was sitting in his car waiting for the AA to come. But all the time looking in the direction of the ladder stairs; then Penny reappearing in a straw hat, agog, shaking him as she chuckled: "Hey, hey, hey . . . better start knitting ... high on poetry but short on prams," and his looking with disbelief, a shy, youthful, baffled look, then its dawning on him and both of them colouring and Penny exclaiming that she had to go out into the garden and feel the forces of nature, because her heart hammered so. She put this excitement down to her black blood and excused herself. A child. Theirs. His seed, consanguinity, perpetuity. The base emotion rising up in Nell then, she who had no right to say so, or to feel so, not wanting this child, stamping it out of existence, crushing it, fetid thoughts aplenty.

Oh, she had reasons, a whole litany of them, his youth, Penny's youth, responsibilities, but the real reason was far more purulent. She did not say anything. She did not have to. Her eyes conveyed her mutiny and he looked back at her with both fear and flounder. This was a big moment, the moment to let him go; all other moments were rehearsals for this. She did nothing. Sat there stone silent, looking at ornaments she had given them that were put out of reach, until he stood up and said, "I'd better go down and see what's what."

Scurried out he did. A child. Inconceivable. Yet conceived. Something as ineradicable as that. A child and her place in his world was usurped. Thinking it, she felt a poison course through her body, brown and off-brown, like water in a clogged ravine. She thought of a day, oh a distant day, years before, when her mother, chastising her—no, not chastising her, consuming her— had in her wild assault burst a sack while gutting a chicken; the poison was of that selfsame colour, tobacco colour, and the selfsame pervading stench. Thinking those things, she thought, too, What pretty names we give to the carnivorousness that is called mother.

In the two weeks after Tristan returned home they tried to be buoyant, tried to make jokes when they had their supper in front of the television. He made a point of talking about Paddy, about plays he directed at school and leading ladies that he had fallen in love with. He had been sent home once for drink, he and a friend called Norrie, and she described the two of them going to a Turkish bath to sweat out their guilt. She kept urging him to see friends, his own and Paddy's. He left notes: "Gone to mow a meadow." Charlie followed him like his shadow. Charlie waited inside the door, mute like an infant in a crib. Charlie knew his footstep two streets away. Charlie was bounced in his arms, flung up to the ceiling, caught on the way down, and then tossed with abandon. He had arranged with his house master that he could bring Charlie back to school and sleep with a neighbouring family. He had not discussed it with her. It was the first wrench in their nearness. She thought, To the outside world we seem near, but something has happened, he is disappointed in me, he believes I am wallowing in my grief, but he doesn't know what it is to be older and isolated. She bought him gifts, bribes. She remembered once long ago in the country she had crossed a meadow to pick a few rhododendrons that took her fancy, the deep red ones. From afar they looked close together, each petal brushing against its neighbouring petal, but close up, that was not the case at all, each petal was on its own little stalk, separate, surviving, the way it is with every living thing.

40

The memorial service was a grand event and many dignitaries were to attend. She had her ticket, a yellow ticket ornamented with the crest of the cathedral. Afterwards they were invited to forgather in the Glaziers' Hall. She shrank from the pomp and stoicism of it—"The Lord is my shepherd; I shall not want." Untruer words never spoken. Tristan decided at the last minute that he would not come up from boarding school, though he did not say why. His grief had become darker and he was having quarrels with people. He and another boy had boxed in the quad. "Please do not write to me for the time being," he had said. Her tribulations were getting to him. He didn't shave. He didn't eat. The headmaster believed it would run its course.

On the steps of the chapel she saw the relatives whom she had last seen so squashed and numb, now loquacious, rallying. They wore hats or headscarves in bright colours. Few were in black. Why hadn't she come to the meetings? Why had she gone into the woodwork? Why? She must know that it was important that everyone fight the fight, that it was not the time for wallflowers.

"I wasn't able," she said, pleading ill health. Ill health! Men on drink. Women on tranquillizers. Families wrecked beyond redemption, and she couldn't give her support. As she turned to escape, a young man approached, touched her sleeve, and in that touch she felt a premonition. He was thin, wore a threadbare gabardine coat, and had the bluest eyes she had ever seen. They reminded her of school ink. His hair, soft brown and closely cropped, was like a shaving brush upon his meek skull. Everything about him shorn, crushed.

"I was the last person with your son."

"Don't," she said. It pierced. A quite different stab to when the news was first broken to her.

"I have wanted to talk to you . . . I have phoned, but I didn't have the guts to speak."

"So it's you," she said, inflamed. In the intervening weeks the phone would ring and be put down, and though at first she thought it was journalists, later she believed it was Tristan, who wanted to give her a pasting, a bit of his mind.

"How could you?" she said.

"Nerves," he said, and laughed skittishly. How she disliked him. How she took that laugh for insolence and hated his little black-heads, wanted to squeeze them out. People were passing on either side and she moved now to join them, to go inside, to suffer the sermons, the fugues, and the hymns, to get it over with, because a rage engulfed her, rage at a young man who had met her son on the boat, had hit it off with him because of their interest in the theatre. He was an actor, yes, an actor, as he stressed. He was determined that she should listen. He had to tell her. Like it or lump it. Yes, for six weeks he had been preparing his confession and here it was: he and Paddy going down to the loo together, both dying for a leak, so deciding to toss for it.

"A leak," she said, affronted.

"Yes, a leak, and we tossed for it and he went in and next thing I know it's happening, I see black, blackness . . . I am being swept into it, sucked into it, and everywhere screaming . . . I go towards this hole of light . . . a slit . . . a hand clutches mine . . . I even think that it might be your son's hand . . . but it isn't . . . it's a woman's . . . probably the fortune-teller that was on board . . . It has rings . . . she had rings . . . We clasp hands, this woman and I, because we are going to die, and if you are going to die it's better to hold on to someone . . . believe me, it is better than being all alone . . . She slips from me, where the hell has she gone . . . I'm calling her, but she can't hear and all I hear is 'Elsa can't swim . . . Elsa can't swim,' and I don't know if I'm swimming but I must be, because I'm moving in this black filthy hellhole . . . I bump into something, it thumps me, and would you believe it, it's a barrel, so I cling to it or it clings to me . . . this barrel and myself in the wilderness and 'Elsa can't swim' in my bloody head . . . A bridge, a fucking bridge, the stone, I touch it, my tombstone, and I'm so fucking wet and winded that I am thankful to be about to die, thankful to give it all up . . . this farce called living."

"Except that you didn't," she said, her eyes now on his wobbling Adam's apple, like a goiter.

"No, I didn't," he said sadly, and withdrew for a second into some corner of his thinking before describing the mercy ship that was lit up like a bus, the arms, several arms hauling him through, except that he didn't want to go, he wanted to be dead. Once in there, a sorry sight, shivering and shaking. He needed a brandy, but the barman said, "If he needs a brandy, someone's got to pay for it," and at first no one did. Then a girl called them all shits, throwing her biker jacket on the counter, saying she'd pay for it, and he said he could still see the sequins on her jacket blinking at him.

"Why in Christ's name did you tell me all this," Nell said, and ran, ran past the people, down the steps, and into a taxi which had just disgorged some smartly dressed mourners. "To the river," she said. "You're on the river, darling," the driver said. He was a big man, with a beam of goodwill on his face, in his voice.

"Farther up . . . Chelsea," she said.

"Oh, you mean the posh place with all them skyscrapers and complete living environment . . ."

"Farther up . . ." she said.

"You don't have to go out for nothing there," he said.

He knows the river, he was born on it, one of your old-timers, used to poach the Queen's swans as a kid. Every single swan accounted for, like her corgis. She was not listening. She was going to the river as if going there was going to solve something, as if a last, or was it a first, battle was going to be waged between herself and her enemy, the water. Of course nothing happened, nothing does. The river had a brisk, business-like gait to it; the water, as it were, snaking along, the patterns on the surface themselves a mimicry of some fish or other. The longer she looked at it, the more cruel and indifferent it was. Glassy on the surface, but fathomless within. New buildings all around it, rising up in their steel-and-concrete imposingness. Suddenly a bit of current. Waves like the blade of a plough, ploughing the surface, gouging it.

"Excuse me." The voice made her jump. She thought it was the young man, the impostor, who had followed her, somehow sniffed out where she had gone, the way a pig sniffs the truffles.

"D'you like the Beatles?" a voice asked. He was a different young man, bearded, a bit creepy. He had some records that he wanted to sell. They were without their sleeves. He hated selling them, but he was hungry, hadn't eaten for days, and when you're hungry you'll do anything.

"Leave me alone," she said, as if he had been going to assault her. He moved back in shock and wished her a pleasant evening. A reptilian hate was taking root in her. Someone was living instead of Paddy, and if she had had a grain of guts she would jump, now, make herself the plaything of the slicing furrows, put an end to the life which she did not have the gumption to live or to die, but kept teetering between both.

41

November again, the holy souls, penance, rain. She would pray
that she could pray, because it might be some help. The rain beat
slantwise down the long office window and soaked into the woodwork. Soaked into the brick of the houses, too, altering their
colour, so that they were like frescoes. She had promised herself
that she would go back to Italy, she hoped with Tristan. Something about seeing frescoes. She dreamt one night that Tristan had
written her a letter of forgiveness on parchment and that it was
headed by a Leonardo da Vinci painting. She believed it was *The
Last Supper*. At least he was thawing. No one ever knows what
sorrow does to another, what form it takes, how twisted it becomes. She dreaded Christmas, breaking-down time. They had
invitations, oodles of invitations, including one from Dolly for a
knees-up and one from a family in Guildford, an author whose
book she had worked on, and one from her boss. Yes, he had made
the break; rather, had made it three times, and each time gone
back to his wife, each time taking a holiday with her, a second
honeymoon, as it was called, and the last time in the Lake District
they almost froze to death and had not the heart left to warm one
another. Miss Flight had won. A bitter divorce and smears in the
newspapers and him getting suddenly older, much older-looking,
the shame of it all being too much, too wounding. They were
welcome, she and her son, to stay overnight. She would ask

Tristan. The one thing that could not happen was for them to be alone. Being alone with someone you love when you are empty is quite the worst, most ghastly thing. When she asked him on the phone, he said, "We'll see, we'll see." He seemed not to want it. Probably a girl. Normally he talked about the girls, their beauty, their prettiness, their little ways, such as who was shy or who loved horseback riding, but this girl, whoever she was, was an enigma. Ah, she could not have foreseen it.

It was a manor house with open fires and plenty to drink. Neighbours called all the time. A big tin of caviar was opened after Mass. An old woman who had come with her family spilt hers and then trod on it, for it not to be seen. Nell felt for her. She herself would be old soon. People were so nice to her; even Miss Flight had taken special trouble with her gifts. Miss Flight had given her a woolly, but a very special woolly, a grey shawl which was half cashmere.

Tristan was a success with them all. He carried in logs, he mended the record player, he put on the records that Miss Flight loved, the jazz records that she danced so beautifully to, so that people looked and thought, What deportment, what deportment. Nell kept having to disappear, in order to cry. Secret crying, like secret drinking. Someone or other called her, called her name, because they knew. Christmas was a time not to brood. At Midnight Mass she had prayed both for him and to him, but went awry. Luckily they had got there late and had to squash in anywhere they could find, so that she was with strangers and it was strangers' hands that she shook and wished peace upon and had peace wished upon her, except that she was in torment. She felt like someone whose only release would be to burst out of her own skin, out of her own life, to bleed into nonexistence as she had once done. She did not think of her parents and Paddy meeting in the afterlife. She couldn't conceive of it.

The turkey was delicious, the stuffing a triumph. Stuffing from a French magazine with unusual things in it, smoked oysters and angelica. She drank champagne, glugged it. Tristan watched her drinking and would give a little cautionary wag of a finger. Upstairs, she cornered him to give him his present. It was a mistake; it meant that she was recalling him to her asylum of woe. It was a little photo album of Paddy and himself from infancy on, charting the passage of time. There were too many words on her card, endearments. He was edging from the room towards the door, down to the others, down to Charlie and the pheasants that he was to help Miss Flight with, to pluck.

"Are you cold, love?"

"I think they want us downstairs." Dancing attendance on Miss Flight, helping with the fire, the crackers, carrying the box of truffles around, telling the old woman the several flavourings. When he kissed her good night and she asked if there was anything wrong, he said, Tush. "Tush" was his word now, both a propitiation and to ward her off. She heard him on the phone to the railway station, making an enquiry about trains to Exeter. In a way she was relieved. They must each grapple with it alone. Each in his dripping cell.

42

It was in an antique market where she often went on Saturdays because the gypsy who had given her the lace runner had moved there, had moved from an outdoor stall because of her arthritis. Was indoors now with her bits and pieces and big floppy angora jumpers which her daughters knit. She went most Saturdays for a chat but never ever to have her fortune told, simply to linger, to kill time looking at bags and brooches, staring at the art deco lamps, things of nature, their fawn globes soft and spindly as toadstools. The gypsy woman talking about her own health, her children's health, allergies and so on, telling Nell that she must get out and about, show her face, get a bit of sparkle back into it; in short, doing everything to be kind. When the first customer came to have her fortune told, Nell made herself scarce. Went to the café a few stalls down. The customer on a milk stool, the gypsy holding the crystal, fondling it as if it were the amber head of a newborn infant.

It is here it happens. She knows it is not he, it cannot be he, yet it is he, identical, down to the blue-grey eyes, to the donkey jacket, to the beret worn at the same angle as the onion man from Brittany wore his. The onion man who used to say that he was Marc Chagall's nephew, which he wasn't. She sees Paddy or his double a few tables away blowing the cinnamon on the milky foam of a cappuccino. He is with two young men, one white, the other dark-skinned, the dark-skinned one thin as a rake, leather amulets about his person. The likeness is too much. She thinks that she will have to get up and tell him. What will he say? What will they say? Perhaps they will laugh at her or think she is mad. She cranes forward to hear what his voice is like. Her mind is beating, beating with a gall that this should happen, that she should come harmlessly for comfort, distraction, and be confronted with this. She is on the point of making a gesture of some sort, because she cannot endure the suspense, when he looks up laughing, a wide laugh, and it is not Paddy, the teeth are different. The shock is too much. The resemblance too great. More than anything, she realises how much she misses him and how much she has buried it. Seeing the face, the skin, the eyes has made him live for an instant, though of course not live, and suddenly she yields; she is only tears, her face a gourd, water coming as from some phantasmagoric source, fierce and fluent and hot, running down her neck, inside her clothes, hot and yet shivery.

The boy looks at her, not knowing why she should be crying so, and others also look, and cups of tea and solaces are brought and someone, recognising that she is a regular on Saturdays, fetches the gypsy woman, who sits opposite saying nothing, a presence the way a nurse is in a sickroom. Still more tears, as if all the sorrow of her life and the sorrow of life itself, the sorrow she knows and the sorrows she does not know have met and mutinied, asking to be heard. In many ways it is a kind of blessing, because she is devoid of thought. She had shed thought, all thought, all memory, transmitted into tears, that came from her eyes, her belly, her stomach, her sex. It had come to this and no one could do anything, not those who came to gaze and got bored, not the woman who sat patiently and said, "Let it out . . . let it all out." It must be the birth of something, she thinks, because after all that crying, it can never be as bad again, or can it?

It went on. It went on, while the shutters came down, the several shutters, the escalating clatter of metal on every side, and lights were quenched and the coffee machine was turned off and the owner of the café stood over them with a few keys, and told them he would be in the pub opposite if they needed refreshments. Yes, people were kind. He pitied her. He winked. Afterwards, long afterwards, it all felt so quiet and so dazed, and she was exhausted as she apologised to the gypsy for having kept her late, for having made her miss her usual train, and now her son or her daughter would be fretting.

"I've kept you," she said, her voice as tired as her brain.

"I like the city at night . . . It's the one thing I miss . . . funny, I miss it," the gypsy said, and then they both got up. There was a stall of clocks, gold, brass, ormulu, tortoiseshell, all telling a different time. She looked at one and another and another. It could be yesterday, could be then, it could be now, it could be before he died, it could be when he lived, it could be tomorrow . . . or never.

"I'll never be right," she said, and looked at a glass dome, inside which was a skeleton clock, the organs so nicely, so perfectly at work, the sunburst pendulum about to give utterance, left right, right left, the little hammer hammering mightily.

"You will," the gypsy said, but in a quashed voice.

43

Easter. Soon the Easter bells ringing out, masculine and feminine ... pewter and lead ... bongs of Resurrection. Oh, to meet the risen. She and Tristan were going to a Russian Mass. She had asked him on the phone. He lost no time with her as he came in with only a small bag. He was saying it as he came through the door, his jacket slung over his shoulder. It was warm, warm as summer—with gnats in little swarms outside.

"I think you had better know," he began, his eyes fixed firmly on her, saying by their expression, "Don't interrupt and don't try to make it easy." She was thinking that he had come home to say that in fact he would rather spend Easter with friends and she would retaliate with what a good thing and how it was not healthy to be hatching indoors with her and how she understood, understood.

"Penny and I are going to live together."

"Penny," she said, and although she had not shrieked, it seemed as if she had.

"Have you been seeing Penny?" she asked with as much composure as she could muster. Her heart was beating, beating against her blouse, as if being wrenched.

"Yes," he said quietly.

Why hadn't she known, why hadn't she been told? When did Penny return to England? Why?

"How did you run into her?" she asked, trying to hide the scalding curiosity that gripped her. In deference or distractedness she was also offering a plate of hot-cross buns.

"She wrote to me after Paddy died," he said, and then blurted it out—that she was having a baby.

"She's having a baby," he said, his voice a little shy and a little solicitous, and above all concerned.

"His?" Nell said, unable to say Paddy's name, unable to join them together.

"Maybe his," he said, and looked away.

"Maybe his but maybe not his . . . What does that mean?"

"She's not sure," he said, his face still turned away, obviously wishing that she would not make it as brutal as this.

"She's a slut," she said. The word had tumbled out of her.

"She's not a slut," he said, sadly and with a disappointed look that also said, "Don't say anything else, you have already said too much." She gripped his arm, deciding that somehow she must reach him, she must reason with him, point out that he was young and that he did not have to take on this legacy, this lie, and in a terrible instant she saw a resemblance to Paddy, the transmitted resemblance of the times when he hated her.

"We can always have the bloods tested," she said raspishly, her voice octaves high.

"What would be the point?" he said—gall in the voice.

"So you're going to live with her?" she said, her turn now to walk away, to swallow the bitter bread of banishment. He said yes, that for now she could not be alone, she had nightmares, she was racked with guilt, that she had tried to kill herself; she was frightened, and going to have a child.

"Do you love her?" she asked, each word cutting cruelly, bitterly, like a hacksaw. He didn't answer. Had he taken on his brother's mantle, and possibly his brother's love? Or was it sacrifice, needless sacrifice?

"Is it pity you feel?" she asked, unable to hold her tongue.

"It's not pity, Nell," he said, and by the tart way he pronounced her name she knew that he was finished with her. In desperation she heard herself revert back to Penny's earlier boast— "high on poetry, short on prams." Would that she had not voiced it. Would that she had not.

"If you saw her you'd believe her," he said, and shouted, in case she needed to know, the lyric name of the maternity ward where Penny was to be admitted and her gynaecologist, who was a woman. Nothing more. When he left the kitchen it was obvious that he was going down to pack. What must she do next?

44

She walks now with a vengeance, with the malice of the desti-
nationless and the pounding of someone who will not concede
that she has nowhere to go. She believes it to be her last walk.
She cannot go on. She might as well never have had children or
a husband or parents—phantoms all. She thinks that whatever
happens, because undoubtedly something will happen, no one
will ever know or should know the spleen within her. This walk
is her last. In the windows she knows so well are the things she
knows too well. A necklace from Africa, each bobbin a golden
acorn, the gold dun like that of icons. Then the wedding dresses
in the dry cleaner's, the same batch or an identical batch, suc-
cessions of them each week, lifelike, ghostlike. Hanging from the
ceiling—cream and ivory and white creations, stuffed with tissue,
ready to float. The tissue gives the arms and the chest a sturdi-
ness so that they seem to breathe. The little white arms are asking to be picked up.

When was she last picked up? Oh, she knows. By a mad, mysterious congruence it coincided with her last cyclical blood. A
white satin quilt in a room in Finland, washing it, rewashing it in
the washbasin, but to no avail. The stain like the vertebrae of a
fish. This, too, a repetition. Everything a repetition. A waltz to
Helsinki, she had called it. He was a big man, like a lumberman,
his arms around her strong, girding, and from him a beautiful

smell that was part woodshavings and part wheat. It was at a conference to which she had been sent. He saw her across the room. Later, at lunchtime, he gave her a little bunch of flowers, gentians, or maybe violets. At dinner they ate raw fish with a dill sauce and then crayfish and afterwards cloudberries. They went to friends of his who had a sauna. His wife was not present, was in southern Italy taking the sun because of her ill health. His wife and daughter.

In the sauna the other women felt their ridges of flesh, squeezed them between thumb and forefinger, and said their husbands wished them kilos lighter. They rubbed salt into her body, vigorous but loving, down her back, on her buttocks; then they made her turn around while they rubbed it into her chest, as if she were a child. She felt a child. The woman whose house it was said she would not have forgiven him for coming with another woman, but she forgave this. Later, when everyone had gone to bed, he brought her out to a plunge pool that was a distance away in the forest, and together they plunged in, the water so cold that it felt as if it were boiling. Then, in a child's bedroom, in a narrow bed, loving her with such avidity, like someone sucking a fruit stone, and making of their one clandestine night many nights, a feast. He would come to England. He would buy a nice house and she could be in part of it, with no one to disturb her except him. A dream. He did not see the blood. He had gone out to prepare breakfast. She held the quilt or that part of it under the tap in the bedroom, begging it, begging it to disappear, to become the colour of a snowdrift like all the rest. She rubbed and rubbed. It went from bright red to dark red and then a sienna colour and then a sullen brown. She tried a pumice stone on it. It refused to give up the ghost. So much in it. A narrative in the satin of a quilt.

He did not follow her to England, but wrote letters, beautiful letters, broken sentences, feeling hopeless with all those kilometres between them. Feeling crazy. Loving and crazy and having to write in another language, but happy, happy about it all. Then a plan for her to follow him to Spain. More crazy. A hotel she went to was not fully finished, wet brown cement in sprawling turds and men with wheelbarrows slowly carting it hither and thither. A foreman in a lather, shouting. The travel agents had got her booking wrong, as the hotel where she intended to be was closed until the spring. He was in an apartment block a few miles away, and she had sent a letter by taxi and was awaiting a reply. It was cold and the little primulas up against a border of fresh concrete looked as if they would not survive. Then came a group of men, very studious-looking and well dressed, some with sheet music, one with a baton. He was the conductor, the one who had inspired them to such extremes of exaltation. Some went so far as to lie down on the new grass seed or the wet cement surround of the pool, to drink in the weak winter sun. The conductor walked alone, talking, gesticulating, while a young man, an acolyte, ran after him with his overcoat, insisting that he put it on. He refused, marched over the newly planted primulas, veered between barrows of cement, talking, exclaiming, a Moses with his tablet of Commandments. Finding himself close by the bench where she sat, he leant over her as if she were a Rhine maiden and spoke in German, spoke heatedly. The acolyte translated. He had discovered that Toscanini had the same brainscan as Puccini, which is why he could conduct *Madama Butterfly* flawlessly.

"Yahw . . . yahw," the conductor said, and then moved closer, eyes demonic, shouting, *"Tiefgreifend . . . Tiefgreifend."*

"What's that?" she said, startled.

"Deep catch . . . deep catch," the acolyte said.

"What's that?" she said again.

"Lachen . . . Frau Lachen," he said to his master, and they both turned away.

On a date tree the young nascent bellies were a pale gold, clustered like berries on a bonnet, except that they spoke of life, fertility, of fruits to come. Looking up she saw him, her lumberman, in a long, modish cardigan, shy, ill at ease, guilty at having left an ailing wife and child, startled by the medley of men speaking German, and going towards him she thought, It is over . . . our fling is over, and yet in their reunion there was a tenderness, the tenderness of those who have passed each other by but who remember it sweetly, the way one remembers a shooting star.

"Your hair," he said. "Your hair is different."

*   *   *

Walking, racing, her glance on the ground mostly, seeing cigarette butts, swirls of dust, and here and there carbuncles in the
pavement where the cement had bulged up. In a restaurant window little meringue cases, not quite sallow and not quite white. A
tiny dish of raspberries catches her eye, each one like a rosebud,
moist. Only nature can touch her now, a fleeting touch at that. To
think that over the months she had thought Penny was a thing of
the past. Now this, this. Was he going for the sake of his brother,
to uphold his brother's troth and so forth, or was he going for the
sake of himself? Passing a half-finished block of flats, she reads a
sign chalked on hardboard: LADS, NO WORK TODAY, GO TO YARD.
Cruelty. Lashings of it. A sudden brainwave, a ruse. She will buy
a bottle of champagne and bring it as a farewell gift, a bribe, and
if he has gone she will bring it to Penny's to patch things up.

"You see," she says to herself, "you are even prepared to lie, to
break bread with those you do not like, simply to cling to him, to
cling; you have become as craven as that."

"But I am doing my best," she answers back, and in an oblong
of mirror at the side of a shut shoe shop, she sees a face that bears
no resemblance to the face of even half a year ago. A wounded
face, eyes stark, upbraiding—all traces of beauty gone. The shoe
shop has closed, but there are shoes left. They stand like solitary
props on glass plinths, with a little tag in front of each one of them.
Circulars and letters cram the passage inside.

"You don't remember me," a voice says. She is in the wine shop
now, having decided to go the whole hog of hypocrisy. She does
not recognise the face or the very blue eyes or the short brown
hair, like the hairs of a shaving brush. She should. He repeats it
and gives his little laugh, his laugh of insolence. Suddenly she does
and gasps at the sheer galling coincidence of it. Why is he here?
Why is she here? Why did she cross the road at that point? Only
because the lights were green and she wanted to walk as fast as she
could, and saw as she sees now a glut of bottles crammed into
wooden barrels, plus lore about wine and wine-tasting, that gives
her the pips.

"I thought you were an actor," she says tartly.

"Not at the moment," he says, and she detects the same little mendicant sneer from which she retreated on the oratory steps. She enquires about wine. He is fluent with description—adjectives rolling off his tongue, false confidence in his thin, hurt eyes as he says in a blasé voice, "South African . . . Bulgarian . . . Italian . . . Californian . . . Lebanese." As if she didn't know. As if she couldn't read. He points to the barrels and she knows why. A barrel saved him. She remembers that. The iron hoop of the barrel cutting his neck. Part of her, indeed an almost vanished part of her, wishes to throw the gauntlet down and tell him her latest bombshell and weep and talk with him. Ridiculous. Feelings have died. Not so, feelings alive and kicking and bucking in her, vicious feelings, growing like a child, a child that swells but does not come out, an alien dementing the walls of her mind.

"I'll have the Macon," she says, to which he asks tersely if she wants the Villages or the Lugny.

"Whichever is cheaper," she says, and detests the remark, as if she is asking him to take pity on her straits. He pounces on it. He has the advantage. He will give her the better one at the lesser price. She doesn't want that. She does not want charity, especially not his. When they tossed the coin, did he choose heads or tails? His eyes are more cavernous than when they last met. The blue is all fear, droplets of fear.

She feels that if at that moment either of them or both of them were opened up, liquid would spill out, gurglings of it, and his would be this vitiated blue and hers a viscous black-red. She vows to smash the bottle on the way home and carry the jagged neck, like a weapon, a weapon she is no longer afraid to brandish. He wraps it and hands her warm coins, coins so warm that they are perspiring. They disgust her.

"So you don't act anymore" is her parting shot.

"No . . . I don't act anymore . . . The thing is, I just don't sleep," he says, and he says it softly, and if there was a moment in this world for any one person to forgive another or to initiate a gesture of reconciliation, it is this moment, except that she can't, she is all balk, blunder, stammer, umbrage, blubber, and hate; so she flees, flees.

45

In the luxury and hush of the chapel, she moves among blues and golds, among pews and escutcheons, in and out between the myriad altars, holding the bottle, skulking, candle flame heaving this way and that, teetering, recovering, swelling, like air being pumped into a bellows; sees the oak-brown of the confessionals, the dropsical expressions of martyrs, always overlooked by sages with sage hands and sage punitive eyes; she sees Virgins, some like queens, some like courtesans, and in recesses naked angels determined to frisk. In the blue dome of the rotunda, a vaporish light, the smell and smokiness of quenched altar candles. There is a barricade of flowers on an iron rest. Waves of incense, a floating presence. Oddments have been forgotten—gloves, rosary beads, a child's knitted boot. Candles have been lit, to beam and intercede for those who have fled to their lunches, or their copulations, or their tennis courts or their gymnasiums. Fronds of light, gleaming, as in a theatre. She kneels by Saint Anthony, he who once brought respite. The bottom of the Infant Jesus fits snugly, fleshily, into the hollow of Saint Anthony's outstretched palm. Comical. In his other hand he holds an Easter lily. She always loved lilies. Not anymore. Both are smiling, as if they share a joke. She cannot pray, and yet she waits the way someone waiting to be sick waits. There are two black boxes on metal stands. One for alms and one in His honour. She cannot give. That is the truth of it. That is her plight. Her sin.

She cannot give. Too much has been taken away from her, everything: her sons, first one and now the other. Galling to see necklaces and lockets and trinkets in the oblong case next to Saint Anthony, offerings from those who can give, mothers such as herself, wives such as herself, daughters such as herself. Hers not the only tragedy, and yet to her the only tragedy. Remembers reading about women in Africa, captive women walking back to their shacks, hundreds of miles back to the ruined village they were plucked from, most of them with child, the foul, forced seed of their captors. How could one love a child like that, and yet they might, their breasts a warm monstrance, their bitter memories dissolved. In a matching glass case are faded blotches on the velvet where other trinkets had been, until a fat priest or a thin priest unhooked them and skedaddled to the pawnshop. She cannot give. She will not give. She would steal the barricade of flowers from the altar except that they are so vulgar, so secular, so vast, so overblown. To think that she thought she might pray. What does one do with grief? What does one do with hate? What does one do with a bastard child seeded from a lewd and vicious captor? What does one do? She thinks of refuse dumps. Not a pretty sight. They are everywhere, only a mile or two from your stately manor or your green-grow-the-rushes lake. A phantasmagoria of ashes, plastic, paper, food, condoms, flowers, mush, the afterbirth of all hope, toil, and aspiration merged into a grotesqueness which cannot itself be destroyed. She thinks that she is like that and calls out to her dead mother, the pity, the raving pity that they had never known that milky oneness; each in her trajectory of dark.

How could he have known? At any rate, he is there chaining his bicycle to the black railing. The blue of the chain transparent, the metal inside like a series of snakes, each coil snug in its socket.

"Mass is finished," she says, harshly, harshly.

"I've just come to say my little prayers."

"Oh, you're religious."

"Let me tell you," he says, and he moves towards her, his hackles out, his moment for retribution. She may think he killed her son.

She may think he cadged a ticket to life. She has another guess coming. He would gladly have died. Yes, lady, to relive the moment before the toss of the coin, the heave-ho, the hole that he squirmed into, is to relive a nightmare every sleeping and waking moment of his life. He knows the worst. He has been there. Death is not the worst. Having to live is, having to live knowing that everyone else has forgotten it, the schamozzle has died down and you're alone and you've lost your three best friends. He laughs, a strange, metallic laugh, and says evidently it was his fate, his karma. His outburst does not frighten her, merely makes her pause for a moment to think.

"Your three best friends?"

He recoils, fears that he has said too much, babbled.

"Say anything . . . say anything," she whispers.

"Well . . . we have dinner," and he looks to see if this is too fantastic, but it isn't . . . "Jim loved soup, so I make soup, tomato or lentil . . . We have it in mugs . . . brown pottery mugs . . . Pasco and I go swimming—he was a great swimmer, the best swimmer of us all—he's teaching me to dive. Then Hugo, the ringleader, our king—he was going to be a rock star, he had all the makings, the smile, the looks, the talent . . . He left a song . . . Well, a bit of a song—'Love Is Gonna Cut You Down.' We put different lines to it . . . different beginnings . . . different ends. 'Love Is Gonna Cut You Down.' I make him an omelette and he throws it back in my face and he says, 'Jeeves, it's runny . . . It's not the way I like it,' so I add this and that to it, a bit of grated cheese, herbs, then I whisk it, put it back in the pan, and I brown it and toss it and say, 'Is that the way you like it, Hugo?' He loves it. He tells me he loves it. I put a few flowers in a pot on the windowsill and I say, 'They're for you, and they're for you, and they're for you.' "

Suddenly he stops and she sees that he is about to cry but that he does not want her to see him, shrinks from pity. So this is what he does with his pain. He regards them as living, or at least living in that region inside himself which matters. Most likely Hugo and he were lovers; yes, they were lovers, because he singles Hugo out, says that he did not want to go to that party, that he woke up and said he'd had a dream in which his boots were too hefty for swimming. They had gone to bed, they had made love, then Hugo's dream, then Hugo ignoring his dream, then down to the pier and meeting the others and meeting Paddy. She can almost touch it, the picture is so real.

"So that's how you manage," she says quietly and with astonishment.

"Sometimes . . . some days are worse. You see, I haven't been to the bottom yet . . . the very bottom," he says.

But she already knows. Then she asks his name. He is called Mitch, because his name is Mitchell.

"Maybe you'll visit me sometime, Mitch," she says, and gives her address shyly.

"Or if I'm in a show, you'll come and we'll have supper." Supper, symbol of another world, a world so far behind both of them, suave and lighthearted.

"So you will be acting?"

"I hope to . . . The thing is . . . at the moment I just don't sleep."

Their bodies more or less fall onto one another, in a sudden embrace. He is all vertebrae, so that it is like holding a musical instrument that is about to break yet won't, will keep faith with something within, innocence perhaps.

46

At home there was no barking. He had left. They had left. What met her on the kitchen floor were the gifts that she had given him: necessities, as she called them. A radio, a blender, a coffeepot, and a packet of fresh coffee beans. Seeing them in their heap, she thought, He has not even acknowledged them, he has gone out and left them there, to show his anger and confirm his separateness. The note had slipped down behind. She read it many times, as if eating the words. The words were like little entities that for some reason reminded her of his first teeth. She read, "Ta for these things, but I don't need them yet. I am never far from you and always at the other end of the telephone. Thanks, too, for everything." He had signed it with love and a little flourish of hasty kisses. It was the P.S. which touched her most of all: "Do you remember one summer we all went to Arezzo?" The light of memory. Sweetness. A wash of words. A baptism. They were like something touching, touching her, a hand, a voice, a breath, a presence from long, long ago, a presence within absence and, yes, within pain, within death. Everything radiant for a moment, as if she reached, or was reached, beyond the boundaries of herself, as if she had known him and he her before, a friendship that transcended time and place and even those little ruses by which we lay claim on one another.

"I can bear it," she said, and looked around at the air so harmless, so flaccid, and so still, a stillness such as she had not known since it had happened, or maybe ever. In the stillness there was a silence, but there was no word for that yet because it was so new; pale sanctuary devoid at last of all consolation.

"You can bear it," the silence said, because that is all there is, this now that then, this present that past, this life this death, and the involuntary shudder that keeps reminding us we are alive.